Susanna G. █████████████████████████ taking up an academic career. She has served as an environmental consultant during seventeen field seasons in the polar regions, and has taught comparative anatomy and biological anthropology.

She is the creator of ██████████████████ ies of mysteries set in medieval C███████████████ loner adventures in Restoration ██████████████ s with her husband, who is also ███████

Praise for Susanna Gregory

'A lively and intelligent tale set vividly in turbulent medieval England'   *Publishers Weekly* on *An Unholy Alliance*

'A good, serious and satisfying read'
                              Irish Times on *A Masterly Murder*

'Excellent . . . the historical research is first rate. All in all, great entertainment for cold winter days'
                              Eurocrime on *To Kill or Cure*

'Once again Susanna Gregory has combined historical accuracy, amusing characterisation and a corking good plot to present a section of British history that is often overlooked: the emergence from the Dark Ages to Renaissance in the field of education and medicine'
                              Historical Novel Society on *A Poisonous Plot*

'Carefully researched, imaginative and evocative . . . this is a gritty but humorous period mystery'
                              Good Book Guide on *The Cheapside Corpse*

'Gregory never fails to impress with her immaculate research, creating a███████████████████████ political backdrop ████████████████████████ tic detail and thrilli███████████████████████
                                                        Strangler

Also by Susanna Gregory

The Matthew Bartholomew series

The Thomas Chaloner series

SUSANNA GREGORY

THE TARNISHED CHALICE

THE TWELFTH CHRONICLE OF
MATTHEW BARTHOLOMEW

sphere

SPHERE

First published in Great Britain in 2006 by Sphere
First published in paperback in 2007 by Sphere
This edition reissued in 2018 by Sphere

1 3 5 7 9 10 8 6 4 2

A CIP catalogue record for this book is available from the British Library.

ISBN 978-0-7515-6952-0

Typeset in Baskerville by Palimpsest Book Production Limited,
Falkirk, Stirlingshire
Printed and bound in Great Britain by Clays Ltd, St Ives plc

Papers used by Sphere are from well-managed forests
and other responsible sources.

Sphere
An imprint of
Little, Brown Book Group
Carmelite House
50 Victoria Embankment
London EC4Y 0DZ

An Hachette UK Company
www.hachette.co.uk

www.littlebrown.co.uk

For Gill Cooper and Mike Smith,
dear friends

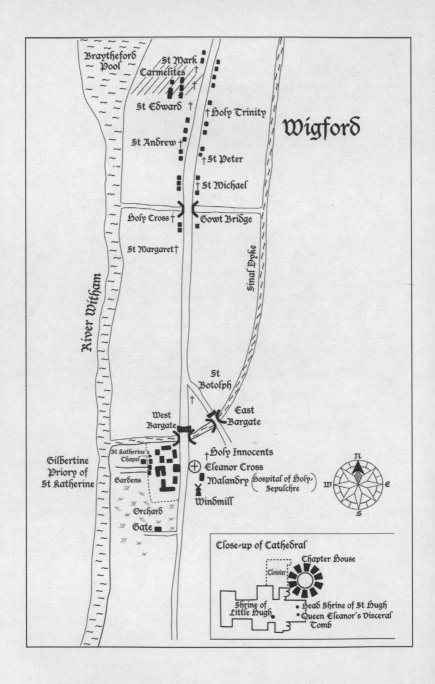

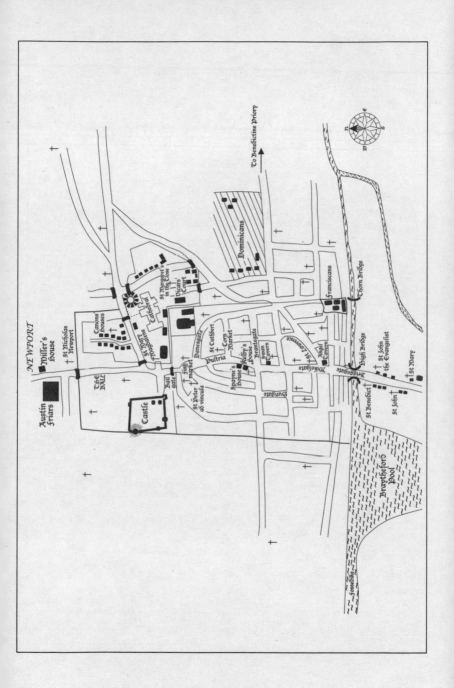

PROLOGUE

The court was full when the sheriff brought the accused from his cell. John Shirlok glanced at the jurors who would try him – twelve local men who shuffled and sighed their resentment at being forced to spend their precious time listening to unsavoury tales of robbery, burglary and murder. They were supposed to be respectable, up-standing citizens of good character, although Shirlok knew that simply meant they were men who had been unable to think of a good excuse to absent themselves. All were wealthy – they wore fur-lined cloaks and thick boots against the bite of late winter – and none would be sympathetic to the crimes Shirlok was accused of committing, but he was not unduly worried. There was no question of his guilt – he had been caught red-handed with stolen property, and that alone was enough to earn him an appointment with the hangman. But he had a plan. No thief worked alone, and Shirlok intended to walk free from the castle that day.

'I bring John Shirlok before you,' intoned the sheriff, quelling the babble of conversation that had erupted while the felon was being fetched from the gaol. 'He stands accused of stealing white pearls, valued at a hundred shillings—'

'Shirlok?' interrupted Justice Sir John de Cantebrig. He was presiding over the court, making sure the trial and its subsequent conviction – he did not think acquittal was very

1

likely in Shirlok's case – followed proper protocols. 'That name is familiar.'

It was his clerk, a clever lawyer called William Langar, who answered. Langar was tall, thin and had spiky ginger hair; his duties were to advise Sir John on the finer points of the law and to make an accurate record of the proceedings.

'Shirlok was due to appear before you two months ago, Sir John,' Langar said. 'But he exercised his right to challenge the jury we assembled. He objected to eleven of them—'

'That was because they were kinsmen of—' began Shirlok indignantly.

'Silence!' snapped Langar. He turned back to the Justice. 'He will make a fuss about any jury if we let him, just to delay his hanging, so I suggest we proceed as planned today. We cannot house thieves in our gaol indefinitely, and he has been enjoying our hospitality for three months already.'

Sir John nodded. He knew all about the devious ploys felons used in an attempt to avoid the inevitable. He glanced at Shirlok, taking in the sly, foxy expression on the man's face, and the way his eyes were never still. He did not think he had ever seen such transparent guilt. 'Very well.'

The sheriff glanced at the parchment he held. 'I was listing the items Shirlok stole, some of which were found on his person – such as the white pearls. Next, there was a chalice worth twenty shillings that belonged to the church at Geddynge . . . '

A murmur of distaste ran through the hall. Theft from a religious foundation was a serious offence. Shirlok heard it, and his composure slipped a little. 'I had nothing to do with taking that cup.'

The sheriff waited for silence, then continued again. The

list was extensive – linen cloth, a brass pot valued at two shillings, an expensive rug, a two-coloured coat, a jug he called an *urciolum*. His monotonous voice droned on and on, and the jurors' eyes began to glaze as their attention wandered.

'We have recovered some of these items, and they are here for your inspection,' concluded the sheriff eventually. He turned to rummage in a box he had brought with him. 'The Geddynge chalice was found in the possession of one Lora Boyner, after Shirlok had sold it to her. She claims she bought it in good faith.'

He held aloft a goblet, reclaiming the attention of the bored jurors – even Sir John had been lost in a reverie about the sorry state of his winter cabbages. The cup was not very big, and its battered, stained appearance suggested it was old. There was an etching on one side, which was worn and faint, although anyone with keen eyes would see it involved a baby.

'That is worth twenty shillings?' asked Sir John, trying to make up for his lapse in concentration by showing some interest. He took the vessel from the sheriff and studied it. 'Is it silver?'

'It is just some old thing,' said Langar dismissively. 'The rector of Geddynge maintains he recently bought it from a travelling friar, but when Shirlok stole it—'

'I *never* took that cup,' protested Shirlok again. 'The other stuff, maybe, but not the chalice.'

'He did – and then he had the gall to sell it to me,' declared Lora Boyner indignantly. She was a squat, muscular person who made her living by brewing ale; Sir John had often marvelled at the way she could lift a full keg as if it weighed nothing. 'He said it belonged to his grandmother, and I believed him – poor fool that I am.'

'Poor fool indeed,' murmured Sir John, thinking what

he would have assumed, had a rogue like Shirlok appeared on his doorstep and claimed he had his grandam's silver for sale.

'And he stole my linen,' added the young woman at Lora's side, speaking because Lora had jabbed her in the ribs with a powerful elbow. Mistress Godeknave was a slender, graceful creature with large blue eyes. 'I am a poor defenceless widow, and cannot afford to lose my few possessions to thieves.'

'How do you plead, Shirlok?' asked Sir John, watching Langar write down the charges.

'Guilty to some of it,' replied Shirlok, trying to stand upright. It was difficult with the manacles weighing him down. 'But I intend to turn approver, and expose the eight men and two women what helped me steal all these years. Deal kindly with me, Your Highness, and I shall give you their names.'

'Speak up, then,' said Sir John, although his inclination was to sentence Shirlok and move on to the next case. He was weary of criminals bucking against the inevitable.

'He is wasting our time,' called one of the jurors, equally keen to be finished before more of the day was lost. Oswald Stanmore was ambitious, determined to make his fortune as a clothier, and because it was market day, he was eager to be back among his apprentices. Next to Stanmore was his youthful brother-in-law, enjoying a break from his studies at the University in Oxford, although Sir John knew why *he* had not been pressed into jury service: Matt Bartholomew had a sharp mind and would ask too many questions. They would probably be perfectly valid ones, but no one wanted to spend all day ironing out details that were irrelevant to the outcome anyway.

'The law compels us to hear what the accused has to say,' replied Sir John. He saw a ripple of annoyance pass through the twelve men. 'Is that not so, Langar?'

4

Langar was thoughtful. 'There have been other instances when criminals have turned approver. But their testimony is nearly always dismissed – mostly because felons are dishonest by definition, so they cannot be trusted to tell the truth. Thus, listening to Shirlok's charges is not mandatory for this court.'

'Not mandatory,' mused Sir John. He was silent for a moment. 'But I took an oath to be fair, even to the lowest of villains. Name your associates, Shirlok.'

There were several weary sighs, and Sir John was irritated to note that one came from Langar, who worked for him and so was supposed to support his decisions.

'First, there is Nicholas Herl,' said Shirlok. He pointed at a thickset man with black hair, who glowered at him. 'We robbed the Walmesford mill together, then set it alight.'

'That is a flagrant lie, Sir John,' snapped Herl. He sounded more annoyed than concerned. 'I am a silversmith – a professional man. Why would I burgle a mill?'

'Not a very good silversmith,' Sir John heard Stanmore whisper to his brother-in-law. 'Did you see those spoons he made for me? Disgraceful workmanship!'

Shirlok was not a fool, and he could see the jury did not like him. In an effort to make himself sound more creditable, he scoured his memory for the Latin he had learned as a child, hoping it would make them revise their low opinions and give him the benefit of the doubt.

'Second, Adam *Molendinarius* received that *urciolum* I stole. Third, "defenceless" Widow Godeknave and Lora Boyner are no innocents, either. With Walter Chapman and that sly clerk who is *Molendinarius*'s brother, they—'

'Liar!' yelled Lora, breaking into the diatribe. She appealed to Sir John, full of righteous fury. 'He is trying to save himself by befouling the names of decent, law-abiding people.'

5

Shirlok pointed at a man who stood some distance from the others he was naming. The fellow wore sombre clothes and carried himself in a way that made Sir John suspect he had once been in holy orders. The country was full of fallen priests, and it was not unusual for them to turn to crime to support themselves.

'Next, John Aylmer took the white pearls I gave him, knowing they were stolen,' declared Shirlok. 'It was probably *him* what stole the chalice, too! He has a liking for such things, because he is a—'

'You are full of deceit, Shirlok,' interrupted Aylmer dismissively. Although he was young, there was an air of dissipation about Aylmer, evident in his ale-paunch and bloodshot eyes. Sir John wondered if loose living had seen him defrocked. 'I am no thief.'

Shirlok continued his malicious tirade, naming others he claimed had helped him burgle houses or who had offered to sell the goods he had dishonestly acquired – ten in total. Predictably, all were outraged, and the hall was soon full of clamouring voices. Sir John quelled them by hammering on Langar's writing desk with his fist. He was used to tempers running high in such situations – although everyone on Shirlok's list had been told exactly why they were obliged to appear at the castle that morning, few folk ever stood quietly when accused of crimes that could see them hanged.

'Everyone indicted by Shirlok is present today, Sir John,' said the sheriff, when it was quiet again.

'And they all assert their innocence,' added Langar, writing furiously.

'It is pure spite,' declared Chapman, an undersized fellow whose only outstanding feature was his penchant for startlingly gaudy scarlet hose. 'There is no truth in these allegations. Shirlok knows he will hang, so he wants others to die with him.'

Sir John studied the ten appellees, noting the expressions on their faces. Herl and Adam *Molendinarius* appeared to be bored, and kept glancing at the hour candle in a way that suggested they resented their time being wasted. Chapman, the other *Molendinarius* brother and Widow Godeknave were anxious and flustered, aware that Shirlok's accusations – even if unproven – might see them strung up in the castle bailey. The debauched Aylmer continued to stand apart from the rest, and Sir John wondered whether Shirlok had included him as an afterthought – the others knew each other, but Aylmer was obviously an outsider. Hefty Lora Boyner and the remaining three were sullen, angry that they had not been permitted to assert their innocence at greater length.

'Did these people know you were a thief, and that the goods you sold them were stolen?' asked Sir John of Shirlok, nodding at Langar to make a note that the question had been put.

'Yes,' stated Shirlok, his firm voice cutting through a new chorus of denials. 'You cannot blame me for stealing when there are folk ready to buy cheap supplies, Your Majesty. I am human, so there is only so much temptation I can bear. *These* are the rascals who should be hanged, not the poor thief.'

'The rest of us manage to resist the seduction of easy wealth,' declared a juror called Stephen Morice, whose reputation for dishonesty – although nothing had ever been proved – and greed was legendary. Sir John tried not to gape at him. 'I do not see why you should be any different.'

'Morice is right,' said Stanmore. 'Men come to me all the time, offering to sell illegally imported cloth at low prices, but *I* say no. A man is responsible for himself, and should accept the consequences of the actions he chooses to take.'

'Well put, Stanmore,' said Morice. 'But we have wasted enough time on Shirlok, and we must hear another two cases before we go home. My verdict is that Shirlok is guilty and these others are innocent. It is clear he named them out of malice.'

'But most of these ten have been thieving and receiving stolen goods from me for a decade, and *I* have just exposed their sins, like the good citizen I am,' cried Shirlok, alarmed by the statement. He appealed to the Justice. 'Let me go, Your Worship, and I promise never to rob in your county again.'

'What say you?' asked Sir John, turning to the rest of the jury. 'Does Morice speak for you all?'

'He certainly speaks for me,' said Thomas Deschalers the grocer, glancing impatiently at the hour candle. A consignment of dried fruit was due to arrive by barge at noon, and it was imperative he was there to check it himself – last time, the contents of one sack had been exchanged for wood-shavings. 'He has admitted he cannot resist easy pickings, and I do not think he can be trusted to live an honest life. He should hang.'

'I agree,' said a portly scholar named Richard de Wetherset. There was an election at his Hostel that day, and he still needed to persuade two more Fellows to vote for him, so he was also eager to be on his way. 'The law is quite clear about what to do with self-confessed thieves.'

'And the others?' asked Sir John. 'These ten he accuses of helping him?'

'No stolen goods were found in *their* possession,' said Deschalers.

'What about the chalice?' asked Stanmore. Sir John saw the clothier's young brother-in-law had prompted him to put the question. 'The sheriff said that was recovered from Lora Boyner.'

'But she received it in good faith,' said Langar, consulting his notes. 'And there is no evidence to suggest otherwise. All the other goods were recovered from Shirlok's house.'

'Shirlok has nothing to support his allegations,' said Deschalers, pretending not to hear Bartholomew urging his brother-in-law to enquire whether the appellees' homes had actually been searched. 'I say we dismiss his testimony.'

Tentatively, Stanmore suggested further investigation, but fell silent when Morice and Deschalers rounded on him – why waste time exploring the claims of a self-confessed criminal? It would mean any thief could accuse whomsoever he liked, just to postpone his execution. Where would it end?

'Then the verdict is carried,' said Langar. 'Shirlok is guilty; the appellees are acquitted.'

Shirlok's jaw dropped as he listened to Sir John intone a sentence of death by hanging. 'But I turned approver,' he breathed, aghast. 'You cannot kill me!'

'You misunderstood the law,' said Langar. 'It does not matter whether you point fingers at the greatest villains in England – turning approver will not affect *your* sentence one way or the other. You lodged a plea of guilty, and there is only one possible outcome.'

'Then I want to change it,' cried Shirlok, as the sheriff's men began to drag him away. 'I am not guilty. I did not take anything after all – it was Chapman, Lora and . . . It was not me!'

'Next case,' said Sir John.

Cambridge, June 1355

A cart clattered along the tangled lanes known as the Jewry and headed for the high street. It was still early, and the

9

wispy clouds were not yet tinged with the sun's golden touch, although the birds were awake and sang loud and shrill along the empty streets. Folk were beginning to stir, and smoke curled lazily skyward as people lit fires to heat ale and breakfast pottage. Bells announced the morning offices, and sleepy monks and friars made their way to their dawn devotions.

Matilde urged her horse to move faster, but the cart was heavy – it was loaded with all her possessions and the beast was not able to move as briskly as she would have liked. When she passed St Michael's Church, her eyes misted with tears. She glanced down the lane opposite, and saw the Master of Michaelhouse striding towards the High Street, his scholars streaming at his heels as he led the daily procession to the church. Matilde could not see whether the man she loved was there, because her tears were blinding her.

She reached the town gate and passed a coin to the man on duty, knowing he would barely look at her: guards were trained to watch who came into the town, but did not care who left it. He waved his hand to indicate she could go, and she flicked the reins to encourage her nag into a trot, wanting to put as much distance between her and Cambridge as possible, before anyone realised she had gone.

Matilde was leaving because she longed for the respectability she knew she would never have in Cambridge. Folk too readily believed she was the kind of woman to entertain men in her house all night, and she wanted something better. In another county, she could begin a different existence, where she would be staid, decent and respected by all. She would be courted by good men, one of whom she would eventually choose as a husband. She could not afford to waste more of her life on Bartholomew, when it was becoming increasingly obvious that he was never going to ask her to be his wife.

She did not look back as her cart rattled along the road that led to the future. She would not have seen anything if she had, with hot tears scalding her eyes. She did not hear the birdsong of an early summer morning, and she did not care about the clusters of white and pink blossom that adorned the green hedgerows. She wondered whether she would ever take pleasure in such things again.

When the service at St Michael's had finished, Bartholomew slipped out of the procession to head for the Jewry. He heard the birds singing and saw the delicate clouds in the sky, and his heart was ready to burst with happiness. He was going to see Matilde, and it was the first day of his new life. The joy he felt told him he should have asked her to marry him years before.

He hesitated when he raised his hand to tap on her door, suddenly assailed with the fear that she might not have him – that the love he had for her was not reciprocated, and she might object to being wed to a physician with few rich patients and a negligent attitude towards collecting his fees. But he would not know unless he asked, so he knocked and waited. There was no reply, and he was tempted to postpone the matter, although he knew he was just being cowardly. He rapped again, then jiggled the latch, but the door was locked. He supposed Matilde had gone to the Market Square, to buy bread for breakfast, so he set off in that direction.

But the traders had not seen Matilde that morning, and nor had her friend Yolande. Then the physician was summoned to his sister's house, where one of Oswald Stanmore's apprentices had a fever. The illness was a serious one, and it was the following afternoon before he could leave his patient and go in search of Matilde again. He was surprised to find Yolande weeping on the doorstep.

'She has gone,' she wept. 'And it is your fault.'

Bartholomew regarded her blankly. 'What?'

Yolande pushed open Matilde's door to reveal a chamber that was empty, with the exception of two benches that had evidently been too large to carry. When he stepped inside, his footsteps echoed hollowly. There was a note on the windowsill, which he picked up with shaking fingers. It said nothing other than that Yolande was to have the remaining furniture, and that the enclosed coins were to pay any outstanding debts.

'She wanted to marry you, but you would never ask her,' said Yolande accusingly. 'It is your fault she has left us.'

He sank down on one of the benches, dazed and numb. 'I came to propose yesterday.'

'But it was too late,' said Yolande harshly. 'She told me she would not wait for ever.'

Bartholomew stood, resolute. 'I will find her. Where would she go?'

'She has a sister in Carcassonne and a cousin in Poitiers, so she may have gone to them. And there was a man who once asked her to wed him – he was rich, not a near-pauper, like you. His name was William de Spayne and he was a merchant, but I cannot remember where she said he lived.'

'Well, try,' ordered Bartholomew curtly. 'It is important.'

'She is more likely to go to her sister first,' said Yolande, sniffing. 'But she once said that if she ever left Cambridge, then no one would ever find her.'

'I will,' vowed Bartholomew with quiet determination. 'I shall leave within the hour.'

CHAPTER 1

Lincoln, December 1356

The sun was setting as the travellers approached the outskirts of the city. Red-gold beams struck the mighty cathedral perched atop its hill, turning its pale stone to a glowing bronze that darkened as night approached. Already, stars were beginning to appear in a cloudless sky, and shadows slanted across the frozen track. Matthew Bartholomew, Master of Medicine at the University in Cambridge and Fellow of the College of Michaelhouse, shifted uncomfortably in his saddle, and was glad the journey was almost at an end. It was unusually cold for the time of year, and early snows dusted the surrounding countryside.

'A magnificent sight,' breathed Thomas de Suttone, gazing at the minster in awe. He was a large man who wore the habit of a Carmelite friar, albeit a very elegant one. One of Michaelhouse's theologians, Suttone preferred to tell others how to practise moderation and poverty than to do it himself. 'A fitting tribute to the glory of God.'

'It is on a hill,' complained Brother Michael, the third of Michaelhouse's travel-weary scholars, regarding it balefully. He was a Benedictine, and his dark cloak and habit were splattered with pale mud. His palfrey stumbled in an ice-filled rut, and a lesser horseman might have been thrown, but the monk had been taught to ride before he could walk, and he did no more than shift in his saddle and adjust the reins. 'We shall have to ascend it on foot, because my poor beast is spent.'

'It is spent because you are so fat,' explained Suttone brutally. 'My animal is not nearly as exhausted, and neither is Matt's. Yours has a far greater load to carry.'

'I am slimmer than I was this time last year,' countered Michael indignantly. He was proud of the fact that the habits he had filled to bursting point eighteen months earlier were now slightly loose, although even the most sycophantic of his friends could not deny that he still possessed a very full figure. Bartholomew encouraged him in his new regime of moderation, because, as a physician, he believed that obese men were susceptible to dangerous imbalances of the humours.

'When the Death returns – which it will – it will carry off gluttons,' stated Suttone matter-of-factly. He was fond of predicting what would happen if the country were ever ravaged by the plague again. Bartholomew stifled a sigh. He was weary of Suttone's gloomy prophecies, and did not like to be reminded of the time when all his medical skills and experience had proved to be useless.

'We are more than a week late,' he said, seeing Michael open his mouth to make a tart response that would almost certainly initiate a quarrel. He was too tired and cold to be caught in the middle of another of their rows. 'Do you think you are still expected?'

'Of course we are!' cried Suttone, offended by the suggestion that the city of Lincoln might not be waiting on tenterhooks for his arrival. 'The Feast of St Thomas the Apostle – when the ceremony installing Michael and me as cathedral canons will take place – is not for another two Sundays yet. It is Wednesday today, which leaves us plenty of time to prepare ourselves.'

'I shall want to look my best,' said Michael, grimacing

14

at his dirt-splattered clothes. 'We will need to commission special vestments, and I might even purchase some new shoes.'

Suttone nodded eagerly. 'I shall do the same. We have been on the road for more than two weeks now, and I am tired of sitting astride this wretched nag and having sleet, snow and rain blow in my face. It has been clear today, but the good weather has come at a price, and I have never known such bitter cold. My feet are frozen to the point where I do not think they will ever move again.'

'It is a pity the same cannot be said for your jaws,' muttered Michael unpleasantly. 'You have not stopped complaining for the last fifteen days.'

'Where shall we go first?' asked Bartholomew, before Suttone could respond to the insult. With dusk approaching, they needed to find lodgings before people closed their gates and retired to their beds for the night. 'The cathedral?'

'Do not be ridiculous,' said Michael scornfully. 'Suttone and I cannot arrive *there* covered in mire and reeking of horse – the other canons will wonder what sort of fellows they have invited to join their ranks.'

'I still do not understand why you two were offered these posts,' said Bartholomew. 'Neither of you have visited Lincoln before, and nor have you done anything to benefit the city.'

Michael glared at him. 'I am Senior Proctor of England's greatest University and a confidant of the Bishop of Ely. Thus, I am an important man, and it should come as no surprise to anyone that a place like Lincoln should want to include *me* among its officials.'

'But you will *not* be among its officials,' Bartholomew pointed out. 'You will be in Cambridge.'

'A non-residentiary canon,' agreed Michael. 'But the

15

cathedral will benefit from having my name in its records and, in return, I shall claim a modest income from the prebendal stall I am to "occupy". Prestige, Matt. It is all about prestige – on both sides.'

'I would have thought being the Bishop of Ely's spy would count against you, Brother,' said Suttone with his customary bluntness. 'I, on the other hand, am one of my Order's foremost scholars, and my family has long been associated with Lincoln. My grandfather was *Bishop* Oliver Suttone.'

Michael regarded him coolly, while Bartholomew supposed that either the long-dead prelate had taken vows of celibacy later in life or – more likely – had ignored them altogether.

'I am not forced to rely on dead ancestors to help *me* win favour,' declared the monk icily. 'And *my* bishop is very well thought of by his peers.'

His comment suggested the same could not be said for Bishop Oliver Suttone, although Bartholomew had no idea whether the man had been a saint or the biggest crook in Christendom.

'Night is drawing on,' said Bartholomew's Welsh book-bearer, kicking his pony forward to speak quietly to the physician. Cynric was the last of the four-man party from Michaelhouse. 'We should not dally while they quarrel again. Remember what happened last night? You and I were hard-pressed to fight off those robbers, and this pair were next to worthless.'

'Michael was not,' said Bartholomew, recalling the competent way the monk had wielded a stave. For a man who had foresworn arms, the monk was remarkably adept with long pieces of wood.

The religious habits worn by Michael and Suttone had deterred most footpads from attacking them on their

16

journey, although the ruthless band that had set their ambush the previous night had chosen to ignore the general consensus that it was a bad idea to raise weapons against men of God. They would be more cautious the next time, though. Cynric was a formidable swordsman, and Bartholomew's recent experiences in France – a country with which England was currently at war – had honed his once mediocre skills to the point where he was more than a match for the common robber.

Cynric sniffed as he rode next to Bartholomew. 'But Suttone distracted me by falling to his knees and squawking prayers. Look at them now – they are debating whether Bishop Gynewell of Lincoln is better than Bishop de Lisle of Ely, and neither is qualified to give an opinion, because they have never met Gynewell. They will squabble for hours, if you do not move them on.'

Bartholomew addressed his argumentative colleagues. 'I can see the city gates ahead. They will close at dusk, so we do not have much time if we want to sleep inside tonight.'

Suttone squinted into the rapidly fading light. 'Bishop Gynewell mentioned gates south of the city in his letter – although he said the first set actually protects a suburb called Wigford, not Lincoln itself. However, he also said the Carmelite Friary is located in Wigford, so we shall stay there.'

'I am not staying with White Friars,' declared Michael firmly. 'They have a nasty habit of fasting or dining solely on fish during Advent – and after a day in the saddle, a man needs red meat. We shall hunt out the Benedictines instead. They have a more sensible attitude to such matters.'

'If you had bothered to read Gynewell's missive, you would know that the Black Monks' Priory is a long way to the east of the town,' argued Suttone. 'Too far to go tonight.

But my Carmelite brethren will not starve two hungry canons-elect and a University physician—'

'Look,' said Cynric, pointing to where someone was lighting a lantern outside a substantial gatehouse. The lamp swung in the gathering wind, and would not burn for long. 'Only a convent would own such a great, thick door. We could ask to stay there.'

'We could not,' said Suttone distastefully. 'According to Gynewell, the first friary encountered from this direction will be Gilbertine.' He almost spat the name of the only religious Order to be founded in England. 'And we all know they are inferior to the rest of us.'

'Then you can find somewhere better tomorrow,' said Bartholomew, spurring his horse forward. The Cambridge Gilbertines were respectable, sober men, and he thought Suttone's prejudice against their Order was unjustified and ignorant. 'But tonight we shall stay here. It is too near nightfall to be choosy.'

Suttone opened his mouth to argue, but the temperature was dropping fast as the sun disappeared, and even he saw further travel would be foolish. He set his pony after Bartholomew, with Michael and Cynric at his heels.

The Gilbertine Priory of St Katherine occupied a substantial tract of land about a mile south of the city, tucked between the main road and the broad River Witham. Like many convents that had been built outside a town defences, it looked to its own security, and was protected by a high wall. Unfortunately, the wall was in a poor state of repair, suggesting it had been built in a time of plenty, but the priory within was currently experiencing leaner times. On closer inspection, the gatehouse was similarly afflicted: there was worm in its wooden door and its metal bosses were rusty. The grille that allowed guards to scan visitors before opening the front door was missing, affording anyone outside an unobstructed view of the buildings within. Bartholomew saw several long, tiled roofs, indicating that the Gilbertines owned a sizeable institution, if not a wealthy one.

Opposite the gate, standing so close to the side of the road that carts would surely be obliged to alter course to avoid hitting it, was a tall structure, liberally adorned with pinnacles and a teetering central spire. It stood twice the height of a man, and reminded Bartholomew of a roadside shrine he had seen recently in France.

'It is probably the Eleanor Cross,' said Suttone, when he saw his colleagues regarding it curiously. He raised his eyebrows in contrived disbelief when Michael regarded him blankly. 'Queen Eleanor – wife of the first King Edward.'

'Ah, yes,' said Michael, struggling to remember his history before Suttone started to gloat. 'When she died, Edward was so distressed that he built one of these monuments at every place her body rested on its journey to Westminster Abbey. The cortege started near Lincoln, I recall.'

'The King left her viscera here, though,' added Suttone, determined to have the last word.

'Her what, Father?' asked Cynric.

'Viscera – innards,' explained Suttone. 'It is a great honour for the cathedral to have them.'

Cynric eyed him in shocked revulsion. 'You English!' he muttered, but not quite softly enough to escape Suttone's sharp ears. 'Disembowelling queens is not the act of civilised men. You are worse than the French – and that is saying something.'

Suttone's eyes narrowed. The book-bearer had been taciturn and deferential before Bartholomew had taken him overseas some eighteen months before, but the experience had changed him – and not for the better. He often voiced his own opinions now, and was not afraid to say exactly what he thought, even when it was rude. Bartholomew did not seem to care, and even sought out the fellow's advice on some matters, which Suttone, a traditional sort of man, found unconscionable. It was true that Cynric's military skills had saved them several times during the journey, but Suttone disliked saucy servants, and he preferred the old Cynric. He opened his mouth to object to being compared unfavourably to the French, but the party had been spotted by the man kindling the lamp – a small fellow with jug-like ears. Like all male members of the Gilbertine Order, he wore an ankle-length tunic of black, covered by a white cloak and hood.

'Are you looking for lodgings?' he asked, coming towards them with open eagerness. 'My name is John de Whatton. We have plenty of beds and food, even for Benedictines and Carmelites, and especially if they can pay.'

'Good,' replied Michael ungraciously. 'I am starving. So is my horse,' he added as an afterthought, when Suttone drew breath to comment on his plague-inducing appetite.

'We have plenty of sweet hay, too,' said Whatton with a cheerful smile. 'However, you may find us in disarray this evening. We have had a death, you see, but you should not let it bother you.'

'I am sorry to hear that,' said Bartholomew politely. 'One of your brethren?'

'No, thank the good Lord. One of the guests. He was murdered.'

'Well done, Matthew,' whispered Suttone venomously, as the Michaelhouse men followed Whatton through the crumbling gatehouse and into the Gilbertines' domain. 'Gynewell wrote that there are *six* friaries and convents in

Lincoln, to say nothing of hospitals that entertain paying guests, and *you* choose the one where someone has just been slaughtered.'

'I do not like the sound of this,' agreed Michael. 'Whatton did not say whether the suspect is under lock and key or still at large. It would be a pity for me to have survived the treacherous journey from Cambridge, only to have my throat cut on arrival. Lord! It is a bitter evening – it would not surprise me to learn there was another blizzard in the offing. But I suppose there are four of us to repel the murderous advances of these Gilbertines, so I suggest we do as Matt says, and stay here tonight. We can always find somewhere better tomorrow.'

'Tomorrow might be too late,' Suttone pointed out darkly.

Michael chose to ignore the comment as he ventured further into the priory. 'This place should please you, Suttone: it looks poor, and you will not want to be too lavishly entertained, lest it encourages the plague to come again.'

'My beliefs about the Death do not lead me to embrace squalor when alternatives are available,' replied Suttone haughtily. 'But we are inside now, and it would be churlish to take one look around and opt to go elsewhere. Some of these Gilbertines might be cathedral canons – future colleagues – and it would be a pity to offend them so soon. I agree with you: we shall sleep here tonight.'

A lay-brother came to take the horses, and Whatton issued a stream of instructions – the visitors' beasts were to be given warmed oat mash and the stable that did not leak. The man nodded in a way that suggested he did not need to be told, indicating the orders were for the guests' benefit, not his. Then Whatton bustled away abruptly, leaving the scholars alone and uncertain what to do next. When Suttone and Michael began a waspish debate about the merits of poverty in religious foundations, Bartholomew took the opportunity to inspect his surroundings before the light failed completely.

The buildings stood around two separate yards, with the chapel and the Prior's House forming a barrier between them. As in most Gilbertine foundations, a nuns' refectory and dormitory lay to the north, while the brothers had a similar set of buildings to the south, along with a two-storeyed hall for guests and a thatched shed for servants. A muddle of kitchens, pantries and storehouses stood to the west, overlooking the neat vegetable plots that ran down to the river. The land to the south of the complex comprised an extensive orchard of fruit trees.

'Who has been murdered?' asked Michael, breaking into the Carmelite's tirade against those who hankered after luxury – with the natural exception of himself, of course. 'Did Whatton say?'

'One of the *guests*,' replied Suttone. 'Clearly, they do not offer much protection for those unlucky devils who are forced to stay within their walls.'

'Look at that!' hissed Cynric suddenly, gripping Bartholomew's arm hard enough to hurt as he pointed. 'Surely, that is a woman? What is *she* doing in here?'

'It is a Gilbertine foundation,' explained Michael. Cynric did not look any the wiser, so he elaborated. 'A dual house – where nuns and brothers live together.'

'Does that mean those ladies will share our beds tonight?' asked Cynric nervously. 'My wife will not approve of that at all, and she is bound to find out. She always does.'

'Well, *I* shall not do it,' declared Suttone. 'Unless there is absolutely no alternative. Here comes Whatton with a friend. Draw your sword, Cynric, lest they have come to kill us.'

'Don't,' countered Bartholomew sharply, when Cynric started to comply.

'God's greetings,' said the newcomer. He was taller than Whatton, and there was something unpleasant about his wet-lipped grin and the mincing quality of his voice. 'You have caught us at a bad time, I am afraid. One of our visitors died this morning, and his friends have been here all day, demanding an explanation. Then several other guests left, because they do not want to sleep in a place where their throats may be cut during the night. So we are now all confusion.'

'Someone's throat was cut?' asked Suttone in alarm.

The Gilbertine's smile slipped a little. 'It was just a figure of speech – he was merely stabbed, so do not worry yourself with unnecessarily gruesome images. I am Hamo, and the prior has asked me to see to your needs during your sojourn with us. I am more than happy to do so.'

'You should be,' remarked Whatton wryly. 'It means an effective promotion to Brother Hospitaller, a post that has been vacant since Fat William died of a surfeit of oysters last year.'

'Fat William was a greedy fellow,' said Hamo, and his grin became a little gleeful. 'He was in the habit of eating the food left by pilgrims for the poor, and Dame Eleanor said God struck him down for his unrepentant gluttony.'

'Then Dame Eleanor sounds like a woman after my own heart,' said Suttone, impressed. 'Does she believe gluttony is the sin most likely to provoke God into sending the Death again? If so, I would like to meet her.'

Whatton raised his eyebrows in surprise: Suttone was not as large as Michael, but he was still a very well-fed man. 'I do not know which sin she deplores the most, but she is a saintly lady, and often weeps when she sees brazen wickedness. Since she walks from here to the cathedral every day – and it is quite a long way – she tends to notice rather a lot of it.'

Hamo clasped his hands in front of him, and adopted an ingratiatingly submissive pose. 'But enough of us. Have you come to Lincoln for the installation of canons, for Miller's Market or to make reparation for sins committed during the Summer Madness?'

'Summer Madness?' asked Bartholomew, startled.

Hamo regarded him oddly. 'People ran insane in August. Did you not hear? It happened all over the country. They fell shuddering and screaming to the ground, and had to be bound hand and foot to prevent them from harming themselves. We took them to the churches, so God could cure them.'

'And did He?' asked Bartholomew, intrigued. He and Cynric had only returned to Cambridge in October, for the beginning of the academic year. The ensuing term had been frantically busy, and neither had had much time to catch up on what had happened in England during their absence.

Hamo nodded. 'For the most part, although we lost a few because they refused to eat or were smothered as they were restrained. However, a number of *very* evil deeds were perpetrated by some sufferers, and many will flock to the cathedral on St Thomas's Day to make amends.'

'What sort of evil deeds?' asked Suttone curiously. 'Gluttony? Avarice?'

'Worse,' replied Hamo. 'One man – a merchant called Flaxfleete – set fire to a rival clothier's storerooms. I am sure *he* will be among the petitioners – he will not want arson on his conscience.'

'The Dean and Chapter have offered a complete absolution from *all* summer sins for the very reasonable price of sixpence,' elaborated Whatton, clearly impressed by such a good bargain. 'And since the Madness was used as an excuse for committing all manner of crimes, there will be a lot of folk eager to take advantage of the offer. It is all in a good cause – the cathedral's roof is very expensive to maintain.'

'We had no cases in Cambridge, but the town was full of the news for weeks,' explained Michael to Bartholomew. 'The sickness struck across all of England, and I am surprised you did not hear the tales when you returned from France.'

'What caused it?' asked Bartholomew.

Michael was startled to be asked such a question. 'I have no idea. An imbalance of humours, I suppose, since that is the explanation you physicians usually give for any ailment that mystifies you.'

'Actually, the Devil was responsible,' countered Hamo matter-of-factly. 'He sent people into fits of twisting and contortions, and made them see things that were not there.'

'*Ignis sacer*,' surmised Bartholomew, drawing his own conclusions. He translated for Cynric's benefit. 'Holy Fire. It is a kind of plague that often occurs after wet, cold winters. It causes a swelling and a rotting of the limbs – and that *does* create an imbalance of humours, Brother.'

'Well, *we* are not in Lincoln to confess sins brought about by Summer Madness,' said Suttone to the Gilbertines. His tone was smug. 'Brother Michael and I are here to be installed as canons.'

Hamo beamed in genuine pleasure. 'I must tell Prior Roger immediately! He will be delighted – he likes to keep favour with the cathedral.' He turned to Bartholomew. 'Are you kin to these two, come to share their moment of honour?'

Bartholomew did not want to tell him the truth, which

25

was that he was looking for the woman he hoped might become his wife. When Matilde had despaired of him ever putting the question that would make her happy and had left Cambridge, he had promptly resigned his Fellowship and had gone to find her, taking Cynric with him. He had visited her relatives in France and on the Italian peninsula, and searched every city, town and village he had ever heard her mention, but all to no avail. Matilde had disappeared as though she had never been born.

When he had returned to Cambridge after almost sixteen months of futile hunting, he learned that Michael – wholly on his own initiative – had destroyed his letter of resignation and arranged a sabbatical leave of absence instead, which meant his job at Michaelhouse was still his own. He had been grateful beyond words, because he liked teaching, and a hall full of eager students had helped ease the emptiness in his heart that Matilde had left.

Then Michael and Suttone had been offered posts as canons in Lincoln, and the mention of that city had jolted a memory in one of Matilde's friends – they had discussed Lincoln once, she said, and Matilde had almost married a man who lived there. Matilde had never talked about Lincoln to Bartholomew, although he knew about the aborted betrothal, and while he doubted he would find her there, he felt compelled to turn the very last stone. And it *was* the very last stone, because he had followed every other lead, even the most unlikely ones. He had waited patiently for term to finish – Michael could not be expected to inveigle a second sabbatical so soon after the first – and then had offered to accompany his two colleagues when they travelled to Lincoln for their installation.

But what should he tell the Gilbertines? No one at Michaelhouse knew why he had gone the first time, except

Michael and Cynric; as far as Suttone and the other Fellows were concerned, he had been seized with a sudden desire to inspect the medical faculties in Padua, Montpellier, Paris and Salerno. Bartholomew was not a monk or a priest in holy orders, unlike most University officers, and so women were not forbidden to him, but chasing them across half the civilised world was not the kind of behaviour expected from scholars nonetheless, and he preferred to keep his business to himself.

'He came to protect us helpless monastics on the long and dangerous road from Cambridge,' explained Michael, when the physician took rather too long to reply to what was a simple question. The monk did not want the Gilbertines to assume there was another reason for the physician's presence, and start to pry. And, since he seriously doubted Matilde would be found in Lincoln, there was no need for anyone to know the real purpose for his friend's journey.

Personally, Michael believed Matilde did not want to be found, and thought Bartholomew should abandon his quest and take the cowl instead. Scholars were not permitted to marry, and if the physician caught his prize, he would be forced to give up his Fellowship. He was a valuable asset to Michaelhouse, which was why the monk had gone to the trouble of arranging the sabbatical in the first place – something he would not have done for any other colleague.

'He defended you against robbers?' asked Hamo doubtfully. Bartholomew's hat and cloak revealed him as a physician, and he wore a leather jerkin of the type favoured by seasoned travellers and soldiers. However, his sword was caked in mud and beginning to rust in a way that would shame a real warrior, and the medicine bag he wore looped over his shoulder would impede his drawing of it.

'We are not overly endowed with good fighting men at

27

the University,' explained Michael, seeing the Gilbertine did not know whether to believe him. 'So, we are obliged to accept whoever offers.'

'Actually, Doctor Bartholomew has recently returned from France,' said Suttone, indignant on Bartholomew's behalf at the slur on his fighting abilities. To underline his point, he deliberately gave the last word a sinister timbre that was potent enough to make both Gilbertines shudder.

'How dreadful,' said Hamo. 'We are at war with the French, so it must have been very dangerous.'

'It was,' agreed Suttone. 'He went to study there, and his devotion to acquiring foreign knowledge meant he was at Poitiers in September.' He pursed his lips meaningfully, glancing at Michael to show that he was wrong to denigrate their colleague's military skills.

'Poitiers?' asked Whatton eagerly. 'There are tales of a great battle there – the Black Prince won a mighty victory. Did you see it? We would love to hear your account, if you were.'

'Such slaughter is hardly a subject for fireside chatter,' said Bartholomew reproachfully.

'It *is,* though,' countered Cynric immediately. 'Most of the great Welsh ballads are about battles, and you have to admit Poitiers was one of the best. I shall never forget the moment when the Black Prince raised his sword after that third skirmish – when we were certain we were doomed because we were outnumbered and exhausted – and tore into the French like an avenging angel. It was a glorious sight and *I* do not mind telling you the story, Master Whatton.'

'But I do,' said Bartholomew quietly. He failed to under-stand how his book-bearer had distilled even the most remote flicker of enjoyment from the bloody carnage.

Cynric, meanwhile, was bemused by the physician's revulsion by what he saw as a bright, shining moment in history. They had discussed it at length, and both knew it was a matter on which they would never agree.

Whatton winked at Cynric in a way that suggested arrangements would be made later. 'How did you come to be in Poitiers – or France, for that matter? Surely, the natives are hostile to Englishmen?'

Bartholomew was not about to admit that he had been visiting members of Matilde's family, but he did not want to lie, either. He told a partial truth. 'Cynric and I were forced to travel with the English army for some of the time. It was safer that way – until French forces trapped us and forced a fight. Poitiers might have been considered a great victory here, but it came at a terrible price – for both sides.'

'While we are in Lincoln, we are hoping to meet an old acquaintance,' said Michael, hastily changing the subject before Bartholomew's distaste for war led him to say something unpatriotic or treasonous. Too late, he realised he had chosen another subject that was painful for his friend, but it would look odd to change what he was going to say, so he pressed on. 'A lady called Matilde, who lived here once. I do not suppose you happen to know her?'

Suttone smiled suddenly and unexpectedly. Everyone at Michaelhouse had liked Matilde, even sour old miseries like the Carmelite. 'Dear Matilde! We all missed her when she left. Do you think she might be here, Brother? It is possible, I suppose. She once told me – after I gave a sermon in which I mentioned my grandfather the bishop – that she considered Lincoln's cathedral to be the finest in the world, so perhaps she does hail from this place.'

'My Order compels me to preach among the laity, so I *do* know a large number of townsfolk,' replied Hamo. 'But

I am afraid there are several women by that name. What does she look like?'

Bartholomew refrained from telling him that she was the loveliest creature he had ever seen. 'I believe she was once betrothed to a merchant called William de Spayne,' he said instead.

Hamo beamed. 'Oh, *that* Matilde – a lady with the face of an angel, and the sweet heart of one, too. I am not surprised you would like to trace her. *She* is an acquaintance well worth keeping.'

Bartholomew gazed at Hamo, aware that his heart was pounding. He had not imagined that the first man he asked would remember Matilde – he had not expected *anyone* to know her, having endured more than a year of shaken heads and apologetic smiles – and he wondered whether his luck had finally turned. 'Is she here now?' he asked, holding his breath as he waited for the answer.

Hamo shook his head. 'I am sorry – she is not. But Spayne might know where she went. You could ask him.'

'He is our current mayor,' added Whatton helpfully. 'And he lives in one of the old stone houses near the corn market. Anyone will tell you how to find it.'

'Not tonight, Matt,' said Michael in an undertone, seeing the physician about to follow their directions immediately. 'It is dark, and only a madman wanders around strange cities after sunset.'

'When was she last here?' asked Bartholomew, trying to keep the eagerness from his voice. It would be hard to wait all night for answers, although he saw the sense in Michael's advice.

Hamo thought carefully. 'It must be six years now. Everyone loved her. There is a deep rift between some of the city officials, you see, and she was one of few who have tried to heal it. But then she just left. She was here one day and gone the next, like a puff of wind, leaving no trace of herself.'

'Just like she did in Cambridge,' said Suttone, shaking his head sadly. Then he frowned. 'Do I recall *you* being especially fond of her, Matthew?'

'No more so than anyone else,' replied Michael briskly, before Bartholomew could answer for himself. 'He is a University Fellow, after all, and not given to hankerings for women.'

Suttone seemed to accept the point, and Hamo began to elaborate on Matilde's abrupt departure from his city. Bartholomew's brief flare of hope had died at the mention of six years. She had been in Cambridge since then, and he suspected her Lincoln friends would know even less about her most recent wanderings than he did.

'Who is *she*?' interrupted Michael suddenly, pointing to where an unusually tall lady in the white habit of a Gilbertine nun was walking towards the chapel, holding a lamp to guide her. The robe accentuated her slim figure, and she moved in a way that suggested she knew she was attracting admiring glances. At her side was an older woman, slightly bent with age, but still moving quickly enough to make her younger companion stride out to keep pace with her.

'That is Dame Eleanor,' replied Whatton, his voice softening with quiet admiration. 'As a child, she was presented to the old queen, who gave her to us. She has been here for nigh on six decades.'

'You mean Queen Isabella?' asked Suttone. 'The wanton wife of the second King Edward?'

'No, the queen before her,' replied Hamo. 'Eleanor – whose memorial stands outside our gate. We are very proud of that, because it is a symbol of the esteem in which our

31

priory is held by monarchs. But *our* Eleanor – Dame Eleanor Darcy – has dedicated her life to Lincoln's saints, and climbs the hill every day to tend their shrines in the cathedral. She is a devout and venerable lady.'

'Is she the one who deplores gluttony?' asked Suttone keenly. 'You mentioned her earlier.'

'What saints?' asked Cynric, as Hamo nodded his answer to Suttone's question. 'Does your city have saints of its own?'

Hamo nodded again. 'They are called Little Hugh and Bishop Hugh, both buried in the cathedral.'

'I meant the *other* lady,' said Michael impatiently, eyes fixed on the apparition in white that glided along the snow-dappled path. 'The younger one.'

'That looks like a woman,' supplied Suttone unhelpfully. 'The Gilbertine Order enrols them in its priories, as you mentioned earlier. It is an odd rule, and I do not consider it a wise one.'

'Women have just as much right to live in this fine convent as men do,' said Whatton coolly. 'And problems with cohabitation occur only when folk are weak and given to fornication. Benedictines could never manage it, and neither could Carmelites, but male and female Gilbertines have been living side by side without trouble or sin for nigh on two hundred years.'

'I applaud your achievement, but who *is* she?' pressed Michael irritably, overlooking the slight to his Order in the interests of learning what he wanted to know.

'Christiana de Hauville,' replied Hamo, glaring at his colleague for his intemperate remarks to honoured guests. 'She is technically a lay-sister, although she is nobly born and owns property in the city. Dame Eleanor has taken a liking to her, and they are often together. As you can see, they are going to the Chapel of St Katherine for evening prayers.'

'Eleanor *says* she has taken Lady Christiana under her wing,' said Whatton. He smiled indulgently. 'Yet it often appears the other way around – Christiana looks after Eleanor. But, suffice to say, they are devoted to each other. It is cold out here. Would you like to come inside?'

'I would like to visit your chapel,' said Michael transparently. 'To give thanks for our safe arrival.'

'You can do it by your bed, Brother,' said Suttone, shooting Michael a look to warn him that the honour of his Order was at stake, and he should not prove the Gilbertines right by ogling the first female who crossed his path. 'Our horses are already installed in a warm stable with a bucket of hot mash, and I would like to do the same.'

'Would you?' asked Hamo, startled. 'I was planning to put you in the guest-hall, and provide you with a supper of roasted goose. But, of course, if you would rather eat oats—'

'The guest-hall will be acceptable,' said Michael, tearing his eyes from the chapel and indicating that Hamo should lead the way. 'And I might manage a sliver of roasted goose, especially if it comes with a few parsnips and a loaf of bread.'

'We are delighted to have you here, and we will cook you whatever you want,' replied Hamo generously. Bartholomew hoped he would not regret the promise: Michael had a formidable appetite. 'Ask for anything, and, if it is in my power to give, you shall have it.'

'How kind,' said Michael, inclining his head. 'You are most hospitable.'

'Yes, we are,' agreed Whatton pleasantly. 'We like guests, especially ones who might leave us a donation to mend our roofs. We suffered badly in the Death – there were sixty of us, but now we are only twelve – and Prior

Roger says we may never recover. The biggest problem is that there are not enough of us to collect the tithes we are owed, and we sink ever deeper into poverty and debt.'

'I am sorry to hear that,' said Suttone. 'But surely you can hire a bailiff to help you?'

'We tried, but they kept absconding with our money,' said Hamo mournfully. He opened the door of the long building that formed the guest-hall. 'Here we are. You shall have the upper room, because it is nicer than the ground-floor chamber. Warmer, too.'

He led the way through a dark, vault-like hall that had bedding piled around the edges, and headed for a spiral staircase. It emerged in an attractive room with clean white walls, wooden floors and the exotic luxury of a stone sink in one corner with a pail of icy water underneath it. He and Whatton set about lighting a fire, while Michael opened a window shutter to inspect the chapel. Bartholomew paced restlessly, thinking about William de Spayne, and hoping, despite the practical part of his mind that told him he was wasting his time, that the mayor might be able to tell him something useful about Matilde.

'You mentioned a Miller's Market when you asked why we had come to Lincoln,' said Suttone conversationally while the Gilbertines busied themselves at the hearth. 'What is that, exactly?'

'It is an annual occurrence now,' said Hamo, rolling straw into a ball for kindling, 'although it does not usually coincide with the installation of canons. Those two events – along with the General Pardon – are why our city is so busy at the moment, and every bed taken.'

'Is it?' asked Michael, thinking about the empty chamber below.

Whatton applied a tinderbox to Hamo's straw. 'Every

convent is bursting at the seams, and every inn seethes with visitors. Except us.'

'That is because our priory is the one farthest from the city, and people dislike walking the extra distance,' added Hamo quickly, seeing his guests' thoughts naturally turn to the man who had been murdered that day.

'You still have not told us what Miller's Market is,' said Michael.

'A merchant named Adam Miller started it five years ago, when he baked cakes and sold them at cost to the town's poor,' replied Whatton. 'The next year, other members of the Commonalty – that is the city's ruling council – followed his example, and the poor had ale and leather goods. And so it has continued, although the promise of cheap supplies encourages evil types – thieves, pickpockets, beggars and scoundrels – to flock here, too.'

'You said you have come to be enrolled as canons,' said Hamo, rather more interested in eliciting information than dispensing it. 'Which stalls will you occupy?'

Suttone smiled with more pride than was right for a man in a vocation that advocated humility. 'Brother Michael will have the Stall of South Scarle, and I shall have the Stall of Decem Librarum – which is valued at six pounds, eighteen shillings and seven pence a year.'

'That is a lot of money, Father,' said Cynric, impressed. 'What will you do with it?'

'As canons, we shall have specific duties to perform,' explained Suttone. 'But obviously we cannot live here, since we have our University teaching to do, so we shall spend a portion of it on paying a deputy – called a *Vicar Choral* – to act in our stead.'

'You will pay him almost seven pounds a year?' asked Cynric, awed. 'May I apply? I can read a bit of Latin – Doctor Bartholomew taught me when we were in France.'

Michael smiled indulgently. 'We only need pay our assistants a fraction of our earnings – our *prebends*, as they are called. The rest we can keep for ourselves. I shall give some to Michaelhouse, some to my mother abbey at Ely, and spend the rest on good wine to share with friends. But Suttone and I do not accept these posts for the money, but because they represent an acknowledgement of our academic prowess.'

'They represent the fact that you have connections to the men who can control these things,' corrected Whatton baldly, making Bartholomew laugh. 'Who is it? The Bishop of Ely? Our own Bishop Gynewell?'

Suttone's face was stony. 'I am related to the Lincolnshire Suttones, who—'

'Gynewell, then,' said Whatton, nodding his satisfaction that he had been right. 'The Suttones are a powerful family in these parts, and Gynewell is obliged to pander to them at every opportunity.'

Hamo beamed in delight, and reached out to grasp the Carmelite's hand. 'Then you and I are kin, Father, because I am Hamo de *Suttone*. I hail from a lowly branch of the dynasty, it is true, but I am proud of it anyway. I had no idea that our humble priory was about to entertain such an auspicious guest.'

'But you both plan to appoint Vicars Choral and join the ranks of Lincoln's many non-residentiary canons,' said Whatton, not as impressed as his colleague. 'Most of your prebends will go to other foundations, and not to poor Lincoln. Still, it cannot be helped. At least you are English. Most of the last lot were French – and us at war, too!'

'Shameful,' agreed Cynric with considerable feeling.

'Whatton mentioned a murder earlier,' said Suttone, glancing towards the door to ensure it could be barred from the inside. 'But he did not say whether you had caught the culprit.'

'We have not,' replied Whatton, standing up as the logs caught at last. 'But there is no need for alarm. I doubt the killer will attack anyone else.'

'How can you be so sure?' asked Michael suspiciously.

Whatton smiled serenely. 'Because of the man Aylmer was – debauched, sly and dishonest. No one was surprised when he was found dead with a dagger in his back.'

'Do you mean *John* Aylmer?' asked Suttone. He swallowed hard. 'From Huntingdonshire?'

Hamo nodded. 'You know him? He was certainly the kind of fellow to stick in a man's mind.'

'He is certainly stuck in mine,' said Suttone weakly. 'He is my Vicar Choral.'

'I cannot wait until tomorrow,' said Bartholomew, pacing up and down in the guest-hall. The Gilbertines had gone, Suttone was out in search of the latrine, and the physician was alone with Michael and Cynric. 'I keep thinking Hamo may be right – that Spayne might know where Matilde is now. If he was going to marry her six years ago, then they were obviously close.'

Michael inclined his head. 'But think about her arrival in Cambridge, Matt. It was roughly six years ago, so she probably went there immediately after she left him. She mentioned this betrothal to you *once*, which suggests that either they parted on bad terms or he did not mean that much to her. Do not rush this. You waited the best part of a term before coming to investigate this particular lead, so surely you can manage a few more hours?'

Bartholomew was not sure he could. The possibility, however remote, that Spayne might be able to help him gnawed at his senses like a worm. 'I know it is dark, but it is not late, and I cannot see Spayne being in his bed before seven o'clock. I am going to see him tonight.'

'It is not wise to wander around strange towns after dusk,' said Michael gently. 'You know this.'

'I will go with you,' offered Cynric, seeing the physician was not to be dissuaded. He stood and slipped his sword into his belt.

Michael looked around for his cloak. 'Then so will I. Cynric can protect you with his blade, and my habit may make footpads think twice about molesting you.'

'It did not work yesterday,' Cynric pointed out ruefully.

'True,' agreed Michael. 'So we shall say a prayer before we go. In the chapel.'

'You mean the chapel that lady went into?' asked Bartholomew, smiling. 'Then go and fulfil your religious obligations, Brother. I do not need an escort.'

Michael was right: it *was* dangerous to explore unknown cities at night, and Bartholomew did not want to put his friends at risk just because he was impatient. They listened to his arguments for them remaining with the Gilbertines, then followed him outside anyway. Snow lay in untidy heaps, where it had been swept, and the ground was slick with hoarfrost.

'You have been more than patient with my hunt,' said Bartholomew, buckling his sword to his waist as they walked across the yard. He never carried weapons in Cambridge, but his travels in France and along some of England's robber-infested highways meant he was now more cautious. 'Both of you. And I shall make you a promise: this is the last time I race off in search of shadows. If I cannot find Matilde this time, I shall concede defeat.'

'I shall hold you to it,' warned Michael, selecting a tortuous route that avoided the bigger drifts. 'You cannot spend the rest of your life haring around countries with which we are at war, and we need you at Michaelhouse. We have students eager to study with you – you taught them more last term than Doctor Rougham managed in a year – and England needs University-trained physicians. If Suttone is right, and the Death is about to come back, the importance of your work cannot be overestimated.'

'You give me too much credit. Physicians were worthless during the plague – worse than worthless, even, since I sometimes wonder whether our advice and practices made it worse. But even if we cannot cure the pestilence, then I suppose there are other ailments to treat. We still have our uses.'

'You do,' agreed Michael. 'Oh, look! We just happen to be at the Gilbertines' church. Give me a few moments to say my prayers, and then we shall visit Spayne together.'

The Chapel of St Katherine was an attractive building, which had been raised by Normans. It boasted small round-headed windows, and the arches in the nave were adorned with brightly painted dog-tooth mouldings. Its chancel was longer than its nave, although not as wide, and its stone floor made their footsteps echo as they walked towards the high altar. It smelled damp, as though the roof was leaking somewhere, and it was icy cold. It was also empty, although a doused but still-warm lamp suggested that Dame Eleanor and Lady Christiana had not long left their devotions.

Michael grimaced before kneeling to recite a psalm of deliverance. Unlike Bartholomew, who enjoyed being on the road and seeing new sights, the monk considered travel a dreadful ordeal, and was genuinely grateful to have arrived in Lincoln unscathed. While he chanted, Bartholomew wondered what it was about Lady Christiana that had caught Michael's attention, thinking she could not hold a candle to Matilde's radiant beauty. But then, he acknowledged wryly, he could not look at a woman without comparing her unfavourably to Matilde these days. It was hardly healthy, and he knew he should stop before he drove himself insane.

'You should leave some coins,' Michael called over his shoulder, as he climbed inelegantly to his feet. 'St Katherine will appreciate them, and we need all the good graces we can muster, since we have to ride home again in two weeks.'

When Bartholomew did as the monk suggested, he saw others had left oblations, too. In pride of place was a silver chalice. It was a simple thing, quite small, and its tarnished appearance suggested it had seen better days. Other people had used it as a receptacle, and several pennies and a ring lay on its bottom. Bartholomew dropped his offering in with them, then stood in the shadows, waiting with poorly concealed impatience for the monk to finish.

Eventually, Michael was ready and they left the priory, ignoring the unhappy strictures of Whatton at the gate, who told them they would miss supper if they took too long. Bartholomew was not hungry, his appetite vanished at the prospect of new information, while in his newly 'slender' form, Michael had trained himself to miss the occasional repast. And Cynric was an old soldier, used to eating at irregular times, and was adept at obtaining what he wanted from locked kitchens anyway.

The first obstacle they were obliged to surmount was a tall, narrow structure known as the West Bargate. It straddled a foul-smelling dyke, and comprised a vaulted arch with a stout wooden gate – the heavy bar that secured the gate from inside gave the building its name – and a guardroom above. Smoke issued from the chimney, and a good deal of hammering and shouting was required before the soldier could be persuaded to leave his cosy domain. Once they had his attention, it cost fourpence to be allowed through, and another fourpence to extract the promise that they would be let out again later, to return to their lodgings.

Bartholomew expected to find himself in the city once they had passed under the West Bargate's dripping portal, and was surprised when the guard said Lincoln was still a mile away: the churches and houses that lined the road ahead comprised the elongated suburb-settlement of Wigford.

The first of Wigford's dozen churches was a stately affair dedicated to St Botolph. Next was St Margaret's, once fine, but now showing signs of neglect. Then came Holy Cross, adorned with a handsome steeple, but with its priest's house a blackened shell at the far end of its churchyard. Some of its parishioners were moving around the ruins with torches, and the rattle of saws and the tap of hammers showed they were rebuilding it, lending their labour once their day's official work was done. A young priest – no more than a boy – had been given the job of stirring the mortar, but he was unequal to the task, and his parishioners' complaints rang in the still night air.

Eventually, after a stumbling walk that took twice as long as it would have done in daylight, they reached a river spanned by a bridge of stone. On the other side was a substantial gatehouse. The building appeared to be several hundred years old, and was the kind of crumbling, unstable edifice that did not encourage people to linger underneath. The Michaelhouse men paid another toll and hurried through its cracked arches, relieved when they reached the city on the other side.

They were pleasantly surprised to find Lincoln far more lively than its suburbs. People were in the streets, and shopkeepers operated by the light of lamps. Inns and alehouses were doing a roaring trade, and musicians entertained frozen admirers with pipes, drums, lutes and rebecs. The performer with the largest crowd was a singer who bawled obscene ballads and encouraged his audience

– a scruffy horde with the pinched look of poverty about them – to join in the chorus. They were watched with rank disapproval by several well-dressed merchants. The scent of roasted chestnuts filled the air, and Michael bought some to eat as they walked, parting with a few to a boy with a mop of golden curls, who agreed to lead them to the house of the merchant called William de Spayne. Michael was unimpressed when it transpired to be up a very steep incline.

'Now you see why I prefer the Fens,' he gasped, as he laboured upwards. 'There are none of these mountains to ascend. Only heathens live in places where there are hills.'

'That is Spayne's home,' chirped the boy, grinning his amusement at the monk's discomfort. 'It is almost opposite the corn market, which always runs late on Wednesdays, as you can see. Spayne's place is called the Jewes House because it was built by the Jews who crucified St Hugh.'

He snatched the rest of the chestnuts and scampered away before the monk could object, while Cynric regarded Spayne's abode with serious misgivings.

'I do not like the sound of this,' he muttered. 'Saints murdered by Jews.'

'He is confusing two stories,' explained Bartholomew, knowing Cynric could be superstitious and not wanting him to take against the city quite so soon. 'St Hugh was a Lincoln bishop who died peacefully in his bed, and who was a good man. *Little* Hugh was a child allegedly crucified by Jews, although since identical stories arose at the same time in Norwich, Bury St Edmunds, York and Gloucester, it makes me wonder whether it was just an excuse.'

'An excuse for what?' asked Cynric uneasily.

'For the expulsion of Jews from England a few years later,' replied Bartholomew. 'And the confiscation of all their goods. The Crown made a lot of money by passing that particular law.'

'And whoever managed to lay hands on this building did rather well out of the Jews' misfortunes,' said Michael. 'It is a very fine house, although in desperate need of loving care.'

'Just like everything else around here, then,' said Cynric, looking around disparagingly.

'Are you going to knock?' asked Michael, when Bartholomew did no more than stare at Spayne's front door. That part of Lincoln was full of stone houses, although Spayne's and the building next door were by far the best. Both were pure Norman, with round-headed doors and windows, and the stocky sense of permanence always associated with that particular style of architecture. The monk was right when he said Spayne's home needed money spent on repairs, though, because the mouldings were beginning to weather, and the window shutters were rotting under cheap paint. The house next to it was in a far better state, although the lamps from the nearby corn market showed scorch marks that suggested it had been in a recent fire.

When Bartholomew continued to hesitate, Cynric knocked for him. The book-bearer jumped back quickly, hand on the hilt of his sword, when it was hauled open by a man wearing a purple cote-hardie – a tight-fitting tunic with flaring knee-length skirts – and a red hat. He was laughing and held a goblet in his hand. Behind him was a hall filled with cheering men.

'Who are you?' he demanded, his humour evaporating when he saw strangers in the darkness outside. 'I was expecting more claret from the Swan tavern, not visitors.'

'Master Spayne?' asked Bartholomew, stepping into the light spilling from the house. Despite his finery, the man was unattractive – no chin at all and eyes that were far too small for his fleshy face – and the physician was not surprised Matilde had rejected his offer of marriage.

The man flushed with anger. 'I most certainly am not! *My* name is Walter Kelby, and you would do well to remember it. Who are you, anyway, and what do you want?'

'Nothing,' said Bartholomew, backing away. There was a strong smell of wine, and Kelby was unsteady on his feet. The physician knew perfectly well that intoxicated men sometimes began fights over nothing, and he did not want trouble. 'I apologise for the intrusion – we have obviously been directed to the wrong house.'

'You want Spayne?' Kelby staggered when he tried to lean against the door jamb and missed. 'Why? Is it about wool? If so, then you would fare better with me, since I offer competitive prices. Come in, and join our revelries. I am Master of the Guild of Corpus Christi, and we are celebrating.'

'Celebrating what?' asked Bartholomew, since the man was obviously itching to tell him.

'Our good fortune. One of us accidentally committed a crime during the Summer Madness, but obviously he was not in his right wits when he did it, so he should not be held accountable for the consequences. But God made Sheriff Lungspee see reason today, and Flaxfleete was acquitted. He will make reparation at the General Pardon, of course – it only costs sixpence, anyway – but it was good to learn he will not be fined by the secular courts for something that was not his fault.'

Bartholomew smiled politely. 'Then we shall leave you to savour your victory.'

'Hurry up, Kelby.' A short man with sharp, rat-like features came to stand behind the merchant, and Bartholomew had the immediate sense that he was dishonest, despite the fact that his sober clothes suggested he had taken holy orders. 'Where is the wine? Master Quarrel said it would be delivered within the hour, and I would kill for a drink.'

'These fellows want to know if I am Spayne,' slurred Kelby. He stumbled when his friend flung an arm across his shoulder, and Bartholomew jumped forward to prevent both from toppling into the street. 'The ground moved! It must have been another earthquake. Is the cathedral still standing? Can you see it, Flaxfleete?'

'It is too dark,' replied Flaxfleete, after a few moments of intent peering. 'But I do not think God will tear up the land tonight. Not after my success in the law courts.'

'Earthquake?' asked Michael in alarm. 'Is Lincoln subject to them, then?'

'We had one during the life of Bishop Hugh, although he died more than a hundred years ago,' explained Flaxfleete. 'The minster was shaken to pieces, and he rebuilt it. Our Guild reveres St Hugh, and we try to emulate his actions.'

'By raising cathedrals?' asked Michael. 'I thought Lincoln only had one of them.'

'I mean we donate money to worthy causes,' said Kelby, fortunately too drunk to know the monk was mocking him. 'Such as providing ourselves with a new guildhall, and buying wine for the cathedral officials. We are good friends with them, unlike some I could mention.'

'Very worthy,' said Bartholomew, before Michael could prolong the conversation with more questions. He started to back away. 'Good evening to you.'

'Who told you Spayne lived here?' asked Flaxfleete curiously. 'One of the choristers – small boys with angelic faces and the Devil's manners? It is the kind of trick they might play on strangers.'

'Why would they do that?' asked Michael, ignoring

Bartholomew's tug on his arm that indicated he wanted to go.

'To inconvenience men who have business with him,' said Kelby. 'God bless them for it.'

'And because *we* are good, honest guildsmen,' added Flaxfleete. 'But Spayne is a member of that vile coven of rich merchants known as the Commonalty.'

'I do not understand,' said Michael. When he saw the monk's interest had been piqued by the two men's odd remarks, Bartholomew sighed and gave up his attempt to cut the discussion short.

'All decent, respectable traders are members of the Guild of Corpus Christi,' explained Kelby patiently. 'Meanwhile, all *corrupt* ones belong to a council known as the Commonalty.'

'Damn them to Hell,' added Flaxfleete viciously. 'So, we and Spayne are enemies, and have been for years. Fortunately, the Guild has more than fifty members, but the Commonalty is only twelve. However, these dozen hold a disproportionate degree of power, and the unemployed weavers favour them because they give charity. One is Adam Miller, you see.' He regarded them with pursed lips.

'Lord!' said Michael, pretending to be shocked. He was amused by the way the merchants kept assuming strangers should know all about their city. 'Not Adam Miller!'

'The very same,' said Kelby gravely. 'The whole town is afraid of *him* and his devious ways – except the weavers, of course. And Spayne is *his* man.'

'Spayne is a criminal?' asked Bartholomew doubtfully. He did not think Matilde would have embarked on a friendship with a man who indulged in illegal activities; she was a woman of considerable integrity.

'Yes, and so is Miller,' said Kelby firmly, leaning so hard against Flaxfleete that the man dropped his cup. 'We are

46

a divided city: the Guild and the cathedral stand for everything good, and the Commonalty represents everything bad. Every honest soul is terrified of Miller.'

Michael was puzzled. 'But I understand a man called Adam Miller finances Miller's Market. He cannot be all bad.'

Flaxfleete waved a dismissive hand. 'As I said, he is popular among unemployed weavers, but we guildsmen and our people are not deceived by his so-called largess.'

'You wear a priest's robes, yet it sounds as though you were tried by a secular court,' said Michael to Flaxfleete, intrigued both by the merchants and their chatter. 'Why? You could have claimed benefit of clergy and been subject to more lenient Canon law.'

'Because I took holy orders *after* the arson incident, and Bishop Gynewell declined to judge me,' said Flaxfleete. It was clear he thought the decision an unreasonable one. 'He said he did not wish to become embroiled in the city's dispute, especially since the buildings I happened to incinerate belonged to my deadly enemy: Spayne.'

'And there is the fact he would not be the first to take holy orders to avoid secular punishment,' muttered Bartholomew to Cynric. 'If that was allowed to happen, every felon in England would wear a habit.'

'Most do anyway,' replied Cynric. He had scant respect for clerics.

'But it was our turn to win a trial presided over by Sheriff Lungspee, in any case,' slurred Kelby. 'Especially after what happened to poor Dalderby.'

'And what was that?' asked Michael.

'A villainous rogue called Thoresby threatened to chop off his head,' explained Flaxfleete indignantly. 'It will not surprise you to learn that Dalderby is a guildsman, and Thoresby belongs to the Commonalty. It was obvious that Thoresby was guilty, but Lungspee pardoned him anyway. It was shameful! Miller certainly bribed Lungspee to get *him* released. Here comes the wine at last.'

'You did not say why you wanted to see Spayne,' said Kelby, lurching to one side to allow a sweating youth to enter his house with a barrel. 'If it is wool business, then you should deal with me instead – and I will even give you a cup of claret while we discuss terms.'

'It is not wool business,' said Michael. 'Although I understand wool is what made Lincoln rich.'

'It *did*,' acknowledged Flaxfleete. 'But times have changed, and we are all suffering from cheap foreign imports – except Spayne, who has trading rights in the upstart port of Boston. Damn him – and damn them, too! Boston is killing Lincoln, and *he* encourages it.'

'You should go sparingly with that,' advised Michael, pointing at the keg. 'My friend here visited France this year, and he says the grape harvest was poor. That claret might make you sick.'

Kelby tried to focus on the barrel, screwing up his face as he did so. 'Well, I have had more than enough for today, so perhaps I will abstain.'

'I have not,' said Flaxfleete, clapping a comradely hand on his shoulder. 'I intend to make this a night to remember – my acquittal *and* the other good news.'

'What other good news?' asked Kelby, trying to focus on him.

Flaxfleete grinned. 'I am saving that to announce later, but you will be delighted, I assure you. We shall be celebrating all night, and I mean to drink until I can no longer stand.'

'My students do that,' said Bartholomew disapprovingly. 'But they are sixteen. An excess of wine leads the black bile to—'

'Come on, Matt,' said Michael, grabbing his arm. 'Or it really will be too late to call on Spayne.'

'He lives next door,' said Flaxfleete, jerking his thumb at the handsome house that stood uphill from his own. 'And you can tell him from me that if there is any Summer Madness next year, he might find more of his storerooms burned to the ground.'

In the darkness of the street, Bartholomew heard a roar of delight as the barrel was presented to the company within. It was loud enough to be heard in the neighbouring house, and he wondered what Spayne thought of the celebration. From what he had been told by the Gilbertines – and what he knew of the disease called Holy Fire – Flaxfleete's claim that his illness had made him incinerate Spayne's buildings was bogus, and Sheriff Lungspee had been wrong to acquit him.

'This is a godless city,' grumbled Cynric, as they walked towards the house Flaxfleete had indicated. 'Disembowelled queens, warring merchants, crucified children. It is not what I expected.'

'Flaxfleete was right: that boy did play a trick on us,' said Michael to Bartholomew, ignoring the book-bearer's unhappy mutters. He grinned. 'If he is a chorister, he will have a shock when he realises he has just started a feud with one of the new canons.'

'It sounds as though Lincoln has enough feuds already,' warned Bartholomew uncomfortably. 'The city feels uneasy, and you should avoid disputes, even with choirboys.'

They reached the house, and the physician stood hesitantly outside a second door that evening. He gazed at it, wondering whether the narrow alley that separated Spayne's home from Kelby's provided enough of a barrier between what sounded to be very determined foes.

Spayne was wealthy, judging from his house, which had new shutters on its windows and a highly polished front door. Snow was piled on the roof in a way that suggested it might slough off at any moment and flatten someone, and it occurred to Bartholomew that Spayne might hope it would, and that its victim would be a neighbour. He tapped on the door, but there was no answer, so he knocked again.

Michael was about to suggest they return in the morning, when they heard a bar being removed and the door was opened by a woman in a long green robe. Beyond her was a handsome hall with fine wall-paintings and polished floorboards. Unfortunately, the chamber's elegant proportions were spoiled by the presence of a crude wooden brace near the hearth, suggesting the ceiling was unstable and needed to be shored up.

'The answer is no,' said the woman coldly. 'The sound of your revelry is *not* disturbing us. You can carouse all night without having the slightest impact on our comfort. Good night.'

She started to close the door, but Michael inserted his booted foot. 'My apologies, madam, but we have no idea what you are talking about.'

She raised her eyebrows. 'Kelby did not send you?'

Michael shook his head.

'He is trying to make as much noise as he can, in the hope of annoying us,' she went on. 'He and his Guild often enjoy raucous meetings, but this one is particularly galling: they are celebrating the fact that Sheriff Lungspee found Flaxfleete innocent of setting my brother's storerooms alight. He claimed it was Summer Madness, but we all know it was not.'

'That is not why we came,' said Michael. 'We are visitors from Cambridge, and I believe Master Spayne may share a mutual acquaintance with us.'

'I am Ursula, his sister, but I am afraid he is out.' Ursula gave a curious half smile. 'Please do not tell Kelby this, but when Will heard there were plans to celebrate Flaxfleete's acquittal, he made arrangements to sleep elsewhere. He asked me to go with him, but I refuse to allow Kelby and his henchmen to drive me from *my* home.'

'I see,' said Michael. He backed away. 'Then we shall return tomorrow.'

'Where is your brother staying, Mistress?' asked Bartholomew, prepared to travel some distance if it meant having answers that night. 'Would it be possible to call on him this evening?'

'He is lodging at the Black Monks' Priory.'

'How far is it?'

Her fierce expression softened. 'Do not venture that way now. The road is haunted by footpads, and the monks always retire early in the winter. They will not admit you, and you will find you have made a wasted journey – if not a dangerous one. Can your business not wait a few hours?'

'Yes, it can,' said Michael firmly. 'We are sorry to have disturbed you.'

'Come back tomorrow. I shall be up *very* early, baking.' She smiled spitefully, giving the impression that she would be doing so as noisily as possible, and that neighbours with sore heads could expect to find themselves woken before they were ready.

'We shall call as soon as we can,' said Michael. 'I hope you manage some rest tonight.'

'That is what a tincture of valerian is for,' she said, shaking a tiny phial at them. 'Will declines to use it when the Guild is at its revels, but I do not mind. He—'

She broke off when a high-pitched shriek issued from Kelby's house, and there came the sound of footsteps hammering on a wooden floor. Lights flickered under the

51

window shutters, and then there was shouting. When Bartholomew looked back at Ursula, she had closed the door, evidently unsettled by the sudden uproar in the enemy camp.

'Murder!' came a braying cry. 'Help us!'

'No,' said Michael, grabbing Bartholomew's shoulder as he prepared to respond. 'We are strangers here. It would be foolish to interfere in something that is none of our business.'

He began to lead the way down the hill. As they passed Kelby's house, the door was thrown open, revealing the lighted hallway within. Flaxfleete lay on the ground, heels drumming, while his friends hovered helplessly above him. He was in the throes of a fit, and Bartholomew knew from the way he was lying that he would suffocate unless he was moved. He pulled away from Michael.

'I am a physician, Brother. I cannot stand by while a man chokes to death.'

'This is not a good idea,' warned Michael, following with considerable reluctance. 'They are sure to remember who visited before this murder – and who was first to arrive when the alarm was raised.'

'It is not murder,' Bartholomew pointed out reasonably. 'He is still alive.'

But when he knelt beside the stricken cleric, he could see it was no fit that afflicted him. Flaxfleete was blue around the nose and lips, he was gasping for breath, and his eyes were wide and frightened in his waxy face. His body twitched convulsively, and he had vomited violently enough to cause bleeding in his stomach. Even as Bartholomew knelt beside him, he knew that all the skill in the world would not save the man. He started to loosen clothing, in an attempt to ease his breathing, but Flaxfleete resisted.

'No,' he whispered, grabbing Bartholomew's tunic and hauling him down so he could speak without being overheard. 'Keep me covered. I am cold.'

It was an odd request under the circumstances, but as Flaxfleete's struggle for air became increasingly frantic, Bartholomew had no choice but to pull the habit away from his neck. As he did so, he saw a strange blue mark on the cleric's skin, on the point of the shoulder. It was not large – perhaps half the length of a little finger – and was the kind of blemish he had seen soldiers make with ink and needles, as a sign of brotherhood. It was a strange thing to see on a merchant-cleric who had probably never seen a battle. Suddenly, Flaxfleete's convulsions reached a critical point, and all Bartholomew's attention was focussed on trying to hold the man's head in a way that might enable him to draw air into his lungs. But it was to no avail, and it was not long before he stood and raised his hands apologetically.

'I am sorry. You should summon a priest.'

CHAPTER 2

'You wear the garb of a physician,' said Kelby, regarding Bartholomew with appalled eyes as he stood in the bright light of his hall. 'I will pay whatever you ask if you save him. Gold, jewels, anything.'

'I wish I could help,' said Bartholomew gently. 'But your friend is beyond my skills.'

'He has stopped twitching,' argued Kelby desperately. 'The fit is over, so he will recover now.'

'He is not moving because he is dead,' explained Bartholomew. 'I am sorry.'

'I shall anoint him,' said Michael. He knelt reluctantly, giving the impression that he wished Bartholomew had heeded his advice and walked away from the whole business.

'He cannot be dead!' cried Kelby. 'He was perfectly healthy a few moments ago, clamouring for wine. You *saw* him. He was waiting for the new keg to arrive, because we drank more than usual tonight, and we ran out. We have a lot to celebrate, what with the acquittal. How could this happen?'

On the dying man's breath, Bartholomew had detected the rank, fishy odour of a substance familiar to most physicians – one that occurred on some rye grain and that was sometimes used by midwives to control post-partum bleeding. It was highly toxic, and Bartholomew had been told by a witch in southern France that it was also the cause of the disease called Holy Fire. His medical colleagues had rejected her explanation out of hand, although he found it more convincing than the commonly accepted perception that the sickness was the Devil's doing.

'Did he suffer from Summer Madness?' he asked. Flaxfleete's symptoms had certainly been similar to those exhibited by folk afflicted with Holy Fire, and people who had been stricken once were liable to suffer future attacks.

Kelby gazed at him. 'You know he did, because we told you about it – it was when he burned Spayne's storerooms. Why do you ask?'

'Do not answer,' murmured Cynric, who had come to stand behind Bartholomew. His hand rested on his dagger, and his eyes were watchful, as though he anticipated violence. 'It is safer to say nothing.'

'You should summon the sheriff,' said Michael. There was definitely something odd about the merchant's abrupt demise, and Cynric was right to advise them to have nothing to do with it.

'Why should we do that?' demanded Kelby. Shock had sobered him up, and although he was still unsteady on his feet, his wits seemed sharp enough. He addressed Bartholomew. 'Are you saying there is something suspicious about poor Flaxfleete's sudden illness?'

'He does not know,' replied Michael before Bartholomew could speak. 'That is why you should ask the sheriff to come. It is *his* job to ascertain what happened, not a passing physician's.'

A tall man with dark hair stepped out of the watching throng and crouched next to his fallen comrade. He wore a priest's robes, and bore an uncanny resemblance to Suttone; as he inspected the dead man, Bartholomew wondered whether he was one of the Carmelite's Lincoln kin.

'This is odd,' said the priest, sniffing the air with a

puzzled expression. 'He smells of fish. The last time I encountered such a stench, it was on Nicholas Herl after he threw himself in the Braytheford Pool. There is a medicine for women that carries a similar reek, although I do not know why Flaxfleete should have swallowed any – just as I did not know why it should have been inside Herl.'

Kelby was bemused. 'Medicine will not harm anyone – it is supposed to make folk better.'

'Many medicines are poisonous when administered wrongly,' said Bartholomew. He did not add that the one imbibed by Flaxfleete must have been unnaturally concentrated to produce such a dramatic result – and to smell so strongly on his body.

Kelby pointed at the wine keg, which had already been broached. 'Did anyone other than Flaxfleete drink from this? Do you know, John?'

The priest was thoughtful. 'He tapped the barrel himself, and swallowed the first cup because someone told him it might be bad. He said he was less drunk than the rest of us, so better able to assess its quality.'

'You do not seem drunk,' observed Michael.

John inclined his head. 'I never touch strong brews. And when men are poisoned while in their cups, it makes me glad I practise abstinence.'

Kelby was unimpressed with his sanctimonious colleague. 'Then, since you are so steady in your wits, you can tell us what happened to Flaxfleete.'

'It would be wrong of me to try – I am no sheriff. But I *can* say Flaxfleete was the only one to drink from this barrel. He downed the first cup in a gulp, declared it good, then poured himself a second. He did not fill the jug for the rest of you, but went back to the table and sat down. *I* was filling the pitcher – at your request, Kelby – when he complained of feeling unwell. And we all know what happened next.'

'What?' asked Bartholomew, earning himself a glare from Michael for his curiosity.

'He said he was cold, even though he was next to the fire,' replied John. 'And that there was a pain in his chest and a numbness in his hands. Then he clutched his head and dropped to the floor. You saw the rest.'

Bartholomew went to the cask, where the familiar fishy odour was just recognisable under the scent of strong wine.

'Is it tainted?' asked Kelby. 'Poisoned?'

Bartholomew nodded. 'Call the sheriff, and let him establish what happened.'

'We shall,' declared Kelby, grief turning to anger. 'Dalderby will fetch him.'

'Me?' asked a fellow with a thick orange beard and an expensive cote-hardie of scarlet and yellow. 'I have a sore foot and will be too slow. Send someone else.'

'You will not mind enduring a little discomfort for Flaxfleete,' said Kelby harshly, shoving him towards the open door. Bartholomew wondered why Dalderby was loath to leave. Was it because he felt unsafe when a fellow guildsman had been murdered? Or was he simply more interested in what was unfolding in Kelby's hall, and did not want to miss anything?

'This barrel came from the Swan,' said John, when the unwilling Dalderby had been dispatched on his errand. 'So, someone from the Swan must have tampered with it – put the medicine inside.'

'Master Quarrel has sold me good wine all my life,' cried Kelby. 'Why would he change now? Besides, can you imagine what impact it would have on his trade, if it became known that he poisons his wares? It was not Quarrel or anyone at the Swan. I will stake my life on it.'

John pointed to the floor. 'Do you see those drops? They run all the way to the door, which means the keg was leaking when it was brought in. If wine was dripping out, then it means something may have been dripped *inside*, too.'

'You are right,' said Michael, as he inspected the trail. 'That does suggest the poison was added when the cask was at the tavern.'

'God's blood!' cried Kelby in anguish. 'Someone will swing for this!'

'I imagine so,' said Michael calmly. 'However, I hope you will remember that it had nothing to do with us. We were talking to your neighbour, Ursula de Spayne, when your friend met his end.'

'That witch,' sneered Kelby. 'It would not surprise me to learn that she poisoned poor Flaxfleete. She has a knowledge of herbs and potions, and regularly offers them to anyone foolish enough to trust her. She hated Flaxfleete and will delight in his death. *She* is the culprit!'

It was a sober supper for the Michaelhouse scholars that night. The meal – provided uncommonly late on account of Bartholomew and Michael going out – was served in the guest-hall's main chamber. Not everyone had taken to his heels after the recent stabbing, and a handful of men huddled near the meagre fire at the far end of the room. Most were poor, as evidenced by their threadbare clothes and thin boots, and it was clear they simply could not afford to go elsewhere. There were baleful glares when Hamo provided them with day-old bread and a few onions, but brought roasted goose for the more valued party from upstairs.

Bartholomew barely noticed them. His thoughts had returned to Matilde, and all he could think was that Spayne might be able to tell him where she had gone. He did not feel like eating, and picked listlessly at the slab of fatty meat

Michael slapped on to his trencher. The monk made up for his lack of appetite by eating more than was wise, and then complained that his stomach hurt. Cynric was withdrawn and morose, and became more so when Suttone began a defensive monologue about the man he had hired to be his Vicar Choral, claiming that John Aylmer was a paragon of virtue, despite Hamo's statements to the contrary.

'What is the matter, Cynric?' Bartholomew asked, pulling himself out of his reverie when he noticed something was bothering his book-bearer. The man had been with him all his adult life, and was more friend than servant. He did not like to see him unhappy.

'I do not like this place,' said Cynric, waving a hand that encompassed guest-hall, convent and city, all at the same time. He saw Suttone had broken off his tirade and was listening. 'You should . . . pay your respects to Spayne, and leave as soon as possible. Tomorrow would be best.'

'You cannot do that, Matthew!' cried Suttone in alarm. 'Michael and I are helpless monastics and need the protection you two provide for our journey home. What is wrong with Lincoln, anyway?'

'It is shabby,' declared Cynric uncompromisingly. 'It looks as though it *was* fine, but has fallen on hard times – just like this priory, in fact. It is also set to be destroyed by an earthquake at any moment, and I am uncomfortable with the notion of murdered saints, queens deprived of their innards, and men poisoned with wine. And Brother Michael was right in what he said: Kelby and his friends may decide to blame *us* for Flaxfleete's death, just because we are strangers.'

'We are going to be canons,' said Suttone indignantly. 'No one would dare offend us with unfounded accusations.'

'*You* are going to be a canon, Father,' corrected Cynric morosely. '*I* am a book-bearer.'

'He has a point,' said Michael to Suttone. His next comment was directed at Bartholomew. 'But we can avoid trouble if we keep to ourselves, and do not meddle in matters that are not our concern. Lord, my belly aches! Are you sure being near that poisoned wine did me no harm, Matt?'

'When you were out, Hamo told me about a rift that is pulling Lincoln apart,' said Suttone, watching Bartholomew prepare his usual tonic for overindulgence. 'Virtually every man, woman and child is either on the side of the cathedral and the Guild of Corpus Christi *or* they support something called the Commonalty. Bishop Gynewell manages to stay aloof, and so does Sheriff Lungspee – but only so he can accept bribes from *both* parties.'

'The *bishop* is neutral?' asked Michael, startled. 'I thought he would side with his cathedral.'

'Apparently, he thinks that if *he* refuses to align himself, then others will follow his example and the bitterness will heal,' explained Suttone. 'Although there is no evidence the ploy is working so far. Still, at least he is trying. He tried to stop the General Pardon for the same reason.'

'You mean the ceremony in which everyone is going to be forgiven crimes committed when they pretended to be afflicted with seasonal insanity?' asked Michael. 'Why would he object to that?'

'Because it is another step in the escalating dissension,' said Suttone. 'First, there was the installation of canons. In defiance, Adam Miller said he was holding his Market on the same day – to entice people towards secular activities. The cathedral immediately responded with the General Pardon. Gynewell tried to prevent it, lest Miller invent something else.'

'Perhaps we *should* go home,' said Michael, sipping the tonic. 'There is almost certain to be trouble, and I am disturbed by the fact that people think I have been honoured with the Stall of South Scarle because the Bishop of Ely arranged it. I do not want to be accused of simony.'

'Do not be so fastidious, Brother,' said Suttone impatiently. 'Michaelhouse is desperate for funds, what with the hall in need of painting and the conclave roof leaking like fury. You should not allow a dubious moral stance to prevent you from taking what is freely offered.'

'What do you think, Matt?' asked Michael. 'Should I put my College before my personal integrity and accept this post? Or should I risk offending my bishop by handing it back?'

'De Lisle will not appreciate his efforts being for nothing,' warned Bartholomew, thinking the monk should have considered such issues before accepting the appointment in the first place.

'True,' said Michael. 'But Whatton made me feel . . . less than honourable about the situation.'

'Ignore Whatton,' advised Suttone. 'Everyone knows the nomination of canons is a political matter, and that greed and favouritism are an integral part of the system. I fully accept that I owe mine to the fact that the cathedral is eager to have a Suttone in its ranks. Besides, we have just spent two weeks getting here, and it seems a pity to return home empty-handed.'

'Make reparation, Brother,' suggested Bartholomew facetiously. 'Take some of this new income and offer a gift to the cathedral, or to one of the city charities.'

Michael regarded him coolly. 'So, your advice is for me to *buy* myself a clean conscience? Very well. I shall see what the silversmiths have to offer tomorrow – assuming it is safe to go out.'

'Do you have a kinsman called John?' asked Bartholomew of Suttone, thinking of the dark-haired priest they had met at Kelby's house and his resemblance to the burly Carmelite.

Suttone nodded. 'A first cousin, once removed. His father was a tanner, but he perished in the Death, God rest his soul. John Suttone is a Poor Clerk.'

'Why *poor* clerk?' asked Cynric curiously. 'Does it mean he earns even less than I get from Michaelhouse?'

'It is a rank in the cathedral hierarchy,' explained Suttone impatiently. 'At the top, there is the dean. He has a Chapter, which comprises the canons, like Michael and me—'

'Not until Sunday,' interrupted Bartholomew.

Suttone ignored him. 'Under us, there are the Vicars Choral, some of whom are in priest's orders and include men like my deputy, Aylmer—'

'But he is dead,' said Cynric gloomily, crossing himself. 'Stabbed in this very room. Right there, in fact, and you can still see his blood to prove it.'

Bartholomew looked to where the book-bearer was pointing and saw a sinister stain beneath one of the beds. He went to inspect it, noting that although an attempt had been made to scrub it away, not much effort had been put into the task. He wondered whether it had been left for a reason – perhaps as a warning to others, or because whoever had been detailed to clean the mess had had an aversion to the blood of a murdered man. People could be superstitious that way.

Suttone continued his lecture on cathedral government. 'And under Vicars Choral are Poor Clerks, who serve the altars, act as recorders for Chapter meetings, bring the dove and so on.'

'Bring the dove?' echoed Bartholomew, bemused.

Suttone shrugged. 'I am not sure what it means, either, but it is an official post, just like my cousin John's proper title is Clerk to Rouse the People.'

'I suppose that means stopping folk from falling asleep

during services,' surmised Cynric. His expression was one of sympathy. 'It sounds an onerous duty.'

'Why did you appoint Aylmer as your Vicar Choral, and not your cousin?' asked Bartholomew curiously. 'I imagine a kinsman would expect to be promoted under such circumstances.'

'I did not want to be accused of nepotism,' explained Suttone. 'However, Aylmer is just a family friend, which is slightly different.'

'He seemed a decent fellow,' said Michael, not pointing out that it was only *very* slightly different. 'Your cousin John.'

Suttone raised his shoulders in a shrug. 'I barely know him. However, he belongs to a city guild, and I do not approve of those. They tend to condone debauchery.'

'The Guild of Corpus Christi certainly does,' said Michael. 'When we were looking at Flaxfleete's body, I saw at least three men slumped unconscious across the table.'

'Dead?' asked Suttone uneasily.

'Drunk. I could hear them snoring – and Flaxfleete was the only one who imbibed from the toxic barrel, anyway. They were lucky he was a selfish fellow who declined to serve his friends before drinking himself. And they are fortunate that John took his time filling the jug. Had he been quicker, there would have been more casualties than just Flaxfleete.'

'You said they accused Ursula de Spayne of tampering with the keg,' said Suttone. 'Do you think they were right?'

Michael finished the tonic with a grimace. 'It is possible, but it would have been a very stupid thing to have done on her part. The dispute between the Spaynes and the Guild seems very bitter, and Flaxfleete's acquittal has done nothing to soothe the antagonism. Ursula and her brother will be the first suspects any sheriff will explore.'

'Anger often drives people to do foolish things,' said

Bartholomew. 'However, I can tell you that being afflicted with Holy Fire does *not* make people dash off and burn their enemies' storerooms – and I am astonished Sheriff Lungspee thinks it did.'

'So is Spayne, I imagine,' said Michael. 'We shall have to be careful when we go to see him tomorrow, and—' He stopped speaking as someone came to hover near them, as if uncertain of his welcome. 'God and all His saints preserve us! Is that Richard de Wetherset?'

A heavyset man with iron-grey hair stood in the shadows. He was dressed in a habit that indicated he had taken major orders with the Cistercians, although the robe was of excellent quality and suggested he did not take too seriously his Order's love-affair with poverty. He was also portly, indicating he did not practise much in the way of abstinence, either. Because it was not a face he had expected to see in Lincoln, it took Bartholomew a moment to place it. De Wetherset had been the University's Chancellor before he found the duties too onerous and had fled to a quieter life in the Fens. However, he had held sway in Cambridge for several years, and Michael had served as his Junior Proctor before the monk's meteoric rise to power under de Wetherset's meeker successor.

Behind de Wetherset was a second man. Like the ex-Chancellor, he was heavily built, and his face was the kind of florid red that suggested too much good living. The skin on his face was puckered, as if marred by some child-hood pox, and even in the gloom, Bartholomew detected a pair of unusually pale eyes. He, too, wore a priest's habit, although his haughty demeanour suggested he regarded himself as something rather more important.

'*I* intend to be Chancellor of our University one day,'

said Suttone conversationally, when the monk introduced him to de Wetherset.

Michael gazed at him in astonishment. 'Do you? You have never mentioned this particular ambition before.'

Suttone shrugged. 'It is a notion I have been mulling over for some time. The present incumbent cannot remain in office for ever, and when he resigns, I shall put myself forward. It will make you *my* Senior Proctor, Brother, but as we are in the same College, I am sure we will rub along nicely.'

Michael was thoughtful. It was common knowledge that Chancellor Tynkell made no decision without the blessing of his Senior Proctor, and that it was Michael who really ran the University. Tynkell was malleable, and seldom argued with the monk; Suttone was more stubborn, and it would require greater skill to manipulate him. Michael's eyes gleamed in anticipation. He enjoyed a challenge, and the last year – with no suspicious deaths to investigate – had been dull.

'Are you still examining corpses on the University's behalf?' asked de Wetherset of Bartholomew, while the monk's clever mind assessed the implications of serving under a different master.

'Not recently,' replied Bartholomew. He was not sure whether the question was de Wetherset's way of initiating a fresh topic of conversation, or whether he was trying to be annoying: when Michael had first asked Bartholomew to inspect bodies, the physician had objected strenuously, and had had to be browbeaten, cajoled or bribed into doing what was necessary. Since then, he had grown used to it, and even enjoyed the work, because there was a good deal to be learned from cadavers. Unfortunately, his medical colleagues considered his discoveries anathema, which meant he was in the frustrating position of not being able to discuss them with anyone who might know what he was talking about.

De Wetherset raised his eyebrows. 'I see. You are not wearing academic garb. Have you resigned your Fellowship at Michaelhouse and become a secular physician? I am surprised: I was always under the impression that you liked teaching.'

'On our journey here, we found his scholarly tabard kept attracting the attention of men desperate for an argument,' replied Suttone, before Bartholomew could reply for himself. 'I suggested he remove it, and we have not been bothered by unwelcome company since.'

De Wetherset gazed at him, not sure whether there was an insult inherent in the Carmelite's explanation. 'Is that so?'

'Matt returned from an extended leave of absence in October,' said Michael pleasantly, before Suttone could add any more. 'He was gone for sixteen months, which meant I was without a decent Corpse Examiner all that time. Do you remember Doctor Rougham of Gonville Hall? I had to make do with him instead, and I am sure innumerable killers went free on his account.'

'They must have done,' said Suttone. 'You investigated several suspicious deaths a year when Matthew was with you, but not one from the moment he left. I cannot believe all Cambridge's killers decided to behave themselves simply because your regular Corpse Examiner was unavailable.'

'A sabbatical?' asked de Wetherset, while Michael frowned unhappily. Suttone was not the first to remark on the abrupt cessation of murders after Rougham had been hired to determine whether or not a death was due to natural causes. 'I hope you did not visit Paris – I recall you studied there before you accepted the post at Cambridge – but we are at war with the French now.'

'We have been at war with the French for as long as I can remember,' replied Bartholomew. 'And that includes when I did my postgraduate training in Paris. But no one

66

cares about the quarrel – in France *or* England – except nobles, kings and mercenaries.'

'You sail remarkably close to treason, Bartholomew,' said de Wetherset with an expression that was impossible to interpret. Bartholomew recalled that he was a dangerous man, who had not been elected to the exalted rank of Chancellor for nothing, and supposed he had better watch his tongue. 'And I think you are wrong. A few months ago, you might have been right, but everything changed after the Battle of Poitiers. The French are angry in defeat and the English gloat in victory, even here, in a place where most people have barely heard of a place called France.'

'That is true,' agreed Suttone. 'The battle has certainly given new life to the conflict.'

'Which foreign universities did you visit?' asked de Wetherset. He held up an imperious hand. 'No, do not tell me – I shall guess. Padua, Montpellier and Bologna, because they are the schools that are most lax about what constitutes heresy. I have been told by more than one Italian *medicus* that anatomy is an intellectually profitable pursuit, and you always did chafe at the boundaries we set you.'

'You were cutting up corpses with your foreign colleagues?' asked Suttone in horror. 'Anatomy is forbidden, Matthew – by the Lateran Council itself. You are a fool to dabble in the dark arts!'

'I did not anatomise anyone,' objected Bartholomew. 'Well, I may have witnessed an examination or two, but I was only one of a dozen physicians and surgeons present. And what I learned allowed me to devise a way to alleviate the pain *you* suffered with the stone last week.'

'Did it?' asked Suttone warily. He reconsidered. 'Well, I suppose might be justifiable under certain circumstances, but please do not do it in Lincoln. Michael and I have our reputations to consider, and they will not be enhanced if you do that sort of thing in front of the general populace.'

'On the contrary,' said the man in the shadows. 'I imagine anatomy would go down rather well with the general populace. The average man has a fascination for the horrible – until one of his number declares it witchcraft, in which case he will hang you without demur, driven by his innate bigotry.'

'Allow me to introduce Father Simon,' said de Wetherset. Simon stepped forward with the kind of smirk that suggested he had already decided the Cambridge men were fools. 'He has been parish priest at Holy Cross, Wigford for the past twenty years – you will have passed it, if you have been to the city – although he has just resigned those duties for something more worthy of his talents. I hear you are to be made a canon, Brother. Well, Simon and I will be joining you in the prebendal stalls.'

'Congratulations,' said Michael, genuinely pleased for de Wetherset. 'Suttone and I knew there were to be five installations, but no one told us the names of the other three candidates.'

'Lincoln wants to honour the University at Cambridge with its nominations this time,' explained Simon. 'Three canonical appointments will go to scholars: you two and de Wetherset.'

'You are not a scholar,' said Bartholomew to the ex-Chancellor. 'You left Cambridge years ago.'

'But not before Brother Michael inveigled me the title of Emeritus Fellow,' replied de Wetherset comfortably. 'So technically, I *am* still a scholar. And, although I spent a few months with my family in the Fens, Bishop Gynewell then offered me the freedom of his cathedral library, and I have been studying theology in Lincoln ever since. People have come to regard me as local.'

'I suppose I can be considered local, too,' said Suttone. 'One branch of my family has lived in the city for years, and my grandfather was bishop. I have cousins in service at the cathedral and—'

'But you do not *live* here,' interrupted Simon coolly. 'That is what is meant by local. Your life is in Cambridge. Mine, however, is here. I have been vicar at Holy Cross for more than two decades, and now I shall serve the cathedral. *That* is what constitutes a local man, not distant kin.'

Suttone bristled, and Michael hastened to change the subject. 'You said three scholars were to be made canons, plus Father Simon. Who is the fifth and last lucky candidate?'

Simon's expressive face darkened. 'A merchant. He is not a particularly good choice, although at least he is in holy orders – unlike some prebendaries I could name.'

'You refer to Canon Hodelston?' asked de Wetherset. 'Who held the Stall of Sleaford, and created a scandal when he announced in his first Chapter meeting that he had not been ordained?'

Bartholomew was mystified. 'If he is not in holy orders, then how does he perform his religious duties at the cathedral? Conduct masses and the like?'

'He appointed a Vicar Choral to do *everything*,' explained Simon disapprovingly. 'He took his vows eventually, but the appointment was a disgrace and it brought shame to the Chapter.'

'His name was Hodelston?' asked Suttone. He shot Simon a cool glance. 'I may not *live* here, but my kinsmen keep me informed of certain people and events. I am not the stranger you imagine. However, the only Hodelston they mentioned to me was a very wicked fellow – accused of theft, rape, extortion and all manner of crimes – but the plague took him.'

Simon sniffed. 'That is the man – as I said, his appointment was a disgrace. However, you are not right about the manner of his death. He died *during* the plague, not *of* it. He had a seizure with frothing mouth and rigid muscles. Some said it was poison. But few mourned his passing, least of all the Dean and Chapter.'

'Hodelston is long-since dead, but the cathedral continues to make dubious appointments,' said de Wetherset unhappily. 'Flaxfleete will not make a good canon. He was accused of arson, and it was obvious that he only took holy orders when he thought he might be fined. The bishop refused to try him in the Church, though, which was a brave thing to do, and Flaxfleete was obliged to throw himself on Sheriff Lungspee's mercy. I imagine bribes changed hands, because he was acquitted today.'

'Flaxfleete?' asked Bartholomew uncomfortably. 'Kelby's friend? *He* is the last canon?'

'So *that* is what he meant, when he said he had a second item of good news to share with his friends,' mused Michael. 'He said it was something that would see more celebration. He must have been referring to his nomination as a prebendary.'

De Wetherset raised his eyebrows. 'You have met Flaxfleete? I suppose I should not be surprised. The Guild of Corpus Christi is influential in Lincoln, and he is one of its founding members. The decision was made to install him a month ago, but nothing could be made official until this accusation of arson was resolved. So, he does indeed have two things to celebrate this evening.'

'Sheriff Lungspee probably acquitted him to level the field after that business with Thoresby,' said Simon. 'Thoresby *was* guilty of threatening to behead Dalderby, and should not have been pardoned. So, because Lungspee favoured the Commonalty over the Guild in that case, he feels obliged to favour the Guild over the Commonalty now.'

'Miller *definitely* bribed Lungspee to secure Thoresby's release,' said de Wetherset with pursed lips. 'I heard three white pearls changed hands. So, Lungspee no doubt accepted a similar sum from Kelby to see Flaxfleete freed. Next time, it will be Miller's turn again. That is one good thing about our sheriff: he is scrupulous about the order in which he allows himself to be corrupted.'

Simon turned to Suttone. 'Have your informative kin told you about the dissent that is currently tearing our city apart?' he asked unpleasantly. 'Or is it something they neglected to mention?'

It was Michael who answered. 'Of course we know about it. On one side there is the Commonalty, which seems to entail an unlikely liaison between a dozen very rich men and some unemployed weavers. And on the other there is the Guild of Corpus Christi, comprising about fifty merchants.'

Simon bristled at the contemptuous tenor of the summary. 'I assume you know about the last mayoral election, too?' he asked, still addressing Suttone. 'You do not need me to explain what happened – why it made the dispute all the more bitter?'

'He does not,' said Michael, earning a pleased smirk from Suttone, who had no idea what Simon was talking about. 'We know it was won by William de Spayne, since he currently holds the title.'

'Spayne was delighted,' said de Wetherset, apparently oblivious to the building tension between Simon and the Cambridge men, 'because it means he is exempted from certain taxes. Kelby was running against him, and was livid when Spayne was announced the winner. Kelby thought *he* had won, you see. He had even been to a silversmith and commissioned a seal.'

'They are *all* turbulent men,' said Simon. 'But I deplore the Guild's sly campaign of slander against Miller. He may be vulgar, but I admire his generosity to weavers who cannot find work. The Guild does not care that folk starve for want of bread. Flaxfleete is particularly mean in that respect.'

'Not any more,' said Michael grimly. 'He is dead.'

'What?' asked de Wetherset, startled, while Simon struggled to mask his own surprise: he was loath to admit that strangers knew something about his city that he did not. 'Lord! Perhaps God struck him down for lying – it was *not* Summer Madness that led him to fire Spayne's storerooms after all. He denied he was even there at first, and only told the truth when he learned he had been seen.'

'Seen by whom?' asked Michael. 'Spayne's friends? If so, then their testimony probably cannot be trusted.'

'By travelling Dominicans with no reason to lie for either side,' replied Simon. 'They were questioned by both Guild and Commonalty, but it was obvious they were telling the truth. There was no doubt in anyone's mind that Flaxfleete did indeed commit a grave crime, and it was a stroke of genius to blame it on Summer Madness.'

'It certainly was,' said de Wetherset. 'It worked.'

'Yes and no,' said Bartholomew. 'It may have seen him murdered.'

When Hamo came to collect the empty dishes and make the beds for the night, Bartholomew, Michael and Suttone, with Cynric trailing disconsolately behind them, retired to the chamber on the upper floor. Uninvited, de Wetherset and Simon accompanied them. There the monk casually mentioned his hope of renewing an acquaintance with Matilde – thinking that if Simon was as well versed in his city's doings as he claimed, then he might have information to share. But although Simon gave the first genuine smile of their acquaintance when he heard her name, he knew no more than that she had once lived in Lincoln and that she had been loved by all. Then Michael gave an account of what had happened when the new keg of wine had arrived at Kelby's home and Flaxfleete had made the mistake of serving himself first.

'And you think Flaxfleete was killed because he set fire to Spayne's property?' asked Simon of the Michaelhouse men. 'How can you know that?'

'We do not,' replied Michael hastily, unwilling to be associated with that sort of claim. 'All we are saying is that the possibility should be assessed before it is dismissed.'

'That is reasonable,' said de Wetherset. 'And there are plenty of suspects to choose from. The Commonalty was furious when it learned about Sheriff Lungspee's decision to acquit Flaxfleete – and Spayne's sister Ursula was so enraged that she is said to have smashed her favourite chamber-pot.'

'Ursula *does* know about toxins,' mused Simon, 'but I cannot see her harming a man with one, not even an enemy from the Guild. There was a case six years ago . . . but I am sure Suttone's kin will have told him about it, so perhaps *he* will elaborate for us.'

Suttone glared at him. 'Their letters dwell on erudite matters pertaining to theology – nothing you would understand. So, I am afraid we shall have to rely on you to provide us with alehouse gossip.'

Simon sneered at him. 'Canon Hodelston's wicked life is classified as theology, is it?' He turned to Michael before the Carmelite could take issue with him. 'Ursula had a friend with a cough, so she concocted an electuary. Unfortunately, this friend was with child and the potion contained some herb . . . what was it now? . . . cuckoo-pint! It was cuckoo-pint. Anyway, the poor woman died, and the midwife said cuckoo-pint should never be given to expectant mothers. It was clearly an accident, but the Guild makes sure Ursula will never forget it.'

Bartholomew was unimpressed. 'It is common knowledge that powdered root of cuckoo-pint is used to expel afterbirth, and only a fool would give it to a pregnant woman. Ursula should refrain from dispensing tonics if she does not know what she is doing.'

'But this woman did not *tell* Ursula she was with child,' said Simon. He lowered his voice to a prudish hiss. 'She was not married, you see. Incidentally, it was your friend Matilde who discovered what had happened, and who insisted that the matter be investigated. She was very angry about it.'

Bartholomew could imagine. Matilde had always championed unlucky women, and the death of a pregnant one from a dose of cuckoo-pint would certainly arouse her condemnation.

'It caused a serious falling out between Matilde and Ursula,' elaborated Simon. 'Some folk said it was Ursula's error that led Matilde to reject Spayne's offer of marriage – and perhaps was the reason why she left Lincoln so suddenly.'

'But this is ancient history,' said de Wetherset. 'Suffice to say that Ursula has a working knowledge of medicine, and was angry when Flaxfleete was exonerated today. She might well have tampered with his wine.'

'I do not see how,' said Suttone. He addressed Bartholomew and Michael. 'You said she was in her house with the doors barred.'

'*I* see how,' said de Wetherset. He smiled at the monk. 'This reminds me of the murders we solved in the University – how we sat and reviewed the evidence with our scholarly logic.'

'How?' asked Michael, more interested in de Wetherset's conclusions than his reminiscences.

De Wetherset's grin faded. 'I was in the Swan earlier this evening, dining with Master Quarrel – he is remarkably learned for a taverner. Anyway, Kelby had ordered two kegs of wine earlier in the day, but then word came that the Guild was so delighted with Flaxfleete's acquittal that another barrel was needed. Quarrel's pot-boy had other work to do first, though, and Kelby's wine stood by the door for some time before the lad was free to deliver it. Ursula could have tampered with it then.'

'Not if she was in her house, trying not to listen to the Guild's revelries,' pressed Suttone.

'Perhaps she was not,' said de Wetherset. 'You can see the Swan from her home, and it would not take many moments to sneak out, tap the barrel, and add some poison.'

'She might have killed the entire Guild,' said Bartholomew, appalled. 'They were all celebrating.'

'I imagine getting rid of *all* her brother's enemies in one fell swoop would have been a tremendous boon to her,' said de Wetherset. 'Of course, that would have been bad for Lincoln.'

'Why?' asked Michael. 'These men do not sound like particularly good citizens.'

'Because it would destroy the balance between the two factions,' explained de Wetherset. 'And the balance is the only thing stopping us from erupting in a frenzy of blood-letting – and I do not mean *your* kind of blood-letting, Bartholomew. I am talking about murder and mayhem.'

'What about you, Father Simon?' Bartholomew asked. 'Have you chosen a side in this dispute?'

'I do not approve of any city pulled apart by discord,' replied Simon. 'However, I dislike the way Miller is denigrated because he is not from an ancient mercantile family, like Kelby's. I suppose I tend towards supporting the Commonalty because I dislike the Guild's smug merchants – it costs little to dispense free bread to needy weavers, but they do not bother. Miller does.'

De Wetherset smiled wryly. 'I stand with neither side, although it may be politically expedient to throw in my lot with the Guild in time. It is favoured by the canons – my new colleagues – you see.'

Simon glared at him. 'That is hardly an ethical reason on which to base your choice.'

'It is as ethical as yours – that you feel sorry for an upstart who is shunned by the older families.'

'But Miller is said to be rich,' said Michael, puzzled. 'Why should Kelby and Flaxfleete take against such a man?'

'Wealth does not confer breeding,' explained de Wetherset. 'Miller is one of the richest men in the city, but you would not want him dining with you – he wipes his teeth on the tablecloth and he spits. And I am not sure his money has been honestly gained. There are rumours—'

'There are always rumours,' said Simon coolly. 'But gossip is for fools and the gullible.'

De Wetherset turned to Michael. 'You see? Everyone feels strongly about this dispute. All I know is that it is important to maintain the *status quo*, so neither party seizes power.'

Simon was thoughtful. 'We all say the same thing about this so-called balance, but is it really true? When a member of the Commonalty threw himself into the Braytheford Pool in a spat of drunken self-pity last Sunday, I held my breath, anticipating the equilibrium would shift and there would be mayhem – the Guild accused of murder, even though Herl's death was a clear suicide. And there were indeed accusations and recriminations, but they amounted to nothing.'

'You may have preached here for two decades, Simon, but my opinion counts for something – and *I* am right,' said de Wetherset with the cool arrogance Bartholomew remembered so well from the man's Cambridge days. 'I say the balance is important, and only a fool would disagree with me.' He changed the subject before the priest could dispute the point. 'I was beginning to think you might not arrive in time, Brother. Most canons-elect come a month early, so they can be fitted for their ceremonial vestments. Such fine garments cannot be run up in an afternoon, you know.'

'The weather is atrocious, and the journey took twice as long as we anticipated,' said Michael, resenting the implication that he was tardy.

'De Wetherset has been extolling your talent for solving murder,' said Simon, with the kind of look that suggested he thought the skill a peculiar one. 'Will you apply your expertise to Aylmer's death? I imagine Suttone will want to know who killed his Vicar Choral.'

'I would,' said Suttone to Michael. 'But I do not want *you* to do it, Brother. It might see us in trouble with the sheriff.'

'I am sure you are right,' said Michael. 'And I have no intention of meddling. I am here to enjoy myself and bask in the glory of my appointment. I do not want to be burdened with secular duties.'

'Good,' muttered Bartholomew. He knew who would be asked to inspect the corpse if Michael agreed to help, and he had no wish to examine bodies when he could be looking for Matilde.

'That is a pity,' said de Wetherset. 'The death *should* be investigated, and I have taken the liberty of informing

Bishop Gynewell about your abilities. He is sure to ask for your assistance, Brother.'

Michael glared at him. 'That was a high-handed thing to have done.'

'You are about to receive a lucrative prebend,' said de Wetherset sternly. 'Surely, you will want to repay that honour by offering Gynewell the benefit of your expertise? If this city has a problem, and it is in your power to eliminate it, then surely you will not deny him?'

Michael continued to glare. 'That is unfair.'

'So is life,' said de Wetherset with an unrepentant shrug. 'I imagine the bishop will want to see you first thing tomorrow morning, so be grateful I warned you in advance. Meanwhile, Simon and I have elected to share this chamber with you tonight, rather than bed in the hall below. Aylmer was murdered by someone who might still be there, and we have no wish to be stabbed as we sleep.'

'He was stabbed as he slept?' asked Suttone in alarm.

Simon shot de Wetherset a withering look. 'No, he was not. His body was slumped across his bed in a way that made it clear he was inspecting his possessions when he was killed.'

'It was not *his* possessions he was inspecting,' said de Wetherset, sharp in his turn. 'You cannot leave the truth unspoken, if Michael is to solve this case. He was holding *your* holy chalice – he may even have been in the process of stealing it – while the rest of us were at our devotions.'

Michael sighed wearily. 'Aylmer was killed while in the commission of a crime?'

Simon grimaced. 'We do not know that. He *was* holding my cup, and perhaps he did have designs on it, but we will never know his intentions, and I am inclined to give him the benefit of the doubt. He was a priest, and so would have been wary of committing evil acts on sacred ground.'

'Was he alone when he was attacked?' asked Michael. 'Were there any witnesses to his death?'

'The bells here are very loud,' replied de Wetherset. 'I think the Gilbertines installed some especially large ones with intention of out-clanging the Carmelites up the road. The upshot is that once the damned things get going for the dawn offices, it is impossible to sleep. Everyone quit the guest-hall this morning, and either left the priory to begin business in the city or went to attend prime.'

'Aylmer did not, if he was admiring other people's property,' Michael pointed out.

Simon inclined his head. 'That is true. However, he definitely accompanied us to the chapel, because he walked across the yard at my side. Then I went to stand near the front, so everyone could hear me singing, and I suppose he must have slipped out later.'

'The killer must have slipped out, too,' said Michael.

De Wetherset nodded. 'Of course. But the chapel is dark in the mornings, because the Gilbertines cannot afford many candles. It is impossible to make out the man next to you, let alone identify which of the brethren, nuns and guests were or were not present. Any of them could have stabbed Aylmer.'

'Except me,' said Simon firmly. 'I was singing and had *I* left, my absence would have been noted.'

'Is that true?' asked Michael of de Wetherset.

De Wetherset raised laconic eyebrows. 'He certainly has a penetrating voice,' he said, giving the impression he was not as impressed with it as was its owner.

'How many people are in this community?' asked Michael, becoming intrigued with the case, despite his resentment at the way in which it was being foisted on him.

'There are twelve brothers and fifteen nuns,' replied Simon. 'The sisters' duties revolve around the six or so inmates of St Sepulchre's Hospital, which is part of the Gilbertines' foundation. And there are a score of lay-brothers who manage the gardens and the sheep.'

'One of the brethren – Hamo, this week – conducts a separate ceremony for layfolk in the hospital,' said de Wetherset. 'I asked whether he had noticed anyone creeping out to murder Aylmer, but he said he had not. He is not overly observant, despite the fact that he loves to gossip.'

'I shall repair to the Carmelite Friary at first light tomorrow,' announced Suttone, horrified by the discussion. 'It will be safer. And Brother Michael intends to foist himself on the Black Monks.'

'You will find both convents are full,' said de Wetherset. 'Do you think *we* would stay in a place tainted by murder, had there been an alternative available? Simon and I will be safe with you, though – *you* cannot be the killers, because you have only just arrived.'

'True,' said Suttone nervously. 'But the same cannot be said for you.'

'De Wetherset is no killer,' said Michael with more confidence than Bartholomew felt was warranted. 'Yet surely, you have homes in Lincoln, if you live here? Why not go there?'

'De Wetherset was lodging with me,' explained Simon, 'but my house burned down last month – we should have been more careful when we banked the fire. Unfortunately, every bed in the city is now taken by folk who are here for Miller's Market, the General Pardon or – as a very poor third – the installation of canons. We have no choice but to stay with the Gilbertines.'

'This poor town,' said de Wetherset softly. 'A century ago, it was one of the greatest cities in the world, but now it is wracked by poverty. The plague did not help, carrying off two in every three of the clergy, and now the Fossedike

– the old canal that gives access to the sea – is silting up, and trade suffers sorely. It deserves better than to be befouled by murder.'

'Two murders,' corrected Michael. 'Aylmer and Flaxfleete.'

'Not to mention the others,' Bartholomew thought he heard Simon mutter.

Bartholomew slept badly that night for several reasons. He was over-tired from the journey; the bed was hard enough to hurt a back made sore by days in the saddle; he was eager to question Spayne about Matilde; he was disturbed to learn that a murder had taken place in the chamber below where he was tossing and turning; and he was uncomfortable sharing a room with de Wetherset and Simon. He had never liked the ex-Chancellor, and had been relieved when the man had left Cambridge. Like Michael, de Wetherset had relished the University's intrigues and politics, and loved nothing more than to scheme and pit his wits against the clever minds of rival scholars. Bartholomew often felt Michael had learned rather too many bad practices from the cunning de Wetherset.

He had also taken something of a dislike to Simon. The priest possessed an arrogant self-confidence that suggested he was used to having his own way, and Bartholomew felt he was exactly the kind of man to kill the hapless Aylmer while claiming to be singing psalms. He distrusted him, and was grateful Cynric and his ready dagger were to hand.

'I am uneasy here,' whispered the book-bearer in the depths of the night, hearing him shift restlessly. 'The servants are a miserable lot, who are raising toasts to the man who stabbed Aylmer – they all hated him, although none would tell me why. And I do not like de Wetherset wanting to sleep in the same chamber with us. He is a crafty man, and there will be trouble for certain.'

'We shall find somewhere else tomorrow,' said Bartholomew. 'We do not have to stay here.'

'Unfortunately, we do,' said Cynric gloomily. 'The servants say these are the last free beds in the entire city. Father Simon was right: folk *have* flocked here for Miller's Market and the General Pardon.'

'How many people were affected by this Summer Madness, then?' asked Bartholomew, startled to learn the disease might have reached plague-like proportions. 'And what sort of things did they do?'

'Theft, robbery, rape, adultery,' recited Cynric. 'Every felon in the county is here, determined to buy absolution for crimes committed during August, when the physicians say no man was responsible for his own actions.'

'I see,' said Bartholomew.

'And the servants say that while we might get one berth elsewhere – if we offer enough money – there is absolutely no chance of finding four together. I do not want to abandon Brother Michael in a place like this. He may need us.'

'What do you mean?'

'They say the bishop *is* going to order him to look into Aylmer's stabbing. Gynewell is appalled by an unlawful death in a convent, and wants the culprit brought to justice. We cannot let him do it alone.'

'No,' said Bartholomew with a sigh. 'I suppose we cannot.'

Bartholomew was jolted from an unsettling dream, in which Matilde was happily married to de Wetherset, by a discordant jangle that made him leap from the bed and grab his sword. Michael was already awake, and sat on the edge of his own bed, reading a psalter.

'Easy, Matt,' he said softly. 'It is only the bells for prime.

De Wetherset said they were louder than normal, and he is right.'

'It sounded like an alarm at the start of a battle,' said Bartholomew sheepishly, setting down the weapon before Suttone, de Wetherset and Simon could see what he had done. They were kneeling next to the hearth, whispering prayers of their own.

Michael closed his book and regarded his friend with concern. 'You have been different since you returned from France – wearing a sword all the time, and drawing it at the slightest provocation. I thought you disapproved of fighting and violence.'

Bartholomew sat back on the bed, and rubbed his eyes. 'I do, Brother, but this city does not feel safe, and you cannot blame me for being wary when a man was stabbed here only yesterday.'

Michael's expression was troubled. 'Cynric approves of your newly honed battle instincts – he worries less now he thinks you can look after yourself – but I am not so sure. It is unlike you.' He saw the physician did not agree, and changed the subject when Cynric approached with a bowl of water. 'Are you coming to prime? Laymen are not obliged to attend, so you can go back to sleep if you like, although that will not be easy with those bells going. It is enough to wake the dead.'

'I hope it does not,' said Cynric with a shudder. 'Although at least then you could just *ask* Aylmer who dispatched him, which would save a lot of time. But what will happen to Queen Eleanor's innards? Would they wake, too, and slither around looking for the rest of her?'

Michael regarded him in distaste. 'What a lurid imagination you have, Cynric.'

'It must come from living among the English for so

long,' sighed the book-bearer unhappily. 'We Welsh do not chop up the corpses of princes, and nor do we have earthquakes or saints crucified by Jews. *We* were on very good terms with the Jews, so a very great wrong must have been done to provoke them to that sort of behaviour.'

Bartholomew followed him down the stairs and through the hall, where the other guests were either readying themselves for prayers, or lying in their beds with their hands clapped to their ears. The bells were even louder in the yard, and when he tried to tell Suttone that his braes were showing under his habit, he was obliged to shout to make himself heard. And then, as abruptly as it had started, the clamour stopped.

'All right,' hissed the Carmelite, adjusting his underclothing while the physician's yell still reverberated around the stone buildings. His plump face was scarlet with mortification. 'There is no need to inform half of Lincoln.'

It was pitch dark and the ground underfoot was frozen hard, although treacherous patches of ice indicated the Gilbertines' main courtyard was more usually an expanse of soft mud and puddles. The air was bitterly cold, and Bartholomew shivered as he drew his winter cloak more closely around his shoulders. Above, the sky was clear, and thousands of stars glittered in a great dome of blackness. A fox yipped in the distance, and trees whispered softly in the wind.

Bartholomew was used to prime being a peaceful, contemplative affair, where the hushed voices of priests echoed around an otherwise silent church, allowing those participating to reflect on the day that was about to begin. Things were different at the Gilbertine convent. The brethren began by marching in to take their places in the chancel, their prior rattling a pair of wooden clappers as he went. Bartholomew knew lepers sometimes wielded such devices, but he had never seen one employed by a religious community, and especially not that early in the morning. Then there was a peculiar whining sound, and a good deal of hissing. Suttone cried out in alarm, and Bartholomew started to reach for his dagger before remembering that he had left his weapons in the guest-hall, in deference to the general rule against bearing arms in churches.

'It is the organ,' whispered de Wetherset, although the Gilbertines' stamping feet and the prior's rattle meant he could have spoken at normal volume and not raised any eyebrows. 'Surely you have encountered them in divine masses before?'

'I most certainly have not,' replied Suttone, resting a hand on his pounding heart. 'Such objects are best left in taverns, where they belong. We have no organs in Cambridge, and nor shall we – especially not once I am Chancellor.'

Bartholomew edged to one side and saw a man operating something that looked like a large pair of bellows. There were more creaks and wails, then a tune of sorts began to emerge. The Gilbertines – men and women together – cleared their throats and stood a little taller. Then the psalm of the day was underway, the Chapel of St Katherine was suddenly awash with such vigorous noise that the physician could not hear himself when he coughed. Suttone leapt in shock at the abrupt cacophony, and Michael started to snigger. Overwhelmed by the volume, Bartholomew moved away, hoping the aisles would render the racket a little less painful. Michael followed, his large frame quaking with laughter.

'What a row! I thought the Michaelhouse choir was bad enough, with its love of the crescendo, but it has nothing on these fellows. Anyone would think God and His angels were hard of hearing.'

'They probably are, if they are obliged to listen to this day after day,' muttered Bartholomew. 'It cannot be good for the ears. Like the ribauld, it will make men deaf.'

'Like the what?'

'The ribauld – a weapon that propels missiles through long tubes by means of exploding powder. The Black Prince had several, and the noise was appalling. The men operating them came to me afterwards, because they could not hear. One never did recover.'

Michael tried to imagine what one looked like. 'Were they very dangerous to the enemy?'

'Not as dangerous as they were to us. They regularly blew up or burned people, and I never saw a missile hit a Frenchman. But they were terrifying to anyone who has never seen one. They spit fire and produce black smoke which, combined with the din, was enough to make some men – and not just the enemy, either – turn and run for their lives.'

Michael shook his head. 'There is something innately distasteful about using exploding devices to harm another person, even the French. The very notion should be anathema to any decent soul.'

Bartholomew nodded, but his thoughts had returned to the noise the Gilbertines were making, and he was considering its implications for Aylmer's murder. 'Everyone is bellowing at the top of his lungs. And while Father Simon is one of the loudest, I am not sure he would be missed, were he to slink away and stab a man who sat admiring his possessions.'

'You do not like Simon, then?' asked Michael, arching his eyebrows in amusement. 'There is an entire convent of suspects to choose from, and you pick holes in his alibi.'

'Because no one else has offered us one yet,' Bartholomew pointed out. 'De Wetherset was cunningly cautious about *his* whereabouts. All *he* said was that the

Gilbertines make a lot of noise at their offices, which is not the same thing as saying he was here when Aylmer was killed. But no, I cannot say I have taken to Simon. He thinks himself better than you, because he intends to be a residentiary canon, and you will have to be an absent one.'

'Well, we will not have to put up with him for long. It is Thursday now, and we can be gone a week next Monday – the day after my installation.'

Bartholomew was startled. 'Will you not stay a little longer? It will not look decent to grab the Stall of South Scarle and make off with its prebend the very next morning.'

'At least I came in person to collect it, which is more than can be said for most of my colleagues. When you were asleep last night, de Wetherset told me that of the forty canons currently in office, only ten have ever set foot in the cathedral. Some live so far away that they might even be dead, for all the contact the dean has with them. They all hire Vicars Choral to do their work.'

'That is what you plan to do,' said Bartholomew, not really seeing the difference.

'But I have made arrangements to hire a *local* man, a fellow named John Tetford, which should please the dean. The foreign canons appoint their own deputies, and they are not always suitable.'

'The dean must find it difficult to maintain order. He will need the support of his Chapter, but if most of his canons are abroad, then he will not have it.'

'I expect that depends on the Vicars Choral. If they are good deputies, his job will be easy enough. My bishop tells me that Tetford will do all he is asked and more, and that he will make an excellent substitute. The dean will probably fare better with him than with me.'

'Probably,' agreed Bartholomew, earning himself an offended glare. 'It is true, Brother. You would be plotting against the dean before the week is out, given your love of intrigue, and he would find himself with a rebellion on his hands, not to mention a rival for his position. He does not know how lucky he is that you are obliged to be in Cambridge. However, none of this tells me why you are so determined to leave Lincoln early.'

'Aylmer's murder,' said Michael in a low voice. 'I do not like the timing of it, and I do not like the fact that he was Suttone's Vicar Choral. Suttone is opinionated and annoying, but he is a colleague, and I do not want *him* stabbed while he gloats over his belongings. And nor do I want you in Lincoln when it is full of felons wanting absolution – not with your current penchant for wearing a sword. It looks as though you want a fight. Everything about our situation feels dangerous.'

'There are the priory's noblewomen,' said Suttone, coming to join them before Bartholomew could comment. He pointed to the back of the nave, where the tall woman in the white habit stood with her head bowed as she listened to the Gilbertines' singing. Her friend, the elderly nun, knelt next to her, holding a candle. Immediately, Michael's eyes lit with interest, murder and unease forgotten.

'I wonder if they would appreciate a philosophical exegesis of this particular psalm,' he mused. 'As a theologian, it is my duty to educate all who might benefit from my expertise.'

'I would not think they need your intellectual skills, Brother,' replied Suttone, apparently unaware of the predatory gleam in his colleague's eye. 'Hamo tells me that Dame Eleanor is quite a scholar herself, while Lady Christiana – the younger one – is a highly valued member of the convent.'

'Because she pays well for the honour of being here?' asked Bartholomew, who knew how such matters worked.

Wealthy ladies often spent time in religious foundations when their menfolk were not in a position to look after them, and it could be a lucrative arrangement for a priory.

'I expect that is the main reason,' agreed Suttone. 'They say she is also upright, kind and popular with children. And Dame Eleanor, whom everyone reveres because she has devoted her entire life to Lincoln's saints, thinks the world of her. Eleanor says Christiana is gracious in adversity.'

'What adversity?' asked Bartholomew.

'First she lost her husband in the French wars, then her mother died. Incidentally, her mother was supposed to remarry, too. She was betrothed to that merchant you met yesterday – Kelby – but passed away before he could escort her to the altar.'

'I would like to meet her daughter,' said Michael, rather dreamily.

'You do not have time,' said Bartholomew, watching him uneasily. 'First, you have a murder to solve, and secondly, you need to be fitted for your ceremonial robes. And then, as soon as you are properly installed at the cathedral, we are leaving. Remember?'

'Are we?' asked Suttone, relieved. 'Good. I do not want to join the ranks of the dead: Aylmer, Flaxfleete and that wicked man who died during the plague – Canon Hodelston.'

'I doubt those deaths are connected—' began Bartholomew.

'You can think what you like, but I know how I feel,' said Suttone curtly. 'And I feel like I want to leave. I shall introduce you to those ladies later, Brother. I see by the way your eyes are fixed on them that you are impressed by their piety.'

'Oh, I am,' agreed Michael. 'Piety is a virtue very dear to my heart.'

* * *

89

By the time the service had been hollered, dawn was beginning to break. It was clear and blue, and the sun was just rising over the flat fields that lay to the east. Every roof was dusted with snow, and the long road that led arrow-straight towards the city was like a gleaming silver ribbon in the gathering light. As the temperature began to rise, a mist formed, and the cathedral sat above it, as though it was hovering. Bartholomew stood by the Gilbertines' main gate and watched spellbound as the first sunbeams touched the yellow stone and set it afire.

'It is like Ely,' said Michael, coming to join him. 'That floats above the morning fog, too.'

'Yes, it does. Did you know that the central spire makes Lincoln's cathedral the tallest building in the world? Yet it is so delicate, it looks as though it is made from lace. Stone lace.'

'I hope you find Matilde soon, Matt,' said Michael, beginning to walk to the refectory to break his fast. 'I do not think I can stand many more of these coarse allusions, in which you compare lovely buildings to women's underclothes. Still, it is better than you prancing about with a sword, I suppose.'

He moved away, leaving the physician staring after him in astonishment.

The refectory was a large hall, with separate sections for each rank of inhabitant: Gilbertine brothers, Gilbertine sisters, hospital inmates, layfolk and guests. It was a hive of activity, and almost as noisy as the chapel. Voices were raised in conversation, pots clattered and there was frequent ringing laughter. Servants scurried here and there, carrying buckets of oatmeal and baskets of bread; although it was plain fare, it was plentiful and wholesome.

'Did you enjoy prime?' asked Simon, coming to sit next

to them. His voice was low and difficult to catch. 'When I was vicar at Holy Cross, I always came here for the dawn devotions, because I find the ceremony so uplifting. It is good to start the day by praising God with all one's heart.'

'You should consider praising Him a little more quietly tomorrow,' suggested Bartholomew. 'You are so hoarse that you can barely speak.'

Simon regarded him askance. 'God gave me speech to extol His name, so that is what I shall do with it. It will recover after a cup of breakfast ale – it always does. You might want to try it yourself.'

'The breakfast ale?'

'Some heartfelt worship. I saw you skulking in the shadows, muttering the psalm as though you were afraid of speaking the words aloud. Brother Michael was no better.'

'He is right,' said Hamo, coming to ensure his guests had enough to eat. 'The Bible should be shouted to the skies, not whispered at the floor. I suggest you return to the chapel after breakfast and practise a few alleluias. I will come with you, and offer some advice.'

'Christ!' muttered Bartholomew when he left. 'The entire town is insane.'

'Do not blaspheme,' admonished Michael sharply. 'I do not hold with undisciplined piety, either, but it does not mean I condone that sort of language in a convent.'

'Sorry,' said Bartholomew. 'From now on, I shall swear only on unhallowed ground.'

Michael glared at him, not sure whether he was being mocked. 'Well, just make sure you do.'

Once the food was on the tables, a tremendous rattling ensued when Whatton waved the wooden clappers in the air, and the hubbub of voices died away. The prior, a tall man with a large head, stood and began to intone grace in a voice loud enough to be heard by even the deafest diner. Then he sat, took a spoon in one hand and gestured with the other that his brethren could commence eating.

'He likes to maintain silence during meals,' whispered de Wetherset. 'They do not mind guests talking, though, as long as they are not too noisy.'

'It is better just to eat,' said Simon, grabbing a pan and helping himself to more of its contents than was considerate. 'They do not take long over meals, and he who chatters goes hungry.'

Michael needed no further warning, and bent his head to the task in hand, managing to put away a monstrous amount before the prior said the final grace. He seized a piece of smoked pork as the platters were being cleared away, and slapped it in the physician's hand.

'It is cold outside, and we have a lot to do today,' he said. 'You cannot wander about on an empty stomach, because if you faint, I have no time to help you revive.'

Bartholomew smiled. It was a ritual they went through most days, ever since Michael had declared him under-nourished after his return from France. He was touched by the concern, but was also aware that the monk's idea of thin was rather different from his own. He tore the meat in half, and they shared it as they left the refectory. They had not gone far before Suttone called them back.

'I just went to pay my respects to Prior Roger de Bankesfeld, and he said he would like to see us in his solar,' he said, rather breathlessly. 'Now.'

'Good,' said Michael. 'We can thank him for his hospitality, and inform him that we intend to stay with our own brethren for the rest of our sojourn in Lincoln. The Benedictines will find a corner for us somewhere. I certainly do not want to join the murdered Aylmer in the charnel house by lingering here.'

CHAPTER 3

Bartholomew and Michael followed Suttone across the yard and entered the house that comprised the prior's lodgings. In the half-dark of the previous afternoon, when they had arrived, Bartholomew had imagined it to be a handsome building, but daylight showed that it, like the rest of the convent, was in sore need of repair. Its roof was all but invisible under a cushion of snow, but the shape indicated it was sagging, and its walls were stained with lichen. Stones were missing from the chimney, and the thick white smoke that billowed out suggested a fire had only just been lit – an early-morning blaze was a luxury the prior did not permit himself. Hamo was waiting to escort them up the stairs to a solar that was pleasant despite its cracked plaster and uneven floorboards.

'Here are the Cambridge men, Father,' said Hamo, prodding Bartholomew when he was slow to follow the others inside – the physician was trying to finish the pork, not being as adept as Michael at devouring lumps of meat at speed. 'Michael de Causton, Thomas Suttone and Matthew—'

'Suttone,' pounced the prior. 'Kin to the great Lincoln Suttones. Hamo says you and he may share common ancestors, and *he* is distantly related to Bishop Oliver Suttone.'

'Oliver was my grandfather,' replied Suttone proudly. 'I have a cousin who has invited me—'

'Do not think of staying elsewhere,' said the prior firmly. 'You are welcome *here*. The Suttones are a respected family, and it is a privilege to have one under my roof for a few weeks. And I intend to make Hamo our Brother Hospitaller today, too, so the Suttones will know I favour them *and* their kin. He will be a vast improvement on Fat William, God rest his soul, because he does not eat as much.'

Hamo's moist lips split in a startled grin, while Bartholomew thought Michael would have to curb his appetite if he did not want to be tarred with the same brush. 'Thank you, Father,' stammered Hamo. 'You will not regret it, I promise, and—'

'I am sure you will be assiduous,' said Roger. He sighed. 'Well, pour us some almond milk, then, man! You are already slacking in your duties.'

Bartholomew studied Roger de Bankesfeld properly for the first time, as the man had been too far away in the chapel and at breakfast. Bartholomew was tall, but the prior was taller – although a good deal thinner – so the overall effect was spindly. He had huge hands with bony knuckles, and big yellow teeth that gave his head a skull-like appearance. He reminded Bartholomew of the grotesque tombs he had seen in southern France, where the sculptors had been overly obsessed with death.

'We plan to stay only a few days, and—' began Suttone.

'It is an honour to receive you,' said Prior Roger with a grin that did nothing to dispel the skeletal image. 'Fortunately, there was something of an exodus after Aylmer's murder yesterday, so we were not obliged to order people to evacuate the best room for you.'

'That is very kind,' said Suttone, swallowing uneasily. 'But there would have been no need for—'

'I *said* it is an honour to receive you,' interrupted Roger with some annoyance. 'And I meant it. Just because we are on the outskirts of the city, and we are a bit short of funds, does not mean we are less hospitable than the other Orders. Well, I accept that the Dominicans are conveniently close to the Bishop's Palace, and the Franciscans have that lovely new guest-hall, but that is all irrelevant. We are very pleased you chose us, when you could have gone elsewhere.'

'The honour is ours,' said Michael graciously. 'However, I am a Benedictine and my brethren will expect me to—'

'You will not want to reside with them,' declared Roger. 'They are deeply in debt, and their guests nearly always go hungry. You do not look like a man who likes to go hungry, Brother.'

'Well, no,' admitted Michael. 'But—'

'And the Carmelite Friary has its drawbacks, too,' Roger went on, addressing Suttone. 'It is too near the river and stinks to high heaven. We are upstream, so do not suffer such miseries.'

From the artful way he spoke, Bartholomew wondered whether the stench that afflicted the White Friars was because of something the Gilbertines did.

'I do not mind a little—' began Suttone.

'And they have a rat problem,' added Roger.

'That is not as unnerving as a murder problem,' Michael managed to interject.

Roger waved his hand dismissively. 'It is the first time we have ever lost a visitor to a killer's blade, although the other convents have had deaths galore. You are better off here, gentlemen. As I said, we are always pleased to have canons-elect sharing our humble abode.'

'You are too kind,' said Michael, although Bartholomew could tell from the glint in his eye that he would go elsewhere if he wanted. 'Not everyone has been so eager to accommodate us during our long and arduous voyage from Cambridge.'

'Not everyone knows how much canons are paid,' Bartholomew was sure he heard Roger mutter. The prior cleared his throat and spoke more loudly. 'I promise you shall have the best of everything.'

'You will,' agreed Hamo. 'And if another convent offers you something we do not have, tell me what it is and I will get it for you. I intend to make your stay as comfortable as possible.' He glanced at his prior, to see if he was being sufficiently obsequious.

'It is our duty to God,' said Roger. He crossed himself. 'Praise His holy name. Alleluia!'

'Alleluia!' shouted Hamo in reply, raising his hands in the air and gazing at the ceiling.

Suttone nudged Bartholomew with his elbow when he became aware that the physician was more amused than religiously inspired by the demonstration, and then did the same to Michael. 'Behave yourselves!' he hissed under his breath. 'They will think us godless heathens if you stand there chortling at their heartfelt expressions of reverence, and they may tell Bishop Gynewell. We do not want to be ejected from our stalls before we have claimed the money that goes with them.'

'You are the godless heathen, if you are only interested in the post for its stipend,' Bartholomew shot back.

'There she is again!' breathed Michael, gazing out of the window when he spotted a flash of white out of the corner of his eye. He moved to one side for a better view. 'Lady Christiana and—'

'And Dame Eleanor,' said Roger, coming to stand next to him. 'We are fortunate to have them in our convent. Dame Eleanor is little short of a saint, and her devotion to St Hugh is legendary. She also prays for Queen Eleanor, whose funeral cross stands outside our gate. God rest her soul.'

'Amen,' chorused Hamo.

'We saw that,' said Suttone. 'It is a—'

'The King is grateful to Dame Eleanor for her care of

96

his grandmother's soul,' said Roger. 'And it is always good to have a king pleased with one of your residents. You should engage Eleanor in a discussion about theology, Brother. You will find her sharp-minded and erudite.'

'And Lady Christiana?' asked Michael. 'Will she benefit from a theological debate, too?'

Roger glanced sharply at him, but answered anyway. 'She lost her husband in the French wars, and the King asked us to look after her until she recovers from the shock. The maintenance he pays for her keep is invaluable, and Dame Eleanor has grown fond of her. They are often together.'

'There is a lot of traffic on the road outside,' observed Suttone, not particularly interested in the convent's females. 'I have counted six carts in the last—'

'They are gathering for Miller's Market,' said Roger, his face darkening with disapproval. 'Wagons have been pouring into the city all week, and the event is not due to start for another ten days. Lincoln is bursting at the seams, but still they come.'

'Very few fairs take place in winter,' said Suttone. 'It must be—'

'I doubt *God* approves,' Roger went on. 'Some will claim Miller is a good man for his generosity, but he did *not* start his fair out of the kindness of his heart. He did it out of spite.'

'The poor probably do not mind,' said Bartholomew. 'They will prefer a festival to a—'

'So, we shall have to make sure our singing seduces them away from their pagan diversions,' said Roger with grim determination. 'A few alleluias will bring them back to their senses.'

'I warned you,' Suttone whispered fiercely to his colleagues, when the prior raised his hands towards the rafters and began to sing in a booming voice; Hamo joined in. 'If you cannot refrain from sniggering, you should leave before he hears you. Say you are unwell.'

Bartholomew was halfway to the door when there was a thundering knock that startled the prior into a blessed silence.

'Who is that?' asked Roger, as if the Michaelhouse men should know. 'I said we were to be left in peace as long as important visitors were with me – and a pair of canons-elect, one of whom is kin to the Suttones, qualify as the most important guests we have had in years.'

The door flew open before Hamo could reach it, and a tiny man bounced inside. He barely reached Bartholomew's shoulder, and his head was covered in a thick mop of wiry curls, some of which twisted into points at the side of his head and gave the uncanny appearance of horns. His ears were large and round, and when he smiled he revealed several missing teeth. He wore the simple robes of a Dominican, although the purple ring on his finger showed he was one who held an elevated position in the Church.

'Good morning, Roger,' he piped cheerfully. 'It is only me.'

'My Lord Bishop,' said Roger with a courtly bow.

Bishop Gynewell skipped across the chamber and presented his episcopal ring for Roger to kiss. He barely reached the Gilbertine's chest, and the tall prior was obliged to bend absurdly low to reach the proffered bauble. The prelate had not come alone, and was accompanied by a handsome young priest who was weighed down with parchment, scrolls and writing materials. When Bartholomew went to help him, the reek of wine was overpowering. The physician concluded, from the clerk's liverish appearance, that he consumed a lot of it on a regular basis. There was something familiar about him, and Bartholomew tried to recall where he had seen him before. Then the memory snapped into place: he had been one of the men slumped unconscious across Kelby's table the previous night. As the physician dived to save a pot of ink from falling to the floor, something hard bumped against his hand. He stepped away smartly, wondering why a man in holy orders should want to conceal a sword under his robes.

'This is a dangerous city,' explained the clerk, guessing what had happened. He glanced at the bishop, to ensure he could not be heard. 'I seldom go anywhere without a blade.'

'Why would anyone attack you?' asked Bartholomew. He thought about the conflict that was tearing the city in half. 'Because you are a Guild member?'

The clerk waved a hand to indicate that was unimportant, and several scrolls pattered on the floor. 'I am not worried about Miller and his cronies – they do not have the wits to best a clever fellow like me. I am more concerned about my fellow priests; *they* are where the real danger lies.'

Bartholomew regarded him uncertainly. 'I do not understand.'

'Have you not heard what happened to Aylmer in this very convent? He was a Vicar Choral and he was stabbed to death, so do not tell *me* canons' deputies are a peaceful band of men. The only way to defend myself is with a sharp sword, and if you visit the cathedral, I recommend you wear one, too.'

He moved away to stand near the door when Prior Roger finished paying homage to his bishop, coincidentally ending up near a tray on which stood several goblets of wine.

'How are you, Roger?' chirped Bishop Gynewell merrily, wholly unaware that his secretary was slyly raiding the Gilbertines' claret. 'Any more murders today?'

'No, My Lord,' replied Roger shortly. 'It was an isolated incident, as I told you yesterday. And we should not be discussing that now anyway.' He flicked his head at his three visitors in an indiscreet way that made Bartholomew want to laugh again.

'Brother Michael, I presume,' said the bishop, turning to beam at the fat monk. 'And you must be Master Suttone. I shall soon count you two among my canons, although I was disappointed to hear you have appointed Vicars Choral and plan to return to your University. Well, that is to say, *Michael* has appointed a deputy. Suttone will have to find another.'

'So I have been told,' said Suttone, bowing over the prelate's hand. 'This is our colleague Matthew Bartholomew. He is a physician.'

'I guessed as much from his bag,' said Gynewell, resting his hand on Bartholomew's shoulder when he stepped forward to make his obeisance. 'I know the scent of valerian and woundwart when I come across it.'

'He used those to treat an injured pedlar we encountered yesterday morning,' said Michael, while Bartholomew regarded the bishop in amazement. 'You are an observant man, My Lord.'

'Thank you, Brother; I shall consider that a compliment.' Gynewell trotted to a chair next to the fire and climbed on to it, folding his legs in a way that made him look more like a pixie than one of the most powerful churchmen in the country. 'I am surprised you have elected to stay with Prior Roger, rather than with me at my palace. I extended an invitation to you, through Bishop de Lisle.'

'Did you?' asked Michael, peeved. 'He neglected to pass it on. However, I—'

'The good brother is settled with us now,' said Roger smoothly. 'He enjoyed our energetic prime this morning, and will want to repeat the experience tomorrow.'

'Will he?' asked Gynewell in surprise.

'It *was* energetic,' admitted Michael. 'But I—'

'All our guests find our style of worship uplifting,' announced Roger uncompromisingly. 'They say it makes a change from the sober muttering of the other Orders.'

'There was certainly no muttering involved,' agreed Michael. 'However, this is the first time I have ever set foot in a Gilbertine House, other than the one in Cambridge and that is a very staid foundation. Are they usually so . . . expressive?'

'This is the only convent I know that praises God at such high volume,' said Gynewell. 'I cannot imagine it is anything but unique.'

'We like to make an impact,' said Roger smugly. 'Why murmur when you can yell, I always say.'

'So do fishwives,' said Suttone in an undertone. 'And it is not seemly.'

'May I have a word with Brother Michael alone, Roger?' asked Gynewell, after several attempts to change the subject had failed, and they were still discussing the Gilbertines' unusual approach to their devotions a quarter of an hour later. 'Please stay, Doctor. What I have to say is not private.'

'No?' asked Roger, settling himself behind his table. 'Then I shall stay, too.'

'It pertains to Cambridge, Roger,' said Gynewell, prodding the fire with a poker. He added several logs and jabbed them until the flames roared. 'You will be bored, and I am sure you have a lot to do.'

'Not really,' said Roger, leaning back comfortably. 'And I am always interested in learning about new and exotic locations. I hear Cambridge sits on a bog, just like Ely.'

'And I hear Lincoln is full of imps,' retorted Michael, irritated by the dual slur on his town and his abbey. 'Little ones, which hurl rocks at the choir during masses.'

Gynewell cackled his mirth, and it occurred to Bartholomew that he looked rather demonic himself, with his horn-like hair and gap-toothed grin. 'The Lincoln imp is a charming folk tale, Brother. But I am starving. Would you mind showing Ravenser here where you buy those lovely red marchpanes, Roger? He can never find the right shop, and I am sure you will not mind obliging your old bishop.'

'And purchase a few Lombard slices while you are at it,' suggested Michael opportunistically. He smiled slyly. 'The Benedictines will certainly provide me with an unlimited supply of pastries if I stay with them. But if the Gilbertines do the same, I shall have no reason to leave.'

Roger stood reluctantly, knowing he was outmanoeuvred. 'The bakeries will open soon, so I shall see what we can do. However, the Black Monks will not give you Lombard slices, Brother. I told you – they have no money with which to pamper their guests.'

'And if they did, they would spend it on themselves,' added Ravenser nastily, swallowing a second goblet of wine before turning to leave.

'I shall come with you, Father Prior,' said Suttone. 'I dislike Lombard slices, and red marchpanes sound unpleasant. I must make sure you buy something I will enjoy, too.'

He, Roger, Hamo and Ravenser left together, and Gynewell grinned conspiratorially at the monk. 'I see you and I will work excellently together, Brother. Roger is a good man, but I did not want to talk to you while he was listening.'

'And your clerk, My Lord?' asked Bartholomew. 'Why did you send him away?'

Gynewell did not seem to take offence at what was essentially an impertinent question. 'We do not need a written account of this meeting – not that Archdeacon Ravenser would have made a decent record anyway. Did you see the state of him? He was at a Guild meeting last night, and they can turn very debauched. Poor Ravenser seems incapable of refusing a cup of wine, but I think he drinks to lessen his desire for women.'

'Perhaps you should try it, Matt,' muttered Michael. 'It would be a lot safer than traipsing across half the world hunting them out.'

'Not necessarily,' replied Bartholomew, thinking about Ravenser's fragile health.

Gynewell glanced at the door. 'They will not be gone long, so we had better speak while we can. Have you heard about this murder?'

'You mean Flaxfleete's?' asked Michael. 'We had nothing to do with that.'

'I know. John Suttone told me you tried to help him. Poor Flaxfleete. He would have made a diligent canon, although I suspect he would have been argumentative in Chapter meetings. But I was not referring to him. I meant Aylmer – Suttone's Vicar Choral.'

Michael sighed wearily. 'Yes, I heard about it.'

Gynewell grinned again. 'De Wetherset says you and Bartholomew were very good at solving murders when he was Chancellor, and thinks you must be even better at it by now.'

'He is exaggerating, My Lord,' said Michael unhappily.

'Perhaps, but Bishop de Lisle also extolled your virtues, and he seldom has a good word to say about anyone. You are exactly the kind of man I would like in my cathedral Chapter, and I hope you will stay with us for a very long time before you leave young Tetford in charge.'

Michael's smile was pained. 'Unfortunately, I have pressing duties in Cambridge, and I am obliged to leave the day after the installation.'

Gynewell's face fell in dismay. 'So soon? There is so much I want to show you!'

'I will return,' said Michael, more kindly. 'In the summer, when the students are no longer in residence, and my own town is quiet. Then I shall spend two or three months here.'

Gynewell's expression was wistful. 'That would be delightful, although it seems a long time to wait. Will you help me with Aylmer's murder? Prior Roger seems content to let the matter lie, but an unlawful killing on sacred ground is a serious matter, and I would like the culprit under lock and key as soon as possible. I shall grant whatever authority you need to investigate.'

Michael frowned. 'Surely you have your own agents for this kind of thing? De Lisle does.'

'Of course, but they are busy policing the felons gathering for Miller's Market, and have no time to look into the death of a man no one liked very much.'

'He was unpopular?' asked Bartholomew, his heart sinking on Michael's behalf. If Aylmer had a lot of enemies, it might be very difficult to locate the real killer.

'It grieves me to speak ill of the dead,' said Gynewell. 'But there is no point in my telling you he was an angel, because he was not. I would not be so concerned, if it were not for this chalice.'

'What chalice?' asked Michael.

'The Hugh Chalice,' explained Gynewell. 'It belonged to St Hugh of Lincoln, so is a very valuable relic. Father Simon has offered to donate it to the cathedral when he is installed, but I am not sure we should accept it.'

'Why not?' asked Michael. 'If it really did belong to St Hugh, it will attract pilgrims. And pilgrims bring trade to the city and will leave donations at his shrine. And the shrine is in *your* cathedral.'

'I know,' said Gynewell. 'But this particular relic has an odd history. The story goes that Hugh was holding it when

104

he died in London's Old Temple. It stayed there for a hundred and thirty years, until my predecessor, Bishop Burghersh, arranged for it to be brought here.'

'Burghersh died years ago,' said Michael. 'Did his arrangements fail, then? And why is it Simon's to donate?'

'It never arrived,' explained Gynewell. 'It was stolen on its journey north twenty years ago, and its where-abouts were a mystery until it reappeared in the hands of a relic-seller recently. It was fortunate Simon hap-pened to hear about it, or one of Lincoln's convents might have snapped it up. However, I cannot help but wonder at the coincidence.'

'What do you mean?' asked Michael.

Gynewell shrugged. 'Let us say I am suspicious. It was missing for two decades, and then suddenly it is about to be presented to the cathedral for no charge. It is too good to be true. In essence, I would like to know where it has been in the interim.'

'Perhaps it is not the real cup,' suggested Michael. 'That is the most rational explanation. You must have come across forgeries in the past.'

'It is no forgery,' declared Gynewell with startling convic-tion. 'I am absolutely convinced of its authenticity. My dean disagrees, though. He held it in his hands, and said it did not instil in him a proper sense of reverence. I asked him to explain further, but he is not very good with words.'

'I understand him,' said Michael. 'We had some bones in Cambridge a few years ago, which were said to belong to a saint. Only the more perceptive of us saw they were not holy.'

'The more "perceptive" of us also knew they had been hacked from a pauper,' added Bartholomew.

'So, Dean Bresley thinks our Hugh Chalice is not the real one,' said Gynewell, off in a world of his own. 'However, I feel with every fibre of my being that he is wrong.'

'Why mention your dean's scepticism if you disagree with him?' asked Michael.

'You cannot investigate the matter properly unless you are fully informed,' replied Gynewell. 'And you should be aware that the chalice has provoked conflict among your future colleagues – the dean doubts its sanctity, but most of the Vicars Choral do not.'

'Thank you for being candid, My Lord,' said Michael. 'But I thought you wanted me to find Aylmer's killer. What has the Hugh Chalice to do with him?'

'It is very simple,' said Gynewell. 'Aylmer was holding it when he was stabbed.'

It was not long before the door opened and Roger entered with a plate of Lombard slices. Bartholomew was keen to go in search of Spayne, but did not want to offend the prior by racing away the moment he arrived with his victuals. He lingered awhile, then made his escape when Michael announced that he was going to begin his investigation into Aylmer's murder. Suttone volunteered to help, but the offer was a half-hearted one, and he was visibly relieved when the monk said the best thing he could do was act as Michaelhouse's ambassador by charming their hosts. Gravely, Suttone agreed to sample the Gilbertines' pastries, all in the interests of establishing friendly relations between the Cambridge College and the Lincoln convent.

'I do not want to stay here,' said Michael resentfully, as they left Suttone to his arduous duties. 'And nor do I want to investigate a suspicious death.'

'Neither do I,' said Bartholomew. 'If Spayne tells me where Matilde might be, I would like to leave as soon as possible. I will not abandon you to investigate this stabbing alone, but I do not want to wait weeks before going after her. The delay might see her slip through my fingers again.'

'We had better get on with it, then,' said Michael. He sighed. 'I did not think accepting a prebendal stall would see me inconveniently beholden to a second bishop.'

'I suppose you can still decline the honour,' said Bartholomew. 'I do not think de Lisle will be very pleased if you do, though. He said he had sacrificed a good deal to secure it for you.'

Michael nodded. 'He was obliged to promote three of Gynewell's archdeacons to posts in his own See in return.' He looked thoughtful. 'But to return to the murder, I am under the impression that it is not Aylmer's *death* that worries Gynewell. What bothers him is the prospect of accepting the Hugh Chalice if it is implicated in a crime.'

'How will you begin your work?'

'By looking at Aylmer's corpse. It lies in the mortuary chapel, and I was hoping you might spare a few moments to help me. I know you are eager to visit Spayne, but I will come with you to interview him, if you oblige me with Aylmer now.'

'I do not need you with me when I talk to Spayne.' Bartholomew was surprised the monk should think he might, given that he had spent the last year and a half making enquiries on his own.

'Do not be so sure,' said Michael. 'He may not want to help you – a man determined to marry the woman who rejected him – but he may be more forthcoming with a monk.'

Bartholomew supposed he had a point. 'Can we see Spayne first, then inspect Aylmer?'

Michael tapped him on the arm with a plump forefinger. 'You dallied weeks in Cambridge after hearing about Spayne from Matilde's friend – waiting for term to end so Suttone and I could travel to Lincoln for our installation. Why the sudden hurry?'

'Because people here knew Matilde, and they have made the search real again.'

'The trail is still six years old, Matt. Be patient, and do not allow your expectations to rise too high. I do not want you crushed with disappointment again – like that time you heard she had gone to Stamford, only to learn she had not been there in a decade.'

Bartholomew nodded. The monk was right, and he tried to put Matilde out of his mind. He was about to follow him inside a low, dismal building, when he spotted Father Simon's pockmarked face. The priest was leaning against a disused stable, in earnest conversation with a fellow wearing crimson hose. When a group of lay-brothers clattered towards them, carrying pails of milk and sharing some ribald joke, Simon started in alarm and shoved his companion out of sight, placing a hand over the fellow's mouth to stop him from speaking. The man put up a token struggle at the rough treatment, but desisted when Simon whispered something urgent. Simon scanned the yard quickly when the cowherds had gone, although he failed to notice Bartholomew watching him. Then he and his companion finished their discussion and parted quickly. Bartholomew was puzzled, wondering why the priest should act so furtively, but then dismissed the incident as none of his business.

'I was about to start without you,' grumbled Michael when the physician entered the chapel, as if the delay had been hours rather than moments. The mortuary was small, dark and smelled of mould. Cobwebs swayed on the ceiling, and the floor was slick with slime. 'Still, you should enjoy this. It will remind you of how you anatomised cadavers with the French all last year.'

'I did no such thing,' objected Bartholomew. 'Well, I suppose there was the occasion when—'

'You can keep that sort of information to yourself,' interrupted Michael tartly. 'I do not want to lose you to an accusation of witchcraft now I finally have you back again. It would be a wretched nuisance. Besides, chopping up human bodies is not a normal thing to which to aspire.'

'Neither is examining them for your investigations.'

'That is different,' said Michael loftily. 'As I have told you before.'

'I cannot see in here,' complained Bartholomew, beginning to resent the wasted time. 'It is too dark and there are no windows to open.'

'We will be poring over bodies until sunset at this rate,' said Michael with an impatient sigh. 'First you dawdle outside, then the room is too dim.'

'Well, it is dim,' Bartholomew pointed out, irritable in his turn.

'Lord, Matt!' snapped Michael, as he stamped outside. He continued to rail as he stalked towards the kitchens, oblivious of the fact that the physician could no longer hear him. 'You are all complaints this morning. Make a start, then, while I fetch a lamp. You should have remembered to bring one yourself. You know perfectly well these places are always gloomy, and I cannot be expected to do everything. You are worse than Doctor Rougham—'

'Who is Doctor Rougham?' asked a low, sultry voice behind him. 'And who is the intended recipient of this bitter diatribe? I hope you will not blame it on Summer Madness. We have not seen a case of that in months.'

Michael spun around and was horrified to see Christiana de Hauville there, a faint smile etched into features that were even more perfect up close than they had been at a distance. Being caught muttering to himself was not how the monk had envisaged their first meeting.

'I was talking to my colleague,' he said, trying to repair

his dented dignity. 'He is always slinking off in the middle of conversations, though, and I expect he has gone to the mortuary chapel.'

'Really?' she asked, amusement tugging the corners of her mouth; Michael berated himself for gabbling and providing more information than was necessary – information that made him sound slightly strange. 'What an odd thing to do.'

'He is a physician and they are apt to be odd, as you will know if you have ever met any,' elaborated Michael. He was surprised to find himself determined that she should not know he dabbled in such sordid activities as inspecting corpses; he was even more surprised to realise how keen he was to make a good impression. He smiled at her, noting that she was almost as tall as he, which was unusual for a woman. 'Do you know where I might find a lamp? Matt needs one for . . . for reading.'

'I shall arrange for one to be fetched,' she replied. There was laughter in her voice, although her face was politely grave. 'I cannot get it myself, obviously.'

'Why not? Do you not know where they are kept?'

'Of course. But I do not perform menial tasks, or so the good brothers keep telling me. Were I to go to the kitchens myself, they would chase me out, like a pig among the cabbages.'

'I would never associate you with pigs,' said Michael chivalrously. 'Or cabbages. But we all need to perform menial tasks occasionally, because they keep us from the sin of pride.'

'Is pride a sin?' asked Christiana. 'I am a noblewoman, and it is considered a virtue in my family.'

'I am the son of a knight myself,' said Michael, unwilling to be thought of as common. 'But I forswore my earthly family when I took holy orders. Perhaps that is why the vows are in place – to ensure we do not confuse filial obligation with something deadly to the soul. Do you have any intention of taking the veil?'

She smiled and he saw white, perfect teeth in a face that might have belonged to an angel. 'I have not decided, Brother. It depends on what the future holds.'

She adopted a helpless pose that indicated she needed assistance, and suddenly there were three brothers and a lay-sister hurrying to see what she wanted. She asked for a lantern and all four scurried towards the kitchens, one sprinting so fast that he missed his footing and took a tumble. When the remaining three reached the door, there was almost an exchange of blows as each fought to enter first.

'Bless them,' she said, watching with a fond smile. 'They are so good to me. Perhaps I *will* take the veil, since I love this place so much; the people are far kinder here than they are in the world outside. Thank you, Hamo. It was very kind of you to do so much running on my behalf.'

Hamo backed away with a silly grin on his face, panting and bowing furiously, while Michael lit the lamp. Then Bartholomew emerged, wondering what was taking the monk so long. He stopped short when he saw the monk cupping his hands over Christiana's as they struggled with the flame together.

'My colleague,' said Michael, making no attempt to move his fingers from Christiana's silky skin. 'The one who sneaks off in the middle of conversations, leaving his friends talking to themselves.'

Christiana inclined her head in response to Bartholomew's bow. 'And the one who likes to linger in mortuary chapels. Reading, apparently.'

'Only if I have a lamp,' said Bartholomew tartly, elbowing Michael out of the way so he could light it himself; the monk was taking far too long over the operation.

Bartholomew studied Christiana covertly, taking in the

fact that her eyelashes were darkened with charcoal, which had the effect of making her skin appear fashionably pale, and the tendrils of gold hair that curled attractively from under her veil were not random escapees, but ones that had been carefully tailored for maximum effect. He could tell from her posture that she fully expected to be the centre of attention. But, he reflected wryly as he glanced around him, people *were* looking at her, and he was among them. He gave his complete attention to the wick, oblivious to the fact that she then used the opportunity to return the scrutiny.

'Have you been here long?' asked Michael, aware that Christiana's interest had moved to a man who was slimmer and far better-looking than himself. Not that it would do her much good – for the physician, there was only one woman.

'Since my husband was killed,' she replied. A tremor in her voice suggested it still pained her. 'I am here until either the King finds another suitable match or I become a nun. I am torn between wishing His Majesty would hurry up, and hoping he never finds a replacement, lest he imposes on me a man I do not like.'

'That is why I took holy orders,' confided Michael, making Bartholomew glance at him in surprise. He had never asked Michael's reasons for taking the cowl, and had always assumed a sense of vocation had led him to do it. 'My family had in mind a match that would have made me unhappy. I have never regretted my decision.'

She regarded him curiously. 'You do not find the life a lonely one?'

'Not at all. I have many friends, and there are ways to alleviate loneliness.'

'The lamp is lit,' said Bartholomew, suddenly seized with the awful premonition that the monk was about to tell her how to break vows of chastity without being caught. 'Come on, Brother. There is not much oil, and we do not have long before it burns out.'

'Would you like me to hold it for you?' asked Christiana, looking from one to the other with wide blue eyes. 'It would be no trouble, and I have never seen anyone read in the mortuary chapel before. I lead a dull life, so I am always eager for new experiences. Even peculiar ones.'

'We can manage, thank you,' said Bartholomew, grabbing Michael's sleeve and trying to guide him away from her.

But it needed a lot more than a tug to shift a man of Michael's bulk. He resisted, and Bartholomew heard stitches snap open. Humour sparkled briefly in Christiana's eyes, but was quickly masked.

'Actually, we are going to pay our respects to Aylmer,' confessed Michael, freeing his arm and clearly preferring Christiana's company to his grim duties in the chapel. 'I did not want to burden you with information about corpses, but perhaps I was being overly protective. You must forgive me.'

She smiled, and Bartholomew was forced to admit she was lovely, although he felt it a pity that she thought so, too. He glanced at Michael, and was alarmed to note how flushed the monk's face had become – and how it wore an oddly dreamy expression Bartholomew had never seen before.

'I shall forgive you, Brother, although only if you agree to tell me no more fibs. I know exactly what you are doing: Bishop Gynewell has asked you to investigate Aylmer's murder.'

The monk's jaw dropped in astonishment. 'How do you know? Gynewell spoke in confidence.'

'Hamo was listening outside the door. The news is all

113

over the convent now, and it will be all around the city by noon.'

'Damn,' swore Michael. 'I had hoped to carry out my commission discreetly.'

Christiana rested an elegant hand on his arm. 'It may not be a bad thing, because now people will know on whose authority you ask your questions. Of course, it may also serve to make the killer more dangerous. You should take special care, Brother.'

'I am always careful,' replied Michael with an unreadable smile. 'In all I do.'

'And so am I,' she replied, while Bartholomew looked from one to the other with growing unease, sure messages were passing between them that he did not understand. 'I shall say a prayer for you. Perhaps you might care to join me at my devotions? I am usually in the Lady Chapel after vespers – not tonight, because there is a vigil for Little Hugh at the cathedral, but I will be there tomorrow.'

'I am sure we shall find plenty to pray about,' said Michael with one of his courtliest bows.

Bartholomew watched him leer appreciatively as Christiana walked away. 'She is a ward of the King, Brother,' he said uncomfortably. 'And you are a monk. This is not a good idea.'

'Are you warning me against praying?' asked Michael archly. 'In a chapel? Really, Matt!'

'You know perfectly well what I am saying.'

Michael regarded him coolly. 'Your quest to find Matilde has led you to assume that every man is consumed with lust. I assure you that is not the case, especially in those of us who have sworn vows of chastity. If you are worried, come with me tomorrow. You will witness nothing amiss.'

'I shall, then,' said Bartholomew, equally cool. He was not astute when it came to romance – his failure to propose to Matilde before she had given up on him was testament to that – but even he had read something in the exchange between Michael and Christiana, and he disliked being considered a fool by his friend.

Michael was not amused. 'You had better examine this corpse, or it will be a skeleton before you provide me with any answers.'

Bartholomew ran a hand through his hair in exasperation. 'I would like that very much, but your lamp has just run out of oil.'

Brother Michael was not Lady Christiana, and it took him considerably longer to locate fuel for the lantern than it would have done if she had been with him. Eventually, a woman from the kitchens offered to help, filling the device with oil and even carrying it to the mortuary chapel, claiming it had a tendency to spill if not handled with a certain expertise. By the time she and the monk reached the building, Bartholomew was stamping his feet and blowing on his hands in an attempt to keep warm in the bitter wind. Michael turned to her.

'Thank you, madam. My colleague is about to conduct an examination, as you no doubt know, since everyone else seems aware of my business here, and you will not want to be a witness to *that*, I assure you. I have seen him do it a hundred times, yet he still possesses the ability to make me shudder.' He glanced coolly at Bartholomew, to indicate there was a double meaning to his comment.

'I do not mind.' She was a sturdy woman in her late forties, with a lined face and a matronly wimple. 'I doubt he will do anything I have not seen before.'

'He might,' warned Michael. 'He has been to Padua, where they are said to practise a macabre form of scholarship called anatomy.'

'I know nothing of the black arts, but I have seen my share of death. It holds no fears for me.'

Michael regarded her curiously. 'Do you work in the priory hospital, then?'

The woman snorted her disdain. 'You obviously think I am one of the lay-sisters. I am not. My name is Sabina Herl, and I am here because my parish priest gave me a week of labour as penance.'

'Penance for what?' asked Michael, intrigued. 'Do not be afraid to tell me. I am a man of God.'

'Lord, Brother!' muttered Bartholomew. 'What is wrong with you today?'

'It was a man of God who got me in this mess in the first place,' she remarked acidly. 'I was caught kissing him behind the stables, and scouring greasy pans is my punishment.'

'What happened to the man of God?' asked Michael.

Sabina nodded towards the mortuary chapel. 'He is in there, although I do not think our tryst had anything to do with the fact that he was stabbed. Poor Aylmer always was an unlucky fellow.'

'Lord!' gasped Suttone, hurrying up to join them. 'I have just been eating those cakes with Prior Roger. I am not sure he is quite sane.'

'He is probably preoccupied,' said Bartholomew, acutely aware that Sabina was listening. While he was more than happy to move elsewhere for the duration of their stay in Lincoln, he did not want it to be because they had insulted the head Gilbertine.

'No, he is insane,' said Sabina matter-of-factly. 'A good many people *are* in this particular convent, which is why my confessor selected it as the place of penance.'

'Penance for what?' asked Suttone immediately.

'Seducing *your* Vicar Choral,' replied Michael.

Sabina looked the Carmelite up and down. 'So, *you* are

the scholar who offered Aylmer that post. We were all rather surprised, since he has always been something of a rascal.'

'He was a good man,' objected Suttone. 'I have known him since he was a boy.'

She smothered a smile. 'And when did you last see him?'

'I suppose it was on his tenth birthday,' admitted Suttone. 'But he wrote to me often.'

She laughed openly. 'Those letters were for you? He had a good deal of fun with them. He fabricated some outrageous lies, but did not imagine for a moment that anyone would believe him.'

'We must be talking about a different man,' said Suttone stiffly. 'My John Aylmer was short, with red hair and a thin scar on his eyebrow, from where he fell from an apple tree as a lad.'

'There is only one John Aylmer,' she said indulgently. 'People will tell you he was wicked and dissolute, but you should not believe everything you hear. He had his faults, true enough, but who does not? And I do not kiss just anyone behind the stables – not even if a man offers me a penny.'

'How about two?' asked Suttone.

'We should be about our work,' said Bartholomew, not sure whether Suttone was making her an offer or just soliciting information. Suddenly, the body in the chapel seemed like a haven of peace in a stormy sea, because at least he knew what he was doing with corpses.

Sabina turned her attention to Michael. 'And you, Brother? Who is to be your deputy?'

'John Tetford. He comes highly recommended by the Bishop of Ely himself. In fact, de Lisle insisted I hire him; I actually had no choice in the matter.'

Sabina smiled, suggesting she thought Tetford would not be much of an improvement on the man Suttone had picked. 'And now you are going to discover who killed poor Aylmer. Well, it will not be easy.'

'Do you have any ideas?' asked Michael.

She shrugged. 'The killer could be anyone. Aylmer was found dead on his bed in the guest-hall. I expect you noticed the dark patch underneath it. I scrubbed as hard as I could, but the stain proved impossible to remove. Hamo says the blood of a murdered man never comes out easily. It taints wood and stone, just as it does the hands of a killer.'

'I wish that were true,' said Michael wistfully. 'It would make my work so much easier. However, I suspect that particular mark *would* come off, with a little effort on your part.'

She shrugged carelessly. 'Perhaps, but it does no harm to let folk know a man died under unusual circumstances there. Were you aware that he was stabbed in the back with his own knife, Brother?'

Michael narrowed his eyes. 'How do you know that?'

'Because I recognised it. Most priests carry weapons in Lincoln, partly because of this feud that is pulling the city in half, and partly because some of the Vicars Choral do not like each other.'

'Stabbed in the back,' mused Bartholomew. 'That means he was either taken by surprise or he did not think he had anything to fear from his killer. Either way, it does not sound as though there was a struggle, especially if he was left holding this chalice.'

Sabina regarded him appraisingly. 'De Wetherset says you have examined the bodies of murdered men in the past, and that you are good at ascertaining what happened to them – as is clear from the conclusions you have drawn without even looking at Aylmer. Do you hire out your services?'

'Why?' asked Bartholomew suspiciously.

'Because Aylmer's is not the only corpse currently

residing in this mortuary chapel,' she replied unhappily. 'There is another, and I would very much like to know how he died.'

Bartholomew regarded Sabina uneasily, not liking the notion that there had been other suspicious deaths in the place where they were obliged to stay, or that de Wetherset had been telling strangers about his expertise with cadavers. 'Another man has died in this convent?'

'No, he was found in the Braytheford Pool. That is the expanse of water where the River Witham meets the Fossedike,' she added, when the physician looked blank. 'It is not far from here.'

'The Fossedike is Lincoln's route to the sea,' elaborated Suttone, proud of the local knowledge he had gleaned from talking to the Gilbertines. 'But Hamo told me it is silting up. Money has been raised to clear it, but the Guild and the Commonalty cannot agree about how it should be done, so the work is never started.'

Sabina was disgusted. 'And meanwhile, the city grows ever more poor. Have you seen how many weavers cannot find work? We will *all* starve if we have no access to foreign markets.'

'Lincoln is a Staple town,' Suttone went on, boasting now. 'That means imported staple goods – like wool, grain and timber – must come here, so Lincoln can claim certain taxes. However, they cannot come if the canal is blocked, and there is now fierce competition from better-sited ports like Boston.'

'Our mayor, William de Spayne, is a Boston man,' added Sabina, 'which gives that horrible Guild another reason to hate him. They say he is pleased Lincoln is suffering, because it means more wealth for his Boston kin. But we are moving away from the point here. If you inspect the second body in the mortuary chapel, Doctor, and tell me exactly how he died, I will give you a penny.'

'You will have to offer him more than that,' said Suttone disdainfully. 'He has been with the Black Prince in France and was rewarded with some plunder. He returned relatively wealthy, and no longer needs mere pennies.'

'Hamo said you are a University physician, so why were you in France?' asked Sabina. 'Was it anything to do with a lady called Matilde? Hamo told me you were asking after her whereabouts, and she once told me she had French kin. Were you there looking for her?'

'He was not, madam,' said Suttone, startled by the assertion. 'He is a scholar, and such men do not hare off to foreign countries in search of women. He went to learn the art of dissection, because it is forbidden in our own universities.'

'Have you seen Matilde?' asked Bartholomew of Sabina, before Suttone could make him sound any more sinister.

Her expression softened. 'Not in six years. She left after she declined Spayne's offer of marriage, although she was a fool to reject him. He is handsome, rich and will make an excellent husband.'

'He has never wed?' asked Michael.

She shook her head. 'Many ladies have tried to snare him, but he is not interested – Matilde broke his heart for ever. But we were talking about France. Did you know Lady Christiana's husband was killed in France? And that is not the worst of it.'

She pursed her lips, waiting for them to invite her to elaborate. Bartholomew did not, because he felt Michael was already too interested in Christiana de Hauville, while Michael demurred, despite his burning desire to hear what Sabina had to say, because he did not want to give his friend the satisfaction of seeing him ask. Thus there was a long pause, until Suttone, shooting his colleagues a puzzled glance for their lack of curiosity, put the necessary question.

'Her mother – another Lady Christiana – was in almost exactly the same position as she is in now,' said Sabina. '*Her* husband was killed in a fight with Scots, leaving her without protectors. She spent a decade in this very convent before a suitable match was found, although the King's idea of "suitable" was that vile Kelby. Now it seems her daughter is destined to follow the same path.'

'Such is the lot of women who marry soldiers,' said Suttone preachily. 'Personally, I think this war with the French has gone quite far enough, although it is probably treason to say so. I cannot even remember what started it now, or why it has continued for so many years.'

'Neither can most of the men who are fighting,' said Bartholomew, not without bitterness.

'So, you made a fortune with the Black Prince,' said Sabina, eyeing his warm winter cloak and sturdy boots. Her eyes lingered on the hem that was unravelling on his tunic. Fine his clothes might be, but he wore them carelessly, and it was clear they would not remain in pristine condition for long. 'I heard Poitiers was very fierce.'

Bartholomew nodded briefly. He did not want to think about it, knowing that if he did, it would play on his mind for the rest of the day – and worse, long into the night. 'Who is the dead man you want me to inspect?'

She was startled by his abrupt acquiescence. 'You will help me?'

He nodded again, ready to do almost anything to change the subject. 'If you like.'

Sabina and Michael followed him inside the dark chapel, this time with the lamp lighting their way. Suttone started to return to the guest-hall, but saw his path would intercept that of Prior Roger, who waved in the kind of way that suggested he might be invited to take part in the next daily office. Abruptly, the Carmelite scuttled inside the mortuary, preferring the company of the dead to spending more time in the company of a man he considered odd. He found his colleagues at the far end of the building, where there was a makeshift altar. Two bodies lay under clean blankets in front of it.

'That is Aylmer.' Sabina pointed at the one on the left. 'The other is Nicholas.'

'Aylmer first,' said Michael, when the physician started to move towards the other. 'You may decide you have had enough after one, and I need all the help I can get.'

Bartholomew peeled back Aylmer's sheet and began. As he did so, he realised he had not examined a body for signs of suspicious death in eighteen months, although he had seen hundreds of corpses in France. Briefly, he wondered whether he might have forgotten some of the skills he had so painstakingly acquired, but it was not many moments before he found his hands working automatically, repeating what they had done so many times before.

First, he assessed Aylmer from a distance, looking at his clothes, hands and footwear. Aylmer had been a beefy, red-haired man in his late forties, which surprised him – he had supposed Vicars Choral were younger. He was clean-shaven, but there were bristles on his jowls that gave him a disreputable appearance. There was a curious crease in the tip of his nose, essentially dividing it in half, and Bartholomew regarded it thoughtfully, aware of a distant memory stirring. When nothing came to him, he resumed his survey. Aylmer's hands were smooth and soft, suggesting he performed no manual chores, although the additional absence of calluses caused by writing implements made him wonder what the man had done to earn his keep.

'How old are most Vicars Choral?' he asked, while he ran his fingers through Aylmer's hair, assessing the skull for tell-tale dents or bumps.

'It varies,' replied Michael. 'Tetford is twenty-three, which is about average for a secular cathedral like this. Aylmer does seem old to be offered such a post, because the pay tends to be low, and most clerks act as Vicars Choral while they are waiting for something better to come along. However, sometimes nothing ever does, and they are doomed to perpetual poverty.'

'Aylmer was the son of my father's bailiff,' supplied Suttone, trying to be helpful. 'He was a bright lad, and I promised to advance his cause. Unfortunately, I have not been in a position to do much until now. I invited him to study with me a few years back, but he would not hear of it.'

'He was not interested in scholarship,' said Sabina. 'Most men consider it a waste of time, and most women agree. After all, you cannot eat a book, can you?'

'He had trouble with a sheriff a few years back,' Suttone went on, ignoring the slight to his chosen profession. 'He said it was a misunderstanding, and I believe him. I invited him to be my deputy, because he already lived in Lincoln, and I wanted to make good on my promise at last. How did he die, Matthew? I would like to know it was not my patronage that brought it about.'

'Your kindness to an old friend had nothing to do with his demise, Father,' said Sabina, before the physician could answer. 'You can rest easy on that account.'

'You sound very sure,' said Michael, regarding her appraisingly.

'I am sure,' she replied. 'I may not have known him for as long as Master Suttone, but I suspect I knew him rather better. The promotion made him happier than I had ever seen him, and had nothing to do with his death. You can blame the dubious business he embroiled himself in for that.'

'What kind of dubious business?' asked Michael.

She shrugged. 'I dare not say much, but bear in mind that he was a member of the Commonalty and a friend of Adam Miller – and Miller's dealings are not always legal or ethical.' She raised her hand in protest when the monk started to ask something else. 'I am sorry, I can say no more.'

Bartholomew ordered the others away before he removed Aylmer's clothes. It was not right to let Sabina watch what he was doing, and Michael was becoming restless – he did not want the monk's impatience to rush him. He opened Aylmer's mouth and shone the lamp down his throat, then moved the neck to test for signs of strangulation. Then he turned the body over and inspected the wound in its back. Making sure no one was watching, he took a surgical knife and inserted it into the hole, moving it gently to assess the depth to which the killing blow had penetrated. When the blade disappeared to the hilt, he pulled it out in distaste. Whoever had stabbed Aylmer had delivered a powerful stroke.

He was setting all to rights again when he became aware of a blemish on the point of Aylmer's shoulder. He moved the lamp to inspect it more clearly, and saw the kind of mark soldiers sometimes scratched on to themselves with needles and ink. It had clearly been made years ago, and Aylmer's physique had changed, so the original cup had probably been taller and thinner than the squat bowl depicted now. Bartholomew rubbed his chin thoughtfully. A cup – and it was identical to the mark he had seen the day before, when he had loosened Flaxfleete's clothes in a futile attempt to save his life.

*　　*　　*

'Aylmer died of a single wound from a sharp implement,' Bartholomew said, after calling Michael, Suttone and Sabina back. 'The blade was long, so I suspect it was a dagger, rather than something a man might use at the table.'

'His own knife,' said Sabina. 'As I told you.'

Suttone was sceptical. 'He had just been made a Vicar Choral, so why would he carry such a weapon? The Church frowns on priests bearing arms.'

Sabina issued a derisive snort. 'First, Aylmer's association with the Commonalty meant he was not popular with men like Kelby and Flaxfleete, and he would have been a fool not to take steps to protect himself. And secondly, the cathedral can be dangerous. Ask any of its priests.'

'Archdeacon Ravenser was wearing a sword when we met him earlier today,' said Bartholomew to Michael. 'Are you sure you should accept a stall here?'

'No,' said Michael unhappily. 'Lord! This was meant to be a pleasant, relaxing diversion, and it transpires that Lincoln is even more turbulent than Cambridge. And your examination has told me nothing I did not know already, Matt. Is there nothing new?'

Bartholomew shook his head, reluctant to discuss the curious drawing in front of the others. The convent was a hotbed of gossip, and he did not want people to know the cup depicted on Aylmer's shoulder was the same as the one on Flaxfleete's – at least, not until he and Michael had considered the significance themselves.

'Now look at Nicholas,' said Sabina in a low voice. 'If you please.'

Bartholomew removed the blanket, and saw Nicholas had been older than Aylmer by about a decade. He had been well built, with soft white hair and old burns on his hands and arms that suggested he had worked habitually with hot materials. He had been dead longer than

Aylmer, and there were signs of corruption around his mouth.

'Tell me what happened to him, Mistress,' said Bartholomew, while he inspected the man's hands.

'I thought that was what I was paying you to do.'

'I mean tell me about the last time you saw him, or what you know of his final movements.'

'He went out for a drink four nights ago, and he never came home. The next day, he was found floating in the Braytheford Pool. He was my husband, and I would like to know whether he flung himself into the water or whether someone pushed him.'

Bartholomew stopped raking his fingers through the corpse's hair and stepped away. 'Your husband? Then I cannot do this while you are watching.'

She shot him a humourless smile. 'Your sensitivity does you credit, but it is unnecessary. Nicholas and I wedded for convenience, not affection. When my first husband died, I hoped to find love a second time, but I never did. So, when Nicholas suggested an arrangement, I accepted.'

'An arrangement?' echoed Suttone distastefully. 'Marriage is a sacred union blessed by God, not something you organise in the marketplace.'

'Oh, really, Father!' she exclaimed. 'Whoever told you that? Look at poor Lady Christiana, waiting for the King to find her a match she hopes will not be too abhorrent. And she is just one of many.'

'Continue your tale, madam,' said Michael, before Suttone could defend himself. 'You and Nicholas arranged to marry. Why? Were you short of funds?'

'Yes. I was a seamstress to Master Dalderby, but he dismissed me when he found out I had friends in the Commonalty – Dalderby is a member of the Guild, you see. I needed a home, and Nicholas wanted a wife prepared to turn a blind eye to his eccentricities, so a liaison between us was the perfect solution. We enjoyed a comfortable, if separate, existence for years.'

'What kind of eccentricities?' asked Michael.

She grimaced. 'It is not right to speak ill of the dead, especially when they lie in front of us. Suffice to say that if Nicholas had been a better silversmith, and if the cathedral artisans had not contrived to take his best customers, then things might have been different. He was a good man, but the city's dispute turned him resentful and sour. He let it spoil his health.'

'Has the feud damaged other men, too?' asked Michael. 'Or just Nicholas?'

'Oh, it has damaged others all right,' said Sabina. 'Some have died in odd circumstances, some have felt compelled to commit wicked crimes against rivals, some are moved to make false promises to God – offering to be upright souls when it is obvious they will fall at the first hurdle. Like Aylmer.'

'I do not understand,' said Michael. 'Aylmer did what? Died in odd circumstances, committed wicked crimes or made false promises.'

'All three, Brother. I was fond of him – and might have taken him in preference to Nicholas, had he not been in holy orders and loath to break his vows with marriage – but I was not blind to his faults. He engaged in more than his share of dishonest activities, but claimed he had a change of heart in the last month – when he was offered the post of Vicar Choral – and was going to make amends. However, he had said such things before, and we all knew it was only a matter of time before he reneged. He was a weak man, at heart.'

Bartholomew was becoming impatient, eager to be on his way to meet Spayne. 'So, Nicholas was found in this lake,' he said. 'Was he floating in the middle, or washed up on the banks?'

'Floating. He had been drinking in the Swan tavern – not somewhere he should have been.'

'Why not?' asked Suttone.

'Because the Swan tends to be frequented by guildsmen, while the Commonalty favours the Angel. He probably went to torture himself by watching the cathedral silversmiths spend their ill-gotten gains. Perhaps someone took against him being there, and decided he should not do it again.'

'You think he was murdered?' asked Michael uneasily.

She raised her hands, palms upwards. 'I do not know. Kelby, who was also in the Swan that evening, told Bishop Gynewell that Nicholas had been maudlin, and talked about tossing himself in the river. And now the priests will not bury him unless they know for certain that he did not commit suicide. So I asked for a few days' grace to find out, which is why Nicholas is here. I do not want him in unhallowed ground without good reason.'

'What do you *think* happened to him?' asked Michael. 'What are your suspicions?'

She shook her head. 'I do not have any: I just want the truth. Was it suicide, because he was low; murder, because he had annoyed someone while in his cups; or accident, because he had swallowed too much ale and staggered off the path? I just want to do the right thing.'

Bartholomew sent them away again before restarting his examination, which met with relief from Suttone and annoyance from Sabina, who wanted to see how her money was being spent. Michael said nothing, and the physician supposed he intended to use the time to assess what they had learned regarding Aylmer. He watched them step outside, then turned his attention to Nicholas.

It was often difficult to determine a cause of death, but

128

he had discovered that drowned men often foamed at the mouth when he pressed on their chests. He pushed now, and watched bubbles emerge from between bluish lips. Nicholas had certainly drowned, although it was not possible to say whether by design or accident. He pushed again, trying to detect the scent of ale. It was not there, but something else was: a pungent, fishy smell. With a start, he suddenly remembered something that had been said at Kelby's celebration, by the priest John Suttone. John had mentioned how he had detected a rank odour on the body of a man who had died in the Braytheford Pool – a man called Nicholas Herl. Simon had mentioned the death of a man called Herl, too, saying he had expected it to shift the balance of power between Guild and Commonalty, and result in bloodshed.

Bartholomew removed the corpse's clothes, noting an unnatural swelling of the feet and a hint of rot – Nicholas had endured a severe bout of Holy Fire, and its symptoms were still evident. The condition was a painful one, so it was small wonder the man had been morose and unhappy. As he was replacing the garments a few moments later, Bartholomew spotted a scar on the point of the shoulder. It was not like the drawings on Flaxfleete and Aylmer, although it was in the same place. He bent to inspect it more closely.

'I doubt his arm will tell you anything useful, Doctor.' Sabina's voice was so close behind him that he jumped in alarm and almost dropped the lamp.

'I am sorry, Matt,' said Michael. Suttone was with him. 'I told her to stay outside, but she wants to make sure she is getting her money's worth. She slipped past me when Hamo distracted us with some Lombard slices.'

'What made this mark?' asked Bartholomew, pointing at it.

129

She frowned. 'I have never noticed it before, but then we never saw each other naked. It is recent, though, because it is still raw. However, during the last month, Nicholas was busier than he had been over the past five years combined, labouring in his workshop all hours of the day and night. It will be a burn, caused by spitting metal, like the ones on his hands. So? How did he die?'

'He drowned,' said Bartholomew, handing Michael the lamp and straightening Nicholas's limbs.

'I know,' said Sabina. 'What I need *you* to tell me is whether it was accident, murder or suicide.'

'I have some questions first. Did he suffer from Summer Madness?'

She regarded him in surprise. 'How did you know that?'

'How badly?'

'He needed to be tied up, to stop him from biting himself, and the only place he became calm was the church. We prayed to St Anthony and he recovered, although he was never fully well after. Why?'

'Did he have trouble breathing? Dizzy spells? Pains in his chest and arms?'

'All those.' She gazed at him. 'But how do *you* know? He never told anyone but me and his friend Will Langar. And what does it have to do with his death, anyway? The Madness was months ago.'

'There is a theory that Holy Fire – Summer Madness – is caused by a toxin, which accumulates in the body and eventually causes a fatal imbalance of the humours. I suspect your husband ingested a large quantity of this substance in August, and it has remained inside him – his swollen feet tell us he was still suffering from its effects. When he swallowed more of the poison, it killed him.'

'Summer Madness is caused by poison?' she said doubtfully. 'How can that be true, when we all know the Devil

130

is responsible? And even if you are right, how could more of this poison have got inside him? No one else has suffered from the Madness for months now.'

Bartholomew shrugged, not looking at Michael, who was drawing his own conclusions about the substance that had now killed two men. 'I have no idea. However, Nicholas's initial dose seems to have been a large one – as evidenced by your description of his illness, the swelling still remaining in his feet, and his continued dizziness. In addition, I suspect he had a natural weakness in his blood that would have made him especially susceptible to the ravages of Holy Fire.'

She was confused. 'I do not understand what you are saying. He drowned *and* he was poisoned?'

Bartholomew nodded. 'The substance was strong on his breath, so he swallowed it shortly before he died. Then, faint and weak, he probably toppled into the water and drowned.'

'But this does not help,' she objected. 'We still do not know where I can bury him.'

'Then think about Nicholas himself,' suggested Bartholomew. 'If he *had* wanted to commit suicide, would he have known where to obtain this poison? And would he have been aware what its effects might be on a body already weakened by its last encounter with Holy Fire?'

Slowly, her face broke into a smile. 'No. He was a simple man, sometimes stupid, and would never have invented such a complex way of doing away with himself.'

'Then you are left with accident or murder, but he can go into hallowed ground, regardless.'

She seemed relieved. 'I shall go to my priest this morning, and order him to bury Nicholas in the church-yard. I think he only made a fuss in the first place because I refuse to lie with him.'

'I hope this is not the same vicar who ordered you to

work here, as penance for kissing Aylmer,' said Michael. 'That would make him a hypocrite.'

She grimaced. 'He has never bothered to hide his failings. But I should not be telling you this, Brother, because he is John Tetford. Your Vicar Choral.'

'Lord!' muttered Michael, as she flounced from the chapel and Suttone regarded him rather smugly. 'Just when I think matters cannot slide any further into the mire, I learn unpleasant details about *my* deputy. It seems we both made poor choices, Suttone.'

'Indeed we did,' said Suttone. 'However, there is something about Sabina Herl that makes me feel she is not telling you the whole truth about her husband's death. It would not surprise me to learn that *she* slipped him poison, then was sorry when she learned he was to be buried in unhallowed ground.'

'What shall we do, Brother?' asked Bartholomew, once Suttone had gone. 'Tell the sheriff that Nicholas and Flaxfleete both died from ingesting the same substance? Flaxfleete's wine came from the Swan tavern, and that was where Nicholas went drinking on the night of his death.'

Michael shook his head. 'From what we have been told of Sheriff Lungspee, it is better to keep out of his way. He is corrupt and everyone knows it. Folk even admire him for taking bribes with commendable even-handedness. Lord, Matt! What a place!'

'Poison is not the only association between Nicholas and Flaxfleete – and Aylmer, too. There is a drawing of a cup on Aylmer's shoulder, which is identical to the one I saw on Flaxfleete.'

'A cup?'

Bartholomew nodded. 'And there is a scar in exactly the same place on Nicholas. The wound was made recently, but dark lines are still visible underneath it. You can see for yourself. It looks as though there *was* a mark, but someone – presumably Nicholas himself – attempted to scratch it off.'

Michael leaned down to inspect it. 'It might be a chalice.'

'When I tried to loosen Flaxfleete's clothes to help him breathe, he asked me not to. I am under the impression that he wanted his mark to stay hidden – that keeping it concealed was important to him.'

Michael straightened slowly. 'And you say his drawing and Aylmer's are identical?'

'More or less. I have seen soldiers disfigure themselves with signs like these, as a declaration of fraternity. But Aylmer and Nicholas were members of the Commonalty, and Flaxfleete was a member of the Guild, which means they were rivals, not friends. It makes no sense.'

'And it is odd that three men with a cup on their arms should die in mysterious circumstances just when the Hugh Chalice miraculously reappears after two decades, too.' Michael rubbed his chin, fingers rasping on the bristles. 'Did you believe Sabina when she said she could not recall how Nicholas came by his injury? They were husband and wife.'

'She also said theirs was an odd marriage, with no affection. Perhaps she was telling the truth, and they never enjoyed each other's body.'

Michael shook his head. 'There is a lot we are not being told here. And I do not like it.'

CHAPTER 4

Daylight did not last long in December, and Bartholomew felt time was slipping away far too fast that morning. The bells were already chiming for the next office, and the Gilbertines were preparing themselves by humming and clearing their throats. He begged hot water from one of the cooks, and washed his hands, trying to rinse away the odour of death that clung to them. He did not want to visit Mayor Spayne smelling like a cadaver.

'There is Father Simon,' said Michael, pointing to where the arrogant priest was hurrying towards St Katherine's Chapel. 'I shall have a few words with him while you change.'

'Why?' asked Bartholomew.

Michael indicated a stain that had not been on Bartholomew's tunic before he had examined the two bodies. 'When you resume your duties as Corpse Examiner in Cambridge, we shall have to invest in some kind of apron. Now you own decent clothes, you need to take better care of them.'

'I meant why do you want to speak to Simon?'

'Because he was the one who found Aylmer's body, and we know from experience that those who discover a corpse sometimes have additional information to impart.'

Cynric had anticipated his master's need to exchange a soiled tunic for a clean one, and was waiting with a spare. Bartholomew removed the dirty garment and donned the replacement as he walked with Michael to intercept

Simon. The priest was not pleased to be waylaid in the yard, claiming he had been warming up his voice in the refectory, and that standing in the cold might reduce its effectiveness.

'A cup of claret usually works for me,' said Michael, who was also proud of his musical talents. 'It combats chilly weather very nicely. But tell me what happened when you found Aylmer.'

'Now?' Simon's eyes strayed towards the chapel. 'I might be late.'

'It will not take long, and I am sure you are eager to co-operate with the bishop's investigation.'

Simon sighed. 'Very well, if you put it like that. It happened yesterday morning, as you know. We were quartered in the guest-hall's main chamber – Aylmer, de Wetherset, I and a dozen others. The bells rang for prime, and we either went to the chapel or left the convent for business in the city. Aylmer walked with me to the chapel. When the service was over, everyone else went straight to the refectory for breakfast, but I was cold and wanted a thicker shift. When I arrived, there was Aylmer, slumped across his bed with a knife in his back. There was blood . . . '

'You did not see him leave the chapel before you?'

'I was praying, Brother. I did not notice anything at all, except Whatton singing flat all through the *Magnificat*. When I saw Aylmer's body, I observed two things: he had died counting the gold that was in his purse, and he was holding *my* chalice – the one I intend to donate to the cathedral.'

'His gold and your chalice were on the bed with his corpse?' asked Michael. Simon nodded. 'Then robbery is unlikely to have been the motive: the thief would not have left such riches behind. What do you think Aylmer was doing with your goblet?'

'Admiring it,' replied Simon. '*Possibly* as a prelude to stealing it. Anyone in Lincoln will tell you he had sticky fingers, and it would not be the first time he made off with another man's property. But we cannot ask him now he is dead, and I dislike maligning a man who cannot defend himself. I refuse to condemn him out of hand.'

'Where is it now?' asked Michael.

'I put it on St Katherine's altar for safekeeping. Even the most hardened of thieves will think twice about taking it now – it would earn him eternal damnation. You probably noticed it when you were in the chapel. It does not look like much, and is showing its age, but holiness still shines through it.'

'How did you come by it?' asked Bartholomew, straightening his clean tunic.

'I bought it from a relic-seller. Do you know its history? How it was in St Hugh's hand when he died in London? Many years later, it was decided that it should be at his shrine in Lincoln, and two friars were given the task of carrying it north. But it was stolen from them in a wicked act of theft.'

'Was it stolen before they left London?' asked Michael. 'Or when they arrived in Lincoln?'

'Neither. It went missing on the journey *between* the two places. In fact, the crime took place near Cambridge, a town they were obliged to pass *en route*. I cannot remember the exact details – this happened twenty years ago, so my memory is excusably hazy – but I recall hearing that these two hapless priests fell asleep under a tree, wearied from the distance they had walked that day, when the chalice was removed from their possession.'

'They travelled on foot?' asked Bartholomew incredulously. 'Carrying a sacred relic?'

'I imagine they did not want to draw attention to themselves with a cavalcade. Anyway, the chalice was stolen, and the thief sold it to a priest in the village of Geddynge – a place that is just a few miles from Cambridge. But Geddynge did not keep it long, because it was stolen again within a few days.'

'By the same thief?' asked Michael dubiously.

'Very possibly. If he knew he could get twenty shillings for it once, then why not retrieve it and sell it for twenty shillings a second time? And a third and a fourth? But no one knows for certain what happened. Eventually, it appeared in the hands of a relic-seller, here in Lincoln.'

'That was very convenient.' Bartholomew tried not to sound sceptical of its timely arrival, just when Simon was about to accept a prebendal stall in the cathedral and was of a mind to make a suitable donation. He did not succeed, and the priest regarded him coldly.

'It *is* the same chalice. I have never been more certain of anything in my life. And if you do not believe me, then ask Bishop Gynewell. He also senses its sanctity.'

'He did say he believed it to be genuine,' acknowledged Michael.

'Of course he did, because it is true. But if you need more proof, then inspect its markings. As even *you* will know, there are two icons associated with St Hugh: a pet swan and a chalice engraved with an image of the Baby Jesus. If you look on my chalice, you will see the carving quite clearly.'

'And you bought it from a relic-seller,' said Michael. 'Had you met this man before?'

'No, he hails from Rome. But I recognised the Hugh Chalice at once, and I am delighted to play a role in putting it where it belongs. The translation will be made on St Thomas's Day, where the cup will take pride of place in *my* installation ceremony, in front of a thousand grateful pilgrims.'

Bartholomew remained unconvinced. 'But it *is* odd that it should appear now, Father, just when you happen to be in a position to make this spectacular benefaction.'

'It is not odd – it is a miracle,' declared Simon, glaring at him. 'And you can think what you like, but as far as I am concerned the only thing that matters is that this holy thing will soon be in the cathedral, where it belongs.'

'You do not have a mark on your shoulder, do you?' asked Bartholomew incautiously. 'Of a cup.'

Simon regarded him with narrowed eyes. 'A mark? What are you talking about?'

'A self-inflicted sign. A scar picked out with ink. One that depicts a chalice.'

Simon regarded him with distaste. 'I know the sort of self-mutilations to which you refer, and they are favoured by men of lesser intelligence. I am offended that you should ask me such a question, but I am also curious. Why do you think *I* should let myself be so scarred?'

Bartholomew shrugged. It had been a stupid thing to ask. Simon was a priest, and had no reason to associate himself with Aylmer, Nicholas Herl or Flaxfleete. 'I have seen others adorned with chalices recently, and your obvious devotion to—'

Simon smiled unexpectedly. 'You are right about my dedication to St Hugh, but any marks I bear are on my soul, not my skin. Do you want to inspect me?'

'No, thank you,' said Michael hastily, when the priest's robe started to come up, revealing a pair of scaly legs. 'Your word is good enough for me, and we do not want you to take a chill when you are about to entertain the Gilbertines with your fine voice. Is this relic-seller still in Lincoln?'

'No,' replied Simon, adjusting his habit. 'He left the city as soon as he sold me the chalice.'

138

'Why did he approach you to make his sale?' asked Bartholomew. 'Why not the cathedral, which might have given him more money?'

'The cathedral has no spare funds, and everyone knows it,' said Simon scornfully. 'Do you have any idea how much it costs to maintain a building like that? The relic-seller knew he would get a better price from an individual. He chose me because I have always made my veneration of the saint public, and because it is common knowledge that I am wealthier than most parish priests.'

'Brother Michael!' called a cheerful voice behind them. It was Hamo, licking his moist lips. 'You must attend nones with me, and afterwards, you shall have more Lombard slices. I said we would look after you, and we mean to do it well. You *will* enjoy your sojourn at our priory, I promise you.'

'I am sure of it,' said Michael politely. 'But I am a man of modest appetite, and I have already eaten seven cakes this morning. That is perfectly sufficient for now. But we were talking about Aylmer's murder. The bishop asked me to investigate, although you already know this, of course.'

Hamo had the grace to blush. 'I did hear Gynewell murmur something when I was polishing the door to Prior Roger's solar.'

Bartholomew was thinking about what Simon – and Sabina – had said about Aylmer's character. He turned to the priest. 'Aylmer was a known thief, yet the cathedral said nothing when Suttone made him his Vicar Choral. Why were there no objections?'

'The appointment of deputies is left to the individual canon,' explained Simon. 'Brother Michael will tell you that. The cathedral has no say in the matter.'

'That is true,' said Michael, 'although someone could have mentioned to Suttone that he had appointed a felon, nonetheless. It would have been polite.'

It was Hamo who answered. 'No one said anything because folk are loath to offend a Suttone by telling him he has made a bad decision. Complaints were certainly aired in Chapter meetings, though, especially by Dean Bresley. Aylmer was disliked, not just because he was a thief, but because he was a member of the Commonalty. That rabble think they can win the town's heart with their Miller's Market, but it will take more than free cakes to alleviate the wrongs *they* have perpetrated.'

'What wrongs?' asked Michael.

'Think carefully before you cast aspersions, Hamo,' said Simon sharply. 'It is because of spiteful chatter that this feud has escalated. Remember how God struck down your predecessor, Fat William, for his venal sins? Well, gossip is just as great a transgression. Watch your tongue.'

Michael sighed. 'I applaud your lofty principles, Father Simon, but if either of you know anything that may help me locate Aylmer's killer, then you must tell me.'

Simon rolled his eyes; he thought Michael was putting too much store in idle talk. 'There are *rumours* that Miller's import–export business is helping to undermine the local cloth trade, but I do not believe them. These are lies invented by the Guild, because *they* want to set the weavers against the Commonalty.'

'That is one interpretation,' said Hamo. 'But even you cannot deny that Miller associates with some particularly nasty people – Thoresby, Nicholas Herl, Langar, Chapman, to name but a few.'

Simon's expression was icy. 'Those are no nastier than Kelby and Dalderby of the Guild.'

'I do not care whether Miller and his friends are servants of Satan,' said Michael, exasperated. 'I just want to know what is *said* about them.'

Hamo answered, his expression gleefully spiteful. 'Miller

and several cronies arrived in Lincoln twenty years ago and, almost immediately, there was an increase in crime – a *lot* of property went missing over the next few months and they became ever more rich. At the same time, they started to infiltrate the Commonalty, and now they run it to suit themselves. Personally, I think they *still* deal on the wrong side of the law.'

'And Aylmer?' asked Michael, ignoring the way Simon shook his head in a way that suggested he thought there was no truth to the accusations. 'Was he one of the men who arrived with Miller?'

'No, he came a few weeks later,' replied Hamo, also ignoring Simon. 'But he lost no time in having himself elected to the Commonalty. Miller was fond of him, and I imagine the killer will be quaking in his boots as we speak. He will be terrified his identity will be exposed, and Miller will come after *him*. He will not appreciate you asking questions that might reveal him, Brother, so you should be careful.'

Bartholomew regarded him in alarm, although Michael remained unmoved. 'If what you say is true, then I shall have Miller on my side.'

'Not necessarily,' said Hamo. 'He will be keen to subject the killer to his own brand of justice, and will try to prevent you from getting to him first. I do not envy you your task.'

It was after noon by the time Bartholomew managed to escape from Michael and climb the hill to see Spayne. He walked briskly, Cynric trotting at his side, and his stomach churned when he considered how important the meeting might be to his personal happiness, despite Michael's cautionary warnings. But his nervous anticipation was all for nothing, because when he arrived, he was informed by a maid that both Spayne and his sister were out.

'Where?' asked Bartholomew, thinking he would collect his horse and ride to meet them.

The maid shook her head. 'I do not know, sir. I can only tell you that Mistress Ursula said not to expect them back until after nightfall tomorrow, and to lock up the house early.'

'You have some very large fires going, lass,' observed Cynric, peering past her into the hall. 'Why would you make such a blaze, if no one is at home?'

'Mistress Ursula ordered them for the snow on the roof,' explained the maid. She led them away from the door and into the middle of the street, where she pointed upwards. 'It fell very thickly a few nights ago, and the weight has made the roof sag. Can you see it? Mistress Ursula said we need to keep fires burning all the time, so the heat will melt it away.'

'It might slough off and land on someone,' said Bartholomew uneasily. 'In Cambridge, we once had a man die when a great mass of ice fell from a roof. We did not find his body for months.'

She crossed herself. 'I will warn Mayor Spayne. Perhaps he can build barriers, to stop folk coming too close. Of course, then the guildsmen will say he is claiming part of a common highway for himself. They will moan if he tries to protect people, and they will moan if someone is hurt. Vile men! Tell me, did you really travel here with a member of the Suttone clan?'

Bartholomew nodded. 'Why?'

Her eyes gleamed. 'It is a great honour – they are so well thought of in these parts. Bishop Gynewell was delighted when he heard one was in holy orders and might be persuaded to take a prebendal stall. *Everyone* likes the Suttone family.'

Bartholomew was amused. 'We had no idea we were in

such exalted company. Have the Suttones taken a side in the city's feud?'

She shook her head. 'They do not come to town very often – perhaps because when they do, the Guild and the Commonalty try to recruit them.' She gave him a shy smile. 'Mayor Spayne had business with Sheriff Lungspee this morning, sir. I doubt he is still there, but one of the soldiers might know his plans for later. You will find the castle on top of the hill.'

Lincoln's main street was so spacious in places that it was able to accommodate a whole string of markets. First, there was an area where corn was traded, which had pigeons picking at the filthy ground and sturdy scales ready for weighing sacks of grain. Then there was the *Pultria*, or Poultry, which was fringed with tightly packed houses and churches. The air was full of clucks, hisses, coos and quacks, and underfoot, feathers, eggshells and bird droppings had been trodden into the mud to form a thick mat. The fish market was next, but the silting of the Fossedike meant it took too long to bring the catch from the sea, and the specimens on display were dull-eyed and smelly. Gulls soared overhead, diving occasionally to snatch a morsel from under the feet of the haggling fishmongers, and cats stalked and crouched in the shadows. Then came the High Market, with ramshackle stalls that sold everything from ribbons to rabbits. It reeked of old urine and decaying meat.

The houses on the high street were mostly handsome, but when Bartholomew glanced along some of the alleys that radiated off it, he saw Lincoln's grandeur was superficial. Groups of men slouched aimlessly against cracked, crumbling walls, and their eyes were dull and flat, as though they were resigned to the hopelessness of their situation. He assumed most were weavers, whose forebears had

143

flocked to Lincoln half a century earlier, when there were fortunes to be made in the wool trade.

'I do not understand,' said Cynric, regarding them with pity. 'This is a rich city, with its great minster and fine Norman houses. So why are its people poor?'

'Apparently, it is because the Fossedike is clogged,' explained Bartholomew. 'It means the weavers cannot send their finished cloth for export, and they are losing out to those who live in more easily accessible ports. I read that royal parliaments were once held in Lincoln, but I do not think His Majesty would be very impressed by what is here now. I have never seen streets more choked with filth, not even in Cambridge.'

'Not even in France,' agreed Cynric. 'And that is a terrible place.'

They passed through the gate that divided the lower part of the town from the plateau known as the Bail. Then they turned left, towards a fortress that transpired to be as dilapidated as the rest of the city. Unimpressed, Cynric announced that to storm it would take no more than a good, hard shove at one of its teetering walls.

'Oh, no!' he breathed suddenly, gripping Bartholomew's wrist in a pinch that hurt. Before the physician could look around, he found himself hauled backwards and pressed into a doorway. 'It is Bishop Gynewell! We do not want *him* to see us.'

'Why not?' asked Bartholomew, rubbing his arm. 'He seems a pleasant man.'

Cynric regarded him in disbelief. 'He is a demon, boy! You only have to look at him to see he is one of Satan's imps – he makes no effort to disguise his horns. And if that is not obvious enough for you, then bear in mind that he likes roaring fires and food made with powerful spices. Ask anyone.'

144

Bartholomew studied him warily, wondering if it was a jest to take his mind off Matilde, but could tell by the earnest expression that his book-bearer was perfectly serious. 'Gynewell is not a demon.'

Cynric's amazement intensified. 'But he *is*! And you should remember it when you visit him – it might save your life. Or better yet, do not enter his domain at all. He might spear you with his pitchfork or rip you to pieces with his claws.'

Bartholomew was about to argue further when Gynewell started to walk in their direction. With a grim face, Cynric gripped Bartholomew's sleeve in one hand, his sword in the other and shot through the door to someone's house. He slammed it behind him and made for the back entrance, ignoring the astonished gaze of the family that was sitting around their kitchen table. Bartholomew grinned sheepishly as he was hauled past them, unable to break free of Cynric's iron grip.

'Hello,' he said, feeling he should make some effort at conversation. 'It is cold today.'

'It is indeed,' stammered the man at the head of the table, while his wife and children sat with mouths agape. 'We shall have more snow soon.'

And then Bartholomew was in their private garden, where Cynric marched down a path and ushered him through the rear gate and into a lane.

'There,' said the book-bearer, closing it firmly. 'We have escaped. The castle is up here, I believe.'

Leaving Bartholomew at a loss for words, Cynric strode towards the barbican's ancient metal-studded door. When he knocked, Bartholomew noticed the wood was so rotten that his fist left indentations. On closer inspection, he saw he could probably hack his way inside with one of his little surgical knives, and knew its neglected defences would present no obstacle at all to a serious invader.

'Mayor Spayne,' repeated the guard who came to ask what they wanted. 'Let me see my list.'

He was a slovenly fellow, with bad teeth and a festering boil on his neck that he kept rubbing with grime-coated fingers. He made a great show of consulting a piece of parchment, which Bartholomew saw was a well-thumbed gaol-delivery record. He was puzzled, wondering why Spayne should be on a register of felons, but then saw the document was held upside down, and realised the 'list' was the guard's way of impressing illiterate visitors with a show of administration.

'I am sorry,' he said eventually, rolling up the warrant in a businesslike manner. 'He left several hours ago.'

'Do you know where he went?' asked Bartholomew, disappointed.

The guard shook his head. 'But Sheriff Lungspee might. Sheriff! Sir! Over here!'

Before Bartholomew could demur, a man with long greasy hair and a shabby leather jerkin started to walk towards them. The physician swore under his breath, knowing it was unwise to draw the attention of city officials after what had transpired at Kelby's house the night before. He started to back away, hoping to avoid the encounter, but Lungspee was too close, and it would have looked suspicious to make a dash for it.

'Look at this,' said the sheriff, proffering a hand adorned with a large emerald ring. 'Have you ever seen a more magnificent object?'

'No, sir,' said Bartholomew, thinking it rather gaudy. He could not imagine wearing such a thing himself. It would be in the way when he examined his patients and he would almost certainly lose it. However, many of his medical colleagues believed that emeralds controlled unruly passions, and he wondered whether he should invest in one for Michael. 'Can I buy one like it in Lincoln?'

'Not these days, unfortunately,' replied Lungspee sadly. 'Flaxfleete gave it to me, although it had nothing to do with his acquittal, you understand. It is even better than the three white pearls I had from Miller, around the time I released Thoresby following the Dalderby affair. What do you think?' He hauled a purse from under his jerkin and showed off a trio of milky gems.

'Very nice. What Dalderby affair?'

Lungspee pursed his lips as he put the jewels away. 'You must be a stranger, or you would know about our town and its troubles. Thoresby threatened to chop off Dalderby's head – he would have done it, too, if I had not stopped him. Then Miller gave me these pearls, and I decided Thoresby had learned his lesson, so I let him out of prison. Dalderby was not very pleased, but I made up for it by looking kindly on his friend Flaxfleete yesterday. It is a delicate business, being sheriff.'

'Yes,' said Bartholomew weakly. 'I imagine it is.'

Lungspee looked him up and down. 'Do you have any items of value you would like to share with me? Your clothes are of decent quality, and a man of good standing always has a few baubles to pass to the sheriffs he meets, especially if he wants a favourable verdict at some point in the future.'

Bartholomew was acutely uncomfortable. Should he oblige, lest he and Michael were accused of foul play over the business with Flaxfleete, or would the fact that they were innocent be enough to see any spiteful accusations dismissed? He glanced at Cynric, who winked and nodded, indicating he thought coins *should* change hands. But Bartholomew had never bribed an official in the past, and was loath to start now.

'Actually, I am looking for Mayor Spayne,' he said, aware of Cynric rolling his eyes in disgust at the lost opportunity. 'Do you know where I might find him?'

'No, I am sorry,' said Lungspee. 'Pleasant man, Spayne. There is only one flaw in his character: his failure to impress his local sheriff with small gifts that demonstrate his affection. Is that all you wanted? You did not come here to tell me your side in a legal matter?'

'No!' said Bartholomew, trying not to sound shocked. He did not think he had ever encountered such brazen corruption. 'I just wanted to speak to Spayne.'

'He left hours ago, and might be anywhere by now. He often journeys to distant villages on business, but since the Guild would dearly love to place an arrow in his back, he seldom confides his travel plans. All I know is that he told me he intends to sleep elsewhere tonight, but that he hopes to be back in Lincoln by tomorrow evening. Of course, if he *were* to die in mysterious circumstances, then a guildsman would not be long in following him to his grave. That is the way of this city, and has been ever since Canon Hodelston died during the plague. That was what started it all.'

'Someone mentioned Hodelston to us before,' said Bartholomew, trying to recall why.

'He was a dreadful fellow, even after he became a priest,' explained Lungspee obligingly. 'Charges of theft, rape and even murder followed him around like flies, and his minster friends were hard-pressed to find something nice to say about him at his funeral.'

'And him a canon, too,' muttered Cynric, shaking his head censoriously.

'Well, someone has to be. But he did do one good thing: he founded the Tavern in the Close. And *that* place is a boon to us all, because it keeps the clerics inside the cathedral precincts at night, and stops them from rampaging through the city.'

'We were told Canon Hodelston was poisoned,' said Cynric, rather salaciously.

'That was the rumour,' acknowledged Lungspee. 'I thought we were better off without him, but his fellow canons took umbrage at his murder and made a terrible fuss. Personally, I think we should all concentrate on more important issues, like draining the Fossedike.'

'Lincoln's link to the sea,' said Bartholomew.

Lungspee nodded. 'Funds were raised for its repair, but they were divided between the Guild and the Commonalty for "safekeeping" and they seem to have disappeared. I would pay for the work myself, but I am struggling to keep this castle in one piece. The King might visit one day, and I should like to show him at least one wall that is not in imminent danger of collapse.'

Bartholomew surveyed his domain critically, trying to pinpoint some part of it that might be sound. 'That round tower looks all right.'

'Dry rot,' confided Lungspee. 'I wrote to the King thirty years ago, telling him we were in a bit of a state, but he did not reply.'

Bartholomew raised his eyebrows. 'Then perhaps you should try again. He may not be pleased if he decides to avail himself of your hospitality, and the roof caves in on him while he is asleep.'

'That would not create a good impression,' acknowledged Lungspee, glancing around dolefully. 'So, if he comes, we shall have to allocate him an upstairs room. From personal experience, I can tell you that it is better to drop through a floor than to have a ceiling drop on you.'

*　　*　　*

149

The following day was cloudy, and it was still dark when Bartholomew was shocked from sleep by the harsh jangle of the Gilbertines' bells. He leapt from his bed, but managed to stop himself from snatching up his sword when he realised it was a call to prayer, not a call to arms. Michael watched, then turned back to his psalter without comment, although his silence said more about his disapproval than any words could have done. They attended the beginning of another deafening prime, but the monk strode out in disgust when some of the Gilbertines started to clap in time to the music. Bartholomew followed him, relieved to be away from the racket.

'It is too much,' complained the monk petulantly. 'It is a chapel, not a tavern. We should sing prime at the cathedral tomorrow, because I do not think I can stand much more of this . . . ' He waved his hand, not sure how to describe it.

After breakfast, he and Bartholomew sat on a low wall near the refectory while he reviewed what he knew about Aylmer. He had not been pontificating for long when Hamo bustled towards them.

'Is anything amiss?' the newly created Brother Hospitaller asked, licking his moist, pink lips anxiously. 'Neither of you ate much, and we would be horrified to think you were dissatisfied with our humble fare. Prior Roger was saying only last night how good it is to have a Suttone under our roof, and he has written to the family, to let them know you have elected to stay with us. They have promised to remember us in their wills, you see, and some have plans to be buried in our chapel. It would be terrible if you were to go elsewhere. And if you did, Prior Roger might demote me.'

'We shall stay,' said Michael, although not very graciously. 'You were right when you said everywhere else is full. Of course, Bishop Gynewell offered us a bed in his fine house, but Matt's book-bearer has encouraged us to decline the invitation.'

This was an understatement. In a startling display of mutiny, Cynric had virtually ordered the scholars to keep their distance from the Bishop's Palace, even threatening to resign if they did not accede to his 'request'. Michael had been inclined to ignore him, but Cynric had been with Bartholomew for many years, and the physician was loath to upset a man who was more friend than servant. Thus Michael had been obliged to do as the Welshman demanded, although he was far from happy about it. Suttone, however, was livid at the loss of a luxurious sojourn, and declared that the book-bearer's new-found confidence after his travels had rendered him impudent and rebellious. It was not really true: Cynric had always had strong feelings on matters of religion, and it was not the first time Bartholomew had been obliged to pander to his superstitions.

'I shall have to give the man a jug of our best ale,' murmured Hamo, pleased.

'When I was inspecting Aylmer's corpse, I noticed a drawing on his shoulder,' said Bartholomew, deciding to see what he could learn for Michael. 'Is that a common habit in Lincoln?'

'I have seen some men mark themselves so,' said Hamo, determined to be amenable, no matter how odd the topic of conversation chosen by his guests. 'There was a sect that scratched crosses all over themselves during the Death, to prevent them from becoming infected. It made no difference, though: they were taken regardless.'

'It is the marks on their souls that count,' said Michael. He clasped his hands in front of him, and gazed skywards in a gesture of monastic piety that was wholly out of character.

Bartholomew was puzzled until Christiana and Dame Eleanor passed by, on their way to the chapel.

'Amen,' said Hamo, adopting a similar pose, but with considerably more sincerity. 'Alleluia!'

'Alleluia!' chorused three Gilbertines who happened to be within hearing distance.

'Aylmer's mark looked like a cup,' said Bartholomew quickly, before the brethren could revisit one of their fervent rites in the yard and expect him to join in. 'Perhaps a chalice.'

Hamo frowned as he lowered his hands to his sides. 'Really? How odd. I never noticed it, but then I never saw him without clothes. Perhaps you should ask Simon. He is considered an expert on sacred vessels, because he is going to donate the Hugh Chalice to the cathedral. It is a pity, because it looks nice on St Katherine's altar, and we shall be sorry to see it go.'

'We have already spoken to Simon, and he was not very helpful,' said Michael, dropping his prayerful posture the moment the ladies were out of sight. 'He told us about the Hugh Chalice's curious travels, but revealed nothing about the man who sold it to him.'

Hamo rubbed his chin thoughtfully. 'Prior Roger might be able to help. He and Simon discussed the Hugh Chalice at length yesterday. You see, Simon *had* kept it in a box under his bed in the guest-hall, but after what happened to Aylmer, it was decided the chapel would be safer. You are honoured guests, so he will be pleased to oblige you with anything Simon may have neglected to mention.'

He began to lead the way to the Prior's House, but Bartholomew glanced at the sky to judge the time. 'I wonder if Spayne will be home yet.'

'His maidservant *and* Sheriff Lungspee told you he plans to be away until this evening at the earliest,' said Michael impatiently. 'And even if he did return sooner than expected, you cannot leave me to investigate alone. If Cynric is to be believed, I have been given a commission by the Devil – and you will not want me on the wrong side of Satan for failing to provide answers.'

'Take no notice of Cynric. He has been listening to too many soldiers around too many campfires. He has always been superstitious, but his reaction to Gynewell is excessive, even for him. We—'

He stopped abruptly when they neared the Prior's House and someone wearing crimson hose scurried past. His head was down and his hood pulled over his face, but the distinctive leg-wear made Bartholomew sure it was the same man he had seen with Simon the previous day. He watched him go, wondering why the fellow should be skulking in so furtive a manner.

'I am about to say a mass for one of our benefactors,' said the prior, when the visitors were shown into his solar. 'A few *kyries* with the organ should rattle his soul free from Purgatory.'

'Did you know Aylmer had carved a chalice into his arm?' asked Michael, declining to comment on the Gilbertines' rumbustious approach to prayers for the dead. 'Matt detected—'

'No, I never saw him naked,' said Roger. 'But I have seen others with marks that sound similar.'

'Where?' demanded Michael eagerly. 'And on whom?'

'On a member of the Commonalty named Thoresby. You may have heard of him – he was recently acquitted of threatening to behead a rival merchant. I saw a cup carved into *his* shoulder when he came to our hospital suffering from Summer Madness. Then there was Fat William, Hamo's predecessor. He had one, and so do a number of canons.' He listed several names that were unfamiliar.

'Does Father Simon have a—'

Roger raised his hands. 'I have no idea.'

'He says not,' said Bartholomew, recalling how the priest had come close to showing them before Michael had become squeamish and stopped him.

'I have never known him lie,' said Roger, 'so there is no reason to disbelieve him. Last summer, when we swam in the river together, I asked Canon Stretle what the carving meant, and he said it was the mark of a foolish young man who should have known better. I suspect it had something to do with the Hugh Chalice. When it was due to arrive in Lincoln twenty years ago, people did some very wild things in anticipation. The fervour died away when it disappeared *en route,* although I suspect it will be resurrected now it has risen from the dead. Just like Christ the Saviour, praise His holy name!'

'Amen,' said Michael, seeing some pious response was expected. 'Simon bought *his* chalice from a relic-seller. Did you ever meet this man, and assess whether he was an honest—'

'No. He always wore a hood, but I had the sense that I *might* have known him, had I been permitted to see his face. Simon said he was from Rome, though, so I am doubtless mistaken.'

'Is he still in Lincoln?' asked Michael.

'Simon told me he left as soon as the sale was made, although I do not think that can be right, because I have seen him several times since.'

'He wore a hood?' asked Bartholomew. 'He does not own red hose, too, does he?'

'Yes,' said Roger, startled. 'How extraordinary you should know that! God does move in mysterious ways! Alleluia!'

'Alleluia, indeed,' said Michael dryly.

* * *

Although Michael was assiduous in scouring the Gilbertine Priory for a man in red leggings, it was clear the fellow was long gone, so he abandoned the search in order to walk to the cathedral and be fitted for his ceremonial vestments. Bartholomew accompanied him, hoping they would meet some canons who might be prepared to talk about Aylmer. Michael complained bitterly about the distance between convent and minster – more than a mile, and some of it up a hill. Then, to take his mind off the exercise, he talked about which Lincoln saints were most likely to answer prayers, confiding that Bishop Hugh was not one of them, because there had been so few miracles at his tomb.

'There have been more at the Shrine of Little Hugh,' he said. 'But I am not sure I believe the story of his crucifixion. Neither does the Pope, because the cult remains unofficial. Of course, the cathedral is unlikely to tell pilgrims that, since Little Hugh is a great source of income.'

'It is a pity there is not a saint who is kindly disposed to investigators,' said Bartholomew. 'You need all the help you can get with this case. You are only supposed to be solving Aylmer's murder, but he is linked to Flaxfleete and Nicholas by the marks on their shoulders, and he died while holding the Hugh Chalice. I have a feeling this might be more complex than it appears.'

'And it has been made more so by the fact that this city is uneasy, and everyone has taken sides. I thought at first that someone had killed Aylmer because he was unpopular, but now I suspect his personality might have nothing to do with it.'

They walked along Wigford's high street, where Michael admired the large houses and dozen or so churches that clustered along it. Many had gardens that ran down to the banks of the River Witham, and, between them, grey-brown water fringed with reeds could be seen. Small boats bobbed on the wind-ruffled surface, carrying goods to the city wharves. Scattered among them were the white flecks of gulls and swans, while ducks dabbled in the shallows.

'I wish Gynewell had not asked you to do this,' said Bartholomew unhappily. 'Hamo was right: you are in danger from two sources – from a killer desperate to avoid detection, and from the Commonalty, who will want to catch him before you do.'

'So Hamo says, but perhaps Miller will be content to see the wheels of justice work.'

Bartholomew thought about his encounter with Sheriff Lungspee. 'The wheels of justice here are rather too dependent on how well they are greased. However, it is always possible that the killer is in holy orders, and will claim benefit of clergy. Then your "wheels of justice" will see him sent to some remote convent to live out his life, and I do not think *that* will satisfy Miller.'

'What makes you think the killer is a priest?' Michael was startled.

'Aylmer died in a convent, which is not a place where anyone can wander as he pleases. And we have been told that the cathedral's vicars never leave home without arming themselves. Of course, we have also been told Aylmer was a criminal, so perhaps he was killed by an associate – a falling-out among thieves.'

Michael rubbed his chin. 'I am acutely uncomfortable with the connections that are beginning to emerge. Not only did Aylmer, Nicholas and Flaxfleete share similar scars, but Nicholas and Flaxfleete were both poisoned after swallowing drinks from the Swan tavern. However, Flaxfleete was a guildsman and Aylmer and Nicholas favoured Miller and the Commonality. They were not friends.'

'Roger said the marks might have been made twenty

years ago, so perhaps they owned different allegiances then. However, these three murders are certainly connected to each other. People have made reference to other odd deaths, too – the wicked Canon Hodelston and Fat William. You must be on your guard, Brother. I shall ask Cynric to stay with you, if I am obliged to leave Lincoln before you are ready.'

Michael glanced at him. 'Do not be too hopeful about Matilde. Folk here remember her, but no one has the faintest idea where she might have gone. Spayne may be the same.'

Bartholomew rubbed his eyes, unwilling to entertain the possibility that his last chance might fizzle into nothing. 'She may have shared secrets with him that are not common knowledge.'

'She confided matters to *you* that she never shared with others, and *you* do not know where she went. Personally, I am inclined to think that if you cannot find her, then no one else will, either. Remember what she told Yolande? That once she had made up her mind to disappear, no one would ever locate her. She is not given to idle boasts.' He sighed when the physician made no reply. 'Are you listening, or are your thoughts so choked with love that you cannot see the logic in what I am saying?'

Bartholomew squinted up at the bright white sky. 'I know all this; I have thought of little else for more than a year. However, I was not thinking about Matilde just now, but Sabina.'

Michael raised his eyebrows. 'Why? She is too old for you, probably past childbearing age.'

Bartholomew gaped at him. 'God's teeth, Brother! I was not considering her in that way! I was actually think-ing about something that happened a long time ago. It has been scratching at the back of my mind ever since we arrived, and I probably should have mentioned it before.'

Michael regarded him uneasily. 'I do not like the sound of this. When you have failed to mention things in the past, the "oversight" has invariably caused me problems. For example, the time you neglected to reveal the presence of a woman in one of our Colleges. And look where that led us.'

Bartholomew grinned sheepishly. 'It is nothing of that magnitude. It concerns Aylmer. When I examined his body yesterday, his face was familiar – that odd crease in his nose is distinctive – and I have been trying to recall where I might have seen it before. Then, during prime this morning, the memory surfaced suddenly. Do you remember what Suttone said about him – about his past?'

'He mentioned a misunderstanding with a sheriff. The comment made Sabina smile. Is that what you meant?'

Bartholomew nodded. 'Many years ago, my brother-in-law was ordered to act as juror for a series of trials at Cambridge castle. It was out of term, and I was home from Oxford with nothing to do, so I went with him. One of the cases involved a man called John Shirlok.'

'Even I know about him,' said Michael. 'He turned "approver" – he named accomplices – but they were acquitted, and it was rumoured that he had simply supplied a list of people he did not like.'

'Aylmer was one of them. I remember his nose among the ranks of the accused. So was Sabina.'

Michael stared at him. 'Are you sure?'

'Yes. She was Sabina Godeknave then, which must have been the name of her first husband – she referred to herself as a widow at the trial. And I have a vague recollection of Nicholas Herl being there, too, gazing out of the window, bored. I cannot remember the names of everyone Shirlok accused, but I know there were ten in total: eight men and two women.'

Michael continued to stare as his own memory began to work. 'You are right. The trial was a significant event because of the large number of people who were involved, and news of it even reached the ears of lowly novices at Ely. Nicholas Herl, John Aylmer and Sabina Godeknave *were* among the appellees. I cannot imagine why *I* did not make this connection.'

'Why would you? It happened twenty years ago, and in a different city. There is nothing to link Cambridge-past to Lincoln-present, except some names in an ancient memory.'

Michael was mulling over the new information. 'If Sabina Herl *is* Sabina Godeknave, then her first husband did not "die" – he was hanged for theft. Sabina was charged with the same crime, but was released for lack of evidence. At the abbey, we were astonished to learn she was later acquitted a *second* time. You said you remember some names, but not all. Who else do you recall?'

Bartholomew rubbed his chin. 'Just two more. Shirlok gave them in Latin, in an attempt to lend weight to his claims, although his pronunciation was all but incomprehensible. They were Adam and Simon *Molendinarius*. As you know, a *molendinarius* is a miller.'

Michael's jaw dropped as the myriad implications of that association rattled about in his mind. 'Adam Miller! God's blood, Matt! What is happening here?'

Bartholomew shrugged. 'Probably nothing relevant to Aylmer's murder. However, it appears that at least some of the people Shirlok accused decided to leave Cambridge, and make Lincoln their new home. The timing fits: the trial was twenty years ago, which was roughly the time Miller arrived here and began to take over the Commonalty.'

'I am not sure about this,' said Michael unhappily. 'Why did they leave Cambridge at all?'

'Probably because the sheriff would have been watching them too closely. I recall *knowing*, with absolute certainty, that the appellees were guilty, despite the verdict. They doubtless moved so they could continue their illegal activities without the eyes of the law on them.'

Michael scratched his tonsure. 'It is possible, I suppose. So, of these ten villains, we know there were two Miller brothers, Aylmer, Sabina and Nicholas. There were five more.'

'I have been wrestling with the matter ever since prime, but nothing has come to mind. I remember poor Shirlok, though. He was sentenced to hang, much to his surprise. The executioner had to do it immediately, because he was already well on his way to being drunk, and would have been totally incapable had it had been left any longer. Shirlok was dispatched within an hour of his trial.'

Michael shrugged. 'He pleaded guilty, and hanging is the only sentence for self-confessed thieves. He cannot have expected any other outcome.'

'He did, though, Brother. He thought naming the others would earn him a reprieve. He was even more astonished when he was convicted but his accomplices were allowed to walk free.'

Michael regarded him thoughtfully. 'You seem to think the verdict was unfair, and I remember being shocked to hear about the acquittals myself. But your brother-in-law was one of the jurors. Oswald's morals are pliant on occasion, but they are not *that* flexible.'

'He was only one of the twelve "good men and true". Another was Stephen Morice.'

Michael grimaced. 'The man whom every Cambridge resident knows to be the most dishonest fellow in Christendom,

160

and who is so brazenly corrupt that he makes Lungspee look like an angel?'

Bartholomew nodded. 'And then there was Thomas Deschalers, the grocer whose death we investigated not long ago.'

Michael frowned. 'He was a sly fellow, too, but the jury was not all bad, because de Wetherset served on it, too. He once confided to me – at a College feast, when he was drunk – that being obliged to pass verdict on Shirlok upset him so much that it was a major factor in him taking holy orders; clerics cannot serve on secular juries. He and Oswald would have seen justice done, though.'

'I am not so sure about de Wetherset: he has always struck me as a man who would do anything to advance his own interests. In essence, though, the whole thing reeked of corruption, and I have often wondered why the appellees were never investigated. Their homes might have been stuffed to the ceilings with stolen goods, but we would never have known, because no one looked.'

'When a man is about to be hanged, he will say all manner of things to save himself, including trying to indict innocent people.' Michael was trying to be fair, by looking at both sides of the story. 'It happens all the time, and Justices must be used to it. So, just because Shirlok's accusations were dismissed does not necessarily mean there was a miscarriage of justice. Right?'

Bartholomew said nothing until they were across the High Bridge. 'When Shirlok was hanged, something odd happened. He was a small man, and kicked for some time before the executioner declared him dead. He was cut down, and his body displayed in the castle bailey, as a deterrent to other would-be thieves. Eventually, the hangman went to a tavern, and I was able to look at Shirlok alone.'

Michael regarded him in distaste. 'You had a ghoulish fascination for corpses even then?'

Bartholomew hesitated. 'I once told Cynric this, but never anyone else.'

Michael was concerned. 'Do not confide in me, if my knowing whatever it is will impede the investigation. Aylmer's murder will be difficult enough to solve, without having restrictions put on it.'

'This has nothing to do with Aylmer. As I stared down at Shirlok's body, he opened his eyes. You see, because he was light, it had taken longer for him to choke than most men, and the hangman was too drunk to notice the signs of life. When I reached out to touch him, he leapt up and ran away.'

The monk could see it was a troubled memory, so tried not to laugh. 'What happened then?'

'Nothing. The executioner told everyone he had buried the body, and I decided not to contradict him, mostly because of an enduring sense that there was something rotten about the whole affair.'

'There is de Wetherset,' said Michael, nodding to where the portly ex-Chancellor was plodding towards them. 'Perhaps we should ask him what he recalls about his duties as a juror that day.'

De Wetherset had attended prime in the Franciscan Friary, and smugly informed the scholars that it was considerably more uplifting than what usually transpired in the Priory of St Katherine. He told them he had attended one rowdy office when he had first taken up residence in the Gilbertines' guest-hall, and had made the decision to subject himself to no more of them.

'Father Simon enjoys that sort of worship,' he went on archly. 'But *I* do not clap when I sing.'

'I thought you liked Simon,' said Bartholomew, surprised

to hear the condemnation in the ex-Chancellor's voice. 'You shared his house before it burned down.'

'It was an economic arrangement that suited us both,' said de Wetherset. 'I would not say we were friends, although I admire him as a man of singular piety. You can see it in his devotion to St Hugh.'

Michael nodded. 'He has spent his own money on a very expensive relic for the cathedral. But what do *you* think of the Hugh Chalice, de Wetherset? Bishop Gynewell believes it is genuine, although his dean is said to be sceptical.'

De Wetherset thought it only natural that he should be asked for an expert opinion. 'Ever since you exposed those false bones in Cambridge, I have discovered a rare talent in myself: I possess the ability to sense an object's holiness. In short, I can identify a fake at ten paces.'

'Can you indeed?' murmured Michael. 'And what do you make of Simon's cup?'

'I have not looked at it. Relics are ten a penny in Lincoln, and I am too busy to inspect them all.'

'We were just talking about the Cambridge trial of John Shirlok,' said Bartholomew, aware that it was something of a non sequitur, but unable to think of another way to broach the subject. 'Michael remembers it creating a stir across the whole shire.'

De Wetherset lowered his voice conspiratorially. 'One of the accused was Adam Miller, and he is still sensitive about the matter, so keep your voice down. But you are right; the case did cause an uproar, and *I* had the misfortune to be a juror, along with your kinsman, Bartholomew. I wondered how long it would take you to make the connection. I was going to prompt you if you had not seen it by this evening, but I need not have worried. You always were a sharp pair.'

'What connection?' asked Michael, bemused. 'Do you

mean the fact that some of the people accused by Shirlok are now living happily in Lincoln?'

'No, *that* is obvious, and I imagine you have known it since you arrived. Miller and his friends came to live here shortly after their acquittal, and never made any secret about the fact that they had been wrongfully accused by a man who was then hanged. The Guild made hay with the information at the time, but not even they dare mention it these days. As I said, Miller is touchy about it.'

Michael's green eyes were hard. 'Actually, we have only just made this particular association, and it would have been helpful to know it sooner. You should have told me that the man whose murder I have been charged to solve was once accused of burglary with Adam Miller.'

'I thought you knew,' said de Wetherset, unrepentant. 'You are an experienced Senior Proctor, and I did not think you needed me to teach you your business.'

'It cannot have been easy for you,' said Bartholomew, cutting across Michael's tart response, 'arriving here to find yourself face to face with people you had judged.'

'It was a shock,' admitted de Wetherset. 'But the trial was years ago, and they bear me no malice – as is right, since we declared them innocent. They invited me to dine with them once, and we had a relatively pleasant evening – if one overlooks Miller's repulsive table manners.'

'Was it an honest verdict?' asked Bartholomew bluntly. 'No bribes exchanged hands?'

De Wetherset was outraged. 'How dare you! No wonder you have not risen very high in the University if you go around putting those sorts of questions! However, since you ask, most of the jury believed Shirlok was making unfounded accusations just to save his neck.'

'Perhaps he was, but even I could see the appellees

were no innocents,' pressed Bartholomew, unmoved by the man's indignation. 'Sabina Godeknave had already stood trial for a theft that had seen her husband hanged, and we have been told that Miller's business in Lincoln is openly shady.'

'That is irrelevant,' said de Wetherset coldly. 'We were not told what the appellees had done in the past, and obviously we could not predict what they would do in the future. We made a good, fair decision based on the evidence available to us at the time. Now, if you will excuse me, my presence is required at the cathedral. I am due to be fitted with my silken cope today.'

'Adam Miller,' said Michael, as de Wetherset started to leave. 'It seems he was the leader of this felonious Cambridge coven. And we know about Nicholas Herl, Aylmer, Sabina and Miller's brother. Who are the other five?'

'You have not learned that yet?' asked de Wetherset contemptuously. Michael glared at him: the ex-Chancellor was beginning to be annoying. 'They are Lora Boyner and Walter Chapman.'

'Of course!' said Bartholomew. 'I remember Lora – a large woman who shouted a lot. She was a brewer and could lift heavy kegs of ale that were too weighty for even strong men.'

'And the remaining three?' asked Michael coolly.

'All dead. Simon Miller and one other man died in prison, and the last two died of a falling pox. However, bear in mind that Adam Miller has made other friends since the trial, and Lincoln's Commonalty comprises more than six members. For example, there is Langar, his legal adviser, who left a post as castle clerk to follow him to a new life.'

Michael continued to glare. 'When we first started to talk, you mentioned another connection you think I should have made. I suspect you are overestimating how helpful

165

people have been to me in this godforsaken place, so you had better tell me what it is.'

'Stolen property, Brother,' said de Wetherset with an impatient sigh that indicated he thought the monk a simpleton. 'One of the crimes for which Shirlok was hanged was the theft of a silver goblet from the church at Geddynge. It was presented at his trial as evidence.'

'I remember,' said Bartholomew. 'It was old, small and tarnished.'

'Quite,' said de Wetherset. His tone became even more patronising. 'And where else have you recently encountered a cup that is "old, small and tarnished"?'

'The Hugh Chalice?' asked Bartholomew, his thoughts whirling in confusion.

De Wetherset clapped slowly and sarcastically. 'At last! I am almost certain that Shirlok's vessel is the same as the one Simon bought for the cathedral, although there was no talk at the trial about it belonging to St Hugh or being stolen from the friars who were transporting it to Lincoln.'

Bartholomew was thoughtful. 'Simon says he bought it from a relic-seller. Prior Roger thinks there was something familiar about this man and his red hose, but Simon claims he is from Rome.'

De Wetherset smiled in his annoying manner. 'Good. And now think about a fellow called Walter Chapman, as you remember him from the trial. What was he wearing?'

'I have not the faintest idea,' said Bartholomew, regarding him as though he were insane. 'And I am astonished you think I should. I cannot possibly be expected to remember a man's clothes after two decades. I cannot even recall what *I* wore then.'

'I can,' said de Wetherset. 'A black tabard with yellow stockings. You looked like a moorhen. But I see I shall have to help your analysis. Chapman wore scarlet hose at the trial, and he still favours the fashion now. *Ergo*, this "Roman" relic-seller, whom Roger thinks is vaguely familiar, is Chapman.'

'There are a lot of questions with that solution,' said Bartholomew, unconvinced. 'First, how did Chapman come by the chalice, since it would have been returned to its owners at Geddynge after Shirlok's trial? Secondly, even if Chapman did manage to acquire it, why wait twenty years before selling it to Simon? And thirdly, why would Chapman peddle it to Simon, knowing Simon intends to put it somewhere where it will be open to public scrutiny? If it is not the original Hugh Chalice – and it does not sound as though it can be – then Chapman is asking to be exposed as a deceiver.'

'Yes,' said de Wetherset patronisingly. 'So, ignore Chapman for now, and concentrate on the man originally charged with its theft: Shirlok. What can you deduce from *his* involvement?'

Bartholomew scratched his head, too interested in the connections he was beginning to see to be offended by de Wetherset's condescension. 'We have been told that the Hugh Chalice was stolen *en route* from London to Lincoln twenty years ago. Shirlok was definitely operating then.'

'Right,' said Michael. 'And Father Simon told us how it was pilfered from the two friar-couriers when they rested their weary bones at *Cambridge*. Shirlok must have found them asleep and taken advantage of the situation. At the trial, it was claimed that Shirlok passed the chalice to Lora Boyner, but she denied knowing it was stolen.'

'You have missed a bit out, Brother,' said Bartholomew. 'Shirlok must have sold it to Geddynge *before* giving it to Lora, because it was Geddynge's priest who claimed he was the owner.'

De Wetherset smiled. 'Exactly! The Geddynge priest bought the cup from a "relic-seller" for twenty shillings. At that price, obviously neither he nor Shirlok had any idea of its holiness. It was removed from Geddynge church within a few days of its purchase, because Shirlok knew that what could be sold once could be stolen and hawked again.'

'Very well,' said Bartholomew. 'But then what? You have established that it was stolen from the friars, stolen from Geddynge, and recovered from Lora Boyner to appear at Shirlok's trial. But how did it get here? After Shirlok had been convicted, it would have been returned to its rightful owner.'

'And who is that?' demanded de Wetherset imperiously. 'Not the Geddynge priest, because he had the misfortune to buy purloined property. And not Lora Boyner, either. So, is the "rightful owner" the cathedral in Lincoln? The Old Temple in London?'

'The two friars?' asked Bartholomew. 'I do not recall them being at the trial.'

'Once the cup was lost to them, they returned to London with their tails between their legs,' said de Wetherset. 'I heard a rumour that they never arrived – God struck them down for their carelessness.'

'Or they were killed by whoever stole the chalice,' suggested Michael. 'Shirlok.'

'So what *did* happen to Shirlok's chalice?' pressed Bartholomew. 'Was it returned to Geddynge, because it was Geddynge's priest who reported it missing? I am sure it was recorded as his property at the trial, regardless of who has real legal title to the thing now.'

Michael snapped his fingers. 'I remember! Everything Shirlok was alleged to have stolen disappeared into thin air when it was in the process of being returned to its proper owners. Shirlok's treasure vanished, and no one ever found out what happened to it.'

De Wetherset was smug. 'Precisely, Brother! So, *now* do you see now why I have not wasted my time examining Simon's cup? With that sort of history, how can it be a genuine relic?'

'Will you come to the cathedral with me, Matt?' asked Michael, as the ex-Chancellor swaggered away up the hill. 'De Wetherset is not the only man due to try on his silken cope today, and I do not trust anyone else to give an honest opinion about my appearance. Strangers might have me processing up the nave in a garment that makes me look fat.'

'Another time,' said Bartholomew, knowing from experience that fittings tended to take a long time with Michael. The monk was particular about such matters, and Bartholomew wanted to spend the day browsing the minster's library. He glanced wistfully at Spayne's house as they approached it. Because the mayor and his sister were away, the window shutters had been left closed, although smoke still billowed from the chimney. The servants were assiduously following Ursula's instructions to keep a fire burning, to melt the snow on the damaged roof.

'There is the Swan tavern,' said Michael, pointing to a large building that stood slightly downhill from Spayne's abode. Above its door was a sign on which a black bird had been painted. It was not an attractive specimen, and the artist had furnished it with a set of teeth that made it look deformed. 'Where Flaxfleete bought his tainted wine, and where Nicholas drank ale before he died. Shall we go inside?'

'We shall not,' said Bartholomew firmly. 'I do not want to be poisoned.'

'No one will harm us,' said Michael, with far more confidence than Bartholomew felt was warranted. 'My throat is parched, and a cup of ale would solve that problem *and* put me in a sober frame of mind for trying on priestly garments.'

Bartholomew followed him with serious misgivings. Inside, the inn was warm and surprisingly respectable. The floor was clean, the main room was fragrant with freshly brewed ale, and the benches and tables were of decent quality. There were even a few women present, indicating it was not some rough city tavern, but an establishment that was rather more genteel. Nevertheless, Bartholomew was still startled to see Lady Christiana and Dame Eleanor there, drinking watered wine from delicately wrought goblets and eating honey-bread from a silver platter. He moved quickly to block them from Michael's line of vision, sure someone would notice if the monk leered at Christiana in such a public place.

The taverner bustled up to them, eyes disappearing into the fat of his face as he smiled a welcome. 'I am glad you came,' he said, ushering them to seats near the fire. 'You are Brother Michael and Doctor Bartholomew, friends of Master Suttone of Michaelhouse. We are honoured to have another Suttone in our fine city. My name is Robert Quarrel, landlord, and I am delighted to make your acquaintance. What will you have?'

'Ale and bread,' said Michael. 'No cheese, though – we slender men tend to avoid cheese.'

Quarrel beamed uncomfortably, not sure how to respond. In the end, he settled for clapping his hands and repeating the order to a pot-boy.

Michael raised a hand to prevent the lad from leaving. 'I saw you on Wednesday night.'

The boy smiled uneasily. 'I saw you, too, sir. I carried a

keg of claret to Master Kelby's house, and you were talking to him at his door. Later, someone started a rumour that Flaxfleete was poisoned and that our wine was the culprit.'

'Do not say such things!' cried Quarrel, anxiety stamped across his chubby features. 'I am a respectable man – I have served as Lincoln's mayor *and* its bailiff. I supply wine to many wealthy patrons and have never had any trouble before. The poison must have come from somewhere else.'

'It was definitely in the keg before it arrived at Kelby's house,' said Bartholomew. 'Drips on his floor attested to the fact that someone had tampered with the seal and it was leaking. Where do you store your barrels?'

'In the cellar,' said Quarrel. 'And no one goes down there except me. I fetched the cask myself, and put it by the door, ready. However, I was enjoying dinner with de Wetherset, and left it for Joseph to deliver instead of seeing to it myself, as I should have done. Perhaps someone did something to it then.'

'You left it unattended?' asked Michael. 'Were you not afraid someone might make off with it?'

'It was not *unattended,* exactly,' objected Quarrel. 'It was by the door, and Joseph would have noticed someone stealing it.'

Joseph looked sheepish. 'I did not watch it constantly, though. Ned went to take Dame Eleanor back to the Gilbertine Priory and left me in charge. I am afraid I was distracted by patrons wanting to talk.'

'Why did Ned escort Dame Eleanor home?' asked Bartholomew, glancing to where she sat. 'Is it usual for pot-boys to abandon their duties to help old ladies?'

Joseph looked defensive. 'It was cold that night, and we were afraid she might slip on ice, so Ned offered to go with her. She is a saint, you see, and it is always wise to curry favour from such folk. She is old and will die soon, and you never know when you might need to petition the saints for a miracle in this world.'

'We watch her because she is dear to us,' corrected Quarrel, slightly shiftily. Bartholomew wondered whether it had been the landlord's own convictions that the boy had so guilelessly repeated. 'And I always encourage my lads to do their Christian duty by helping others.'

'How much wine did Kelby buy from you?' asked Michael, smothering a smile.

'Three kegs,' replied Quarrel. 'I had delivered two earlier in the day, and he told me he would send for the last one if it was required – he did not want to pay for three if he only used two. But they were celebrating Flaxfleete's acquittal, so more was imbibed than was anticipated. The keg was not waiting by the porch for long, Brother – an hour at the most.'

'What can you tell me about Nicholas Herl?' asked Michael, changing the subject.

Quarrel seemed surprised. 'He was a bitter man, but he became oddly gleeful in the month before he died. He usually drank in the Angel, which suited us – we would rather not have belligerent patrons if we can help it – but he chose to come here the night he died. He was sullen and angry over something. He drank too much, and was found the next morning in the Braytheford Pool. The priests said it was self-murder, although his wife does not believe them.'

'He was also poisoned,' said Bartholomew baldly, seeing no reason to keep it quiet.

'Sweet Jesus, no!' Quarrel was clearly appalled, and glanced around furtively before lowering his voice. 'I hope you will not make this public, because it could ruin me. You can see for yourself that this is a respectable place. We do not murder our customers!'

172

'It does seem pleasant,' agreed Michael, looking around appreciatively. He suddenly became aware that Christiana was there. '*Very* pleasant.'

Bartholomew watched with a sinking heart as Christiana sensed she was being admired, and turned around. She raised her eyebrows when she saw Michael, and whispered something in her companion's ear. Then she stood and came towards them, Dame Eleanor in her wake. She glided, rather than walked, and Bartholomew was left with the feeling that she knew the eyes of every man present were on her, and that she expected nothing less. Pointedly, he fixed his own attention on her friend. Dame Eleanor had a kind, brown face and eyes that twinkled. He stood, to offer her his seat.

'Good morning, Brother,' said Christiana with a smile that made her appear vaguely wanton. She plumped herself down in the place Bartholomew had vacated for the old lady. 'I thought you had eaten breakfast with the Gilbertines.'

'I came for ale to slake my thirst,' replied Michael with the air of a martyr. 'I shall touch no food; I am not a greedy man.'

'I am sure of it,' Christiana replied. Her tone was grave, but her eyes sparkled with mischief. 'Do you like this tavern? I inherited the building from my mother, and Master Quarrel has rented it from my family for the past thirty years. It is said to be one of the finest inns in the county.'

'In England,' said Eleanor, perching on the end of the bench, where there was not really room for her. To avoid being crushed, Christiana shifted closer to Michael than was decent.

'We have excellent taverns in Cambridge, too,' said Michael, making no attempt to move away. 'You must come and sample a few.'

Old Dame Eleanor frowned her puzzlement. 'How do you know, Brother? I thought our universities forbade alehouses to its scholars – to keep hot-blooded youths away from sober townsfolk.'

'I am no hot-blooded youth,' said Michael, aware that Christiana was looking at him with amused eyes. 'Well, no youth, at least, and—'

'He is obliged to visit them, to make sure students do not break the rules,' Bartholomew explained hastily, before the monk could confide something he might later regret. 'He is our Senior Proctor.'

'I sensed, the first time I met you, that you were more than a mere monk,' said Christiana with an expression that was distinctly flirtatious. 'You are also a man of power, which explains why Bishop Gynewell is so eager to honour you with a prebendal stall.'

'I do own a certain influence in the University,' admitted Michael in a modest understatement. 'Although I am a humble man.'

'Then we shall leave you to your humble duties,' said Dame Eleanor, hoisting Christiana to her feet with surprising strength for an elderly woman. 'Whatever they might be. But St Hugh will wonder what has happened to me if I do not tend his shrine soon. I have prayed there every day for the past sixty years, except when I was stricken with the plague and he cured me.'

'Were you healed by Bishop Hugh or Little Hugh?' asked Michael in a transparent attempt to delay their departure. 'Only I have heard there are more miracles at the tomb of one than the other.'

'It is not for me to compare them, Brother,' said Eleanor gently. She turned to her friend. 'It looks like snow, so you should not tarry here long, Christiana. Go to the market while the weather holds, and then return to the Gilbertines without delay. My old bones sense we are in for a blizzard, and I will worry if I think you are out.'

Christiana smiled fondly as Eleanor hobbled out. 'She is a very dear lady, although I suspect I am better equipped to deal with a little snow than she is. I am younger and fitter, after all.'

'Yes, but *she* is a saint, My Lady,' said Quarrel seriously. 'And blizzards mean nothing to them. I imagine she could quell one with a mere wave of her hand, if she were so inclined. Would you like Joseph to accompany you? With Miller's Market so close, there are far too many rough types descending on our city.'

'I will escort you,' offered Michael chivalrously, standing and proffering a sturdy arm. 'Matt needs a bit of ribbon for his spare tunic, and I always like exploring new markets.'

Christiana smiled and stretched out an elegant finger to touch his arm. 'No, Brother. You must repair to the cathedral and be fitted with your canonical vestments. Who knows, perhaps St Hugh will touch your heart and order *you* to remain in Lincoln, as he did with Dame Eleanor all those years ago. Then we might have many outings together.'

She left, with Joseph carrying her basket. Only when her graceful figure could no longer be seen did Michael turn his attention back to the landlord. 'So, you have no idea how Nicholas Herl or Flaxfleete came to be poisoned?'

'None at all,' said Quarrel firmly. 'And I assure you it was nothing to do with my beverages. I am heartily sorry for both deaths, but my wine and ale are innocent of harming any man.'

CHAPTER 5

Michael and Bartholomew left the Swan and walked up the hill towards the cathedral. Bartholomew gazed at it, admiring the way it loomed above the city, dominating its steep, narrow streets. Then he skidded on some rotten vegetable parings, and focussed his attention on the road instead, noting that there seemed to be more unemployed men in the upper reaches of the city than there were lower down. They clamoured at the scholars as they passed, offering labour in exchange for food.

As they ascended, Michael began to pant like a man twice his age, and even Bartholomew was forced to admit that the climb was a stiff one. They passed a group of pilgrims attempting to make the journey on their knees, and Michael remarked tartly that reaching the summit on foot was penance enough. Several took him at his word and stood in relief.

'I think Quarrel was telling the truth,' said Bartholomew, waiting while the monk caught his breath. 'You could see his was a respectable tavern, and he would not risk what must be a good living to dispatch someone like Nicholas. If Nicholas had been stabbed in an alley, I might say Quarrel had rid himself of an unwanted customer, but he would never do it by poisoning a man's ale. And I do not think he tampered with Kelby's wine for the same reason.'

'I am inclined to agree. So, someone else must have taken advantage of the unattended barrel. Kelby was drunk, and probably did not order the third keg discreetly, so the killer

176

would have known exactly where it was going. I can only assume that one of the Commonalty did it, intending to strike a fatal blow at the Guild. Or should we assess Ursula de Spayne's possible role a little more carefully?'

'Did she have time? She was answering the door to us when the barrel would have been poisoned.'

'Actually, she was not. First, Quarrel said the wine sat by the door for an hour before Joseph delivered it, so she may have already done her worst by the time she spoke to us. Secondly, she took ages to reply to your knock, so perhaps she was still out – in the process of slipping through her back door – when you were trying to summon her to the front.'

'So, she saw the keg, guessed it was destined for Kelby, and slipped the poison – which she just happened to have with her – inside? Then she re-stoppered the barrel so no one would notice it had been broached, and dashed home to talk to us about noisy neighbours?'

'Well, someone must have had poison to hand.'

'She was not breathless,' argued Bartholomew. 'And she would have been, had she been racing up and down these hills. I do not think it was her.'

'Then perhaps it was her brother,' said Michael. 'I met a fellow Benedictine yesterday, and he maintains very strongly that Spayne was at his priory from about two o'clock on Wednesday afternoon. But when I pushed him, he admitted that they were busy with sacred offices all day. In essence, Spayne could have slipped out, doctored the barrel and returned with no one the wiser. Thus Spayne has no real alibi, and he and his sister are the obvious suspects for Flaxfleete's murder.'

'How could Spayne have known that Kelby would want more wine, and that the keg would be left in a place where tampering was possible?'

'He lives here, Matt. He probably knew exactly what Kelby had ordered – Kelby may even have told him, just to gloat. And Quarrel strikes me as a man of habit, so it would not take a fortune-teller to know that he would haul his keg from his cellar and leave it for his lad to deliver.'

Bartholomew sighed. 'I do not see Matilde making friends with a murderer.'

'Perhaps that is why she declined to marry him,' suggested Michael. 'She found out what he was really like, and fled Lincoln while she could.'

Bartholomew turned to another matter that had puzzled him. 'You told de Wetherset that the property recovered from Shirlok – and presented at his trial as evidence of his guilt – went missing immediately afterwards. How did you know that?'

'How do you not? It was a huge scandal, and the whole county talked about it for weeks after.'

'I was probably back in Oxford by then. What happened?'

'The goods disappeared on the day of the trial, although they were not actually missed until the various owners contacted the sheriff some weeks later, demanding to know why they had not been returned. The sheriff had dispatched them on a wagon, but none reached their intended destination. Searches were made, but nothing was ever recovered.'

Bartholomew frowned. 'When I was looking at Shirlok's body in the castle bailey, I recall seeing a cart being loaded with the items he had stolen. There was property relating to the other cases that had been heard that day, too. The sheriff wanted it all off his hands as quickly as possible. He ordered the jurors to help with the heavy work, but they objected strenuously, and the only one he actually snagged in the end was de Wetherset – who was furious about it.'

'So, you saw Shirlok's ill-gotten gains leave the castle?'

Bartholomew nodded. 'It was all very chaotic, because a few of the acquitted felons had been kept in gaol until the trial – obviously, the sheriff had not trusted them to appear on their own recognisance. They were being released at the same time, and there was a lot of fuss and noise. It was only when they had all gone that Shirlok made his own bid for freedom.'

'So, any of these villains could have made off with the property at that point? It was being piled into a wagon under their very noses?'

'The sheriff drew a line in the mud with his boot, separating the cart from the milling crowd in the bailey, and said he would shoot anyone who crossed it.'

'Was he serious?'

'Oh, yes. The jurors' refusal to help with the loading had put him in a foul mood, and he was a surly man at the best of times. He was itching to vent his temper on someone. Had Miller or anyone else put so much as a toe over his line, he would gladly have loosed an arrow.'

'So, Miller and his friends could not have taken the hoard, then?'

'I sincerely doubt it. The sheriff was watching them like a hawk.'

'Well, someone did – and whoever it was found himself in possession of the Hugh Chalice, as well as a chest of stolen property.'

'Assuming this cup *is* the Hugh Chalice, Brother. De Wetherset does not seem to think so.'

'Perhaps he will change his mind once he sets his "special skills" to work – especially if the bishop is convinced of its sanctity. He will not want to annoy his new prelate.'

Eventually, Bartholomew and Michael reached the top of the hill, where they passed through the gate that led to the

Bail – the plateau that housed the minster and the castle. The Church had ensured its property was better defended than its secular counterpart, and its precincts were surrounded by a high, crenellated wall that was relatively new and in good repair. The resulting enclosed area, known as the Cathedral Close, was massive, and contained not only the minster itself, but two churches and a chantry; the chapter house; cloisters; offices for the dean, precentor, treasurer and sacrist; and living accommodation for the canons, Vicars Choral, choristers, and the clerks and scribes who undertook the onerous task of overseeing the largest diocese in the country.

Dominating all was the cathedral. From a distance, its nave and chancel had appeared low, dwarfed by the tower with its soaring spire, but Bartholomew saw this was an illusion, and the main body of the building was actually impressively lofty. He began to walk around the outside, gazing up at the mighty buttresses, the intricately carved pinnacles, and finally the ancient frieze on the splendid west front. Michael went with him, for once voicing no objection to the extra walking.

When they had finished admiring the exterior, they entered the building through a gate near the south transept, and were immediately assailed by the familiar scents of incense and candle wax, along with the musty smell of damp: somewhere, a roof was leaking. Bartholomew gazed at the ceiling high above, a celebration of colour and carvings. The vaulted nave drew the eye to the chancel screen, which was a joyful jumble of gold, red and blue, and everywhere the stone eyes of saints and angels watched the people who came to pray, do business, chat to the priests or shelter from the cold weather. Michael led the way towards the central crossing, his footsteps echoing in the great vastness of empty space.

'I always feel so tiny in places like this,' he whispered. He was not easily awed, but Lincoln's grandeur had impressed him. 'They tell me I can enjoy as many Lombard slices as I like, because however large I grow, I will always be insignificant.'

'Go and stand next to a beehive then,' suggested Bartholomew practically. 'That should curb any abnormal desires to eat enough to fill a cathedral.'

'You have no sense of the magnificent,' said Michael irritably. 'This is a building fit for God, and I am honoured to be one of its canons.'

'It is splendid,' acknowledged Bartholomew. 'Especially those two rose windows.'

'Bishop Gynewell told me they are meant to represent eyes. The Bishop's Eye faces south, inviting in the Holy Spirit, while the Dean's Eye looks north and shuts out the Devil.'

'You had better not mention that to Cynric, or he will turn it all around and have the bishop ushering in Satan. He has taken a dislike to Gynewell.'

'Cynric is a superstitious fool, and so are we for letting him talk us out of a sojourn at the Bishop's Palace. It would be far safer – no one has been stabbed in Gynewell's guesthall. God's blessings, madam. I hope the saints were not too distressed over your late arrival this morning?'

Bartholomew turned to see Dame Eleanor standing nearby, and noted the way her eyes twinkled with amusement at the monk's mild irreverence. 'They seem to have survived the inconvenience, thank you. I have just finished my devotions at the Head Shrine and am about to tend Little Hugh.'

'I am ashamed to confess that I have been too busy to inspect these famous sites so far,' said Michael. 'But perhaps you might show us now? Can we accompany you to Little Hugh?'

Obligingly, Eleanor took them to the South Choir Aisle. Several pilgrims knelt next to a large stone sarcophagus, and the floor around it was carpeted with leaves and dried flowers. It comprised two sections: a sealed tomb-base, containing Little Hugh's bones, and an ornately carved canopy above. The canopy was topped by a wooden statue of a child bearing the marks of crucifixion; the relevant parts were picked out in red paint, and were graphic enough to make Bartholomew wince. Pilgrims had left gifts of jewels, coins and prayers scribbled on scraps of parchment; they had been shoved through the canopy's carved tracery, and could be seen piled untidily within.

'I sweep up every day,' whispered Dame Eleanor, gesturing to the vegetation-strewn floor. 'But I have not had time to do it this morning, hence the mess. Meanwhile, the priests are supposed to collect the written prayers from inside the shrine, because they are the only ones allowed to touch them. They read them aloud, then burn them on the altar, to send them heavenward. All the other oblations go straight to the treasurer, who is trying to raise enough money to repair the roof in the north transept.'

'What is that?' asked Michael, pointing to a pottery flask that stood just behind the statue. 'Do pilgrims leave offerings of wine for the boy, then?'

Eleanor passed it to him. 'Holy water, Brother. The bishop gives me a jug of it each week. Some I sprinkle on the shrines I have undertaken to serve, some I dab on particularly needy pilgrims, and some I sip when I feel the need for God's strength inside me. I am nearing seventy years of age, and attribute my good health to the saints and holy water. Will you make a petition to Little Hugh?'

Bartholomew backed away. There was something about the tomb that he did not like, and he was uncomfortable with the notion that the child's 'crucifixion' had been used to justify a massacre of innocent Jews. 'I would rather see the other shrine,' he said evasively, trying not to hurt her feelings. 'Bishop Hugh's.'

St Hugh of Lincoln had not died a grisly death, like so many others who had been canonised, but he had been a good man, whose honour and integrity had been a bright blaze in a dark world. His massive tomb stood near the High Altar, but his cranium had been separately interred in the Angel Choir – a peaceful area east of the sanctuary, which Hugh had built himself. The Head Shrine was a grand affair surrounded by rough wooden railings, to keep eager pilgrims at bay. It comprised a large, solid plinth topped by a richly decorated chest that held the skull itself. The chest was fitted with handles, so the relic could be removed from its base, and carried about in religious processions.

Pilgrims clustered around it. Some knelt quietly, others issued demands for cures, and others still thrust hands and arms through its stone pillars in an attempt to get as close to the saint's mortal remains as possible. Many had lit candles, and the Angel Choir was full of their wavering light, which turned honey-coloured stone to gold. Several clerics were present, both at the Head Shrine and the nearby Visceral Shrine of Queen Eleanor. Among them was Archdeacon Ravenser, the bishop's debauched scribe. He was in the process of removing a thick white candle from his sleeve, which he then passed to a Vicar Choral in a sleight of hand that would have impressed the most skilled of pickpockets. After a moment, he produced a second one, and then a third, all of which were lit and set in pride of place on the altar dedicated to St Hugh. Michael frowned before disappearing for a few moments. When he returned, his expression was stern.

'The High Altar seems to be missing three of its best candles,' he said sharply, having slipped up behind

183

Ravenser without being heard. The archdeacon jumped in shock at the voice so close to his left ear. 'I wonder why.'

'I have no idea,' replied Ravenser, quickly regaining his composure. 'John Suttone is in charge of the High Altar this week. I expect he forgot to collect them from the sacristy. Right, Claypole?'

His friend, a toothy fellow who wore a sword openly with his religious vestments, nodded. 'We are only the poor souls detailed to look after St Hugh's head – in a corner of the cathedral so draughty that the Host blows all around the altar.'

'It is a grim part of the building,' agreed Ravenser, rubbing red eyes and looking as though he needed a good night's sleep. 'That old lady in the Gilbertine habit who escorted you here – Dame Eleanor – says the wind is St Hugh's spirit, chilling all those with evil hearts. She says it never cuts through her, implying she has a pure one, I suppose.'

'Well, she does,' said Claypole. 'And that is why it is unreasonable for her to expect us to follow her example. We are mere mortals, and her standards are impossibly high.'

'You do not look as though you try very hard,' said Michael, looking them up and down.

Before either could reply, the choir started to sing, and the voices of boys soared through the chancel, complimented by the lower drone of Vicars Choral and canons. Bartholomew glanced up at the carvings of angels high above, and his imagination led him to wonder whether it was celestial voices that rang so beautifully along the ancient stones.

'The dean is not warbling, thank God,' said Claypole, cocking his head to one side. He grinned at Michael. 'We can tell, because none of the glass is vibrating in its frames.'

'The dean sings like an old tom cat,' laughed Ravenser.

'But you must excuse us. It is time to say prayers for the canons who died in the plague – which was all except two, Brother.'

He walked away and Claypole followed, leaving Bartholomew staring after them uneasily. Ravenser's words had sounded vaguely like a threat. Michael was not paying any attention to the archdeacon and his crony, however; he was listening to the music.

'It makes me see what a long way from perfection I am with my own efforts at Michaelhouse,' he said wistfully. '*My* choir will never sing like that.'

'These are professionals,' Bartholomew pointed out, not liking to admit the monk was right: the Michaelhouse chorus could rival the Gilbertines for enthusiasm, but without the benefit of any redeeming talent. 'Do not underestimate yourself, Brother; you have performed little short of a miracle already.'

Michael's eyes narrowed, and he reached out suddenly to grab someone in the process of darting behind a pillar, apparently as part of a game of hide-and-seek. His captive wore the blue gown of a chorister, which, added to his mop of golden curls, gave him a cherubic appearance.

'*Where* does Mayor Spayne live?' asked the monk mildly, lifting the boy so his feet dangled in thin air. Michael was a strong man, and held the struggling lad as though he was as light as a kitten.

'Oh,' said the chorister sheepishly, recognising him and promptly abandoning his startled bid for freedom. 'Did I point you in the wrong direction, sir?'

'You did,' said Michael evenly. 'Now why would you do that?'

'It was not you I meant to annoy,' said the boy, hanging quite comfortably at the end of Michael's outstretched arm. 'It was Flaxfleete. I do not like him, even though he is a member of the Guild and they give us marchpanes on the first Sunday of every month.'

'Was a member,' corrected Michael. 'He is dead, so will not be dispensing sweetmeats again.'

The boy's jaw dropped. 'Truly? Was he so angry with you for calling at the wrong house, that he challenged you to a fight? With swords? Or perhaps one of those new ribaulds they are using in the French wars? I would like to see men do battle with a pair of those!' He jerked in the air as he made several violently descriptive gestures with his hands. Michael set him back on his feet.

'I did not kill Flaxfleete,' said Michael. 'I am a monk, so I do not carry arms.'

The boy shot him a look that told him to try his claims on someone more gullible. 'Our canons and Vicars Choral are also men of God, but *they* would never think of leaving home without a weapon. I am going to have a sword when I am fourteen.'

'You do not intend to take holy orders, then?' asked Michael, amused.

The boy shot him another withering look. 'I am going to be a philosopher. Dame Eleanor tells me I have sharp wits, and will do well at a university.'

'And how will owning a sword help you with your studies?'

The boy smiled cheerfully. 'I will be able to defend my arguments better if I have a sharp blade.'

'You *will* do well at a university,' said Bartholomew, raising his eyebrows. 'I think some of my students feel the same way.'

'Tell me why you have taken a dislike to Flaxfleete,' said Michael. 'And why you send innocent victims to his door, just to annoy him.'

The boy shrugged, unabashed. 'I liked Aylmer, because he let me pick cherries from his trees last year. Flaxfleete hated Aylmer, so I hated Flaxfleete. Besides, Flaxfleete only became a priest because he thought he might hang for arson otherwise. He was a snivelling coward, not a true man at all.'

'Why did Flaxfleete hate Aylmer?'

The boy shrugged again. 'Probably because Aylmer was Miller's friend, and Flaxfleete is Kelby's. Adults take their squabbles very seriously, although they should just challenge each other to a duel and have done with it. That is what I would do.'

'What is your name?' asked Michael, watching him parry and thrust with an imaginary weapon.

'Hugh Suttone.' He pointed to the High Altar, where John Suttone – the cleric they had seen at Kelby's celebration – was sweeping the floor. 'That is my brother. He is the Clerk who Rouses the People, and this week he is in charge of the High Altar.' There was pride in his voice.

'We are friends of your cousin,' said Michael. 'The one who is to be installed as a canon.'

'Thomas,' said Hugh, with clear disdain. 'My brother was offended when Thomas picked Aylmer to be his Vicar Choral. He said it should have been him. Do you think Thomas will choose John now Aylmer is dead? We were talking about it this morning, and John said the situation was looking a bit more hopeful.'

Michael tapped him gently under the chin. 'Possibly, but you should not say this to anyone else. You may make people think John killed Aylmer, just to get his appointment.'

'He did not, though,' said Hugh. 'I thought the same thing, you see, so I asked him, but he said he has killed no one. He never lies, so he is definitely innocent. Excuse me, Brother. The dean is coming, and I do not want him to lecture me about running in church when I am supposed to be singing.'

He was gone in a flash, leaving Michael quaking with astonished laughter. 'I should hire him to help me with my investigation. There is something to be said for blunt questions.'

'Yes, but perhaps not *that* blunt, Brother.'

Deans were the men who headed a cathedral's hierarchy, and the office was thus an important one. Lincoln's was a short man with a perfectly round head, which was bald with the exception of a thin fringe around the sides and back. His eyes were oddly small for the size of his face, which made him appear furtive. A strange clanking sound emanated from his robes as he walked, and Bartholomew saw Hugh dart from the shadows to grab a coin that appeared to have rolled from the dean's person. He expected the boy to keep it, and was surprised when he trotted to the Head Shrine and dropped it through the railings. Dame Eleanor saw the gesture, too, and patted his shoulder encouragingly.

Three waddling canons intercepted the dean before he could reach Michael and Bartholomew, and the intense, whispered discussion that followed looked as though it might continue for some time, so the two scholars took the opportunity to visit the High Altar while they waited for it to finish, admiring the glitter of gold from a vantage point near Little Hugh's shrine. When he spotted them, John Suttone came to pass the time of day.

'I saw you with my young brother,' he said, with a humourless smile that made him look very like Michaelhouse's Suttone. 'He is a rascal, so I hope he was not insolent.'

'Not today,' replied Michael. 'Although the last time we met, he sent us to Kelby's house when I had actually asked him for directions to Spayne's.'

John grimaced. 'He cannot help himself where mischief

is concerned. I am sorry I did not make myself known when you tended Flaxfleete on Wednesday, but I had no idea who you were. Bishop Gynewell tells us you have been asked to find Aylmer's killer – hopefully before the installation ceremony. Is it true?'

Michael nodded. 'And young Hugh tells *me* you are not the guilty party, despite the fact that you have a powerful motive – you might benefit from Aylmer's untimely death.'

John looked alarmed. 'I have killed no one! And you are wrong to think I have a motive. Cousin Thomas overlooked me once, and there is no reason to suppose he will not do so again.'

'What about your cathedral colleagues? Do any of them have a reason to kill Aylmer?'

John was surprised by the question. 'Of course! Most of us prefer the Guild to the Commonalty – an honoured few have even been invited to join its ranks. Conversely, Aylmer was a fully fledged member of the Commonalty, and so naturally people here distrusted him.'

'Was their "distrust" enough to see him killed?'

'I imagine so.' John's expression became a little spiteful. 'Will you talk to them all? There are thirty Vicars Choral, ten Poor Clerks, twelve choristers, and a dozen chantry priests. Oh, and there are eight archdeacons, too. You will be busy, Brother.'

'I have faced greater challenges in the past,' said Michael, unperturbed. 'But the dean has finished talking to those three fat canons now. We have not met, so will you introduce us?'

John made a choking sound that Bartholomew assumed was a smothered gulp of laughter at the monk's description of his new colleagues – or perhaps it was a gasp of disbelief that such a portly fellow should so describe men who were, after all, considerably slimmer than him.

189

'His name is Simon Bresley,' said John, controlling himself. 'He and the bishop are the only cathedral men who do *not* stand against the Commonalty. Gynewell refuses to be drawn to either side, while Bresley often accepts invitations to dine with Miller and his cronies.'

'Why would he do that?'

'Ask *him* – the rest of us do not understand it at all. Dean Bresley, may I present Brother Michael? And this is his friend Doctor Bartholomew, who tried to save Flaxfleete two nights ago.'

Bresley nodded a polite greeting, but his attention was clearly elsewhere. 'The music,' he explained, when Michael asked if anything was amiss. 'It is so beautiful this morning that one might be forgiven for forgetting that it emanates from the throats of devils.'

John gave another of his grim smiles, as if anticipating what was coming next, then turned to Michael. 'Some of my High Altar candles were stolen this morning, and I need to replace them. Please excuse me.'

'Devils,' repeated the dean when he had gone. 'And by "devils" I mean Poor Clerks, choristers and Vicars Choral. They may sing like angels, but they swear, fight, spit, talk through the divine offices, and carry swords under their robes. They are more like pirates than men of God.'

'These are serious charges,' said Michael. 'As a canon, I shall speak out against such practices.'

Bresley gazed at him with burning hope. 'Will you? It would be nice to have someone on my side in the war against sin. Just last week, I was obliged to fine Ravenser and Claypole for rape *and* being absent from their duties – both very serious matters.'

Bartholomew gazed warily at him. 'Especially the rape. Who was she?'

'One of the ladies who lives in the Close,' explained the

190

dean. 'There are several of them, and they save the Vicars Choral the bother of going into the city after dark for their vices. Listen!'

Michael cocked his head, although the music was insufficient to distract Bartholomew from his horror at the dean's revelations. 'Simon Tunstede's *Gloria*,' said the monk. 'My favourite setting.'

'How is it possible that such a heavenly sound can come from such wicked creatures?' asked the dean. He led them to the Angel Choir, and pointed to the pier above the Head Shrine. 'One such fiend was turned to stone many years ago.'

Bartholomew started in shock when he saw the carved imp. 'That is Bishop Gynewell!'

'Hush!' breathed Bresley, looking around uneasily. 'You are not the first to have noticed the similarity, but he does not like it. It is coincidence obviously, since the imp lived many years before Gynewell was born. However, no prelate appreciates being told that he bears an uncanny resemblance to a demon, so watch what you say.'

'It is a rather unsettling likeness,' said Michael. 'No wonder he is sensitive about it.'

'Cynric will feel vindicated,' murmured Bartholomew, still gazing up at the statue. 'He will see it as proof, right down to the horns.'

'It is a pity you plan to be a non-residentiary canon, Brother,' said Bresley. 'You look like the kind of man who knows how to keep order among unruly clerics. I understand you are a proctor.'

Michael nodded. 'And if my University is ever suppressed, or I despair of scholarship, I shall come here and teach you how to control spirited young men.'

'Then I shall write to the King immediately, and ask him to put an end to the *studium generale* at Cambridge,' said Bresley with a tired smile. 'God knows, I could do with you.'

'I am sure the bishop told you that I have been charged to investigate Aylmer's death,' said Michael. 'Do you have any ideas regarding his killer?'

Bresley shook his head. 'Although Aylmer's appointment was unpopular with virtually every cleric in the minster. They interpreted it as a sign that Miller had started the process of invading their domain.'

'I am told you side with Miller,' said Michael.

'I have attempted to befriend him, in the hope of reducing the animosity between the two factions. Some folk claim I betray my colleagues by taking such a stance, but they are wrong. Indeed, Miller's company at dinner is invariably an ordeal. He is not mannerly, and I am obliged to endure spitting, teeth-wiping, nose-picking and belching in my quest for an end to the hostilities.'

'So *you* did not mind Aylmer's nomination as a Vicar Choral?'

'On the contrary, I minded very much. While such a move *could* have ameliorated the trouble between Guild and Commonalty, in this case it would have made matters very much worse. Aylmer was debauched and dishonest, and would not have made a good deputy – although he probably would have fitted in with his new colleagues well enough, given time. Like attracts like, after all.'

'Did anyone else object to him?'

'The Guild, obviously. They also thought it was the Commonalty's way of clawing into their territory. Kelby and Dalderby complained to the bishop, but Gynewell told them the decision belonged to the relevant canon. It is fortunate for your friend that he is a Suttone. Everyone likes the Suttones, and will forgive them a good deal.'

'I understand you have voiced an opinion about the Hugh Chalice,' said Michael, turning to another matter. 'You are wary of its sanctity, unlike your bishop.'

The dean nodded unhappily. 'Gynewell said he could feel the holiness emanating from it, but I could not. I still had the urge to . . . well, suffice to say that I think it is just a goblet.'

'The urge to what?' asked Bartholomew.

'It does not matter. When – if – the real Hugh Chalice does come to Lincoln, I shall know it.'

Michael raised his eyebrows. 'How?'

Bresley grabbed the monk's arm suddenly. 'Hell's teeth! Look who is heading our way! I must bid you good morning, gentlemen, because I have no wish to talk to *him* this morning.'

Dean Bresley was gone before Michael could open his mouth to say he had not finished asking questions, and his place was taken by a grinning priest with freckles and an arrogant swagger. His clothes were of the finest quality, and he wore spurs on his boots, which sat oddly with his monastic attire. So did the sword that was concealed – but only barely – under his fur-lined cloak.

'Brother Michael, I presume?' he said, bowing. 'I am John Tetford. You were kind enough to appoint me as your Vicar Choral. Did you like our singing? I was the solo tenor.'

'Very nice,' said Michael. 'Why are you carrying that weapon in a church?'

'Because I might meet Ravenser,' replied Tetford, un-abashed by the censure in Michael's voice. 'He is in here somewhere, and you will not want me run through before I can take up my duties.'

'Why does Ravenser mean you harm?' Michael's expression was cold and angry, and Bartholomew saw that his first real foray into his new cathedral had left him far from impressed.

'There was a misunderstanding over a lady,' replied

Tetford with a careless grin. 'It will not happen again, not now I know what kind of man *she* allows in her bed. I have standards, you know.'

Michael eyed him balefully. 'You confess to enjoying women now, as well as to harbouring violent feelings towards your fellow clerics?'

'Self-protection, Brother. And I will not attack Ravenser unless he attacks me first. However, I shall cut back on the encounters with the fair sex, if it makes you happy.'

'Yes, you will,' said Michael sternly. '*I* have standards, too, and if I find you breaking *any* of the cathedral's rules, I shall dismiss you and appoint another deputy.'

'You can try,' said Tetford insolently, 'but I doubt my uncle will allow it.'

'Your uncle?' asked Bartholomew.

'The Bishop of Ely,' explained Tetford. 'Well, he *refers* to me as his nephew – along with my several cousins – but the reality is that he has no siblings of his own, so I am sure you can guess the real nature of our relationship. He will not cast stones.'

'De Lisle will not favour you for long if you bray about his youthful indiscretions,' said Michael icily. 'He is ambitious, and will not let a "nephew" stand in his way. So, behave yourself – unless you want to be branded a bastard, and prevented from holding any sort of office in the Church.'

Tetford turned sullen. 'You are a tedious man. Uncle said you were fun, but I do not think I shall invite you to my alehouse of an evening. You can go somewhere boring and respectable instead, like the Swan.'

Michael tried not to gape. 'You run a hostelry?'

'The Tavern in the Close. It is a lively place, only ever frequented by clerics – and the occasional lady, of course. Gynewell and the dean keep trying to close it down, but they will never succeed. People enjoy it too much, even the dean, on occasion. Everyone needs fun from time to time.'

'You have until next Sunday to mend your ways,' said Michael, struggling to regain his composure. 'You will shut the Tavern in the Close, resist female company, and decline strong drink. If you do not, I shall appoint another Vicar Choral. De Lisle will not object when he finds out why.'

'He already knows my foibles, Brother,' said Tetford smugly. 'You and I can have a contest of wills if you like, but be warned that you will not win. You would do better concentrating on finding out who killed Aylmer. I assume Gynewell asked you to oblige him with an investigation? He told me at breakfast yesterday that he intended to do so.'

'He told *you*?' asked Michael in patent disbelief. 'Why would he do that? He seems a decent man, and I do not see him wasting time in idle chatter with lowly Vicars Choral.'

Tetford did not seem offended by the insult, but his grin faded and his voice dropped to a murmur. 'Do not tell my colleagues this, but I liked Aylmer – he was fun. So, I asked Gynewell what he planned to do about the murder. At the same time, I happened to mention what Uncle has told me about your investigative skills. You had better find Aylmer's killer, Brother, or I will not be the only one disappointed.'

'Is that so?' asked Michael unmoved. 'And who else will have me quaking in fear, pray? Gynewell certainly did not issue threats when he gave me this commission, and Bishop de Lisle is too far away to care whether I succeed or fail.'

'I refer to Adam Miller. He and his Commonalty hold a lot of power in this town. You will not want to begin your new appointment by annoying *them*, and Aylmer was one of their number.'

'Then how do you know *they* did not kill him?' asked Michael. 'A falling-out among thieves?'

'They are not thieves,' said Tetford, glancing quickly behind him, to see whether anyone had heard. 'They call themselves merchants, so watch the name-calling, please. Langar sued the last man who referred to Miller as a felon, and the courts forced Kelby to pay an entire year's profits to make reparation for the insult.'

'Langar,' mused Michael. 'He is—'

'I suppose you might have come across him, if you were in Cambridge two decades ago,' interrupted Tetford before Michael could say what he knew. 'He was a law-clerk at the castle there.'

Bartholomew was puzzled. 'If I recall correctly, a clerk called Langar advised the Justice over the Shirlok case, and—'

Tetford flung out a hand to silence him, looking around in alarm. 'Do not even *whisper* that name in Lincoln! Everyone knows that a man called Shirlok made untruthful allegations against Miller and some of his friends in Cambridge, and was hanged for it, but Miller is sensitive about the incident, even today. Not even his deadliest enemies dare mention it these days, and if you want to see your University again, I recommend you follow their example.'

'We shall bear it in mind,' said Michael coolly. 'It was not the trial we were discussing, though: it was Langar. How did he come to leave his post with a Justice to work for a "merchant"?'

Tetford remained uneasy. 'I was told the Justice died shortly after Miller's acquittal, and Langar decided to enter private practice instead. He came to Lincoln, and is Miller's legal adviser. Can we talk about something else?'

Michael turned to Bartholomew. 'This is becoming very

196

complicated. There are connections everywhere, and I cannot decide which are significant and which are irrelevant.'

Bartholomew was troubled. 'This might be important, though. If Langar was involved in the Shirlok trial, then he knew Aylmer twenty years ago.'

Tetford was clearly unsettled by the discussion. 'If you must ignore my advice, then at least keep your voices down. It is Friday, and the members of the Commonalty always come to light candles at about this time. Miller might hear you, and while I shall be more than happy to inherit your prebendal stall when he kills you, my uncle will be sorry to learn you dead and I do not want him upset.'

Michael glared. 'I doubt someone like you will ever be installed as a canon. But time is wasting, and I have a lot to do today. I was told to come here for a fitting. Where are the vestments?'

Tetford gestured to a nearby tomb, over which several garments had been slung. 'It is my responsibility to find you something suitable and arrange for any necessary alterations. I was expecting someone smaller, however, and I am not sure we have anything big enough for you.'

Michael's eyes narrowed. 'Is your Chapter composed of insignificant men with no stature, then?'

'It is not your height that is the problem,' explained Tetford bluntly. 'It is your width. Try on this alb, Brother. It is the largest we have.'

Glowering indignantly, Michael stepped forward and allowed Tetford to put the garment over his head. Albs were ankle-length robes with wide sleeves, but the one Tetford gave Michael barely reached his knees and was embarrassingly snug. Bartholomew looked away, not wanting to be seen laughing.

'I cannot wear this,' objected Michael, aghast. 'It would not be big enough for Little Hugh!'

'It is tight,' agreed Tetford. He was thoughtful for a moment, then brightened. 'I know a lady who is very skilled with a needle. She might be able to take a few strips from an old altar frontal, and make this longer and wider. She is rather good, and no one will notice her repairs, especially if we all drink to your health the evening before the installation. No one notices much after a night in *my* tavern.'

Michael glared at him. 'If this is just an excuse to visit women with my blessing, I shall not be pleased. You may see her – although not at night, obviously – but I shall expect to be presented with an alb that fits. What about my almuce? Canons are supposed to wear fur-lined almuces.'

Tetford rubbed his chin as he considered the garment that covered a priest's shoulders. 'I had better discuss that with Rosanna, too.' He held up a green item with gold trimmings. 'However, you will like this. It is the special cope of Deuxevers cloth.'

Michael slipped into it, and was relieved when it fitted. 'At last! I was beginning to think I might have to go through the ceremony stark naked.'

'I found it in a chest belonging to a canon who died several years ago. It was in the attic of my alehouse, so do not be too damning about such places. If I had not been an innkeeper, I would not have found the box, and you might well have gone to the Stall of South Scarle in a state of nature.'

'Who was this canon?' asked Michael. 'I shall say a mass for him tomorrow.'

'I doubt even your prayers will save Hodelston from the fires of Hell,' said Tetford cheerfully. 'He was a dreadful fellow, well past redemption.'

Michael hauled the garment from his shoulders and

hurled it away. 'Hodelston? He died during the Death! And you hand me his cope to wear? Matt!'

'You cannot catch the plague from clothes after all these years,' said Bartholomew, hoping it was true. 'And I was under the impression that Hodelston did not die from the pestilence anyway.'

'He was probably poisoned,' agreed Tetford, picking up the cope and thrusting it into the monk's reluctant hands. 'And you are not in a position to be choosy, Brother, so just be grateful we have found *something* that fits. Well, we are finished just in time, because Miller is coming this way and he is making gestures that suggest he wants to talk to you.'

'Perhaps he is, but I do not care to meet *him*,' said Michael, beginning to move in the opposite direction.

Tetford grabbed his arm. 'I am fond of my uncle, so I shall give his spy some good advice: do not run, because Miller will assume you are afraid of him. And he has a nasty habit of extorting money from timid people. Master Miller! Good morning.'

'Maybe it is,' replied the man who had approached them. He sounded cagey. 'Or maybe it isn't. It depends.' He leaned to one side and spat on the cathedral's fine stone floor.

Instinctively, Bartholomew went to stand next to Michael, his hand resting on the hilt of his dagger. Adam Miller was squat and heavy, like a bull, and the three people at his heels carried enough weapons to equip the English army. Bartholomew recognised all four, although they were older than when he had last seen them. Miller had suffered most from the ravages of time. His skin had turned leathery and he had lost all his teeth except four yellow lower incisors; what little hair that remained was white.

Behind him stood the man Shirlok had named as Walter

Chapman, a skinny fellow in his red hose, who looked just as disreputable as he had in Cambridge two decades before. Bartholomew wondered what Simon had been thinking of, to buy a relic from someone like Chapman, since everything about him screamed that he lived on the wrong side of the law – just like Miller, in fact.

Next to Chapman was the man who had kept the record of the Cambridge trial so many years ago, the ginger-haired clerk called William Langar. He had clearly done well for himself, because he was by far the best dressed of the quartet, and his fingers were adorned with so many rings that Bartholomew could only suppose he hired a scribe to write for him now. His eyes were dark and unreadable, and Bartholomew had the sense that he was deceitful.

The last person was a burly matron with a square face and small eyes, who gripped a stave as though she was considering braining someone with it. Lora Boyner, thought Bartholomew, recalling the way she had yelled her innocence when Shirlok had made his accusations. In all, they were a disreputable crowd, and he sincerely hoped they would not remember him.

'This is Brother Michael,' said Tetford, bowing and grinning in a way that suggested he was terrified. Bartholomew wondered whether he knew about Miller's exploitation of faint-hearted men from personal experience. 'And his colleague Bartholomew. I would introduce you to their friend, Thomas Suttone, but he is not with them, and—'

'Thank you, Tetford,' said Langar softly. 'You may leave us now.'

Miller spat again when Tetford had scuttled away. Bartholomew itched to reprimand him, but there was something about the easy way the man held his weapons that stopped him. Miller might be old, but the physician sensed he was still a formidable fighter, and there was no point in starting a brawl he would not win by asking him to gob outside. He suspected the man's cronies were equally adept with their weapons, with the possible exception of Chapman, who just looked like a petty thief.

'I understand you have instigated a special market, for the poor,' said Michael pleasantly, when no one else said anything. 'What a charming notion. December is cold and gloomy, and it is heart-warming to hear of merchants being generous in such a cheerless season.'

'Thank you,' said Miller, revealing his four fangs in a smile. His eyes remained cold. 'I had to do something, because people were frightened of me, and it was becoming difficult to get anything done.'

'Fear has its advantages,' said Langar in a sibilant hiss that was infinitely more sinister than his friend's gravely tones. 'It means people are willing to do whatever we ask. However, it also means that sometimes they are so nervous, they make mistakes. And that is a nuisance. I suggested the Market as a good way to alleviate the problem.'

'It is working,' said Chapman. 'The unemployed weavers love us now. Unfortunately our largess has had unforeseen consequences: other folk have flocked to the city to take advantage of our generosity, and it is proving difficult to exclude villains.'

'I am sure it is,' murmured Michael, thinking that Chapman was probably in a good position to recognise them, since he was so clearly one himself. It occurred to him to ask how he had come by the Hugh Chalice, but decided Chapman was more likely to be persuaded to tell the truth when his friends were not looming protectively around him. 'Why are people so afraid of you?'

'Because those who displease me have accidents,' replied Miller darkly.

'And he is very easily displeased,' added Lora in a voice that was even deeper than Miller's.

'If you take our meaning,' said Chapman, fingering his dagger.

'But I did not come here to make threats,' said Miller. Langar stared at his shoes and the physician was under the impression that he was trying not to laugh at his friends' crude tactics. 'I came to ask if you know who murdered Aylmer. He was my friend, and I was vexed when I heard he had been stabbed. I want the culprit.'

'I have not identified the killer,' replied Michael. 'But then I have barely started my investigation.'

'You sound confident, though,' said Langar thoughtfully. 'Are you?'

Michael shrugged. 'I shall do my best.'

Miller spat again, and wiped his mouth on the back of his hand. 'When you find the rogue, I shall expect you to tell me his name immediately. Before you tell the bishop.'

'Why would I do that?' asked Michael, startled.

Miller sighed in a way that suggested he thought the monk was stupid. 'Because if the culprit is a clerk – and Aylmer had plenty of enemies in holy orders – the rogue will claim benefit of clergy. I do not want to traipse to some remote monastery to stick my dagger in his gizzard. I want to do it here.'

Michael raised his eyebrows in astonishment. 'You want me to confide in you, so you can murder him if he is a priest? And you are asking me to do this in a cathedral? A sacred House of God?'

'Yes,' said Miller, bemused in his turn. 'What part do you not understand?'

'Nothing,' said Michael, defeated. 'I shall bear your request in mind.'

'Thank you,' said Miller. 'I appreciate your co-operation

and will do something nice for you in return. I learned from Sheriff Lungspee that a favour deserves a favour, and it is a lesson that has served me well. Or would you prefer money? It is your choice.'

'Neither,' said Michael, affronted. 'Canons-elect do not accept bribes.'

Miller was as offended by the response as Michael was by the offer. 'No canon – elect or otherwise – has refused them in the past, and I do not like my generosity rejected.'

'We shall give you time to reconsider,' said Langar, keen to avoid a confrontation that would serve no purpose. 'And while you investigate Aylmer's death, I shall look into Nicholas Herl's. Both were members of the Commonalty, and we are determined to know what happened to them.'

'His wife told us what you found when you inspected Herl's body,' said Miller to Bartholomew. 'We are grateful for your help. Are you fastidious, like the monk, or will you accept a reward?'

Bartholomew heartily wished he had declined Sabina's request. 'There is no clear evidence of foul play,' he said, avoiding the question. 'Herl's death may have been an accident.'

'I concluded the same, in the light of your findings,' said Langar. He gave a humourless smile at Bartholomew's surprise. 'Your monk is not the only one with the wits to unravel mysteries.'

Chapman grinned at the scholars. 'Langar was a law-clerk, and knows many cunning tricks. It was his cleverness that made us what we are today – combined with Miller's talents, of course.'

Bartholomew suddenly became aware that Langar was studying him rather intently. 'You look familiar,' said the lawyer. 'I know you hail from Cambridge, but have you been there long? John Suttone told us his cousin was a fairly recent arrival, and I know from Tetford that Brother Michael has only been there a decade. But what about you?'

'He and I became Fellows at almost the same time,' said Michael, before Bartholomew could reply for himself. 'He studied at Oxford first, then Paris.'

Langar was too clever to be misled, and regarded the physician thoughtfully. 'No, I never forget a face, and you *were* in Cambridge when ten good people were accused of wicked crimes by a rogue called Shirlok. I was a clerk at the time, employed to keep records for the Justice. But Miller, Aylmer, Lora, Chapman and dear Nicholas suffered from Shirlok's mean tongue.'

'You forgot to mention Sabina,' said Chapman, while Miller's face creased into a bleak scowl. Bartholomew saw Tetford had been right to warn them against discussing the trial: it *was* still a sore point with the man. 'Shirlok tried to indict her, too.'

'I did not forget,' said Langar coldly. 'I just choose not to utter her name. Hateful woman!'

'Shirlok named my poor brother, Simon, too – God rest his sainted soul,' said Miller angrily. 'And three others, also now dead. It was a wicked business, but right prevailed, and we were released. Thank God for English justice.'

'Amen,' said Bartholomew, drawing on his recent experience with the Gilbertines and ignoring the startled look Michael shot him. He intended to follow Tetford's advice and stay well away from discussing the case with Miller, especially given his own suspicions about the 'English justice' that had been meted out that day.

Langar continued to stare. 'It was a painful incident for Master Miller, so I am sure you can be trusted not to mention it to any guildsmen. They know what happened, of course, but there is no point in giving them cause to resurrect the matter.'

'There is nothing to mention,' said Michael soothingly. 'It was a long time ago, and we are more interested in what happened to Aylmer this week. Do *you* have any idea who might have killed him?'

It was Miller who replied. 'Dean Bresley might have done it, to prevent him from becoming a Vicar Choral. Aylmer was a bit of a thief, you see, and holy men take against thieves, which is unkind. After all, Jesus was crucified with two of them, and they all went to Heaven. Then there is Bishop Gynewell, who also objected to Aylmer on moral grounds.'

'Gynewell would hardly have asked me to investigate, if he was the culprit,' said Michael, deciding not to comment on Miller's singular interpretation of the scriptures.

Langar gave a sly smile. 'Or he might have asked you to investigate specifically to *conceal* his guilt. Do not take everything at face value, Brother.'

'It was Hamo,' said Lora with malicious satisfaction. 'He disliked Aylmer being in his convent, and asked Prior Roger to eject him. Roger was going to do it, too, until we passed him a few coins.'

'And *there* is another possibility,' said Langar. 'Prior Roger, killing an unwanted guest *after* Aylmer's non-refundable rent had been paid. Roger needs money desperately, but he also has a duty to preserve his convent's integrity. And even Aylmer's best friends cannot tell you he was a saint.'

'Then there is the sanctimonious John Suttone,' added Miller. 'There is no way he can be as ethical as he would have everyone believe. It would be unnatural. And his fellow priests would kill their own grandmothers for a penny. Although I understand that position, because my grandam—'

'We have other suspects, too, beside clerics,' interrupted

Langar, before Miller could incriminate himself. 'Dalderby is angry with us, because Thoresby was acquitted of threatening to behead him.'

'And *Kelby* would do anything to hurt me,' said Miller. He spat again. 'He once called me a pugilist. I had to ask Langar what it meant, and was offended when he told me.'

'Of course,' said Chapman helpfully, 'if the killer manages to confound you, Brother, you can always eavesdrop at the General Pardon, and see if anyone confesses to the murder.'

'The killer will never confess here,' said Miller scornfully. 'No felon wants the cathedral priests to know about his most intimate crimes. I certainly do not.'

'God's teeth,' breathed Bartholomew when they had gone. 'That was unpleasant! Miller, Chapman and Lora are bullies in positions of power, and I am not surprised they are obliged to hold fairs to win people's favour. But Langar seems dangerous. I imagine Chapman was right when he said Miller's coterie rose on the back of his cunning. Miller might be the man who appears to be in charge, but I will wager anything that the real master is Langar.'

Michael shook his head. 'Langar is sly, but there is no great strength in him. He may be full of ideas and plans, but it is Miller's brutality that keeps them going. Regardless, I see why de Wetherset said we would not want to dine with them: the minster is awash with spit.'

'I wish Langar had not recognised me from Shirlok's trial. I told you there was something corrupt about that day, and I imagine *that* is the reason they ordered me not to mention it to anyone here.'

'Very likely, so take Cynric with you if you go out after dark. We do not want you stabbed to ensure your silence. I intend to leave Lincoln as soon as I can, and your murder would delay me.'

206

'I am pleased you have my welfare at heart, Brother.'
'Always, Matt. Always.'

Bartholomew was unsettled by the danger he felt they were in, and wanted to analyse logically what they had learned. It was already late afternoon, and there was not much daylight left, so they began to walk back to the Gilbertine Priory, discussing the case as they went.

'I wonder if Gynewell knew what he was asking when he ordered me to find Aylmer's killer,' said Michael unhappily. 'Or perhaps he dislikes the notion of having a canon foisted on him who is an agent for a rival bishop, and hopes the investigation might see me killed. Meanwhile, Langar's concern over what you might have seen in Cambridge all those years ago indicates that you are probably right when you say there was something odd about the verdict.'

'No one else seems suspicious of it, though,' said Bartholomew. 'The tales in Lincoln seem to revolve around the fact that they were accused in the first place, not about the legitimacy of the acquittal. We should ask de Wetherset what really happened that day. He *must* know the truth – he was a juror.'

'No, we should not,' said Michael firmly. 'That might tell Miller you are asking questions about the incident. Besides, de Wetherset told us Miller invited him to dinner, and it sounds as though they had a merry old time convincing each other of their mutual harmlessness.'

'Or money exchanged hands in return for de Wetherset's silence. He was very indignant when I asked whether he had been bribed, and that level of outrage is often indicative of a guilty conscience.'

'Or indicative of the fact that you had just accused him of being corrupt. He was a University Chancellor, Matt, and while you may not have liked or trusted him, there are moral boundaries across which some men will not pass.'

'However, they may not be the same limits as those set by honest men,' Bartholomew pointed out. 'But you are right: there is no point in quizzing de Wetherset, because he will not give us truthful answers anyway. Why should he, when admitting to corruption might mean his stall is withdrawn?'

'And more importantly, he may tell Miller about your interest, and that is something we should definitely avoid. This may come as a surprise to you, but you are my friend, and I do not want to lose you to an assassin's dagger. You must leave de Wetherset and Miller alone.'

'They are both connected to Aylmer, Brother. How will we solve his murder if you plan to keep clear of them? And there is the Hugh Chalice. I still do not understand how that fits into your case, although I am sure it is significant, since Aylmer was holding it when he died.'

Michael rubbed his chin. 'I wonder why he did that. It belonged to Simon, not him.'

'The consensus seems to be that he was going to steal it.'

'Right. And *that* means the murder may have nothing to do with Miller or his shady acquittal, and more to do with the fact that someone objected to Aylmer laying sticky fingers on a sacred object.'

'Simon is the obvious candidate. He says he has an alibi in his singing, but he does not.'

Michael agreed. 'The Gilbertines work themselves to such a state of ecstasy that I doubt they have the faintest idea what anyone else is doing.'

'Did you notice that de Wetherset has changed his story? What he told us initially – that he attended prime with Simon in the convent on the day of Aylmer's murder – was not what he said this morning. Today he claimed he had joined the Gilbertines on his first day as a guest in their priory, but found it too noisy, and has opted for something quieter ever since. *Ergo,* he is lying about something.'

'I wondered whether you had picked up on that. Now, why he would tell us untruths?'

Bartholomew pulled his cloak more closely around him when a snowflake spiralled down and landed on his cheek. A second followed, and he saw they were in for another cold night. Dusk was on them, and lights were already burning in the Wigford houses. They passed the Church of the Holy Cross, and he saw the blackened shell of the priest's house in its graveyard. He recalled that de Wetherset had lived with Simon before a blaze had driven them to take refuge with the Gilbertines.

'Cynric made some enquiries about that in the taverns,' he said, nodding towards the ruin. 'Sheriff Lungspee was able to deduce that the cause was accidental – a brazier had been left burning by mistake. Simon and de Wetherset managed to escape with their belongings, and Simon's successor is lodging with a relative until the house can be rebuilt.'

Michael glanced at him. 'You sound unsure. Do you think they let the fire rage deliberately?'

Bartholomew shrugged, then nodded. 'The inferno made everyone sorry for Simon, and he was immediately offered a prebendal stall. You have to wonder whether he had been promised such an honour, but it was taking too long to come, so he drew attention to himself with a misfortune – a misfortune that did not cost him any of his possessions, given that he still had plenty of money to buy the Hugh Chalice.'

'And I am sure Chapman charged him a princely fee,' mused Michael.

'Perhaps de Wetherset is willing to lie for Simon because he was warned of the conflagration and it saved his life.

209

Or perhaps it was de Wetherset's carelessness that caused the fire.'

'Possibly, although I still cannot see him engaging in such unsavoury activities. However, none of this is relevant to Aylmer – unlike the Hugh Chalice. Shall we go to see it?' Michael's voice was oddly casual. 'We are almost at the Gilbertine convent, thank the good Lord. It is cold out tonight. Can you see that frost sparkling on the Eleanor Cross?'

Bartholomew glanced at it, and remembered poking icicles off Matilde's eaves with a broom handle – she had been afraid they might fall and hurt someone. He wondered whether she had recruited someone else to do it now, and whether she would be settled with another man when – and if – he ever found her. Suddenly, the night seemed colder and darker, and his prospects of happiness bleak.

The physician followed Michael through the Gilbertines' main gate, where they were saluted cheerfully by Hamo, and then across the yard to the chapel. The ground was frozen hard, and dusted with new snow. Inside, candles and lamps gave the chapel a cosy feel, although the air was frigid, and his breath billowed in front of him. Then he saw why the monk had been so keen to inspect the chalice. Vespers had just ended, and one of the congregation had lingered to say additional prayers.

That evening, Christiana de Hauville's slender form was accentuated by a tight, front-laced kirtle, and her fret – the net that covered her hair – was of gold. Although she was kneeling, she still managed to adopt the current fashionable posture for women, with abdomen thrust forward and back curved, which was meant to reveal them as ladies of breeding and style. Because all the Gilbertines had gone to their refectory for something to drink, Bartholomew could only suppose the display of courtly deportment was for Michael's benefit. The monk's expression was unreadable as he made his way towards her, and Bartholomew watched uneasily.

Christiana was not alone, however. When the monk would have gone to kneel next to her, a figure stepped out of the shadows and intercepted him. It was Sabina Herl. She held a basket over her arm, and looked bored and cold.

'I have been told to act as chaperon,' she said, and the tone of her voice suggested she was not very happy about it. 'Dame Eleanor is still at the cathedral, and Hamo says that Lady Christiana should not be here alone in the dark, despite the fact that this is a convent, and you would think she would be safe.'

Bartholomew saw a grimace of genuine annoyance flick across Christiana's beautiful face, and supposed she had objected to the Brother Hospitaller's cosseting, too.

'I see,' said Michael, hands folded in his wide sleeves. 'Well, she is not alone now, because I am here.'

Sabina was amused. 'I do not think Hamo would accept you as a suitable substitute for Dame Eleanor, Brother. But why did you come? To pray? To admire the Hugh Chalice?'

Before the monk could reply, Christiana stood, took the cup from the altar, and came to hand it to him. Their fingers touched briefly, before she returned to the cushion on which she had been kneeling. She was clearly aware that she cut a fine figure from behind, because her hips swayed provocatively and she did not need to look around to know Michael's eyes were fixed appreciatively on them.

'What do you think?' asked Bartholomew. The monk regarded him askance. 'Of the chalice, Brother! What do you think of the chalice?'

211

Michael tore his attention away from Christiana's trim shape, and looked at the goblet. 'It is very small, and too tarnished to be handsome, although someone has tried to buff it up. Is it silver?'

Bartholomew shrugged. 'I have no idea how to tell. However, I do know that some kinds of tin can be made to gleam like precious metals.'

Michael turned the cup over in his hands. 'Even if it is silver, it is thin and light, and I doubt it is worth much for its weight alone. Is there a carving on it? My eyes are not good in dim light.'

'It is worn, but I think there might be a child with a halo around its head.'

Michael squinted at it. 'As Simon told us so condescendingly, a Baby Jesus etched on a chalice is often associated with St Hugh – it is one of his icons. I suppose that might mean it is authentic.'

A shadow suddenly materialised at the physician's side. It was Cynric. Michael leapt so violently that the goblet flew from his fingers and clattered to the floor. Christiana turned to gape at him, and Sabina issued a shriek of alarm, so the monk hastened to cover his clumsiness by pretending he had done it on purpose.

'It *is* silver,' he pronounced authoritatively, bending to retrieve it. 'See how easily it dents?'

'Be careful, Brother!' breathed Cynric, round-eyed with shock. 'St Hugh may not like his relic tossed about like a turnip. Of course, it is probably a fake, but you would be wise to be wary, nonetheless.'

'You should not creep up on people like that,' hissed Michael irritably, once Christiana had turned back to her prayers. 'And how is it that *you* are suddenly in a position to make declarations about the authenticity of sacred cups?'

212

'I have a good sense for what is holy,' objected Cynric, hurt by the reprimand. 'And a good sense for what is *un*holy, too. Speaking of unholy, did you see Bishop Gynewell's statue in the cathedral? It is in the Angel Choir, looking longingly at Queen Eleanor's Visceral Tomb. It is probably trying to work out how to get inside and earn itself a meal.'

'Gynewell does not like to be reminded of the similarity between him and the imp,' said Michael. 'So you had better keep your thoughts to yourself, unless you want to feel the end of his pitchfork.'

'You think he might attack me?' asked Cynric, appalled. 'He is definitely one of Satan's own. Master Quarrel of the Swan tavern told me that the fellow likes so much hot spice in his food, it is inedible to mere mortals. And he wears a Dominican habit to conceal his tail.'

'Quarrel told you that?' asked Bartholomew, startled.

'Not the bit about the tail,' admitted Cynric. 'That is my own conclusion. You see, I have been in alehouses all afternoon, listening to gossip for you about Aylmer. Since I was there, I decided to ask a few questions about Gynewell, too. I went to the Swan first, then the Angel. The Swan is preferred by guildsmen, and the Angel is frequented by the Commonalty.'

'What did you find out?' asked Michael. 'About Aylmer, I mean, not Gynewell.'

'He arrived about twenty years ago – a few weeks *after* Miller – and immediately started work as Miller's scribe. Then Langar came, and was better at clerking, so Aylmer elected to dabble in various other trades instead, but was never very successful. Apparently, he always *said* he was in holy orders, but no one believed him, so he was obliged to take his vows again a month ago. He was accused of theft, see, and needed to claim benefit of clergy. It is all wrong, if you ask me, and there will be a rebellion. People do not like priests tried by different rules to the rest of us.'

'So you have been saying for years,' said Michael, well aware of Cynric's seditious sentiments. 'What did he steal?'

'A cup,' said Cynric. 'It *may* have been the Hugh Chalice, but the men at the Swan could not be sure. The fellow who lodged the complaint was Flaxfleete, but he withdrew his accusation when the property was returned. Word is that the bishop did it.'

'Did what?' asked Michael, confused. 'Stole whatever it was that Aylmer was accused of taking?'

'Returned it to its rightful owner,' said Cynric impatiently. 'And the other thing I learned was that Aylmer was good at Latin, and mocked priests who were not. They did not like that at all, apparently, especially John Suttone and Simon. I shall try listening to gossip in a few more taverns tomorrow.'

'No,' said Bartholomew worriedly. 'Miller suspects I witnessed Shirlok's trial, and Michael's investigation has a dangerous feel to it. You will not be safe in these places.'

Cynric regarded him askance. 'I can look after myself. The only thing *I* fear is Bishop Gynewell. So, I had better say a few incantations, to ward him off.'

While he went to kneel next to Christiana, Michael approached Sabina, who was rubbing chicken droppings off the eggs in her basket. 'You are freezing,' he said sympathetically.

She nodded, blowing on her hands. 'I do not understand how Lady Christiana can kneel for so long in here. Dame Eleanor is the same. They both spend hours at shrines and in chapels.'

'You said you were ordered to work at this priory as penance for kissing Aylmer behind the stables,' said Michael. 'How long did you say you had known him?'

'I did not confide that particular detail. Why? Would you like to steal a few kisses from me, now he is not here?'

Michael glared at her. 'How long have you known Aylmer?' he repeated.

She sighed. 'We were friends for years. He was fond of Nicholas, and often visited our house.'

'But your Nicholas died before Aylmer did,' said Michael thoughtfully. 'So Aylmer could not have been killed by *that* jealous husband.'

Sabina's expression was wry. '*Especially* not by that one. Nicholas loved Langar, not me.'

'Nicholas was Langar's lover?' asked Michael, startled.

Suddenly, Bartholomew had the answers to several questions – why Sabina had never seen the scar on her husband's shoulder, and why she had been willing to marry a man she did not love. Nicholas had given her a home; she had reciprocated by providing him with a respectable image; and they had both gone about their separate lives unfettered. And the physician recalled Langar's angry reaction when Sabina was mentioned earlier that day; the lawyer had been envious of the relationship Nicholas had shared with his wife, regardless of the fact that it had almost certainly been chaste.

'You and Nicholas were still friends, though, which is why you are keen to know how he died,' he said. 'And you also mentioned that you would have preferred to marry Aylmer, but he was in holy orders. He took his vows a month ago, when he was accused of stealing from Flaxfleete.'

She shook her head. 'He *re*took his vows a month ago. He was in holy orders for more than two decades, although he lived a riotous life, and few believed he was a priest. That is why he would never marry me; he said it was a step *too* far along the road of sin. However, Langar's affair with Nicholas should tell you why he is investigating *that* death, and why he is happy to let you find Aylmer's killer. He cannot do both, and has chosen the one that is important to him.'

'Could Langar have killed Aylmer?' asked Michael. 'Perhaps he thought it was Aylmer who gave Nicholas the poison that saw him topple into the Braytheford Pool and drown.'

'Aylmer did not hurt Nicholas, because he was with me that night, and Langar knows it. Hence Langar did not kill Aylmer, which is a pity for all of us. It would have made for a neat solution, and once Langar is gone, Miller and the Commonalty will fall. I would love to see Langar hang.'

'That is an interesting reaction from a woman who was accused of dire crimes at Miller's side,' said Michael. 'De Wetherset told me. I am sure you recall that he was one of the jurors.'

She stared at the floor. 'It is true, to my shame. Aylmer always said he wanted to escape from Miller and his cronies, but he never did anything about it. I have, though. I no longer take part in their evil dealings, and I am becoming a good daughter of the Church.'

'A good daughter who kisses ordained priests behind the stables?' remarked Bartholomew.

She pulled a face at him. 'I am human, with human failings. None of us is perfect.'

'Did Aylmer seem different before he died?' asked Michael, not very interested in her feeble attempts to walk the straight and narrow.

She nodded. 'He was thoughtful – contemplative. He was moved by the offer of Vicar Choral, and I think he was going to do his best for Master Suttone. He was weak, though, and the likes of Ravenser and Tetford would have urged him to mischief before long, so I doubt his good intentions would have lasted. I loved him dearly, but he was not a man for self-restraint.'

'What about the other flaws in his character,' said Michael, 'such as his dishonesty?'

'He did steal, on occasion,' she admitted. 'But I was working on that.'

'Working for how long?' asked Michael archly. 'You have known him for at least two decades, given that you were both named by Shirlok in Cambridge.'

'Shirlok,' she repeated softly. 'There is a name from the past!' She shivered, and pulled her cloak around her shoulders.

'I will guard Lady Christiana while you go to the kitchen with Cynric and Matt for a hot posset,' offered Michael generously. 'It is cold in here, and your fingers are blue. Do not worry about propriety – her virtue will be quite safe with me. I am a monk, after all.'

'But you are also a man, and Hamo said—'

'Hamo will not mind *me* playing chaperon,' asserted Michael firmly. '*I* am a Benedictine, so my morals are above reproach. Go to the kitchens, child, and warm yourself before you take a chill.'

Sabina hesitated only a moment before nodding her thanks, and Bartholomew thought he saw a sparkle of tears as she turned to leave. He wondered whether she was touched by Michael's 'thoughtfulness', or whether she still grieved for the deaths of old friends. Obediently, Cynric rose to escort her, although Bartholomew was not so easily dismissed. He hovered in the shadows.

'Do not gulp your posset,' called Michael after Sabina, as he moved towards his quarry, 'or it will do you no good. And I am in no hurry to leave.'

CHAPTER 6

In the still silence of the chapel, Bartholomew watched Michael stalk towards Christiana, and kneel next to her, placing his hands together in an attitude of prayer. Christiana glanced at him out of the corner of her eye, and Bartholomew saw her start to smile. Michael was not the most handsome of men, and was too fat to be truly attractive, but he possessed a certain allure that appealed to women. Bartholomew lingered uncertainly, not sure whether to leave them to their own devices – they were both adults, after all – or whether he would be a better friend to Michael by staying.

'Good evening, Brother,' simpered Christiana. She turned in surprise when she heard the rustle of Bartholomew's cloak. 'Doctor! I thought you had gone with Sabina.'

'So did I,' said Michael meaningfully.

'He invited me to pray with him,' lied Bartholomew, suddenly determined not to go anywhere.

'I am sure I did not,' said Michael, eyeing him coolly. 'And Prior Roger wants you to visit his hospital. There is a perplexing case of tertiary fever.'

'He said nothing to me,' said Bartholomew. 'And it must be very perplexing indeed, since nobody has tertiary fevers at this time of year.' He expected Christiana to be irritated by his stubborn refusal to leave, and was surprised to see a flash of amusement in her eyes.

'Do not stand so far away,' she said, ignoring Michael's frustrated grimace. 'Join us. We can talk about something

Hamo told me – that we all have a mutual acquaintance in a lady called Matilde.'

Bartholomew nodded as he approached. 'Hamo remembers her living in Lincoln six years ago.'

'I arrived here about a month before Mayor Spayne asked Matilde to be his wife,' said Christiana. Her expression became distant, as though she was lost in memories. 'I was preoccupied with my own troubles at the time, but I recall that quite clearly – a woman made an offer of marriage by a man she did not love. It was at that point when I realised the same thing might happen to me, once the King decides I have had long enough to recover from my grief.'

'Matilde did not love Spayne?' asked Bartholomew. 'How do you know?'

She regarded him in amusement. 'We women can tell such things, Doctor. Besides, she would have accepted his offer had she loved him, given that he is handsome, rich, kind and gentle. Her standards must be very high. As are mine.' She included Michael in her next enigmatic smile.

'You have avoided being trapped so far,' said Michael.

'Yes, but my period of grace is coming to an end. His Majesty is beginning to be exasperated.' Christiana sighed. 'I adored my first husband, and would like to feel at least a modicum of affection for the second. My mother was on the verge of marrying a man she despised, and I saw how miserable it made her.'

'Kelby,' said Michael, remembering what Suttone had told him. 'Unfortunately, she died before the ceremony could take place.'

'She did not "die", Brother,' said Christiana softly. 'She took medicine to ease a cough, and it killed her. She was with child, you see, but did not tell anyone. She swallowed

219

the electuary she was given, but it contained cuckoo-pint, which is dangerous for ladies in such a condition—'

'That was your mother?' asked Bartholomew, startled. 'We heard Ursula de Spayne had prescribed an inappropriate remedy to a pregnant woman, but no one told us her name.'

Christiana nodded. 'It was her. Matilde and my mother were friends, and Matilde was furious when she learned what Ursula had done. But, perhaps Ursula was as much a victim as anyone. My mother was deeply unhappy about the match with Kelby, and told me she would rather die than marry him. She would never have taken her own life, so she did the next best thing: she asked Ursula for a tonic, and she neglected to mention her pregnancy.'

'How could she have known Ursula's remedy would have such a deadly effect?' asked Bartholomew doubtfully. 'And I do not mean to distress you, but bringing about the premature expelling of a child is not an easy end.'

Tears sparkled in Christiana's eyes, and she rubbed them away impatiently. 'She was a devout woman, and saw her suffering as penance for what was so dangerously close to self-murder. She had been caring for the hospital inmates here, so had some knowledge about the medicinal properties of plants. I think she knew exactly what she was doing when she asked for that particular electuary.'

'If your mother did not love Kelby, then who was the father of her child?' asked Michael.

Christiana managed the ghost of a smile. 'That is an ungentlemanly question, Brother! However, not all couplings take place with both parties willing, and my mother was given an unpleasant glimpse of her life to come.'

'I am sorry,' said Bartholomew. 'Did Matilde know about . . . ?'

'My mother's rape? I doubt it. It is not the kind of thing

220

one chatters about, and Matilde would have been very angry. She would have said or done something to make matters worse. If you know her, then you will be aware that this is true.'

'She would not have ignored it,' acknowledged Bartholomew. 'Did your mother tell you all this?'

Christiana nodded. 'To warn me against taking a man *I* do not like. Our lives had been parallel until then – both married at fifteen, and widows ten years later. She urged me to take the veil rather than accept a man who is unworthy, and she told me why. I have shared this with very few people, and I am uncertain why I am confiding in you now. Perhaps it is because you have a kind face, Brother.'

Michael inclined his head. 'Your confidences are safe with us.'

'It is not really a secret, although you will appreciate the subject is a painful one for me. So, based on her advice, I informed His Majesty that I would rather become a nun than accept a man I do not like, and since the Crown will not benefit financially if I join a convent, he is prepared to grant me a degree of leeway.'

'There is nothing wrong with life in the cloister,' said Michael.

'Maybe not for men, who can enrol at universities and ride across the country to accept lucrative honours. But women are locked away until they grow old enough to be abbesses, at which point they prefer to stay at home by the fire. It is no life for a lady with an enquiring mind.'

'There are ways around those difficulties,' began Michael. 'I am—'

'Did Matilde tell your mother where she might go, if she ever left Lincoln?' blurted Bartholomew, certain the monk was about to regale her with a list of ways to enjoy amorous liaisons without being caught, and equally certain he would be no friend if he let him do so.

Christiana dabbed her eyes with her sleeve, and took a deep breath, relieved to be discussing something else. 'Matilde once expressed a desire to see Cambridge, and she said she had kin in Poitiers.'

'She is not at either of those places now,' said Bartholomew unhappily.

Christiana regarded him with a puzzled frown. 'You told Hamo that you just hoped to renew an acquaintance with Matilde, but it seems to me that you want to do rather more than that.'

'Everyone at Michaelhouse loved Matilde,' said Michael when Bartholomew hesitated, trying to think of a way to reply without revealing too much about his intentions. 'And we were concerned when she left Cambridge so abruptly. All we want is to be sure she is safe and happy.'

'She once told us a story,' said Christiana. Her eyes became distant again, as if she had transported herself to another time. 'It was about a woman about to be pressed into an unwelcome marriage, but she conspired to disappear so completely that no one ever knew what happened to her. Matilde's purpose was to show my mother that there was an alternative to life with Kelby, but it also proved to me that she knew how to make herself vanish, too. I was under the impression she had done it before – perhaps even that it was her own story she was telling.'

Bartholomew nodded. It was not the first time he had been warned that Matilde had known what she was doing when she had left Cambridge. And she *had* once confided to him that she had escaped a betrothal by running away.

'Disappearing can be useful in a convent,' said Michael conversationally. 'A wise monk or nun always knows how to find a quiet spot, away from enquiring eyes.'

'Is that so?' asked Christiana, wide-eyed. 'And how might that be achieved, when one's every move is watched? Hamo and his brethren are very solicitous of me.'

'Do you know anything about Aylmer's death?' asked Bartholomew, determined to prevent the monk from teaching her sly tricks. Michael shot him an unreadable glance.

Christiana folded her hands in her sleeves. 'I heard the uproar when Father Simon found the body. My first instinct was to assume Simon had killed him – he is a rough sort of fellow for a priest – but he says he was in the chapel when Aylmer was killed, so I suppose he must be innocent.'

'Who else do you think might have been responsible?' asked Bartholomew.

'I could list dozens of men who wanted Aylmer dead, but those with the strongest motive are at the cathedral. They did not want him as a Vicar Choral, and there were fierce arguments in Chapter meetings about it. Here is Sabina, back already. I must leave you, gentlemen.'

'Why?' asked Michael, disappointed.

She touched his wrist with her fingertips. 'I have religious duties to attend. I may not have taken holy orders yet, but I still set myself daily chores. It has been a pleasure talking to you.'

When she had gone, Michael gazed at the hand she had brushed, then raised it to his cheek.

When the Gilbertines' bells clanged to life at five o'clock the following morning, Bartholomew pulled the blanket over his head in a futile attempt to muffle the racket. During a brief interlude, when the ringers took a break, the chamber was filled with Michael's nagging voice, ordering Cynric to kindle a lamp so he could read his psalter. From his bed,

Suttone declared that rowdy bells would bring the next wave of plague, while de Wetherset and Simon seemed to be embroiled in a private battle to see who could issue the most fervent prayers. Going back to sleep was clearly going to be impossible, so Bartholomew forced himself up, exchanging a weary grin with Cynric at his colleagues' antics.

When the crashing clappers were finally stilled, the Michaelhouse men, with de Wetherset and Simon at their heels, left the guest-hall and crossed the yard, Simon heading for the chapel and the others for the gate. Michael had been serious when he had declared a preference for prime at the minster, while Bartholomew wanted to visit Mayor Spayne as soon as it was light, hoping to catch him before he went out to work.

'Where are you going?' cried Hamo, breaking into a run to intercept them. Whatton was behind him. 'You cannot leave! It is Saturday, and we always have extended singing on Saturdays.'

'In that case I am definitely going to the cathedral,' muttered Michael. He cocked his head. 'Lord! I can hear the racket from here, and all the chapel doors and windows are closed.'

'And only half the brothers and nuns have arrived so far,' agreed Suttone. 'The others are still walking from their dormitories, and have yet to add their voices to the cacophony.'

'What is that cracking sound?' asked Bartholomew in alarm. Cynric drew his dagger.

'It is the clapping psalm,' explained Simon, beginning to slap his own hands together. Hamo and Whatton joined in, and Bartholomew edged away uneasily when Simon began to warble at the top of his voice: '*O clap your hands together, all ye people; O sing unto God with the voice of melody!*'

'That is the spirit,' cried Prior Roger, as he emerged from his house. He carried his rattle, and gave it a few experimental shakes. 'We shall praise the Lord with music and a great multitude of sound! Where are you going, Brother? The chapel is in this direction.'

'We shall walk in silence,' declared de Wetherset, after he, Bartholomew and Michael, with Cynric trailing behind, had managed to persuade Hamo to open the gate and let them out. Suttone had been less convincing with his excuses, so was condemned to remain. 'We have had a narrow escape and should give quiet thanks. What will Roger think of next? Speaking in tongues?' He shuddered.

The cathedral was a solid, black mass on the skyline, although delicate needles of yellow showed where candles had been lit in some of the windows. A cockerel crowed in the garden of one house they passed, and people were beginning to stir, despite the fact that it was still dark; when dawn came late, some duties needed to be performed by lamplight. The air was warmer than it had been the previous day, and there was a hazy drizzle in the air. It was melting some of the ice, and the scholars took care to walk in the middle of the road, to avoid being hit by falling icicles.

They arrived at the Close, where they were admitted by a sleepy lay-brother. They made their way to the minster, and stepped into the vastness of the nave. The scent of incense and damp wafted around them, and old leaves whispered across the stone floor in the draught from the door. As canons-elect, Michael and de Wetherset were expected to celebrate the divine office with the bishop at the High Altar, while Bartholomew went to listen from the Head Shrine, and Cynric expressed a desire to compare the carving of the imp with its episcopal original. Their footsteps echoed as they walked, and the building was a haven of silence and peace.

It was too early for pilgrims, so the Head Shrine was quieter than it had been the day before, and only three people were present. The sword-wearing priest, Claypole, was asleep, wedged into an alcove with his long legs stretched comfortably before him. Meanwhile, the dissipated Archdeacon Ravenser moved lethargically among the candles, trimming wicks and scraping spilled wax from the floor. His eyes were bloodshot and his complexion yellow, as if he had enjoyed another riotous night with too much wine. Dame Eleanor was kneeling in front of the shrine itself.

'She has been here all night,' whispered Ravenser, as Bartholomew approached. 'Keeping vigil for the Feast of St Lucy, which is today as you will know. I cannot imagine how she stands it. She must be an angel, because I do not think any mere mortal could bear the tedium. Give me a tavern any day.'

Bartholomew refrained from pointing out that the old lady looked a good deal more pert and fit after her night of prayer than Ravenser did after whatever he had been doing. Dame Eleanor saw the two men looking at her, and beckoned them forward. Unwilling to be included in what might transpire to be an invitation to some lengthy prayers, Ravenser hastily busied himself with his candles.

'Listen to the choir chant the responses,' said Dame Eleanor softly, when Bartholomew went to stand next to her. 'Can you imagine anything more beautiful?'

'It is certainly more tuneful than Prior Roger and his ear-splitting ensemble.'

She frowned when she became aware of Claypole's lounging posture. 'That wicked young man is asleep *again*, and I have woken him twice this morning already! If he went to bed earlier, he might stay awake for the duties he is paid to fulfil. He is lucky Ravenser is of a mind to be diligent this morning.'

'Is Ravenser not usually diligent, then?'

'I think he prefers non-secular activities to religious ones, although he has been working very hard this morning. I can only assume it is penance for some sin committed during his latest revelries.'

Bartholomew suspected that Ravenser was simply trying to make a good impression on a woman generally regarded as a saint in the making. With practised movements, the archdeacon laid out the vessels for mass, slapping his hand down sharply when a sudden draught caught the Host and flipped it into the air. He placed a paten across it, so it would not happen again. Dame Eleanor returned to her prayers, while Bartholomew let the choir's singing envelop him. He could hear Michael's baritone among the lower parts, and de Wetherset's creaking tenor. Then there was another voice, this one discordant and jarring. Claypole woke with a start.

'The dean,' Bartholomew heard him mumble to Ravenser, 'sings like a scalded cat.'

Eleanor shot them an admonishing look when they started to guffaw, causing Ravenser to complete his duties and leave hastily. Claypole, meanwhile, heaved himself upright and rubbed his eyes. When a burly canon sauntered past, Claypole went to talk to him, and Bartholomew noticed that while Ravenser's weapon had been mostly concealed under his robes, Claypole wore *his* sword brazenly, and did not care who saw the unusual addition to a priestly habit. Claypole and the canon leaned nonchalantly against a nearby wall, and Bartholomew assumed, from their vaguely obscene gestures, that the discussion had little to do with religion.

'Christiana is their only hope,' said Eleanor, following the direction of his gaze. 'When she is here, they at least *try* to act like men of God.'

'They seem a quarrelsome rabble,' said Bartholomew.

The old lady winced. 'They should be ashamed of themselves. And they will regret their wicked ways when the plague comes again, and those with black souls face God's judgement. Your friend Master Suttone told me last night that the worst sinners will be struck first.'

She went back to her prayers, so Bartholomew left her and began to wander around the cathedral. The milder weather had not yet percolated inside the building, and it was bitterly cold. He wondered how an elderly woman like Dame Eleanor coped with the chill. Still listening to the music, he passed the spot where Cynric was inspecting Queen Eleanor's Visceral Tomb, and aimed for the South Choir Aisle, walking briskly in an attempt to warm himself up. Dawn was breaking, but the first glimmerings of light had not yet touched the shadowy corridor, and the only light was from a single brazier.

When he reached the tomb of Little Hugh, he saw Christiana there, lighting a candle. He hung back, loath to disturb her, and watched as she stepped up to the statue and grabbed the flask of holy water that stood behind it. Furtively, she removed a second jar from under her cloak, and emptied its contents inside the first, replacing both vessels smartly when voices echoed along the aisle. Bartholomew ducked behind a pillar as Claypole, John Suttone and Ravenser approached; Christiana dropped quickly to her knees and put her hands together. The three priests loitered in a way that indicated they wanted her attention, shuffling and coughing until she had no choice but to look around. When she did, they vied for her attention like besotted schoolboys.

'Please,' she said gently, resting her hand on Ravenser's arm and smiling sweetly at Claypole and John. 'I want to pray, and I cannot do it while you three fuss and fidget behind me.'

'Perhaps we can help,' offered Claypole, unwilling to be dismissed. 'We *are* priests, after all.'

'Yes,' she said thoughtfully. 'Perhaps you might. I would like to light another candle for my mother, and I would like a wreath of leaves to place on Little Hugh's statue. The old one is sadly wilted. Would you be kind enough to fetch them for me?'

They shot away to do her bidding, but then she became aware that yet another person was lingering in the shadows. She sighed, and there was a weary expression on her face.

'Do I have to devise errands for you, too, so I can pray uninterrupted?'

'Is that what you are doing?' asked Bartholomew. 'Or are you here to exchange Dame Eleanor's holy water for something else?'

She grimaced in annoyance. 'You saw me, did you? Damn! I add wine to her water occasionally, because I have learned that it eases the ache in her legs brought on by the cold. She does not know, and I would rather you did not tell her. She believes a small miracle takes place when it happens – that Little Hugh is watching over her – and I would not like her to think otherwise. Look.'

She handed the jug to him, and while he thought Dame Eleanor would probably disapprove of being deceived, he supposed it was being done with the best of intentions. He tasted the contents, and was not surprised the old lady enjoyed it: Christiana had been generous in her mixing, and there was far more wine than water. It was good quality claret, too, and he supposed it might well help to keep the aches of a cold winter morning at bay.

'It is very strong,' he observed. 'Does she ever fall asleep halfway through the morning?'

Christiana looked surprised. 'Well, yes, she does, but that is just her age. Is it not?'

'Reduce the amount,' he advised. 'Excesses of wine are unhealthy too early in the day.'

Her face burned red with mortification. 'I am not doing her any harm, am I?'

'Not if you practise moderation. Indeed, you may be doing some good.'

She smiled, relieved. 'Dame Eleanor is the best of friends to me. I was lonely and frightened after my mother died, but she was kind and patient, and taught me to take pleasure in serving the saints in this magnificent cathedral. I do not think I would have survived without her.'

Bartholomew backed away. 'Then I will leave you in peace.'

The physician continued his circuit of the minster. When he reached the nave, he saw Tetford hurrying towards the chancel, rubbing his eyes as though he had overslept. He was carrying the alb he was supposed to be altering for Michael. Ravenser approached him, fingering his dagger. Tetford's hand dropped to his own belt, then scrabbled about in alarm when he realised he had forgotten to arm himself. Ravenser whispered something and, with a heavy sigh of resignation, Tetford produced a thick beeswax candle from the satchel he carried over his shoulder. Ravenser snatched it from him and darted towards Christiana, not seeing the obscene gesture Tetford made at his retreating back. Eventually, Bartholomew's wandering brought him to the Angel Choir again, where he had started. It was possible to see through the carved screen to the sanctuary beyond, and he found Cynric there, looking from Bishop Gynewell to the stone imp in its lofty niche.

'Coincidence,' said Bartholomew, before the Welshman

could whip himself into too much of a frenzy. 'Some of the angels have faces similar to living people, too.'

'But angels are heavenly beings,' Cynric pointed out. 'And Gynewell is one of Satan's imps. Just look at him! His horns are particularly noticeable today.'

Bartholomew wanted to contradict him, but Cynric was right. The bishop had evidently risen in a hurry, and had raked his fingers through his hair to 'tidy' it. As a result, the twisted curls at the sides of his head looked very much like horns in the unsteady light of the candles, and the way he hopped about behind the altar did little to enhance a sense of episcopal dignity, either.

'If Gynewell is a demon, he will evaporate in a puff of smoke when he touches the Host,' he said.

Irony was lost on Cynric, whose eyes gleamed in eager anticipation. 'I will stay here and watch, then. I have never seen a devil consumed by flames, and it would make a good tale to tell of a winter night – along with my accounts of Poitiers. Perhaps there will be another earthquake, too, like the one that brought down the old cathedral. It probably happened when Gynewell first arrived. It is common knowledge that the denizens of Hell are hundreds of years old.'

Bartholomew looked through the screen and saw that Michael and de Wetherset were virtually the only ones paying any attention to Gynewell's mass. The Vicars Choral were clustered around Tetford, who was relating some anecdote about the alb he held; they sniggered loudly enough to attract a stern glare from the dean. The Poor Clerks were sitting against a wall, half asleep, while the choristers – young Hugh among them – darted about in some complex, but relatively soundless, game of their own. They did not even stop when it was time to sing, trilling the notes as they ducked this way and that. Bartholomew could not imagine such antics permitted at Michaelhouse, and suddenly experienced a sharp desire to be back there again, among familiar things and faces.

Eventually, the rite was over, and Bartholomew waited for Michael to emerge. He watched the monk shake his head when Gynewell skipped towards him and asked a question, but then the bishop's attention was caught by the dean, who was in the process of removing something from the altar. Gynewell took Bresley by the arm and hauled him away to one side. Tetford passed unnecessarily close to them, and made some remark that had the dean blushing furiously. Bartholomew looked away. Lincoln was as bad as Cambridge with its petty quarrels, rivalries and feuds.

'You should forget you saw that,' said Tetford, when he reached the physician. He leered slyly, as he stooped to ensure a lock was secure on an oblations box. 'The dean, I mean.'

'Saw what?' asked Bartholomew.

Tetford grinned. 'With an attitude like that, you would make a good canon yourself. I intend to be one soon. Perhaps I shall be given Brother Michael's Stall of South Scarle.'

Bartholomew regarded him uneasily. 'Canons are installed for life, so I doubt it.'

'Maybe he will resign,' said Tetford with a careless and unconvincing shrug. 'But now I am a Vicar Choral, there is no reason why I should not aspire to be a prebendary. And, once I am a full member of the cathedral Chapter, I shall do something about that dean.'

'Something like what?' asked Bartholomew, wondering whether it was a threat on Bresley's life – and on Michael's.

'That is in God's hands,' said Tetford, striding away.

*   *   *

As soon as the mass had ended, and the streets were beginning to fill with the dim, grey light of pre-dawn, Bartholomew and Michael went to Spayne's home. While the monk tapped on the door, then fidgeted impatiently for his knock to be answered – he disliked being kept waiting – Bartholomew stood back and inspected the house. It was a fine building, larger but not as tall as Kelby's home next door. The window shutters looked new, and were brightly painted.

By contrast, Kelby's abode was suffering from the same air of neglect that afflicted the rest of the city, and lacked the care that had been lavished on its neighbour. Loose tiles hung from its roof, and its chimney leaned in a way that suggested it might not survive the winter. The whole shabby edifice told a story of a merchant in financial decline – that while the wool trade might have allowed men to secure fat fortunes in the past, it was more difficult to make profits in the present economic climate. Thus Kelby could not afford to have his façade replastered, or even apply a coat of paint to conceal his rotting timbers. Would encroaching poverty among the mercantile classes intensify the feud between Guild and Commonalty? Bartholomew imagined it would, and that jealousy might well induce resentful guildsmen to burn down the storehouses of their wealthier rivals.

And Spayne? Bartholomew examined the mayor's house more closely, and on reflection decided the gleaming paintwork and new shutters were more indicative of urgent repair than meticulous maintenance. There were scorch marks on the beams at the left side of the building, suggesting a recent conflagration. When he took a few steps to look down the narrow alley that separated the two houses, he saw Spayne's walls were dark with soot, and the yard at the end of the house contained a burned-out shell. He had assumed the storehouses Flaxfleete had ignited were in some distant place, perhaps near the river, and it was with a shock that he realised they were actually at the back of Spayne's home. It put the crime in an entirely different category – one that suggested Spayne's goods might not have been all Flaxfleete had intended to incinerate.

'Do not tell Spayne the real reason why you want to locate Matilde,' said Michael suddenly. 'He may be the jealous type, and might refuse to help you because she slipped through his own fingers.'

'I know,' said Bartholomew. His months of searching in France, the Italian peninsula and remote parts of England had taught him that not everyone was inclined to be sympathetic to his quest.

Michael shot him a sidelong glance. 'Then let me do the talking. Some people are like the traders in the Market Square at home – they have ways of knowing when you really want something, and they raise the price accordingly. I suspect you will learn more from Spayne if the questions are put by someone who is not quite so desperate for answers.'

Bartholomew was sure he was right, and the fact that Lincoln – and Spayne – represented his last hope meant it might be difficult to conceal his true feelings. 'Thank you, Brother,' he said gratefully.

Eventually, the door was answered by Ursula. She gave a cool smile when she recognised her visitors, but stood aside so they could enter, gesturing them into the hall within. It was a fine room, although its proportions were marred by the addition of a heavy pillar near the central hearth, and there was a pan at one end to catch drips from a leaking roof. Windows opened to the front and back of the house, although the rear ones were shuttered, indicating that Spayne probably did not want to look into a yard containing the charred remains of his warehouses.

234

'You are probably wondering about that brace,' said Ursula, although Bartholomew was actually staring at a cushion embroidered in a bold, flamboyant style that was almost certainly Matilde's, and Michael was admiring a dish of sugared almonds. She pointed to the wooden post. 'It is to stop the house from tumbling about our ears. When Flaxfleete burned our storehouses, the blaze damaged the roof in our home, too. The weakened timbers are buckling under the weight of the recent snows.'

'Can you not mend it?' asked Michael, glancing up uneasily.

'Not as long as the ice is up there, apparently. The builders say it will collapse if they step on it now, and we are all waiting for a thaw. Only then can work begin to repair it.'

'Then I hope winter ends early this year,' said Bartholomew politely, when she paused for sympathy. 'Is your brother home?'

'Yes, and he is eager to meet you. He says any friends of a member of the Suttone clan can consider themselves friends of his. He is with a customer at the moment, but will come as soon as he is finished. Meanwhile, he has asked me to entertain you while you wait. Would you like some wine?'

'Not at this hour in the morning,' said Michael, lowering his ample rump on to Matilde's cushion. 'Ale, if you please. And perhaps a little bread. Unless you have any Lombard slices? Lincoln does produce rather fine Lombard slices – better than Cambridge, I am forced to admit. Did you hear about the death of your neighbour on Wednesday?'

She winced at the abrupt change of topic. 'Not our neighbour, unfortunately. That would mean Kelby is dead, but we have only lost his henchman, Flaxfleete. Still, the loss will blunt Kelby's claws. It has not stopped him accusing my poor brother of murdering Flaxfleete, though. He claims Will gave Flaxfleete another bout of Summer Madness, so it is a good thing Will was staying with the Black Monks that night. They will swear he did not leave them, not even for a moment.'

'How do you think Flaxfleete died?' asked Michael, not mentioning the fact that he had already ascertained the Benedictines were able to do no such thing.

She grinned. 'I imagine he was struck down by God, because he was going to demand absolution for burning our sheds at the General Pardon, when we all know he was not sorry at all.'

A servant arrived with a platter of pastries, and Michael leaned forward to claim the largest one. 'Are you sure he was unrepentant?' he asked, fingers hovering as he made his choice.

'Of course I am,' she snapped irritably. 'He said Summer Madness made him do it, but no other sufferer was seized by a desire to commit arson.'

'People are saying that *you* killed Flaxfleete,' said Bartholomew, tugging the cushion from under Michael and inspecting it more closely. It was definitely Matilde's handiwork, although it was frayed in places and had been repaired, suggesting it was several years old. 'Because you have a motive, and it is known that you have dispensed strong substances in the past.'

'I know,' she said with a rueful sigh. 'I made *one* mistake, and the Guild will never let me forget it. A woman came to me with a cough. She was with child, but did not mention it when she asked for a cure. I gave her a remedy, but it served to bring the babe early and both died. It was not my fault. If she had been honest about her condition, I would *never* have given her an electuary containing cuckoo-pint.'

'Flaxfleete was killed with a different poison,' said Michael. 'It was—'

'Cuckoo-pint is *not* poison,' snapped Ursula defensively. 'It just has harmful effects on people in certain conditions. I hated Flaxfleete, but I am not so foolish as to kill him in so obvious a manner. Besides, I heard the toxin was in a wine keg, and while I detest guildsmen with a passion, it would be lunacy to murder them all. I would hang, because unlike Flaxfleete, *I* cannot claim benefit of clergy.'

'Neither did he,' Michael pointed out. 'He was acquitted by a secular court.'

'Only because there was an outcry from decent folk when he demanded a Church trial. Quite rightly, Gynewell refused to do it. But God struck Flaxfleete down for his wickedness anyway.'

'God had nothing to do with it,' said Michael. 'It was a human hand that put poison in his wine.'

'Well, it was not mine, and it was not my brother's,' stated Ursula firmly. 'You can search our house from cellars to attics, and you will find nothing to prove us guilty.'

After Ursula's impassioned declaration, there was an uncomfortable silence, so she went to see what was taking her brother so long. Bartholomew stood in the window, staring across the cobbled street to the corn market, wondering what he would do if Spayne refused to help him. He thought about his own sister's delight when he had returned from France in October, and how he had been touched by the warmth of the welcome provided by his Michaelhouse colleagues. He had been missed by family and friends, and it had been good to see them again. Would he be content to keep his promise to Michael, and return to the College that had been his home for so many years, or would he always be wondering whether one more journey might earn him what he really wanted?

'What can I do for you, gentlemen?' came a deep voice from the doorway.

Mayor William de Spayne was a man who commanded attention. He was tall, well muscled and his thick, red-gold hair and beard were neatly trimmed. His eyes were brown, and the combination of dark eyes and fair curls served to render him outstandingly attractive. His clothes were expensive and well cut, but it was his quiet dignity that set him above the other Lincoln merchants. The moment he walked across the room to greet his guests, Bartholomew understood exactly why Matilde had allowed herself to be courted by such a fellow.

'We have come from Cambridge,' said Michael, when Bartholomew said nothing. 'One of our dearest friends was Matilde—'

'Do not speak that name!' cried Ursula, coming to take her brother's arm protectively as a stricken expression crossed his face. 'Not in our house. Is this who you meant when you said we had a mutual acquaintance? I would never have invited you in if I had known.'

'She was . . . a . . . ' Spayne suddenly seemed unable to speak coherently.

'Will loved Matilde, but she accused *me* of poisoning that woman I was telling you about,' said Ursula.

'The older Christiana de Hauville was betrothed to one of my most bitter rivals,' explained Spayne in a voice that was unsteady. 'Ursula was accused of bringing about her death, because Lady Christiana's demise meant Kelby lost his future wife.'

'He lost her dowry, too,' said Ursula spitefully. 'And that is what really annoyed him.'

'And his heir,' added Michael. 'The dead child is said to have been his, too.'

238

'But Christiana did not *tell* me about that,' said Ursula bitterly. 'Her death was not my fault!'

'All right,' said Michael. 'We believe you. However, I fail to see what this has to do with Matilde.'

'Christiana was Matilde's friend, and it was Matilde who made the fuss about her death,' said Ursula resentfully. 'The whole affair was extremely unpleasant.'

'Matilde is not . . . ' Spayne whispered, blood draining from his face as something occurred to him. 'You have not brought me bad news about her . . . health?'

'She was well when we last saw her,' said Michael. 'And as lovely as ever.'

Spayne closed his eyes in relief. 'Thank God,' he muttered. 'I could not bear it if she . . . But you must forgive me. I did not know you came here to talk about Matilde, and hearing her name after so long has been a shock. I . . . Matilde and I . . . '

'Will believed she would consent to be his wife,' said Ursula, when he faltered into silence. 'But she refused him, and left Lincoln the following day. He tried to find her, but she once said she would never be located once she had gone, and she was right. So, she went to Cambridge, did she?'

'I went to all the places where she had kin,' said Spayne softly. 'None had heard from her in years, so I was forced to concede defeat. Is she happy in Cambridge? I hope she is happy.'

'I think she was,' said Michael, when Bartholomew still said nothing. 'But she is no longer there.'

Spayne's expression was sad. 'I shall not go after her, Brother. Her abrupt disappearance made it clear that she wanted to sever all ties with me, and I respect her wishes. She is a kind, good woman, and I feel myself honoured that she befriended me for a while.'

'We were her friends,' blurted Bartholomew. 'But she left before . . . she left suddenly.'

Spayne raised his eyebrows. 'She abandoned you, too? I understand how that feels! And now you are looking for her? Well, I wish you luck, but do not hold too much hope. When she disappears, she does so very completely. I hired men to search the length and breadth of England – not to drag her back and force her to take me, but to invite her home, to live among the friends she had made here. I was even ready to leave Lincoln myself, if she did not want me in the city. But none of my hunters were ever able to deliver the message, so I am here and she is not.'

'Will you tell us where her kin live?' asked Bartholomew. 'You may know some that we do not, and she may be with them now.'

'Why are you looking for her?' asked Spayne warily. 'Are you agents for some other jilted man?'

'No,' said Michael soothingly, while Bartholomew gripped the cushion and let the monk do the talking. 'As Matt just said, she was our friend, and we were concerned when she disappeared so suddenly. All we want is to make sure she is safe. We had hoped to find her here, in Lincoln, and we were deeply disappointed when we learned she has not been seen for six years.'

Spayne stroked his beard for a while, regarding his visitors with troubled eyes. 'No,' he said eventually. 'I am sorry, but if she left you, it means she does not want to be found.'

'We are concerned for her welfare,' insisted Michael, while Bartholomew gazed at the mayor in dismay. 'You do her a disservice by not telling us what you know. And besides, she was so happy in Cambridge that every fibre of my being tells me that she *wants* to be found and encouraged to return.'

'That may well be true, but *I* do not know that, and I will not meddle in her life again.'

'It would not be meddling,' snapped Michael, becoming annoyed. 'And she will certainly thank you if you assist us. She left over a misunderstanding of intentions – one that can be rectified just by talking to her for a few moments.'

'No,' said Spayne firmly. 'I will not do it. But tell me about her, and how you came to be close. It warms my heart to learn she found happiness, even if it was not with me. Come and share a cup of wine. Anyone who earned Matilde's good favour can consider himself a friend of mine.'

Bartholomew did not want to reminisce with one of Matilde's former beaux, but it would have been churlish to leave, and he harboured the hope that Spayne might let something slip while he talked. Michael was a skilled interrogator, and had an uncanny knack for making people reveal secrets they later wished they had kept. He saw determination in the monk's face, and knew he would do his best. Michael set to with a vengeance, and encouraged Spayne to talk all he liked. The merchant obliged with an eagerness that showed he still felt his loss very keenly.

As Spayne described his courtship, Bartholomew became aware that he was a man of culture and intelligence. He was also a skilled lutanist and an accomplished dancer, which suggested Matilde had probably had a good deal of fun in his company, too. Bartholomew tried to dislike him, but there was nothing in the man's manners to offend, and he thought that under other circumstances, he and Spayne might have developed a friendship.

Ursula listened to the fond ramblings with pursed lips, obviously disapproving of the woman who had broken her brother's heart, but too wise to say anything bad. Michael recounted some memories of his own, which made Spayne laugh. He had a rich, deep chortle that was infectious. Then he asked Bartholomew about his work, and expressed

241

an interest in his treatise on fevers – a vast tome that had taken most of the physician's spare time before he had abandoned it to search for Matilde. It was still at Michaelhouse, packed in a chest and jealously guarded by his students. Bartholomew was impressed to learn that Spayne was familiar with the work of several Arab scholars, and they began a lively debate about Ibn al-Nafis's controversial theory regarding the pulmonary circulation of the blood, which sent Michael to sleep and Ursula out to do some shopping.

When she returned, she offered her guests dinner, although not with very good grace. Spayne talked all through the meal, outlining his observations about the furious debate that was currently raging among scholars regarding the nature of Blood Relics – if Christ's blood was holy, it would have risen with Him at His Resurrection, and it was therefore impossible for cathedrals and churches to possess drops of it in phials. Not all theologians agreed, and the Dominicans and Franciscans had ranged themselves on opposing sides of a schism that threatened to rip the universities apart. Michael had strong opinions about it, but found himself hard-pressed to refute Spayne's arguments for the other side. Then the monk saw Ursula closing the window shutters, and realised it was nearly dusk.

'We have been talking all day!' he exclaimed, jumping to his feet in horror. 'There was so much I was going to do, not least of which was making sure Tetford has seen to my ceremonial alb. And then there is the small matter of the murder Gynewell told me to investigate. He will wonder what sort of man he is going to install, if he learns I have been debating Blood Relics instead.'

Spayne smiled. 'You are a scholar, so he should expect you to be diverted by intellectual pursuits.' He surged forward suddenly, grabbing the monk's arm and easing him away from the brace near the hearth. 'Mind the pillar, Brother. The house is quite safe as long as it is in place, but the carpenter says the roof might collapse if we move it. I would not like it jostled accidentally.'

'I had no idea it was so dangerous,' said Michael, edging away in alarm.

'Well, you do now,' said Ursula unpleasantly. 'Flaxfleete may be dead, but his legacy lives on.'

Spayne shot her an admonishing glance. 'There is no need for bitterness. Besides, the carpenter said the roof will be perfectly all right as long as his post is here. Of course, the additional weight of all this snow is not helping, but the rafters cannot be mended until the weather clears, and . . . I should not burden you with my problems.'

'And I have a killer to catch,' said Michael, moving towards the exit.

'Flaxfleete's?' asked Ursula. 'Good. You can prove I had nothing to do with it.'

'The feud between Guild and Commonalty is no game of my choosing,' said Spayne, as he opened the door for them. A blast of cold air whipped in, so he closed it again while he finished what he wanted to say. 'Kelby has never liked me, but my election as mayor made matters far worse.'

'He resents Will's success in the wool business,' added Ursula. 'But he does not have the financial vision to make a similar fortune himself.'

'It is a pity your dispute has drawn the entire city into a maelstrom of conflict,' said Michael.

'The rift is years older than me and Kelby,' said Spayne, startled by the disapprobation in the comment. 'I only took sides when he started to seduce cathedral officials with free wine. It upset the balance between the two factions, so I threw in my lot with Miller, to make them equal again.'

Michael was unconvinced. 'I have met Miller, and I would not like him holding sway in any town I was obliged to live in.'

'He may be vulgar, but he spends a lot of money on his Market, all of it to benefit unemployed weavers. And he built six houses in Newport, which he rents at low cost to those without work. The Guild's only "charity" is buying wine for debauched Vicars Choral to guzzle.'

'Kelby knows we occupy the moral high ground,' elaborated Ursula, 'which makes him hate us even more. Did we tell you how he gloated when Matilde left? He is shallow and mean, and no gentleman would have said the things he did. Personally, I cannot imagine why Matilde rejected Will: he is the richest man in Lincoln, he is handsome, and he has been elected mayor on several occasions – legally elected, not like when Kelby tried to falsify votes and have himself declared the winner.'

'Ursula, please!' cried her brother, embarrassed. 'You make it sound as though Matilde made a mistake, and we both know she did not. She did not love me, so she was wise to decline my offer.'

'I understand you stayed with the Black Monks on the night when the Guild celebrated Flaxfleete's acquittal,' said Michael, changing the subject.

Spayne smiled. 'I do not mind keeping company with the Benedictines on occasion. It is good to sleep on a hard bed and listen to the bells calling God's servants to their nocturnal prayers. Do you not agree, Brother?'

'Of course,' said Michael, who never encumbered himself with uncomfortable mattresses if there was a way to avoid them, and did not often keep the night offices, either. 'Did you know Flaxfleete was poisoned?'

'Was he?' asked Spayne, while Ursula pursed her lips

and glared, as if daring Michael to accuse her again. 'Poor man. He was always in Kelby's shadow, but he was not a bad fellow.'

Ursula was contemptuous. 'His fire cost you a fortune in burned wool.'

'Enough, Ursula,' said Spayne tiredly. 'He is dead, and we should let him rest in peace – and perhaps some of this feud will die with him. God knows I am weary of it. I wish you luck in uncovering his killer, Brother.'

'Actually, I am not looking into Flaxfleete's death, but Aylmer's,' said Michael. 'He was to have been the Vicar Choral of our friend, Thomas Suttone.'

'I heard Aylmer had secured the favour of the Suttone clan,' said Spayne, stroking his beard. 'We were all very impressed to learn he had inveigled such noble patronage, but we were astonished, too. He was a member of my Commonalty, but I cannot say he was someone I trusted.'

'We have been told he was a thief,' said Michael baldly.

Spayne nodded agreement. 'Miller was obliged to pay Sheriff Lungspee twice to acquit him of charges of burglary, while he was one of ten men and women named for dishonest dealings at a court in Cambridge. You will know about that, I imagine, since you live there.'

'It happened long before we became scholars,' said Michael smoothly, immediately assuming Spayne was fishing for information to pass to Miller, his ally against the Guild. 'So, we know nothing about it – and nor do we want to. Ancient history does not interest us.'

'You are very wise,' said Ursula. 'Miller does not like anyone discussing it, and he successfully sued Kelby for slander when *he* once made reference to it in a speech at a Guild dinner.'

Spayne shot her a look that warned her to watch her tongue. 'De Wetherset told me Aylmer died holding a silver chalice – the one Father Simon intends to donate to the cathedral. Did you know Simon was sold that chalice by a local man?'

Michael nodded. 'A fellow called Chapman, whom Simon *claimed* was a Roman relic-seller, but who actually transpires to be one of Miller's colleagues. One of *your* colleagues, too.'

'Chapman is *not* my colleague,' stated Spayne firmly. 'He is a member of the Commonalty, but only because is he is a friend of Miller. I would object to his association with us, but he travels a lot, so seldom attends meetings anyway. I decided to let his "election" pass, in the interests of harmony.'

'Why did you ask whether we knew it was Chapman who sold Simon the cup?' asked Michael.

'Because, like Aylmer, Chapman is not always honest,' replied Spayne. 'If he did hawk this goblet to Simon, then it is unlikely to be the real Hugh Chalice. I wanted you to know, because it may be relevant to your investigation. I am trying to assist you.'

'Thank you,' said Bartholomew, when Michael regarded the merchant rather suspiciously.

'It is the truth, Brother,' insisted Spayne, noting the monk's wary response. 'I have no reason to lie to you. However, you may not find others as helpful. People here are apt to stretch the truth.'

'Not only here,' said Michael. 'I seem to encounter lies wherever I am.'

By the time Bartholomew and Michael left Spayne – and he only relinquished them when they promised to visit him again – the sun had set, and Michael gave up any notion of pursuing his investigation that day. It was late enough that even those merchants who traded by lamplight were beginning to close their premises, and Bartholomew felt the city was oddly deserted as they walked down the hill towards the Gilbertine Priory. The only people out were men he assumed were workless weavers, who did not look as though they had anywhere else to go. Nervously, he wondered whether they were massing to cause mischief – to attack the homes of guildsmen for not supporting them in their time of need.

'It is Saturday night,' explained Michael, seeing him glance around. 'It is always quiet then, because no trading is permitted on Sundays, and shopkeepers tend to shut early. However, it is unnerving to see the city quite so empty, when we have only seen it teeming with folk.'

Bartholomew rested his hand on the hilt of his sword. 'We should be safe enough.'

Michael regarded him uneasily. 'Are you thinking of challenging a few night-felons, then? Do you imagine it will ease the frustration you feel over Spayne's refusal to help you? As I have pointed out before, you have grown rather too eager to don a weapon these days, Matt, and it is unlike you.'

'I always wear a sword when I travel,' said Bartholomew, surprised by the admonition. 'And so do most men who value their lives. But I was actually thinking that your habit might afford us some protection, along with the fact that people here are oddly in awe of the Suttone clan, and seem to respect us because we arrived in company with one. I was not thinking of fighting anyone.'

'I am glad to hear it. Violence has always been abhorrent to me. It used to be to you, too, before you went to war.'

'I did not "go to war". I just had the misfortune to be in a place where two armies met. And I assure you it is not an experience I am keen to repeat.'

'I do not think Gynewell will be very impressed with my investigation so far,' said Michael, after they had walked in silence for a while. 'I spent most of the day listening to a merchant lust after a woman who is far too good for him.'

Bartholomew stared at the monk in astonishment. 'He did no such thing! The memories he shared with us showed them both in a good light.'

'That is what he wanted us to think, but I could see what was really in his head. He is a mean, bitter fellow, who has decided that Matilde will not find happiness with her friends, because he did not.'

'I beg to differ. He is still obviously hurt by her rejection, but he is an honourable man.'

'He is a rascal, and if you were not so determined to believe that Matilde's taste in men is impeccable, you would see it, too. He is cunning, with a mind like a trap, and the likes of you and I will never catch him out. Did you hear him denigrating Aylmer and Chapman? And they are his friends – fellow members of his Commonalty! If he is so vociferous against men who are on his side, I dread to think what his enemies must be obliged to endure from him!'

Bartholomew was bemused by the force of his convictions. 'If you found him so objectionable, why did you spend so long in his company?'

Michael sniffed. 'I wanted to get his measure, and I hoped he might let something slip about Matilde. He is too wily, though, and I was able to deduce nothing. Perhaps we will do better next time.'

'Next time? You are prepared to see him again?'

'I would give a good deal to see you content, even spending hours of my valuable time with a rat. Did you hear his excuse for throwing in his lot with that felon Miller?' Michael's voice became mincingly mocking. '"I wanted to maintain the balance between factions." Who does he think he is dealing with, to imagine we would be fooled by such rubbish? He is a detestable, odious villain.'

'He cannot be all bad, or Matilde would not have been his friend.'

'She is not here, though, is she? Perhaps *that* is why she left: she found out what he is really like. The wretched man has information that may see you two reunited, and he will not share it, out of simple spite. I shall do all in my power to worm it out of him, but I am not overly hopeful. I suspect the only way we shall ever best him is by resorting to blackmail.'

'Michael!'

'Do you want Matilde or not? If she is worth spending months among the French, then she is worth digging around in Spayne's dubious existence. I see you find it distasteful, so leave it to me. I shall find a way to make him part with his secrets.'

'No,' said Bartholomew forcefully. 'You are to be made a canon a week tomorrow. You cannot risk your reputation by engaging in criminal activities. I will not let you. Not even for Matilde.'

'Very well,' said Michael stiffly. 'I shall teach you how to do it yourself. But I do not want to discuss that villain any more tonight. Let us talk about what we have learned of Aylmer instead.'

Bartholomew tugged his mind away from Spayne. 'He was a member of the Commonalty, and its leaders want his death avenged. And you have discovered that his association with Miller made him unpopular – along with his fondness for other people's property. Even Spayne could not find a good word to say about him.'

Michael grimaced at the mention of the man he had taken against. 'What do you think of Langar the Lawyer as the killer? Perhaps he was jealous, because Aylmer visited his lover Nicholas a lot.'

'Sabina, who detests Langar and who would probably love to see him hang for murder, does not think so. Besides, Aylmer visited Nicholas's house to see her, not Nicholas.'

Michael was sceptical. He sniffed. 'So *she* says, but does she have any evidence to prove Langar's innocence? No, she does not. And have you considered the possibility that Langar was jealous of Aylmer's promotion to Vicar Choral, and decided to make sure he never enjoyed it?'

'That would be self-defeating,' argued Bartholomew. 'Aylmer had been appointed to a place where he could watch the doings of the Commonalty's enemies. Langar would never spoil an opportunity that would see his faction with an advantage over its rivals.'

'Well, you can think what you like, but *I* am unwilling to eliminate Langar and his cronies just yet. They remain on my list of suspects for the murder, along with Spayne, who—'

'Spayne?' echoed Bartholomew in disbelief. 'Now you really are allowing personal dislike to run riot. You would do better looking at the men who live in the place where Aylmer was killed, and who had ready access to him: the Gilbertines.'

'They are certainly worth perusal,' acknowledged Michael. 'And Hamo's alibi is especially dubious, because I spoke to the hospital inmates, and they are unable to say exactly when he arrived to say mass for them. He could well have stabbed Aylmer before attending to his religious duties.'

'Meanwhile, Whatton is a quiet, unassuming fellow, and no one would notice if *he* escaped from the chapel. The building is always dark, there is a colossal amount of noise, and everyone is so transfixed by his alleluias that you could probably discharge a ribauld with no one any the wiser.'

Michael nodded. 'And that conclusion means *none* of

the Gilbertines have a solid alibi. The same can be said for Father Simon, who remains my prime suspect, because it was *his* cup Aylmer was holding when he died. Why would someone kill Aylmer but leave a valuable chalice with his body? It makes no sense.'

'De Wetherset is on my list,' said Bartholomew. He raised his hand when Michael started to object. 'He *lies*, Brother. He told you he saw Simon in the chapel that morning, but he could not have done, because he later let slip that he never attends prime with the Gilbertines. And if he cannot vouch for Simon, then Simon cannot vouch for him. What is not to say that *he* did not catch Aylmer stealing his friend's cup, and stabbed him?'

Michael was thoughtful. 'I suppose he may have learned a few secrets by watching us investigate murder in Cambridge, and he is certainly wily enough to know how not to leave clues.'

'How will you eliminate some of these suspects?' asked Bartholomew. He did not like the notion of Michael meddling with such folk. It was different in Cambridge, when there was an army of beadles under the monk's command and a friendly, understanding sheriff always ready to help. But in Lincoln, they were alone, with only Cynric to protect them.

'Ask questions, I suppose, although it is difficult to know where to start. I will talk to Simon again, and try to get some proper answers about this chalice. Perhaps that is where the solution lies.'

'Especially when you consider that drawing on Aylmer's shoulder. I am certain it is significant.'

'Aylmer, Nicholas and Flaxfleete. All murdered. Two with poison and one with a dagger. Perhaps if I find the killer of one, I will know who did away with them all.'

* * *

251

Lincoln was swathed in a thick pall of fog the following day, so dense that Bartholomew could not see the Chapel of St Katherine from the refectory next door. He had intended to accompany Michael to prime in the cathedral, but one of the hospital inmates was suffering from a lethargy, and by the time he had finished the consultation, Michael was nowhere to be found and the physician was obliged to endure the Gilbertines' high mass instead. With gritted teeth, he listened to them howl and clap their way through several psalms, and was shocked when Prior Roger suggested singing in the vernacular.

'Come on, Doctor!' he shouted, leaving his place at the altar and coming to mingle with his joyous flock. 'It is a lovely Sunday, and you are blessed with the ability to raise your voice to the Lord! Sing His praise with all your heart. Alleluia!'

Bartholomew took several steps away when Roger waved his rattle, making a deafening racket that served to make his brethren shriek all the louder. Hamo was yelling so loudly that his voice was cracking, while even Simon seemed slightly taken aback at the fervour exploding around him.

'I think I would rather—' began Bartholomew.

'Is there a particular psalm you would like us to trill?' asked Roger, almost screaming to make himself heard. 'Hamo has translated some into English, so the lay-brothers can join in.'

Bartholomew looked longingly at the door. 'The patient in the hospital will need—'

'Praise the Lord!' yelled Roger, almost delirious in ecstasy. He raised his hands in the air, and closed his eyes. As soon as Bartholomew was sure it would be a moment before he would open them again, he made his bid for escape, racing up the nave and flinging open the gate to freedom.

'Steady!' exclaimed Dame Eleanor, who was passing by outside. 'You almost had me over.'

'I am sorry,' said Bartholomew, slamming the door behind him and leaning on it, in the hope that it would prevent Roger from coming after him.

She cackled her amusement when she understood what was happening. 'You are not the first man to rush screaming from one of the priory's Sunday masses. Roger is a very dear man, but his style of worship is not to all tastes.'

'Would you like me to escort you to the cathedral?' asked Bartholomew, keen to leave the convent.

She patted his arm. 'You are kind, but I usually go later on a Sunday, and Christiana has already agreed to walk with me. Do not be afraid that Roger will hunt you out. He will be so engrossed in his ceremony that he will have forgotten about you by now. It is almost time for the organ – yes, I can hear it starting up now – and he always becomes rather animated once that is going.'

'Lord!' muttered Bartholomew, not liking to imagine what Roger might be like, when 'rather animated'. 'If ever I do take the cowl, I will never choose the Gilbertine Order.'

'As far as I am aware, this is the only Gilbertine house that enjoys such passionate worship. There is Michael, about to visit the cathedral for his Sunday devotions. You should go with him, since he is investigating a nasty murder and this can be a dangerous city. He is a good man, so please look after him.'

'I will try,' said Bartholomew, watching the monk and Christiana emerge from a building he thought was a disused brewery. Michael was laughing at something she had said, and the physician thought it was no wonder they had been impossible to locate earlier – a defunct brew-house was not an obvious place to look. 'But I do not think he wants my company at the moment.'

'He and Christiana are only flexing their wits in bright conversation,' said Eleanor indulgently. 'Do not worry about your friend's virtue. Christiana would never harm him.'

'It is not him I am worried about.'

She chuckled again. 'Christiana can take care of herself. She has been repelling passionate suitors for six years, and has become rather adept at it.'

She headed for the gate, and Christiana broke away from Michael to join her. Bartholomew could not help but notice how the younger woman moved her hips in a way that was sure to keep the monk's attention. Bartholomew went to stand next to him, but Michael only turned to face his friend once the two women could no longer be seen through the mist. He seemed surprised to find Bartholomew regarding him with arched eyebrows.

'What?'

'You know what.'

'I was just making sure Lady Christiana did not slip on ice. The convent yard is very slippery, and it would not do for her to fall and injure herself.'

'No,' agreed Bartholomew. 'She is likely to break bones, while old Dame Eleanor would simply bounce back up again. What is wrong with you, Michael? You are like a lovesick calf.'

'You know nothing of such matters,' said the monk loftily, 'or you would not be riding all over the known world in a futile attempt to locate the woman you let slip from your grasp.'

Bartholomew was taken aback. 'That is an unkind thing to say.'

Michael was unrepentant. 'It is true, though. Besides, you forget that I am bound by vows of chastity, so do not preach at me. And I am not—'

He stopped suddenly, and when Bartholomew followed

the direction of his gaze, he caught a glimpse of scarlet. 'Chapman?' he asked, straining his eyes in the swirling fog.

Michael nodded. 'Now what would he be doing here, when all the brothers are howling their devotions in the chapel? I doubt he has come to admire the quality of their music. After him, Matt!'

Bartholomew regarded him coolly, still smarting from his remark about Matilde. 'You go.'

'Very well.' Michael began the waddle that passed for a sprint in his eyes, calling over his shoulder as he went, 'If he draws a dagger, I shall scream. Rescue would be appreciated.'

Rolling his eyes at the brazen manipulation, Bartholomew trotted after him. It did not take long for him to catch up with and then overtake the lumbering monk, and he reached the building around which Chapman had disappeared far more quickly. He stopped, trying to see through the layers of mist. Then he glimpsed a flicker of movement and broke into a run. His footsteps were oddly muffled in the damp air, but they were enough to make his quarry glance behind him. Then there was a flash of crimson and Chapman took to his heels. Bartholomew ran harder, racing past the hospital and into the gardens beyond. Ahead was a gate, and Chapman was in the process of hauling it open when Bartholomew caught him. He grabbed the man by the shoulder and pushed him up against the wall.

'All right!' Chapman shouted, raising his hands to show he was unarmed. 'I give up!'

'What are you doing here?'

Chapman glared. 'I came to see Simon, but he is in the chapel, so I decided to come back later.'

'If your purpose was innocent, then why did you run?'

Chapman pointed to Bartholomew's sword. 'I always flee from armed men.'

'What did you—?'

Suddenly, there was a dagger in Chapman's hand, and he slashed at Bartholomew without warning. The physician jumped back, instinctively reaching for his blade, but it was a cumbersome weapon, and not quickly hauled from its scabbard. Chapman's knife scored the thick material of his sleeve. Then the relic-seller reeled and slumped to his knees, gripping his head. Michael strolled up, wiping mud from his hands. He grinned, to show he was pleased with the accuracy of the stone he had lobbed.

'I had him,' said Bartholomew, bending to inspect Chapman and deciding it had been surprise, not injury, that had made him topple. 'You did not need to break your vow to forswear arms.'

'A pebble does not constitute "arms", Matt, and this fellow is a sly fighter. I am not sure you would have won, which I confess pleases me. I was beginning to think you had turned into something of a warrior, and I am relieved to see you still reassuringly inept.' Michael turned to the relic-seller, who was staggering to his feet. 'So, we meet again, Master Chapman.'

'What do you want?' demanded the felon, trying to resist when Bartholomew removed the dagger from his hand. 'You have no right to accost innocent men and chase them through gardens.'

'I daresay you are right,' said Michael. 'But are you an innocent man? There seems to be an odd confusion about you. On the one hand, you are Miller's friend and a member of the Commonalty, but on the other, you have made a living by selling relics to gullible priests. Like Father Simon.'

'However, there is something peculiar about your dealings with Simon,' Bartholomew continued. 'Prior Roger has seen you with him – as have I – but Roger did not

256

recognise you as a man who has lived in Lincoln for the past twenty years, while Simon himself told us you were from Rome. Why is that?'

'I *have* been to Rome,' said Chapman sulkily. 'And I *do* sell relics on occasion. I sell lots of things, mostly for Miller, who says I have a talent for it. Since I often carry goods of considerable value, it is sometimes prudent to disguise myself, and *that* is why the prior did not recognise me.'

'Then does Simon know you as Walter Chapman or as someone else?' asked Michael.

'I have never told him my name. He did not ask for it.'

Bartholomew regarded Chapman thoughtfully, not sure what to believe. Lincoln was a large city, so Simon was unlikely to know everyone who lived in it. However, Chapman was a member of the Commonalty, so enjoyed a modicum of local fame, and Prior Roger had noticed something familiar about him. Had Chapman really managed to deceive Simon, who had seen him at much closer quarters? Or had Simon lied?

'Does Simon know you are a member of the Commonalty?' Bartholomew asked.

'I have no idea, and it is none of your business anyway. Stand aside, or I will tell Miller you manhandled me. And you do not want *him* to think badly of you, believe me.'

'Tell me about this cup you sold Simon,' said Michael, ignoring the threat. He put one hand on a nearby sapling and leaned on it, effecting a casually nonchalant pose. Bartholomew saw the whole thing begin to bend under his weight, and icicles and water began to shower downwards.

Chapman flinched when a clot of snow landed on his head. 'It is not a "cup". It is the Hugh Chalice – a relic worthy of great veneration. It belonged to the saint himself.'

'How do you know?' asked Michael. The tree leaned at

a more acute angle, and the monk was obliged to shift his hand to avoid toppling over. 'We have been told that the Hugh Chalice disappeared while being carried to Lincoln from London, so how can you be sure it is the same one? Or are *you* the thief who took it from the couriers twenty years ago?'

Chapman was outraged. 'I am no fool, going around stealing holy things! However, if you must know, I recognised it when it appeared for sale at a market in Huntingdon. I brought it here and sold it to Simon, because Lincoln is where it belongs.'

'You recognised it?' asked Bartholomew suspiciously. 'How?'

'Because it is distinctive,' replied Chapman. 'Old and tarnished, with a carving of a baby. Look for yourselves. It is in St Katherine's Chapel, awaiting its translation to the cathedral.'

'That does not answer my question,' said Bartholomew. 'How did *you* know it was the Hugh Chalice? Had you seen it before?'

'In London,' said Chapman, licking his lips nervously. 'I travel a lot, and I saw it in the Old Temple there. That was *before* the saint made it known that he wanted it brought to Lincoln.'

'But the saint allowed it to be lost *en route*,' said Michael. 'And I am under the impression that he has permitted a very large number of thieves to lay hands on it.'

Bartholomew regarded the monk uneasily. He was coming dangerously close to mentioning what they knew of Shirlok's trial, and it was not a good idea to discuss the case with a man who would almost certainly repeat the conversation to Miller.

Chapman gazed earnestly at Michael. 'St Hugh was angry when it failed to arrive at his shrine – rumour has it that

258

he caused robbers to kill the two careless couriers on their homeward journey. He has rectified matters now, though, and *I* am the vessel he chose to help him. Brother, please! You will have that tree over in a moment.'

Michael released the hapless sapling, surprised that he had managed to push it so far out of alignment. He tried to tug it upright, but it continued to list, and Bartholomew suspected it always would. While Chapman picked shards of ice from his clothing, Bartholomew addressed the monk in an undertone.

'Is he telling the truth? Could part of Shirlok's hoard have appeared for sale in Huntingdon? Huntingdon is not far from Cambridge, where the goods went missing.'

Michael shook his head. 'It is too much of a coincidence – the goblet stolen after a trial in which Chapman was acquitted, and then appearing in the same villain's hands two decades later. Besides, he does not look like a truthful man to me.' He stepped forward to speak to Chapman again. 'De Wetherset tells me that shortly after your Cambridge trial, a lot of property went missing. Among the items that disappeared was a cup that he says looks remarkably like the Hugh Chalice.'

'Poor de Wetherset,' murmured Bartholomew uneasily. 'I hope you have not put him in danger.'

'It *was* the Hugh Chalice,' said Chapman softly. 'And it was Shirlok who stole it from the couriers. But then St Hugh intervened. He caused Shirlok to be caught, and everything he had stolen to be seized by the Cambridge sheriff. Then he caused the chalice to appear in Huntingdon when I happened to be there, knowing I would bring it home.'

Michael raised his eyebrows. 'I see. Did *you* have anything to do with its disappearance from Cambridge, before it so conveniently arrived in Huntingdon?'

Chapman bristled with indignation. 'I did not! As it

happens, I was detained after Shirlok's trial, because of a misunderstanding over some other goods, and the cup went missing when I was in still in gaol. I will swear on anything you like – even the Hugh Chalice – that *I* did not steal it.'

'What about your co-accused?' pressed Michael. 'Or Langar? Could they have—'

'No!' snapped Chapman. 'And they will be furious if I tell them the sort of questions you are asking. And now, if you will excuse me, gentlemen, I have business to conduct.'

CHAPTER 7

The mist seemed thicker than ever as Bartholomew and Michael left the Gilbertine Priory and began to walk to the cathedral for High Mass. It encased them in a cocoon of grey-white, so they could not even make out the churches and houses to either side of the road, and fine droplets clung to their clothes and hair. Bartholomew could taste the fog in his mouth, touched with a hint of wood-smoke, although it was missing the malodorous taint of the marshes he had grown used to in Cambridge. Michael was reviewing what they had learned about the chalice and its travels, but the physician's mind was fixed on the various diseases and ailments that might be carried in such a miasma. It was a long time since he had lost himself in a reflection of medical matters; mostly, he thought about Matilde in his free moments.

They reached the Cathedral Close, where the bells were pealing, announcing that Bishop Gynewell had arrived and was ready to begin the sacred rite. Michael went to his place in the chancel, and Bartholomew stood in the nave to listen to the singing. That day, the music was sporadic in quality and volume, and he saw why when he noticed that a number of those supposed to be taking part in the ceremony were actually wandering about on business of their own. Tetford was with Master Quarrel of the Swan and money was changing hands – Michael's Vicar Choral was laying in supplies for his tavern. Tetford saw the physician watching and turned away.

Young Hugh, cherubic in his gown and golden curls, was racing up and down the aisles with several friends, chased by a flustered-looking man who was evidently the choirmaster. The boys considered it fine sport until Dame Eleanor, abandoning her customary spot at the Head Shrine, beckoned them towards her. She spoke a few quiet words that had them hanging their heads in shame before traipsing obediently towards their exasperated teacher. Hugh lingered uncertainly, so she added something that made him grin, then sent him after his cronies. Bartholomew saw Claypole observing the episode with a malicious smile, hand on the hilt of his sword.

'Nicholas Bautre was made choirmaster two years ago,' he said when the physician approached. 'He is worthless, and I should never have been dismissed in his favour.'

'You were dismissed?' asked Bartholomew. 'Why?'

Claypole looked sullen. 'I lost my clothes and all my vestments at the gaming table. It was my own fault – I should have chosen the white stones over the black. Dean Bresley decided to make an example of me, and had Bautre appointed in my place. It has been disastrous for the cathedral, because Bautre cannot even get the boys to stay put during the mass, let alone teach them music.'

'They have a poor example in the adults,' said Bartholomew. 'Not many clergy are in their places, either. They are either in the nave doing secular business, or they have not bothered to come at all.'

Claypole shrugged. 'It is the dean's responsibility to maintain discipline, so you can blame him. He is a sanctimonious fool! What is wrong with the odd game of chance of an evening?'

'Presumably, he has a problem with you arriving for your duties with nothing to wear.'

Claypole pulled a disagreeable face. 'He is in no position to preach, given what *he* does in his spare time. Perhaps he appointed Bautre because he *knew* the choir would run amok, and it means his own voice can be heard. He is singing now.'

Bartholomew winced as a response was issued several tones too high, creating a discordant clash that had the other choristers faltering uncertainly. 'Lord help us!'

Claypole grinned. 'I had better get back to St Hugh's head before Dame Eleanor admonishes me again. The dean can ride me all he likes for insolence and irregularity, but I do not like it when she does it. She has a knack for making me feel ashamed – and she might tell Lady Christiana.'

He moved away, but was intercepted by Ravenser, who was weaving up the nave in a manner that suggested he was drunk. He leaned heavily on Claypole, and laughed raucously at some joke of his own making. A woman joined them, and Ravenser whispered something that made her slap him.

It was some time before Michael emerged from the chancel. His face was bleak. 'The dean has just given me a complete catalogue of offences committed by Vicars Choral and Poor Clerks. It seems I am about to be installed in a den of vice. And speaking of vice, here is my deputy.'

'Your alb, Brother,' said Tetford cheerfully, flinging a garment at Michael in such a way that it landed on his head. 'Rosanna could not believe the dimensions I gave her, and is keen to meet you for herself. I intend to introduce you.'

'No, you will not,' said Michael, hauling the vestment from his face. 'I am not some prize bull, to be produced on demand for the entertainment of women of easy virtue. And you agreed to give them up, if you recall. Or had you forgotten my threat to dismiss any assistant whose character is tainted?'

Tetford snorted his disdain. 'Which saint will you hire,

then, Brother? Dame Eleanor? She is the only one around here who reaches your lofty standards. What do you think of the alb?'

Michael glared at him, but declined to waste his breath with further recriminations. Bartholomew stepped forward and helped him hoist the garment over his shoulders. The length was good, and the seam was barely visible thanks to some talented sewing, but it was nowhere near large enough around.

Tetford took it back with an unkind snigger. 'Rosanna will think I am playing a game with her when I say it needs to be made bigger still. Or would you rather I abstained from her company, and you can be installed as it is? It makes you look fat, so I would not recommend it.'

'It will take more than a morning away from women to save *your* sinful soul,' declared Michael angrily. 'And I am not fat, I have big bones. Tell him, Matt.'

'Massive ones,' agreed Bartholomew obligingly. 'Will the alb be ready in time for the ceremony? There is only a week to go.'

'It will be tight – and I do not mean the alb,' said Tetford. 'Christ in Heaven!'

Somewhat abruptly, he turned and strode away with the robe over his arm. Bartholomew turned quickly, and saw Ravenser and John Suttone coming towards them. Although he was obviously inebriated, Ravenser had still remembered to arm himself, and he fingered his dagger as he nodded a cool greeting to the scholars.

'My Vicar Choral seems nervous of you, Ravenser,' remarked Michael. 'I told him to disarm, but I can see from here that he is wearing a sword under his habit.'

'He should be nervous,' said Ravenser, narrowing his eyes when he spotted Tetford hurrying away. He began to follow, drawing his sword as he did so and calling over his shoulder, 'There are rules in the Cathedral Close, and he broke them.'

'What rules?' asked Michael of John, watching Tetford break into a run. Ravenser lumbered after him, but it was not long before he gave up the chase, putting his hand to his head as if the exercise had been too much for the delicate state of his health. 'Would they be the monastic ones of chastity, obedience, humility and poverty?'

'Tetford has certainly broken those,' replied John, watching his colleagues' antics in distaste. 'And you can add theft, fornication and insolence, too. But in this instance I think Ravenser refers to who has rights to a certain lady. It is anathema to me, of course. *I* do not indulge in licentious behaviour.'

'Of course,' said Michael dryly. 'Would you like me to tell our friend Suttone about his cousin's virtuous character? He is looking for a new Vicar Choral, now his original choice is murdered.'

John regarded him icily. 'I am naturally virtuous. It is not something I enact simply because there is a post of Vicar Choral on offer. Good morning, Brother.'

'Poor Dean Bresley,' said Bartholomew, while John stalked away, head in the air. 'If all his clergy are like the ones we have met, his life must be like a foretaste of Hell.'

'Speaking of Hell, here comes the bishop. Or is it the stone imp from the Angel Choir?'

'Brother Michael,' said Gynewell, skipping towards them. His curly hair gleamed in the dull morning light, and so did his eyes. 'Have you found Aylmer's killer yet? The dean said you questioned some of the Vicars Choral after High Mass.'

'I did,' said Michael. 'However, my task has not been made easier by the fact that you were not entirely open with me. It would have been helpful to know that Aylmer was a member of the Commonalty *and* that he was friends with unsavoury men like Adam Miller.'

Gynewell was rueful. 'I see you have questions, but this is not the place to talk. Come to my house, and we shall discuss it there.'

The Bishop's Palace was a sumptuous set of buildings that stood in the shadow of the cathedral. It boasted a stately hall with a great vaulted undercroft, which was the prelate's private residence, while a range to the west held rooms for the clerks and officials who managed his diocese. The complex stood on a series of terraces that afforded fine views of the city, while the cathedral loomed protectively behind. The palace was made from honey-coloured stone, and its thick walls and sturdy gates suggested its builders had an eye to security, as well as to beauty and comfort. It formed a stark contrast to the shabby poverty of the town that huddled outside its well-tended grounds.

'A tavern would have been more convenient, My Lord,' said Michael irritably, as he followed Gynewell down a narrow path with steep stairs that provided a shortcut between palace and minster. The dampness of the fog made it slippery, and it was not an easy descent. 'I understand the Close is rather well supplied with them.'

'I am a bishop,' said Gynewell archly. 'I do not frequent alehouses – and especially not the Tavern in the Close, which is more brothel than hostelry.'

Once they reached the bottom, he led the way to a fine hall. At the far end was a massive hearth, in which a fire blazed so fiercely that it was difficult to approach. The window shutters were closed against the winter cold, and flames sent shadows dancing around the room, giving the impression that some of the figures in the wall-tapestries were alive and moving. None of the hangings depicted religious scenes, and some were openly pagan. Bartholomew glanced at the diminutive bishop uneasily, then realised he was allowing himself to be influenced by Cynric's prejudices.

Gynewell headed straight for the fire, where he climbed into a throne that was placed directly in front of it, waving his guests to a bench on one side. Both bench and chair were well supplied with cushions, all of them red. The bishop leaned down and took a bell in both hands, giving it a vigorous shake that made Bartholomew afraid he might burst into song, like the Gilbertines. After a moment, the door opened, and young Hugh marched in.

'Yes, My Lord?' the lad piped, doffing his hat.

'It is your turn for bishop-duty, is it?' asked Gynewell amiably, raising one of his short legs to cross over the other as he basked in the heat. Bartholomew wondered how he could stand it. 'Or have you been assigned an additional spell of servitude for some act of mischief?'

'Dean Bresley was cross because I accidentally dropped Master Bautre's music in the stoup,' said Hugh. 'And the ink ran, so he cannot read it, which means we cannot practise the *Te Deum* today.'

'I understand there is an archery practice this afternoon at the butts,' said Gynewell with a grave expression. 'You will have to go there, instead of singing Bautre's latest composition.'

'What a pity,' said Hugh with a perfectly straight face. 'What would you like me to fetch you, sir?'

'Some wine – hot, of course. And a few of those red cakes the baker delivered yesterday. Oh, and bring my pitchfork, will you?'

Hugh left obediently, while Bartholomew regarded the bishop with renewed unease. 'Pitchfork?'

Gynewell leaned forward to prod the fire into even greater fury, then sat back with a contented sigh. 'Red cakes are best served toasted. Bishop de Lisle knows my liking for them, and he once gave me a miniature pitchfork, just for that purpose.'

When Hugh returned, heavily laden with a tray of wine and nasty-looking pastries, Gynewell showed off his 'pitchfork'. It was the length of a man's arm, and beautifully crafted to mimic the double-tined tools used for moving hay. Its handle was bound in crimson leather, to prevent the user from burning himself, and Bartholomew suspected de Lisle had considered the gift an excellent joke.

They had done no more than be served a cup of scalding wine, so liberally laced with spices that it turned Bartholomew's mouth numb, when there was a tap on the door. It was the dean. He sidled in as though he was about to burgle the place, eyes darting everywhere. He jumped guiltily when he saw Michael and Bartholomew.

'Come in, Bresley,' said Gynewell genially, waving the dean to the bench and presenting him with a cup of wine. Bartholomew saw it was a wooden vessel, rather than one of the set of silver goblets with which he and Michael had been provided. 'You know you are always welcome.'

'I am not sure I want to be welcome in *this* company,' muttered the dean unhappily. 'Tetford has just informed me that Brother Michael plans to hold a wild celebration in his tavern the night before his installation. He said Christiana de Hauville has been invited, because the good Brother has developed an improper liking for her. However, Lady Christiana is a woman, so should not be in the Close after dark. It is not right.'

Michael regarded him in open-mouthed shock, while Gynewell speared a pastry with his fork and began to cook it.

'I have tried on several occasions to shut that den of

iniquity,' said the bishop, 'but each time I issue an order of suppression, Tetford finds a way to circumvent it. Still, I shall prevail in the end. I have better resources and infinite patience. Try one of my cakes, Brother.'

He passed a smoking morsel that the monk accepted without thinking, more concerned with the slur on his character than with food. 'My Lord, I harbour no impure thoughts about Christiana de Hauville. I hope you do not believe these wicked aspersions.'

'She is an alluring woman,' replied Gynewell, 'and lesser men than you have been smitten with her charms. But I shall trust you, if you say you are made of sterner stuff. Do you like the cake?'

Michael took a bite mechanically. 'You will find me as pure as the driven—' His protestations of innocence stopped abruptly, and his face turned dark. He reached for his wine, took a gulp, then started to choke. Bartholomew leapt to his feet, but Michael flapped him away.

'The red cakes are full of pepper,' explained Bresley dolefully, watching the monk's sufferings with unhappy eyes. 'And the bishop is the only man in Lincoln who can stand them. I should have warned you, but my mind was on other matters. I am sorry.'

'I suppose they are an acquired taste,' admitted Gynewell, regarding the puce monk anxiously. 'Are you all right, Brother? Shall I summon Hugh to bring you something else to drink? Water?'

Michael shook his head, tears streaming down his face, and when he spoke, his voice was hoarse. 'Your water is probably full of brimstone. Do you consume nothing normal men deem edible?'

Gynewell regarded him in a way that suggested he thought the question was an odd one. 'I dislike bland flavours. If you are going to eat something, you may as well taste it, I always say. You should try my devil's eggs. Now those *are* highly spiced.'

'You refer to him as *your* Devil?' asked Bartholomew uneasily.

Gynewell stoked up the fire. 'Shall we talk about Aylmer's death? I am a busy man, and do not usually spend my valuable time chattering about victuals.'

Michael recovered once Hugh had brought a jug of ale from the kitchens. When it arrived, it was so cold there was ice in it, and Gynewell shuddered in distaste as the monk sipped. He dismissed Hugh for the day, waving away the lad's gratitude, while Bresley regaled the company with a gloomy litany of the various vices enjoyed by the residents of the Cathedral Close. When his lips had regained some feeling, Michael brought the discussion back to his enquiry.

'My Lord,' he said huskily. 'You were about to explain why you had neglected to mention Aylmer's association with criminals when you asked me to investigate his murder.'

'Aylmer *was* a member of the Commonality,' acknowledged Gynewell, while Bartholomew held his breath, expecting the bishop to take umbrage at the admonitory tone. 'Then Suttone wrote to offer him the post of Vicar Choral. He was moved to tears. He came to me and said he intended to renounce his evil ways, and was determined to live the life of an honest man.'

'And you believed him?' asked Michael doubtfully.

'Actually, I did,' replied Gynewell, choosing to ignore the dean's derisive snort. 'He immediately left Miller and took a berth in the Gilbertine Priory – the convent farthest from Miller's domain.'

Michael was exasperated. 'But this is relevant! It means

Miller may have killed Aylmer, because he was angry at being rejected by a man he had known for years.'

'That assumes Miller knew about Aylmer's change of heart,' said Gynewell. 'And Aylmer confided in no one here but Bresley and me.'

'He told Sabina Herl,' countered Bartholomew. 'So, what is to say he did not mention it to other members of the Commonalty, too?'

'Sabina is different,' argued Gynewell. 'She has also moved away from Miller, and is trying to forge an honest life. Aylmer probably asked her how to go about it.'

'I seriously doubt Aylmer shared his plans with the Commonalty,' said Bresley. 'They were delighted when they heard one of their own was to become a cathedral official, and would not have been pleased had he then told them he planned to end their association. I imagine he intended to live quietly in the Close until they forgot about him.'

Michael was thoughtful. 'Miller is keen to know the identity of Aylmer's killer, so perhaps you are right – he did not know he was in the process of being abandoned. If he had, he would not care about vengeance.'

'Bresley did not believe Aylmer was sincere,' said Gynewell, glancing to where the dean was inspecting the wooden cup with more than a casual interest. 'And he argued against the appointment.'

'Were there similar objections to me choosing Tetford?' asked Michael uneasily.

Bresley nodded. 'Plenty. And now you have met him, you will understand why.'

'Tetford was Bishop de Lisle's choice,' said Michael. 'Not mine.'

'I suspected as much,' said Gynewell. 'They are clearly kin, and de Lisle is famous for his nepotism. I doubt Tetford will stay with us long, though; he will leave the moment something more lucrative is offered. That is the advantage of Vicars Choral – they can be promoted if they are a nuisance, preferably to another diocese. Do not worry, Brother. We shall send him to Ely in a few weeks and so be rid of him.'

Michael scrubbed at his eyes. 'You are very kind – to me and to Tetford.'

Gynewell shot him a mischievous grin. 'I was young once, Brother, and all Tetford needs is a firm hand.'

'You will not succeed in taming the fellow,' warned Bresley. When Bartholomew looked at him, the wooden cup was nowhere to be seen. 'He is beyond redemption.'

'Have you heard anything about Flaxfleete's demise?' asked Michael. He saw the surprise in the bishop's face at the change of subject, and hastened to explain. 'I believe the deaths of Flaxfleete, Aylmer and Nicholas Herl might be connected.'

Gynewell raised his eyebrows. 'Really? Well, there are two tales circulating regarding Flaxfleete at present: the Guild maintains that Ursula de Spayne poisoned him, and the Commonalty just as firmly assert that he died from a recurrence of his Summer Madness.'

'His affliction was unusually severe,' added Bresley helpfully. 'The other victims only harmed themselves, but Flaxfleete was compelled to commit arson in his delirium.'

'What about Nicholas Herl?' asked Michael.

Gynewell tugged thoughtfully on one of his horns. 'Herl was probably a suicide, who drank too much, then threw himself in the Braytheford Pool. He never really recovered his health after his bout of Summer Madness, so no one was surprised when he was found dead. Langar and Sabina have been petitioning me to bury him in a churchyard. They say he was out of his wits, so not responsible for himself. I think I shall oblige. I dislike the Church's inflexibility where self-murder is concerned.'

'Three deaths within a few days of each other,' said Michael. 'And I understand there have been others, too.'

Gynewell thrust another cake on his pitchfork. 'There have, but this is a large city and men are mortal. Not every demise is suspicious.'

'Canon Hodelston,' said Bresley. 'Rapist, burglar, extortionist and liar. His was the first odd death, although no one mourned *his* passing. He was even more evil than my current batch of priests.'

'That was seven years ago, Bresley,' said Gynewell impatiently. 'It cannot possibly have a bearing on Aylmer, and saying it does will lead Brother Michael astray.'

'Herl, Flaxfleete and Aylmer had a mark on them,' said Bartholomew, watching the bishop eat the smoking delicacy. 'A cup, which looked as though it had been scratched into their skin years ago. Do you know anything about that?'

Gynewell exchanged a bemused glance with Bresley. 'Do you mean the kind of sign that is inflicted voluntarily, or a brand that was not?' asked the dean.

'It was probably something they agreed to,' replied Bartholomew, sounding more certain than he felt. 'I suspect it symbolises membership of some secret fraternity.'

'If these scars were confined to Herl and Aylmer, you might be right,' said Gynewell. 'They were certainly the kind of fellows to cut themselves in a demonstration of manly affection. The problem is Flaxfleete: he hated the Commonality, and would never have associated himself with them. If it was a cup they marked on themselves, do you think it was something to do with the Hugh Chalice?'

Bresley's tone was wistful. 'That went missing years ago, and has not been seen since.'

'I told you the dean and I disagree about this,' said

Gynewell to Michael. 'I believe the one Father Simon intends to give us is genuine. Bresley does not.'

'I wish it *was* real,' said Bresley morosely, 'but I feel nothing when I hold it, except something that should not be there. So, it is still missing, as far as I am concerned. Simon says he bought it from a Roman relic-seller, so we have been unable to question the fellow ourselves.'

'Actually, he had it from Walter Chapman,' supplied Michael. 'Miller's red-legged friend.'

Gynewell's jaw dropped. 'Then the Hugh Chalice is the only genuine thing he has ever handled, because he usually deals in fakes. The Commonality would disagree, but I am afraid it is true.'

'No wonder I have the sense that it is just a cup,' said Bresley. 'And not even a very nice one.'

'This is all very perplexing,' said Gynewell with a frown. 'But if Simon's chalice *did* come from Chapman, then I wonder if Chapman heard about it – and then somehow acquired it – because of the stink Flaxfleete made about its disappearance. That makes sense.'

'Not to me,' said Michael. 'I have no idea what you are talking about.'

Gynewell tossed the remains of the cake into the fire, where it disappeared in a flurry of sparks. 'A month ago, Flaxfleete accused Aylmer of breaking into his house and stealing a silver cup. However, Aylmer's dishonest history does not mean he was responsible for *every* theft in the town, so I went to speak to Flaxfleete, and he agreed to drop the charges.'

'But it might have been true,' said Michael. 'Aylmer *could* have stolen the goblet from Flaxfleete, then given it to his friend Chapman to sell to Simon.'

Gynewell shook his head. 'Aylmer did *not* steal the cup, because I found it in the cathedral crypt. I took it back to

Flaxfleete – not realising it was the Hugh Chalice, of course – which is why he was willing to withdraw his complaint against Aylmer.'

'But *Chapman*'s attention might have been drawn to the goblet because of the fuss Flaxfleete made about its loss,' surmised Bresley. 'He recognised it as something that could be hawked to a gullible fool who would believe it was a relic. So, he stole it from Flaxfleete after you returned it.'

'Wait,' said Michael, holding up his hand. 'I am confused. Are you saying Flaxfleete had the Hugh Chalice first? It was stolen from him – possibly by Aylmer – and was found in your crypt? You returned it to Flaxfleete, on the understanding that all charges against Aylmer would be forgotten, and it next appeared when Chapman sold it to Father Simon a month ago?'

'Yes,' said Gynewell. 'That is an accurate summary of its travels, as far as I understand them. However, I suspect *Flaxfleete* did not know it was the Hugh Chalice, either, or he would have made a far greater commotion when it went adrift.'

'Thank God he did not,' murmured Bresley fervently.

'I never liked to ask Flaxfleete how the cup had gone from him to Simon,' said Gynewell. 'I was afraid that if I did, it might give him an excuse to harass Aylmer again, and I did not want trouble.'

'He never made a second complaint of theft,' said Bresley. 'So we must assume that either he did not notice Chapman had taken it from him, or he died before he could tell anyone about it.'

'Or he was poisoned to make sure he remained silent permanently,' said Gynewell soberly.

'Perhaps we can go back a little,' said Michael, breaking into their discussion. 'You say you found the chalice in the crypt? What was it doing there?'

'Perhaps it wanted to be in the sacred confines of our cathedral,' said Gynewell, in a way that made Bartholomew certain he was not telling the truth. 'These relics have a habit of making their own way to the places where they want to be. Have you seen it yet? Did you feel the sanctity it oozes?'

'I did not,' said Michael shortly. 'I think Simon has been cheated.'

'Hear, hear,' murmured Bresley.

'The Hugh Chalice is genuine,' said Gynewell in a voice that suggested further debate was futile. 'I have never been more sure of anything in my life.'

Michael spent much of the day in the Close, questioning clerics about Aylmer. Bartholomew kicked his heels restlessly, not sure what to do. He was eager to ask questions about Matilde, but did not know who to approach. Then he recalled that the cathedral would keep records of the masses it was paid to conduct for the souls of the dead, and wondered whether Matilde had commissioned any. It was a feeble hope that she might have bought prayers for some hitherto unknown friend or relation, but he was desperate and willing to try anything. He obtained Gynewell's permission to trawl through the minster's accounts, and was conducted to the library, where details of the cathedral's business arrangements were stored on great dusty scrolls.

He soon learned the task was a hopeless one, but persisted anyway. While he scoured the rolls with a growing sense that he was wasting his time, he overheard a group of canons discuss the growing bitterness of the town's poor. The weavers were beginning to mutter more loudly against the selfishness of the Guild, and the canons were terrified that Miller's Market might end in a riot. If that happened, then the minster and its clerics might become targets, too, because of their friendly relations with the Guild.

Bartholomew left with the sense that Michael could not have chosen a worse time to be installed, and was uneasy enough that he went to the town butts to practise his shooting. He had the awful feeling that his fighting skills might be needed, although he was relieved the monk was elsewhere, and not in a position to comment on his new-found preoccupation with martial pursuits. He was not surprised to see Hugh and his fellow choristers there – or to note that their aim was considerably better than many of the adults – but he had not imagined archery was something to be enjoyed by cathedral officials. There were so many clergy jostling for a turn that the townsfolk found it hard to break through them, and there was a good deal of bad feeling. And when Miller and his cronies arrived, it was only a matter of time before someone was shot.

The victim was a guildsman, and Bartholomew recognised him as the fellow who had been sent to fetch the sheriff when Flaxfleete had died – there were not many men in the city who sported large orange beards. His name was Dalderby, and he howled pitifully, despite the fact that it was only a flesh wound. His friends formed a protective cordon around him, and Bartholomew saw they carried some very expensive and sophisticated weapons. So did their allies from the cathedral.

They were solidly outnumbered by the mass of poor folk, headed by members of the Commonalty, but the balance was redressed by the fact that few of them were armed. They had shared bows when they had practised their shooting, and there were not half a dozen weapons among the entire mob. Bartholomew supposed, from their hungry, sullen expressions, that they were the same unemployed weavers who gathered in the streets to ask for work each day. He eased to the back of the crowd when it looked as though a harmless Sunday pursuit was about to turn dangerous.

'You must make your peace with God, Dalderby,' announced a surgeon, after a cursory glance at the wound. He was a nondescript fellow with long, greasy hair, who had been standing with Miller when the 'accident' had occurred. Bartholomew assumed he was a member of the Commonalty.

'Does he have time for such a lengthy process, Master Bunoun?' asked Langar. An expression of deep concern was etched into his face, so no one could castigate him for being facetious. 'His crimes are very great, and it would be terrible for him to meet his Maker only part shriven.'

'I could prolong his life with an elixir,' declared Bunoun importantly. 'And, if he pays me in gold, I *may* be able to work a miracle. What do you say, Master Miller? Should I attempt to save him?'

Everyone waited in silence as Miller pondered the question, spitting from time to time. Bartholomew itched to inform Dalderby that the wound was not mortal – that it only needed to be bound with a healing poultice for a complete recovery – but he knew better than to interfere.

'For the love of God, man!' cried Kelby, when Miller's inner deliberations extended longer than was kind. 'Do you want *another* death on your conscience? Let Bunoun do his work.'

'I did *not* kill Flaxfleete,' said Miller, eyes glittering. He hawked again, aiming perilously near to Kelby's feet. 'But *you* dispatched Aylmer and Herl, so that puts me two murders behind you.'

'I did not touch either of them!' shouted Kelby. 'I would not sully my hands.'

There was an ill-humoured murmur from the crowd,

and fingers clenched into fists. Bartholomew was certain Dalderby's would not be the only blood shed that day.

'Please, Miller!' begged the stricken merchant, ashen with fear and pain. 'I promise never to mention that business with Thoresby again. He *did* threaten to behead me, and we all know it, but I will agree to forget about it, if you let Bunoun give me his cure.'

'What do you say, Thoresby?' asked Miller of a puny, rat-faced fellow who stood grinning his delight at the situation. Bartholomew had seen him shoot the offending arrow, although – fortunately for the chances of a peaceful conclusion – no guildsman had. 'Shall we be merciful?'

'No,' said Thoresby. 'Let him die. His accusations saw me in court, and I did not like it.'

Miller regarded the injured man dispassionately, then turned to Langar, listening as the lawyer murmured in his ear. There was absolute silence, as everyone strained, without success, to hear what was being said. Eventually, Langar spoke.

'Cure him, Master Bunoun. The Commonalty is not a vengeful organisation, and *we* do not engage in spiteful retaliation. We leave that to the Guild of Corpus Christi.'

Bartholomew watched a massive amount of money change hands – more than he had charged even his wealthiest patients for the longest and most intricate of treatments – and then left the butts before more trouble erupted. He met Michael exchanging forced pleasantries with Spayne near the fish market, and was appalled when the monk started to question the mayor closely about the current state of his finances. The physician brought the discussion to an abrupt end, declining Spayne's offer of refreshment with the excuse that he wanted to read a scroll he had borrowed from the library.

'What did you do that for?' demanded Michael,

resenting the unceremonious manner in which he had been dragged away. 'Spayne was given some of the money the King sent for draining the Fossedike, and I want to know what he has done with it. He has certainly not spent it on the canal; in some places, it is so shallow you can walk across without getting your feet wet. That sort of information would persuade him to part with what he knows of Matilde.'

'I do not want you to resort to blackmail,' said Bartholomew firmly. 'It is not right, and it could be dangerous. I have just seen a guildsman shot by one of the Commonalty. Tensions are running high, and it is stupid to risk being caught in the middle.'

'It might be your only chance,' argued Michael. 'And it is not unethical – I am merely using the wits God gave me to extract information that a decent man would have parted with willingly. Time is short, Matt; we do not have the luxury of tiptoeing around the man.'

'If you were not going to be installed next Sunday, I would recommend we leave Lincoln tomorrow,' said Bartholomew unhappily. 'I have never felt so vulnerable or so alone, not even at Poitiers. At least I could recognise the enemy there.'

'I recognise them here,' said Michael grimly. 'The problem is that there are so many of them.'

Being installed as a canon was not just a case of donning new robes and reciting oaths of obedience during a grand ceremony. There were administrative matters that needed to be resolved, too, and Michael found himself trapped at a desk in the scriptorium under a growing mound of parchment. Bartholomew helped him, afraid that if it was not completed, it would delay their departure the following Monday. They worked until the light began to fade, and left when Michael confided that he did not want to walk back to the Gilbertine Priory after dark.

They met Bishop Gynewell near the market called the *Pultria*. He was hopping up the hill like a mountain goat, Dean Bresley labouring at his side. He carried the equipment needed for Extreme Unction, and Bresley said they had been summoned to Robert Dalderby, who had suffered a grave wound at the butts. Surgeon Bunoun professed himself in fear for his patient's life.

'Did he?' asked Bartholomew, astonished. 'Does he lose many victims with minor wounds, then?'

'No more than any other leech,' replied Gynewell. 'He often recommends last rites to his patients, and when they recover, he demands a higher fee for snatching them from the jaws of death.'

'His tactics have made him extremely rich,' said Bresley. His expression was wistful. 'He owns some lovely gold spoons. I have had them in my hands on several occasions. I often meet him when Miller invites me to dine, although he has an unpleasant habit of talking about diseases while we eat.'

'I know someone else who does that,' said Michael, glancing at Bartholomew. 'It is probably a ploy to put us off our food, so there will be more for themselves.'

Gynewell frowned uneasily. 'I hope you are not planning to walk to the Gilbertine Priory alone.'

'It is only just four o'clock,' said Bartholomew. 'Hardly late. And it is not even dark.'

'It will be soon,' said Gynewell, passing his sacred vessels to Bresley. 'I shall escort you.'

'No, thank you,' said Bartholomew hastily, not wanting the bishop's company once night had fallen. The visit to the palace had unsettled him, and although he knew he should not allow Cynric's suspicions to interfere with his reason, he felt the prelate had too many odd habits to be ignored.

'They do not need such cosseting, My Lord,' said Bresley impatiently. 'No one will harm them. They are friends of the Suttone clan.'

'Why are the Suttones so revered?' asked Michael curiously. 'They do not live in Lincoln, and nor have they taken sides in the city's quarrels.'

'And there you have your answer,' replied Gynewell. 'If they did reside in the city, people would see their faults, and the veneration would fade. But they are far enough distant that they can do no wrong. Also, the fact that they stand aloof from the dispute is important: both sides hope they might be recruited, which would tip the balance permanently. However, the family know what will happen if they declare an allegiance, and they have no wish for bloodshed.'

'They are good men,' said Bresley. He shifted the bishop's accoutrements in his arms, and a silver brooch dropped from somewhere inside his robes to clatter to the ground. Gynewell pounced on it, and Bartholomew was bemused when he slipped it in his own purse. Bresley did not seem to notice.

'I think I *will* come with you, Brother,' determined the bishop. 'Just to be on the safe side.'

'People know he is a friend of the Suttones,' insisted Bresley. 'He will be quite safe. And what happens when you reach the convent. Will he walk back with you, so *you* are not alone?'

'Cynric is waiting near the High Bridge,' lied Michael. 'We do not need any other guard.'

'I wish that were true,' said Bartholomew, when Gynewell and Bresley had gone. 'There was a good deal of ill-feeling at the butts, and folk see you as an addition to the cathedral's ranks.'

'They would not have noticed me at all, if Gynewell had not ordered me to investigate a murder. I would have been with Suttone, being feted as the friend of a man who hails from such a well-loved family. *He* is not obliged to interview criminals who call themselves Vicars Choral, and nor is he obliged to sit with a demon and eat cakes that sear the inside of his mouth. It still hurts.'

'Gynewell unnerves me,' said Bartholomew. 'He *sounds* sensible and decent, but his appearance and habits are hard to overlook.'

'I would have taken issue with you this morning, but the cake incident has made me reconsider. I found I did not want him with us on that long, lonely road to the Gilbertine Priory.' Michael chuckled ruefully. 'We are worse than Cynric! What do we expect him to do? Rip out our innards with his claws? Spear us with his pitchfork?'

Bartholomew laughed. 'We will be ashamed of ourselves in the morning, when we are not surrounded by shadows. Poor Gynewell!'

'We should not discuss him now, or we will be nervous wrecks by the time we reach the convent. We shall talk about the Hugh Chalice instead. Are Gynewell and Chapman right, and it is making its own way to where it thinks it belongs?'

'It will only be able to do that if it is genuinely holy,' said Bartholomew. 'And you said it is not.'

'But I cannot be sure,' said Michael, exasperated. 'I cannot be sure about anything in this case. I do not recall ever being so confused.'

Bartholomew considered what they knew. 'Aylmer *may* have stolen the thing from Flaxfleete, although we can hardly ask either of them now, but we *do* know that he died with it in his hands. It was clearly important to him, which means it may hold the key to his murder.'

'True. I will talk to Lady Christiana again, and ask whether she has heard any rumours about it. It is lodging with the Gilbertines, after all, and that is where she lives.'

'No, I will ask her,' said Bartholomew firmly. 'You can talk to the gossiping Hamo instead.'

Michael gazed at him with round green eyes. 'That is not fair.'

'But it is wise. I have seen the way you look at her.'

Michael gave a sudden leer. 'All right, I admit to admiring her. She is a splendid woman, and it does no harm to enjoy the beauty of God's creations.'

'Then enjoy them a little more discreetly. I am not the only one who has noticed you think God has done a rather good job with this particular part of His handiwork.'

Michael was dismissive of the advice. 'She will be perfectly safe with me.'

'But will you be safe with her?' mused Bartholomew. He stopped walking and turned suddenly. They were by the High Bridge, and dark alleys full of hovels radiated off to the left and right. It was not a respectable part of the city. 'What was that?'

'Rats,' said Michael, after a few moments. 'This city is full of them, especially near the river.'

They crossed the bridge, and strode through Wigford, Michael for once making no complaint about the rapid pace the physician set. Lights gleamed inside houses, and in several churches evening prayers were in progress. They caught snatches of Latin as they walked. Bartholomew glanced behind him frequently, although it was now too dark to see whether anything was amiss.

'There is the Gilbertine Priory at last,' breathed Michael in relief, when he spotted the familiar gate looming in the blackness. 'I wish you had chosen us lodgings nearer the city. If you had, I might not have been ordered to look into the murder of this one's guests.'

'Do not be so sure. When I was in the library, John Suttone told me the Gilbertines are not the only ones with problems on that front. There was a stabbing at the Dominican Friary last night, and two men brained each other with kitchen pots at the Carmelite convent.'

Michael regarded him with troubled eyes. 'Yet more murders for me to investigate?'

Bartholomew shook his head. 'Sheriff Lungspee caught the Dominicans' knifeman, while the two who fought with pans are in the Gilbertines' hospital. They—' He stopped a second time.

'You are making me uneasy, Matt,' complained Michael, walking faster. 'Here is the door. Hammer with the pommel of your dagger, while I make sure no one creeps up behind us.'

Bartholomew did as he was told, but there was no reply. Then he thought he saw a shadow next to the Church of Holy Innocents opposite. He peered into the darkness, but nothing moved and he supposed he had imagined it. He turned to the gate and knocked again.

'No one is going to answer,' he said, when a third pounding met with no response. 'They must be singing, so cannot hear us.'

'What shall we do?' asked Michael. 'Shout?'

'That will do no good. We must find another way in – quickly. It does not feel safe out here.'

'No,' agreed Michael, heading for the alley that ran around the rear of the compound. 'It does not.'

The lane was narrow and pitch black, and Michael swore foully when he fell and twisted his ankle. His language degenerated even further when he put his hands in a bed of nettles. Bartholomew urged him to lower his voice, afraid the racket might attract unwelcome company, but the monk was too agitated to be calmed. The clamour became even more furious when the physician started to pull him to his feet, but then dropped him abruptly when he heard something behind them. Bartholomew spun around and drew his sword in one smooth movement.

'You never used to be able to do that,' said Michael, from his patch of weeds. 'If you were ever obliged to use a weapon, you were all fingers and thumbs.'

'Someone else is here,' said Bartholomew. He darted forward to make a lunge in the darkness, returning moments later with someone wriggling ineffectually in his grasp.

'You never used to be able to do that, either,' muttered Michael. 'You would have been like me, and waited to see what happened before launching wild attacks.'

'Let me go,' shrieked Tetford, trying to free himself. 'I am a priest.'

Bartholomew released him so suddenly that he stumbled. 'Then why were you following us?'

'I came to tell Michael that I have closed the Tavern in the Close,' said Tetford, brushing himself down, to indicate he did not appreciate being manhandled. 'Completely. I sent the women away, and sold my remaining stocks of ale and wine to the bishop.'

'I see,' said Michael, holding out his hand so Bartholomew could help him up. 'Does Gynewell intend to take up where you have left off, then?'

'Of course not. He does not approve of the place, and was delighted when I told him my decision. He will give the ale to the poor, and use the wine to celebrate your installation.'

'I saw you buying something from Quarrel only this morning,' said Bartholomew sceptically.

'That was then,' said Tetford. 'This is now. A lot can happen in a day.'

Michael picked leaves from his habit. 'Matt is not the only one who is wary of your sudden capitulation, and my suspicions are not allayed by the fact that you feel compelled to tell me in a shadowy alley. Why not come in daylight, like a normal man?'

'Because I wanted you to know as soon as possible,' replied Tetford. 'And sometimes it is safer to move around this city in the dark, anyway. Miller was not very pleased when he learned I no longer need the ale Lora Boyner brews for me, but that is too bad, because I have made the firm decision to dedicate myself to God and to the furtherance of my career, although not necessarily in that order.'

'You remind me of Bishop de Lisle,' said Michael, with the ghost of a smile. 'Is he is the reason you have decided to be virtuous? Has he written to you?'

'There was a letter,' admitted Tetford. 'He said that if I am a good Vicar Choral, he will make me an archdeacon in a year. It will not be fun, but I shall do my best.'

'Did Aylmer confide that *he* wanted to abandon his dissolute life, too?' asked Bartholomew. 'You are the only priest who has admitted to liking him, so it is possible that you traded secrets.'

Tetford nodded. 'He wanted to leave the Commonalty and escape Miller. I am not sure he had the willpower to do it, though – he was not like me. Forgive me for asking, Brother, but why are you wallowing in nettles in a dark and dingy lane?'

'We are locked out. Matt is going to climb over this wall, then go and open the front gate for me.'

'Is he now?' muttered Bartholomew.

'I can help you there,' said Tetford. 'The rear door is nearly always open at night. I know, because the Gilbertine cook boosts his income by selling illicit rabbit pies, and I buy . . . I *bought* them for my tavern. We usually did business at that gate. Follow me.'

They walked a short distance until they saw an opening in the gloom. Tetford produced a lamp from the foliage, indicating his visits to purchase the cook's pies were suspiciously frequent, and lit it to illuminate their way. Bartholomew was unimpressed when he saw that not only was the door unbarred, but it was actually open. It was hardly conducive to good security.

'Thank you, Tetford,' said Michael, stepping inside. 'And now we shall bid you a good night.'

Tetford followed him, holding the lamp aloft to reveal a thick growth of fruit trees. 'Will you take a drink with me before you go? Here is a flask, and I propose a toast to our success: you as an absent canon, and me as your deputy.'

'And if I drink, will it seal our agreement?' asked Michael. 'You will carry out your duties without recourse to running taverns and lusting after women?'

Tetford nodded and started to pass the flask to Michael, so he could take the first gulp. Suddenly, it exploded in his hand, sending red liquid flying in all directions. He gave a cry of alarm, and Bartholomew saw a figure move among the trees. Another missile thudded into the gate behind them.

'Down!' shouted Bartholomew, leaping forward to drag Michael into the long grass. When Tetford joined them, it was with an arrow protruding from his chest.

'How many?' whispered Michael, trying to keep his voice steady. The orchard was silent, except for the occasional snap as someone trod on a dead twig. Their assailants were drawing closer.

'Three or four. I cannot really tell.'

'Can you reach that branch near your leg? Hand it to me. We will not go without a fight.'

'Keep down!' hissed Bartholomew, grabbing his arm in alarm. 'An arrow killed Tetford, but it was a crossbow bolt that hit the wineskin. I can hear someone rewinding it, and the lamp Tetford dropped is throwing out enough light to make you a perfect target.'

'Here they come,' said Michael. Ignoring the physician's advice, he scrambled to his feet and went on the offensive. There were three men, hooded and masked against recognition. The largest carried a sword, and the other two held daggers. Bartholomew saw the crossbow discarded in the grass. It took time to arm such a weapon, and its owner had abandoned it in favour of a blade.

Bartholomew lunged forward to parry the blow the swordsman aimed at Michael, and twisted his hand in a move he had learned from Cynric, which sent his opponent's blade skittering from his hand. He heard a muffled curse, and the fellow backed away to retrieve it. He turned to the other two, making a series of sweeping hacks that drove them before him like sheep. The smallest turned and fled. The way he did so suggested the encounter had terrified him, and told the physician that the plan had obviously been to shoot their victims, not engage them in hand-to-hand combat.

Meanwhile, the first assailant had managed to locate his dropped weapon, and came at Bartholomew a second time. And then the physician realised he was facing a more formidable opponent than he had thought – the ease with which the fellow had been disarmed had been misleading, and he approached with a series of fancy manoeuvres that made the air sing. Bartholomew was dimly aware of Michael doing battle with the last man off to his right, wielding his branch like a windmill, and screeching a series of expletives

Bartholomew had never heard him use before. The monk looked vast compared to his attacker, and Bartholomew hoped his superior strength would see him victorious.

'Who are you?' he shouted, hoping the racket they were making would raise the alarm in the priory, although he did not hold much hope. His furious hammering at the gate had not brought an answer, so there was no reason why yelling and the clash of arms should.

Predictably, there was no reply. The man charged at Bartholomew, driving him backwards faster than was safe in the dark. Bartholomew stumbled over the root of a tree, and the attacker used his momentary lack of concentration to lunge with a deadly stab. Bartholomew twisted away, kicking his opponent's ankle as he did so, making him stagger. Then the fight began in earnest. Bartholomew parried blow after blow, feeling his arms burn with fatigue: the sword was one he had been given by a soldier before Poitiers, and was too heavy for prolonged wielding. Further, the faint light thrown out by the lamp was beginning to fade, and once they could no longer see properly, the chances of being hit were much greater.

Suddenly, Michael's attacker released a bark of satisfied laughter: the monk had lost his footing. Bartholomew saw the dagger rise, and was aware of Michael trying to jerk away. Then there was a blood-curdling howl that made Bartholomew's opponent leap in shock. It was Cynric and his Welsh battle cry. The book-bearer raced to where the monk now lay unmoving in the grass, the knifeman hovering above him, blade raised. The dagger started to descend. Cynric issued a scream of rage and his violent tackle sent them both spinning to the ground. Cynric tried to climb to his feet, but the grass was slick, and by the time he had hauled himself upright, the man had gone. There was an urgent snap of twigs as the fellow thrust his way through the trees, aiming for the river. Cynric followed.

Meanwhile, Bartholomew tore into his own opponent with slashing swipes that had him backing away in alarm. He heard a grunt of pain when the sword glanced the fellow's arm, but it was only the flat of the blade that had struck him. When a pounding of feet suggested Cynric was coming back, the attacker lunged in a way that made Bartholomew stumble, then disappeared into the darkness. The physician whipped around and headed towards Michael.

'Brother?' he whispered, resting his hand on the monk's chest. He could feel nothing under the thick layers of cloth. He grabbed Michael and shook him, but the massive body was too much for his weary arms.

'Have they gone?' asked Michael softly.

'Where are you hit?' asked Bartholomew hoarsely. The lamp had dimmed to a pathetic glow, and he could barely see. He searched the monk for wounds with fingers that shook.

'Have they gone?' repeated Michael, more loudly. He jerked away suddenly. 'Ouch! Have a care, Matt! You just jammed your thumb in my eye!'

'Are you hurt?' Bartholomew felt exhaustion wash over him, as it had done after Poitiers.

Michael sat up. 'No. I knew I could not win once I dropped the stick, so I thought the safest thing would be to pretend I was dead. I let myself tumble to the ground and lay still. Did I fool you, too?'

'Are you insane?' snapped Bartholomew, relief making his temper break. 'The man was about to plunge his dagger into your heart. He would have done it, too, if Cynric had not arrived.'

'Would he?' asked Michael, shaken by this news. 'I had

my eyes closed. He would not have believed me dead if I was watching him, so I had them firmly shut. I did not see anything.'

'Christ, Michael!' shouted Bartholomew furiously. 'That was a damned stupid thing to do!'

'Steady now! There is no call for blasphemy. Everything is all right.'

'Everything is *not* all right! Tetford is dead, and you were attacked by men intent on dispatching you. Jesus wept, Michael! I cannot believe you did something so indescribably stupid.'

'I am sorry I alarmed you,' said Michael gently, resting his hand on his friend's shoulder. 'But it is over, and God must have been watching His own, because we are both unscathed. Here is Cynric.'

'They escaped,' said the Welshman resentfully. 'They know this area, and I do not. I am sorry.'

Bartholomew climbed to his feet, pushing Michael away when he tried to help. He was still fuming, aghast at the thought that if Cynric had arrived a moment later, Michael would not be alive to patronise him with insincere apologies.

'You fought well,' said Cynric, slapping him on the shoulder in soldierly camaraderie. 'A year ago, a swordsman like that would have skewered you, but this time you were actually winning.'

'I am a physician,' said Bartholomew, rubbing a shaking hand across his face. He was beginning to feel sick. 'Not a warrior. I am not supposed to cross swords with people. And I injured one; he will have a nasty bruise on his arm tomorrow.'

'Good,' said Cynric maliciously. 'It will make him easier to identify. Who were they? Miller and three criminals from the Commonalty? Kelby and a trio of guildsmen? Or four wraiths summoned by Devil Gynewell, because he failed to get you when you were in his lair earlier?'

'Three,' corrected Bartholomew. 'One with a sword, one who started with a crossbow but reverted to daggers, and one who almost knifed Michael.'

'And the one who shot the arrow,' said Cynric, pointing to Tetford's body. 'I had a look for the bow, but I could not find it, so the archer must have taken it with him. None of the three who fought you carried one, so there must have been a fourth man, too.'

Bartholomew was too tired to think about it. 'Shall we go inside? It is not safe here.'

'You had better stay while I fetch a stretcher,' said Cynric. 'We cannot leave Tetford's body out here unguarded, not with Gynewell on the prowl. Demons feast on the flesh of the recently dead.'

'You really do know some dreadful things, Cynric,' said Michael. 'Go, then; we will wait. Tell them to hurry. I doubt our assailants will return tonight, but there is no point in taking chances.'

'Are you sure you are unharmed?' asked Bartholomew, when Cynric had gone.

Michael assumed a pitiful expression. 'No, these nettle stings are very painful. I wonder if Lady Christiana will agree to tend me with cool cloths. If she does, please do not offer to do it in her stead. You do not have a woman's healing touch.'

Bartholomew felt some of his anger drain away. 'You are incorrigible, Brother.'

Once Tetford had been taken to the mortuary chapel, and Michael had given Prior Roger a terse report about how they had been attacked, Bartholomew lay on his bed and stared at the ceiling. He did not imagine for a moment that he would sleep, and each time he closed his eyes, he saw the monk lying in the grass with the dagger poised above him. He knew his dreams would teem with uneasy thoughts that night, and considered resorting to the wine Roger had insisted they accept in an effort to make amends for the 'mishap' in his convent's garden. But he disliked drinking himself to sleep, so he abandoned the bedchamber and joined the others talking in the guest-hall below.

The room was full. Not only were there several new residents, driven to the Gilbertines by virtue of the fact that there were no other beds available anywhere in the city, but Suttone, de Wetherset and Father Simon were there, too. So was Prior Roger, his skull-like face white with shock as he asked Michael to repeat the tale. Michael declined, so Cynric obliged, giving an account that was far more colourful than the reality. For once, Roger did not interrupt, but listened in rapt horror.

The door opened, and Whatton and Hamo entered, the hems of their habits damp from searching the grounds. Whatton was full of questions and speculation, but Hamo was uncharacteristically quiet.

'I fell over,' he said, when Roger demanded an account of his explorations. 'I hurt myself.'

'Can I do anything to help?' offered Bartholomew tiredly.

Hamo shook his head. 'I will be better in the morning. In fact, I shall retire now.'

'You did not recognise these villains?' asked Roger of Michael, when Hamo had gone.

Michael shook his head. 'Tetford dropped the lamp, and all I could see were shadows. They had hoods over their faces, too. I do not know how we shall identify them.'

'One will have a bruised arm,' said Cynric. 'I shall look

at the limbs of every man in Lincoln tomorrow, if need be. No one attacks my—'

'I doubt the culprits will be out and about,' predicted Roger. 'Not if they know that sort of inspection is in effect. You will only trap them by cunning. Personally, my money is on Miller. I heard you declined to accept a favour from him, Brother, and he will not have liked that. No man appreciates his bribes being rejected, because it makes him feel soiled. Do you not agree, de Wetherset?'

De Wetherset was not amused to be singled out for such a question. 'I would not know.'

'All yours are accepted, are they?' Roger turned back to Michael. 'These felons were bold, entering my convent for this evil work.'

He walked to the table, and poured himself some wine. As he went, Bartholomew saw his boots were muddy. Had *he* been out in his gardens with bows and daggers, determined to dispatch the man who was investigating the death that had occurred in his domain? Bartholomew thought about Hamo, retiring to bed because he had taken 'a fall'. Meanwhile, Whatton and others were wet and bedraggled from their search of the grounds, making it impossible to determine whether they had been out before or after the attack. If Prior Roger or his Gilbertines had been responsible, then it was a clever tactic to start a hue and cry – to provide a legitimate excuse for any bruises or inexplicably soiled clothing.

'You should not have accepted Gynewell's commission,' said Suttone to Michael. 'I could have told you it would lead to trouble. Sin stalks our country, and the Death—'

'Fetch more wine, Whatton,' ordered Roger. 'Then go to the gatehouse and ask why the porter did not answer Michael's knock. I will relieve him of a week's pay if he was sleeping.'

'He may have been locking doors,' said Whatton. 'I have ordered regular patrols, since there are so many vagabonds arriving for the Market, and that means he is not always at the gate.'

'You need to employ more porters, then,' said Michael. 'And just closing your back gate at night would be an improvement on your current security.'

'That is always locked,' said Roger indignantly. 'The cook sees to it, and he is very reliable.'

'Except on those occasions when he is baking pies for the Tavern in the Close,' muttered Michael.

Within moments, Whatton returned in a state of agitation, reporting that the guard was so deeply asleep, no one could rouse him. On going to examine him Bartholomew detected claret and poppy juice on the man's breath, and knew they would have no sense from him that night.

'I doubt he will tell us much in the morning, either,' said Whatton, holding up a wineskin. 'This is still half full, which means that he passed out before he could finish it. It must be very strong.'

It occurred to Bartholomew that he should sit with the porter, to make sure he was not ordered to lose his memory as soon as he opened his eyes. 'He will know who gave it to him,' he said, to test the Gilbertines' reactions.

Whatton's expression was vaguely triumphant. 'I doubt it. People often leave anonymous gifts at our door – to be distributed to the poor – and it will not be the first time a guard has helped himself. Look at Hamo's predecessor, Fat William, who ate anything he could lay his hands on, and died from a surfeit of oysters. Any sort of ale or wine left will almost certainly be sampled by our porters.'

'And folk in the city know it,' added Roger. He turned to Suttone. 'It could happen anywhere, Father, so I hope this unfortunate incident will not encourage you to leave us.'

'Leave you and go where?' asked Suttone, to Roger's satisfaction. 'Every bed in the city is taken.'

'So, someone *wanted* us to go to that rear door,' mused Michael, when he and Bartholomew were alone again and in their room. Cynric came to sit with them, anticipating that his expertise might be needed in analysing what had happened. 'Where an ambush was waiting.'

Bartholomew ran a hand through his hair, frustrated by so many questions and no real answers. 'We had already started looking for another way in when Tetford offered to guide us to that particular gate. Was he part of it, do you think, and was shot by mistake?'

Cynric did not think so. 'If he knew what was about to happen, he would have stayed in the lane. No man steps willingly into a dark place, knowing there are nocked arrows waiting.'

'Perhaps they were expecting Matt and me, and were confused by the presence of a third person,' suggested Michael. 'Their quarrel killed Tetford, but that still left two of us ready to fight them.'

Cynric nodded. 'They were obliged to resort to blades, which they had not anticipated. They were unprepared, explaining why two fled before the fighting really began.'

'We helped them, of course,' said Bartholomew bitterly. 'Michael screeched up a storm when he fell in the nettles, warning them that we were coming. And while Tetford probably was *not* part of the ambush, his intentions were not entirely honourable, either. Here is his wineskin.'

Michael took it. The crossbow bolt had gone clean through the middle, and it was empty except for a dribble of liquid in the bottom. Bartholomew indicated he should sniff it.

'Fish?' asked Michael, wincing. The scent was powerful and unpleasant.

'Poison,' replied Bartholomew. 'The same substance that

saw Nicholas Herl drown in the Braytheford Pool and that gave Flaxfleete his fatal fit.'

'Tetford offered it to me,' said Michael aghast. 'Are you saying he was trying to commit murder?'

'Possibly,' said Bartholomew. 'Assuming he knew the wine was tainted.'

'He wanted me to drink it first,' said Michael unsteadily.

'True, but that may have been simple good manners. A dead canon does not need a Vicar Choral, so I suspect you would have been more useful to him alive.'

'Perhaps he wanted the Stall of South Scarle itself,' suggested Cynric, 'and did not like the notion of spending a year as a deputy. Men have killed for a good deal less. I am more worried about the other four, though, Brother. Tetford is no longer a problem, but these others may try to harm you again.'

'You seem to think the attack was aimed at me. Why not at Matt?'

'Because I am not the one charged to find Aylmer's killer,' answered Bartholomew.

'But you are here to search for information that may help you locate Matilde, and I have already told you Spayne does not like it.'

'None of our attackers was Spayne.'

'Did you see their faces? No, because they were careful to keep them hidden. The tall swordsman who tackled you could easily have been Spayne. I imagine he was trained to use a blade in his youth.'

'And do not forget Miller,' said Cynric to Bartholomew. 'You denied knowing anything about Shirlok's trial, but there is nothing to say he believed you. He is sensitive about it, and may want to silence you before you say anything. Then you both declined to accept his bribes on Friday. And *then* you had that set-to with Chapman this morning.'

Bartholomew did not argue, because Cynric was right. 'So there were two separate attacks on us tonight: the quartet with daggers, bows and sword. And Tetford with poison.'

Michael nodded. 'I think we can safely say that someone does not want us here.'

CHAPTER 8

The next day was windy, and rattling window shutters woke Michael long before dawn. He tossed and turned for a while, then noticed Cynric sitting by the hearth, prodding life into the dying embers of the fire. He went to sit next to him, stretching chilled hands towards the feeble glow. They were not alone for long. The gathering gale disturbed Simon, de Wetherset and Suttone, too. They clustered around the blaze, talking in low voices, so as not to disturb Bartholomew, although Michael knew it would take more than wind and a discussion to rouse his friend. Bartholomew was a heavy sleeper, and very little woke him once he was asleep – the notable exception being the Gilbertines' bells.

'You really heard nothing of our fracas?' asked Michael, recalling the racket they had made.

'You know how loudly they sing here,' replied Suttone. 'It is enough to wake the dead, and I heard nothing else at all. The only reason Cynric did was because he was in the kitchen.'

'I was one of the warblers,' said Simon. 'So I heard nothing but my own sweet music.'

De Wetherset was thoughtful. 'Now I see how easy it must have been to dispatch Aylmer. When he was stabbed, he probably uttered no more than a startled gasp, which would have been inaudible to anyone except his killer.'

'Someone wants my investigation to fail,' said Michael. 'Or perhaps Spayne dislikes us looking for Matilde.' He did

300

not mention his suspicions about Miller, because that would entail discussing the Shirlok trial, and the physician's wariness of de Wetherset was beginning to rub off on him.

'Mayor Spayne would never hire killers,' declared Simon. 'He is not that kind of man.'

'Then what about *you*, Father?' asked Michael. 'Since Aylmer's death is intricately associated with your Hugh Chalice, you have a very good reason for not wanting the matter probed too deeply.'

Simon glared at him, offended by the bald accusation. 'I told you: I was at my devotions, both when Aylmer died and when you were attacked last night. I am involved in neither incident.'

'Lincoln is home to dozens of unemployed weavers who are desperate for money,' Michael went on. 'I imagine it would be easy to find someone willing to kill in exchange for a good supper.'

Simon regarded him coldly. 'I imagine so, but that assumes I am afraid of what your investigation might reveal, and I am not. The Hugh Chalice is genuine, and if you say it is not, you will be wrong.'

'Michael will not denounce the Hugh Chalice,' said Suttone confidently. 'It is real, so there *cannot* be any evidence to the contrary.'

'How do you know it is real?' asked Michael, startled by the conviction in his colleague's voice.

'Gynewell told me, and he is a friend of the family. *He* would never be deceived by a false relic.'

'This particular cup has undergone some very sinister travels,' said Michael, deciding not to address Suttone's peculiar rationale. 'Ever since it was stolen twenty years ago.'

'Perhaps, but its movements cannot be relevant to its sanctity,' argued Suttone. 'The bishop and Simon are right:

301

it *does* have an aura. I feel in my heart that it is the genuine article.'

'People said the same thing about the Cambridge relic – the one dubbed the Hand of Justice,' said Michael. 'And I learned then that men's beliefs are something quite different from the truth.'

'You should see to your friend,' said de Wetherset, after a few moments during which the debate became quite heated. 'You are virtually yelling and still he sleeps.'

Concerned, Michael went to the physician's bed and touched his shoulder. When nothing happened, he prodded him hard with a forefinger, relieved when he stirred and sat up.

'What is the matter?'

'Nothing,' replied Michael. 'I was just making sure you have not been poisoned. There seems to be a lot of it about these days.'

'Poisoned with what? We have had nothing to eat or drink since we left the Bishop's Palace.'

'Ignore me, Matt. My nerves are all afire this morning. Lord! There go the Gilbertines' bells. I am tempted to ask Cynric to steal their clappers. That would stop them in their tracks.'

Michael was unwilling to leave the convent before it was light, so was obliged to attend prime in St Katherine's Chapel. Bartholomew stood at the back until he was sure Prior Roger had noted his presence, then slipped away to read in the refectory instead. After a breakfast in which the Michaelhouse men were served smoked pork and boiled eggs but everyone else had oatmeal pottage, he and Michael went to look at the chalice again. Michael stared at it for a long time, shaking his head.

'I am not the best of monks, but I should be able to tell a brazen fraud from something sacred. I suspect I could gaze at this thing until Judgement Day and be none the wiser. What do you think?'

Bartholomew inspected it closely. 'St Hugh died about a hundred and fifty years ago; this cup is thin, battered and tarnished, and might well be that old.'

'Is that a yes or a no to its authenticity?'

'It is an "I have no idea". I do not feel the urge to fall to my knees, but I do not want to pick it up and toss it out of the window, either.'

'St Hugh really did own a chalice with a carving of the Baby Jesus on it – it was recorded by his chronicler. So perhaps we should give it the benefit of the doubt.'

'You did not come, Michael,' came a soft voice from behind them. The monk jumped in alarm and spun around. 'You said we should meet last night after vespers. I waited an hour, but you never came.'

Christiana looked especially lovely that morning, her cheeks pale in the flickering light of the candles. She wore a cote-hardie of gentian blue, which almost exactly matched the colour of her eyes. Uneasily, Bartholomew wondered whether she had abandoned the Gilbertine habit she usually favoured in order to remind Michael that she had not yet taken monastic vows, and all they entailed.

'Lord!' exclaimed Michael in horror. 'It slipped my mind.'

Her expression was incredulous, and Bartholomew saw she found it hard to believe that she could 'slip' anyone's mind. He imagined it would be a stunning blow to her ego. 'You *forgot* about me?'

'Not forgot,' hedged Michael uncomfortably. 'My attention was snagged by another matter. Someone tried to kill me last night.'

Her jaw dropped in shock. 'I heard a commotion, but no one told me what it was about.'

She gasped in horror when Michael told her what had

303

happened and she learned how close the attack had come to succeeding. With a sense of unease, Bartholomew saw she had definitely developed a soft spot for the fat Benedictine.

'This is terrible!' she cried, aghast. 'You must hurry to the Shrine of Little Hugh immediately, and ask him to watch over you. I shall do the same. And tell the bishop to appoint someone else to do his dirty work. Giving him answers about Aylmer's death cannot be worth your life.'

'No,' agreed the monk. 'However, I shall be on my guard now, and will not be easy to dispatch. Of course, it may not have been me these villains wanted.'

Christiana regarded Bartholomew doubtfully. 'Why should you be a target?'

'Spayne knows he would like to find Matilde,' explained Michael, keeping his suspicions about Miller to himself, 'but he refused to help, even though he may have some idea as to where she might have gone. Perhaps he decided that killing Matt was the best way to ensure the hunt for her ends.'

'That does not sound like Spayne,' said Christiana. Her expression became wistful. 'Dear Matilde. I shall never forget her kindness to me when my mother died. Perhaps it was my grief that prompted her to persecute poor Ursula so vigorously. I never did tell her my contention that my mother determined her own destiny. I intended to, but she was gone before I had the chance.'

'Have *you* given any more thought to where Matilde might be?' asked Bartholomew after a short silence, during which the cathedral bells began to chime in the distance. 'I would be grateful for even the smallest piece of information. And so would Michael,' he added as an afterthought.

She frowned thoughtfully. 'She must be very important to you.'

'To both of us,' replied Michael smoothly. 'She is a good friend, and all we want is to be sure she is safe.'

'Then Dame Eleanor and I will make a list of all the places she ever mentioned,' said Christiana with sudden determination. 'We are no Mayor Spayne. *We* will help you find her.'

Bartholomew smiled gratefully, promptly revising his unflattering opinion of her. 'Thank you.'

Her own smile faltered as she returned her gaze to the monk. 'Your story of dangerous felons attacking you with knives will play on my mind all day, Brother. Were you hurt?'

'Yes.' Michael held up his hands, swollen from their battle with nettles. 'I was badly stung.'

'And you have given him nothing to alleviate the pain?' cried Christiana, turning on Bartholomew. 'I thought you were a physician!'

'I found him a dock leaf,' he said defensively.

'It was rough – and so is he when he wields them,' explained Michael to Christiana, in a voice that came very close to a whimper. 'And I had suffered enough.'

'There is a balm in the hospital,' said Christiana kindly. 'I have used it on nettle rashes myself. Come with me, dear Brother, and we shall soon have you feeling better. Dame Eleanor will be there, so do not worry about propriety.'

'I shall not,' promised Michael.

'What is in this poultice?' asked Bartholomew, starting to follow.

'Dock leaves,' replied Christiana, with a wry grin. 'But a gently applied paste is far more soothing than being rubbed with foliage. I will show you, if you like.'

'You need not come, Matt,' said Michael airily. 'I shall be perfectly happy with Lady Christiana.'

'I am sure you will,' murmured Bartholomew, watching them walk away together.

With Michael ensconced with Christiana, and the hospital doors firmly closed against any would-be intruders – even Cynric could not hear what was going on inside, and he was a far more experienced eavesdropper than Bartholomew would ever be – the physician found himself at a loose end. He did not want to visit Spayne again, despite the open invitation, since he suspected he would never have what he really wanted from the man. It was not his duty to investigate the death of Aylmer, and he had no idea how to move forward on it anyway. And the other murders were none of his affair – he did not think anyone would thank him for meddling, and, given the events in the garden the previous night, he was inclined to stay away from the whole business. He was restless, even so, feeling as if he should be doing something, and his sense of unease was exacerbated by the growing agitation among Lincoln's citizenry. The talk in the convent, by the tradesmen who came to deliver victuals, and by the people who passed the gate outside, was full of the brewing crisis between Guild and Commonalty.

'I thought we would be riding to Matilde by now, having new clues as to her whereabouts,' said Cynric, standing next to him at the guest-hall's window and staring across the yard. 'I shall enjoy watching Brother Michael canonised, but it is not what I was expecting to be doing next Sunday.'

'Not canonised, Cynric,' said Bartholomew. He shivered. Heavy grey clouds scudded across the sky at a vigorous lick, and the wind roared through the trees. It was going to snow again, and there would be a blizzard. 'He is not a saint yet. And he never will be, if he allows himself to be seduced by Lady Christiana.'

'She is not seducing him!' exclaimed Cynric, shocked. 'What a thing to say! He is a monk and she is a widow. They would never engage in lewd behaviour.'

'Of course not,' said Bartholomew, recalling that the Welshman was apt to be prim. 'I wonder if Spayne would be more forthcoming if he knew my real reason for trying to find Matilde.'

'I imagine that would make him even less helpful. Brother Michael thinks he might have guessed anyway, which is why he is being stubborn – if he cannot have her, then neither will you. I could visit his house and have a poke around if you like. He might have written down her whereabouts, lest he forgot.'

'I doubt it. It is not the sort of thing one commits to parchment. Besides, it is not a good idea to burgle the houses of wealthy merchants, Cynric. People are hanged for that sort of thing.'

'Like Shirlok was, twenty years ago in Cambridge,' said Cynric, somewhat out of the blue. 'I heard Miller talking about it in the Angel tavern yesterday. I told you I was going to listen to a few—'

'You eavesdropped on Miller?' Bartholomew was aghast. 'That was rash! The man is dangerous.'

'You took me to Poitiers,' said Cynric wryly. 'Is Miller more dangerous than that?'

'He was talking about Shirlok, you say?' asked Bartholomew, declining to admit that the book-bearer had a point. He supposed Langar recognising him in the cathedral had prompted a discussion of the old case, which made him uncomfortable, since it meant they had been bothered by it. Perhaps Michael was right, and the Commonalty *had* decided to prevent the matter from being raised again, so had tried to dispatch the man who might do it.

Cynric nodded. 'They were recalling how fast they had left Cambridge after the trial. Lora Boyner was bemoaning the abandonment of expensive brewing equipment, and Miller kept telling his cronies – Langar, Chapman, Surgeon Bunoun and others – how he hates being reminded of the whole affair.'

Bartholomew frowned, puzzled. 'They were acquitted, so there was no need for them to go. Do you remember what I told you about Shirlok? That he was still alive after his hanging?'

'Of course. It is a splendid tale, and I often tell it at Christmas. It scares the wife, see. But you are not the only one who knows he still lives. So do the Commonalty. Or some of them, at least.'

Bartholomew was startled. 'How do you know that?'

'Because of what I heard in the Angel. They were mulling over the whole affair, from the moment they learned that Shirlok intended to betray them, to their arrival in Lincoln a few weeks later.'

'Did any of them *see* Shirlok after his execution?' asked Bartholomew, thinking the man would have been a fool to make himself known to them – but that did not mean he had not done it.

'Langar has a lawyer friend who claimed to have seen Shirlok racing along the north road after his hanging, so *Langar* knows the man was not properly dispatched. He was telling the others – who do not believe this tale – that Shirlok might come to Lincoln one day and make a nuisance of himself.'

'Not if he has any sense. They will kill him.'

'Sabina agreed with Langar, although it pained her to take his side.'

'Sabina? She told us she was trying to distance herself from her old associates. Why would she be with them in a tavern?'

308

'From her sullen manner, I suspect she was ordered to join them. After Sabina had been dismissed, Langar told his cronies that she might *invite* Shirlok to Lincoln. She has turned against her old friends, he says, and he believes she might use Shirlok to damage them. He really hates her.'

'She is not very keen on him, either,' said Bartholomew, recalling how both had leapt at the opportunity to defame the other. 'Of course, Shirlok's resurrection was twenty years ago, and a lot can happen in that time. He might have died of natural causes – or the plague.'

'But he might not. He might be in Lincoln, avenging himself. First Nicholas Herl, then Aylmer.'

'Why? All they did was deny his accusations. It was the court that sentenced him to hang. And, even if Shirlok does believe Miller is responsible for his "death", he will not have waited two decades to make his feelings known. Also, it seems to me that Miller and company are the ones with the grudge: *they* were the ones who were named as accomplices.'

'Langar thinks Shirlok will come to Lincoln because of the Hugh Chalice,' said Cynric, dismissing the physician's reasoning with a wave of his hand. 'He thinks Sabina procured it to entice him here.'

'I doubt it. If anyone made the chalice reappear, it is Chapman. However, I suppose we should not overlook the fact that Sabina's lover Aylmer was holding it when he died.'

'*Or* that Aylmer was accused of stealing it from Flaxfleete a month ago. I do not want to stay indoors all day. Shall we see if we can find out a bit more about this Hugh Chalice? It is obviously relevant to Aylmer's murder, and anything we learn might help Brother Michael.'

Bartholomew did not relish the prospect of a morning

inside either, even though it was starting to snow, and supposed he might as well put his time to good use. He reached for his cloak and threw it around his shoulders. 'Where do you suggest we start?'

'With a visit to Miller's house,' replied Cynric promptly. 'He asked Brother Michael to keep him informed about the investigation. We shall go and tell him a few lies – and pry at the same time.'

Bartholomew removed the cloak and sat down. 'That would be wildly dangerous. Besides, Miller asked *Michael* to tell him about the enquiry, not us, and he is not interested in details, anyway. All he wants is the identity of the culprit, so he can kill him. He made no secret of his objective.'

Cynric, however, was not easily dissuaded from a course of action, once he had decided on it. 'You can distract Miller with witty conversation, while I have a look in some of his rooms.'

'No!' insisted Bartholomew, appalled by the notion of doing something so reckless. 'What would happen if he caught you? And what if he *is* the one who tried to kill us last night? It would be like walking into the lion's den.'

'Brother Michael cannot leave Lincoln until he has solved this case, and I think Lady Christiana might distract him. She is lonely and sad, and he is a kind man who finds it hard to refuse a damsel in distress. If you do not help him, he may be here until summer.'

'He will not leave at all, if we disappear and he feels obliged to locate our bodies. Or if he accuses Miller of murdering us and ends up choking on poisoned wine himself.'

'Miller will not harm you if you visit his house with a few friends,' said Cynric, thinking fast. 'Ask Suttone and de Wetherset to go with you. He can hardly dispatch three scholars with no one noticing. And if he does, I can always tell Brother Michael where to start hunting for corpses.'

'That is reassuring, Cynric. And what shall I tell Suttone and de Wetherset when they ask why we are all going to the home of the man who may have tried to kill me last night?'

'You will think of something,' said Cynric comfortably. 'You physicians are very resourceful.'

Bartholomew was not an easy liar, and could think of no reason at all why de Wetherset and Suttone should accompany him to Miller's house. Eventually, it occurred to him that he could offer Miller a free horoscope, as an act of goodwill to a man who was generous to Lincoln's poor, and claim he needed de Wetherset and Suttone to help him with the calculations. It was a ruse he imagined de Wetherset would see through in an instant, but as it happened, he was not obliged to use it: when he went to find them, he discovered they had gone out. Cynric was disgusted, and grumbled until Bartholomew suggested visiting the cathedral and talking to the Vicars Choral about Tetford instead. He also wanted to return the scroll he had borrowed from the library.

They walked through Wigford and crossed the High Bridge, struggling against a fierce wind that swept into their faces. People clutched billowing clothes, and hats were blown away, forcing owners to scamper after them. One was Dame Eleanor, who was obliged to trot most of the way down the hill before she managed to retrieve her hood, then was faced with the prospect of climbing up it again.'

'I thought you were with Christiana and Michael in the hospital,' said Bartholomew uneasily.

Surprise winked in her hazel eyes. 'She told me *you* would be with them! Clever Christiana! I think she has taken a liking to Brother Michael.'

'And he has one for her,' said Bartholomew, trying not to sound concerned.

'Do not worry,' she said, patting his hand. 'They know what they are doing, and it gives me pleasure to see colour in her cheeks at last. She smiles too seldom these days.'

'She is unhappy? I thought she liked her life here.'

'A convent is no place for a spirited woman. And she is worried that the King will foist an unlovable husband on her. There is only so long His Majesty will leave a valuable heiress unclaimed. Look at what happened to her mother.'

'She was betrothed to Kelby.'

'He was more influential six years ago than he is now, and he inveigled himself an interview with the King. Then he said that if he could marry Christiana, he would give His Majesty half the dowry. Christiana did not love Kelby, and her daughter saw how miserable the situation made her.'

'She carried his child,' said Bartholomew, recalling that Kelby had staked his claim early.

Dame Eleanor's expression was pained. 'Actually, she let him take her, because she was already pregnant with the child of the man she really loved. She endured Kelby to protect the fellow.'

'She had a lover?' he blurted, startled.

Her expression was bleak. 'I am a nun, who has sworn vows of chastity, but *I* could not find it in my heart to condemn her for daring to claim a little happiness, and neither should you.'

Bartholomew wondered who it was, but it was hardly a question he could ask, and he had no reason for wanting to know, other than curiosity. 'Your Christiana says she will take the veil if the King forces her into a match she does not want,' he said instead.

'She might, but only as a last resort. There are other options yet.'

Bartholomew regarded her uneasily. 'She is not thinking that Michael might . . . ?'

'There is a difference between distilling pleasure from a man's company and falling in love. I do not see your fat friend as her beau idéal, and I am sure his honour will remain intact.'

'Let us hope hers does, too,' muttered Bartholomew disloyally.

Eleanor smiled as someone approached, pulling a cap from his fair curls. 'Good morning, Hugh.'

Hugh effected a courtly bow, then spoiled the effect with a cheeky grin. 'I am going to collect devil's cakes for Bishop Gynewell,' he chirped.

'Devil's cakes?' echoed Cynric, shooting Bartholomew a pointed look.

'Monday is devil's cake day at the palace,' explained Hugh, as though it was the most natural thing in the world. 'Can I fetch some for you, My Lady?'

Eleanor shook her head. 'They are far too spicy for my old teeth. Put your cap on, Hugh. There is snow in the air, and you might take a chill.'

Obediently, the lad jammed the hat on his head. 'Father Simon gave me an apple this morning for delivering a prayer to St Hugh. He is so busy with preparations for his installation that he forgot to leave it, and he asked me to do it instead.' There was a sly gleam in his eye that did not go unnoticed by the observant Eleanor.

'You mean the written prayer he inserts into the Head Shrine at the beginning of every week?' Her eyes narrowed. 'And where did *you* leave it?'

Hugh's face was the picture of innocence. 'He just said with St Hugh.'

'You are a wicked boy,' said Eleanor sternly, although there was no real sting in her voice. Hugh looked suitably chastened, though. 'You know perfectly well which shrine he meant, and I can see from your face that you gave his prayer to Little Hugh instead. You must put it right immediately.'

Hugh sighed, caught out. 'All right. I will do it after I have collected the bishop's pastries.'

He skipped away, although not towards the bakery: the freedom of an errand was too good an opportunity to squander, and he was clearly intent on enjoying it to the full.

'Christiana tells me you are concerned about Matilde,' said Eleanor, when he had gone. 'Apparently, she left Cambridge too suddenly, and you would like to ensure she is safe and happy.'

Bartholomew nodded. 'It seems she left Lincoln suddenly, too.'

'Yes, just after Christiana's mother died. She thought Ursula had prescribed the wrong potion deliberately, although she had no proof. My Christiana believes her mother swallowed the cuckoo-pint to avoid marrying Kelby. Then, the day after Christiana's funeral, Spayne proposed to Matilde.'

'That does not sound like good timing.'

'Yes and no. He felt her slipping away from him, and wanted to arrest the process. She did not love him, though, for all his good looks and riches. Other women cannot imagine why she refused such a man, but Matilde is a lady for whom a handsome face and untold wealth mean very little.'

'Why did she not love him?' asked Bartholomew, wondering whether the same might apply to him. He had assumed she was fond of him, but she had never told him so, just as he had never told her. And while he could not offer 'untold wealth', the gold he had been awarded for his actions at

314

Poitiers meant he was no longer poor, and he had assumed a degree of financial security might make a difference to her decision. But perhaps it would not.

'She did not know why. It was just one of those things.'

'Do *you* know where she might have gone?'

'Christiana is preparing a list and I shall give her my ideas. You can have it when it is complete.'

'Why not tell me now?'

She regarded him astutely. 'Is there some urgency in this quest, then? There is more to your search than just ensuring she is well?'

'No, My Lady,' replied Cynric, before Bartholomew could think of a good way to answer for himself. 'It is just that the roads are getting bad for travel, and we want to be on our way as soon as we can.'

'You will not leave before Michael's installation, though, and we shall have our list to you before then,' said Eleanor.

Bartholomew was not sure whether Cynric had been fully believed, so he changed the subject before she could ask him anything else. 'You were about to walk up the hill. Is there something I can do for you, to save you the journey?'

'I need to see Ravenser or John Suttone, who are duty librarians this week. I must return the book they loaned me, because someone else wants to read it.'

'I can do that.'

She relinquished a slim volume, which she had kept protected under her cloak. 'Do not give it to the dean, though. He may offer to see it back on its shelf, but you must hand it to Ravenser or John.'

'Why not the dean?'

She regarded him oddly. 'Because he is forgetful,' she replied after a moment.

With the natural curiosity of the scholar for any book, he unfolded the cloth in which it was wrapped. 'Hildegard

315

of Bingen – her mystical visions. And there is an appended chapter by Trotula. I have always admired Trotula.'

She was surprised. 'There are not many physicians who regard her a worthy authority, and I am inclined to think they are right. That particular epistle contains her thoughts on childbirth, and I found it confusing and contradictory. It is obvious she was no scholar, not like Hildegard.'

'Why are you interested in childbirth?'

'I am not, but the scribe who copied the Hildegard found himself with a few empty pages at the end of the tome, so he added the Trotula to use them up. It is a common practice in scriptoria, as you know. So, when I finished the Hildegard, I discovered a short essay all about how some plants can be used to a mother's advantage, but how misuse can kill. There is one particularly horrible herb called wake-robin, which Trotula said brings fits and death. It did not make for pleasant reading.'

Bartholomew nodded. 'Wake-robin can also expel the afterbirth in cases where it sticks. Midwives use a little at a time, over a period of hours. However, I am seldom required to prescribe it.'

And he was even less likely to be asked now Matilde had gone, he realised with a pang. She had often summoned him to help ailing prostitutes with labour problems, but they were unlikely to come of their own volition. Such matters were the domain of midwives, who were jealous of their territory.

Eleanor shuddered. 'What a dreadful responsibility these women bear. Some must kill by accident, despite their very best intentions.'

'Not with wake-robin. Good midwives know how much to use and when to stop. Motherwort is another example. A little settles the womb, but too much brings on a lethargy that—'

Eleanor stopped him hastily. 'Enough, Doctor, please! I have no stomach for your trade, which is why I prefer to *pray* for the sick than to tend them physically. Are you sure you do not mind walking up the hill on my behalf?'

'I have to return a scroll to the library anyway. And Cynric is always eager for an opportunity that might end in an encounter with Bishop Gynewell.'

Cynric's sense of humour did not stretch to irony, and he was bemused by Bartholomew's comment. He spent most of the journey up the hill regaling the physician with reasons why it was wise to avoid Gynewell, a feeling that seemed to have intensified as he had learned more about him. Hugh's mention of devil's cakes had been carefully analysed, and Cynric had convinced himself that the baker had summoned culinary assistance from Hell, to create fare suitable for a demonic palate. Bartholomew listened with half an ear, recalling how Matilde had smiled at Cynric's fixations and prejudices. She would certainly have derived plenty of amusement from his theories regarding the hapless prelate.

They reached the cathedral, where they walked through its echoing expanse, looking for the duty librarians. However, Ravenser and John were nowhere to be found, and the Vicars Choral supervising the pilgrims at the Head Shrine and Queen Eleanor's Visceral Tomb said they had not seen them all day. Cynric crossed himself, as he gazed up at the carved imp.

'Do you think it chose that spot, so it has a good view of these regal entrails?' he asked. 'Everyone knows demons are interested in guts, and that imp is perfectly positioned to devour Queen Eleanor's when they rise up on Judgement Day. She will not be able to stop him, not while the rest of her is in London. By the time she gets here, it will be too late.'

Bartholomew fought the urge to laugh, and led the way down the South Choir Aisle, past Little Hugh. Unusually, the child's tomb was devoid of petitioners, so he stopped to look at it. Through the delicate tracery in its side, he could see the gifts that had been inserted – coins, prayers on pieces of parchment, jewellery, and flowers that had withered. Few were near the edges, and he supposed that either pilgrims made sure their offerings were shoved well into the middle, or people – hopefully cathedral officials – had removed the more readily accessible items for safekeeping.

He saw a new piece of white parchment, and supposed it was the one Hugh had put there. Cynric noticed it, too, and before Bartholomew could stop him, he had drawn his dagger and speared it out.

'I doubt that cheeky lad will bother. Make sure it is the right one, and I will put it in its proper place. Both saints will be pleased, and we need their good graces with that bishop on the loose.'

'I cannot read a man's private petitions,' said Bartholomew, shocked. 'Only a priest can do that.'

Cynric sighed. 'I shall do it, then, although it will take me a while. Despite your teaching, I am still slow at Latin.' He jumped out of the way when Bartholomew made a grab for it. 'Fortunately, Simon has big writing. It is just a list of names, though. Look.'

'No!' Bartholomew lunged a second time, but was no match for the agile Welshman.

Cynric frowned in concentration. 'Simon asks the saint to remember him at his canonisation. Then he asks for a blessing on someone called *pater et mater mea, mortuum*'

'His parents,' said Bartholomew. 'Dead parents. Stop it, Cynric. This is highly unethical.'

'Then there is a bit I damaged with the tip of my dagger. It says *ami . . . Christi . . .* possibly with another *mortuum.*

Hah! It must say *Christiana amantes, mortuum*. That means his dead lover, Christiana. So, now we know the real father of the older Christiana's child.'

Bartholomew's jaw dropped at the liberal translation. 'Rubbish, Cynric! It could mean all manner of things, including *amicus Christi* – Christ is dear to me. And the declension of amator—'

Cynric was not interested in grammatical niceties. 'Next, his *sorora* – sisters! – again with a *mortuum*, and a *frater* called *Adam Molendinarius*, with no *mortuum*. That must be his brother . . . '

He stopped backing away abruptly, allowing Bartholomew to snatch the parchment from his unresisting hand. The physician folded it quickly and posted it back inside the tomb, giving it a hard shove that saw it well beyond the reach of men with knives. He suspected Cynric was right, and young Hugh would not bother to rectify his mischief, but better the prayer lay in the wrong shrine than left in a place where it could be retrieved and pored over by nosy visitors.

'His brother,' said Cynric softly. 'His *brother*, Adam *Molendinarius*.'

'The miller,' translated Bartholomew. 'Adam the miller.'

'Adam Miller,' repeated Cynric. 'Simon is Adam Miller's brother.'

'It is a common name, Cynric, and a common occupation. Although . . . '

'Although Miller had a brother who stood accused with him at the Cambridge court,' finished Cynric. 'He was acquitted with the others. Michael told me. I am sure *his* name was Simon.'

'Coincidence,' said Bartholomew. 'They look nothing alike, and how can you believe a priest and a fellow like Miller are related? Besides, Miller told us himself that his brother is dead – died in prison.'

'Probably a lie,' said Cynric, happy to dismiss facts that did not fit his theory. 'Simon told you he came to Lincoln two decades ago. That means he and Miller fled Cambridge together and came here to rebuild their lives. And Simon – oddly for a religious man – elects to side *against* the cathedral and *with* Miller, whom he says is misunderstood and the subject of unkind rumours. I am right here, boy.'

'What if you are?' asked Bartholomew. 'What difference does it make?'

'A lot,' declared Cynric. 'Or they would not have gone to such pains to conceal it.'

Bartholomew and Cynric argued about Simon's possible family ties and past lovers until they reached the room that housed the cathedral's books, when Cynric fell sullenly silent. The library was open, but neither Ravenser nor John were in it. Bartholomew was tempted to leave scroll and book on one of the desks, but he was bound by his promise to deliver the Hildegard into their hands and no on else's. Claypole occupied the large table in the centre of the room, in earnest conversation with several friends. He stopped talking when Bartholomew tapped on the door, annoyed by the interruption. The physician noticed he had exchanged his sword for a dagger, and supposed Tetford's death must have reduced the need for a larger weapons.

'Try their houses,' he replied curtly, when Bartholomew asked politely for the duty-librarians' whereabouts. He looked as though he had taken a leaf out of Ravenser's book, because he was pale and heavy-eyed, as though he had had one too many cups of wine the previous night. 'They live in Vicars' Court.'

'I am sorry Tetford is dead,' said Bartholomew, somewhat provocatively. It had occurred to him that Claypole's obviously delicate health might have been a result of him celebrating the event. Claypole made a moue of impatience when a burly canon called John de Stretle stood to speak.

'Thank you,' Stretle said. 'We are sorry, too.'

'Very,' said Claypole insincerely. He lowered his head and pointedly started to whisper again. Bartholomew heard the name 'Bautre', and when 'inept' followed it, he supposed he was plotting against the man who had been promoted to the post that had been his.

'We shall miss his running of the Tavern in the Close,' added Stretle, ignoring Claypole and continuing to address Bartholomew. 'Although he did inform us yesterday that he planned to shut it. His uncle, Bishop de Lisle, offered some sort of financial incentive for a year of seemly behaviour, but Tetford would eventually have found a way to have the reward *and* live his life as he pleased. He was a clever fellow, and liked his fun. It is a damned shame he is dead.'

Another fat canon grimaced. 'I was shocked when he announced his resignation. I felt like shoving a knife in him myself! Life in the Close will not be the same without his genius for entertainment.'

Others nodded heartfelt agreement, and Bartholomew saw it was the loss of lively evenings they mourned, not the man who had provided them.

'I doubt Ravenser will be a worthy successor,' predicted Stretle gloomily. 'John Suttone would have been better, and it is a pity he declined our offer. I thought I made a convincing case, too.'

'You did,' said the fat canon. 'However, while he would have managed the books with consummate skill, he would have imposed too many restrictions for our liking, especially concerning women—'

His words were lost amid a sudden hammering. Claypole had an inkwell, and was banging it on a wall to regain their attention. 'We came to talk about Bautre, not the damned alehouse. Now, where were we?'

Bartholomew left, trying to mask his distaste for the men and their plotting. He started to feel sorry for Michael, having connections to such a place, before he realised the monk would revel in the intrigues and double-dealing, and might even make them worse. He and Cynric walked around the outside of the cathedral, then followed a paved lane south until they reached the quiet yard known as Vicars' Court. Ravenser and John were standing in the middle of it, yelling at each other. They stopped when Bartholomew approached. John was stiff and angry, but Ravenser shot the physician a grin that suggested he was glad of the interruption.

'Dame Eleanor would like to return this,' said Bartholomew, handing over the book.

'Good,' said John, taking it. 'Father Simon has requested it from tomorrow, as material for his inaugural sermon on the Choirs of Angels.'

'God's blood!' muttered Ravenser. He reeked of wine, despite the early hour. 'That promises to be tedious. I have read some of Hildegard's ramblings myself, and they are all but incomprehensible.'

'It is not worth perusing, then?' asked John, turning it over in his hands. 'I thought I might look at it tonight, since the Aristotle is out with the dean, and Gynewell has Dante's *Inferno.*'

'You let the dean have a book?' asked Ravenser, horrified. 'Are you mad?'

'He asked for it,' said John defensively. 'And I did tell Gynewell.'

'Well, if Gynewell knows . . . ' Ravenser turned to Bartholomew. 'We were sorry about Tetford.'

'Were you?' asked Bartholomew. 'I thought you did not like him.'

'True, but I did not want him dead.'

'He had closed his tavern and sold his stock,' said John. 'I think he was serious about wanting to be a decent Vicar Choral, although the others were sceptical.'

'Who will benefit from his death?' asked Bartholomew. 'You, John? It means Michael is now looking for a replacement deputy, as well as Suttone.'

John grimaced. 'I *would* like to be promoted, but not at the cost of my life. And the deputies appointed by you Michaelhouse men seem to meet untimely ends.'

'And I will not benefit, because I am an archdeacon, so senior to a Vicar Choral already,' added Ravenser. 'Obviously, neither of us killed Tetford.'

'I hear you plan to take over his tavern, though,' said Bartholomew, thinking that was an extremely good motive for murder. By all accounts, it was a lucrative and popular enterprise.

The archdeacon nodded, pleased. 'The canons asked John to do it, but when he declined, I put myself forward. If Tetford were alive, he would want me to take up where he had left off.'

'He would not,' countered Bartholomew. 'He was frightened of you.'

'We had a recent – and temporary – misunderstanding over a lady called Rosanna,' said Ravenser stiffly. 'But we were friends before she booked us both on the same night and he refused to bow to my seniority, and we would have been friends again, once our tempers had cooled.'

'Lord!' muttered Bartholomew.

'Anyway, I have laid in a stock of the Gilbertines' famous rabbit pies *and* rehired our favourite serving wenches,' Ravenser went on. 'I shall open tonight.'

'You should experience the Tavern in the Close for yourself,' said John, although there was a gleam of spite in his eye as he spoke – he had not extended the invitation because he was being nice. 'Bring your friend the monk. You will have an interesting evening, I promise.'

'Do come,' said Ravenser, graciously including Cynric in the invitation, too. 'The ale arrived an hour ago. It is from Lora Boyner, who produces the sweetest brew in the city. And Kelby has donated three kegs of good claret for the occasion.'

'The last time I saw someone drink wine provided by Kelby, it was poisoned,' said Bartholomew.

'Poor Flaxfleete,' said Ravenser insincerely. 'Come at five o'clock tonight. You will have to knock, since the Close is locked at dusk, but John will wait for you, and let you in.'

'*I* will take you up on your offer,' said Cynric keenly. 'I like good ale as much as the next man.'

Bartholomew did not reply, but he was tempted to go, just to see what happened when the prudish Welshman learned he had agreed to spend an evening in a brothel.

The market area called the *Pultria* was always busy on Mondays, and the steep street was a stark contrast to its silence of the previous day. It was full of people, despite the snow that was now falling in earnest, and traders used bells, rattles and voices to attract customers to buy their wares. Bakers' boys with trays of pastries weaved among the crowds, although the fragrant scent of their goods was lost among the more powerful reek of chickens and geese. Women from the outlying villages sat in huddled heaps on the ground with winter-brown vegetables displayed in front of them, and carts vied for space with the animals that were being taken to the slaughterhouses.

Most of the people who thronged the stalls were poor. Some knew the traders, and addressed them by name, pleading for credit, but others were labourers from the farms and estates outside the city, or vagrants attracted by the prospect of Miller's Market. Many of the locals had a pinched, dull look about them, and Bartholomew heard one trying to sell a blacksmith his oldest child.

Cynric liked markets, even ones that sold chiefly birds and eggs, and the physician trailed after him for want of anything better to do. He heard people talking enthusiastically about Miller's fair, and rather less keenly about the installation. A few folk claimed they would absent themselves from the fair because it would take place on a Sabbath, and Bartholomew supposed they were guildsmen – or in the employ of them – taking a stand against the Commonalty. One person particularly vocal in denouncing Miller's event was Kelby. He was with his friend Dalderby, who wore a massive bandage around his upper arm: Surgeon Bunoun was obviously of the belief that a patient liked something to show for his sufferings, and that the size of the dressing was directly proportional to the sophistication – and expense – of the treatment.

'Sunday trading is a sin,' announced Kelby. 'And anyone who attends Miller's Market will be damned in the eyes of God.'

Bartholomew watched uneasily as Ursula de Spayne overheard and stalked towards him. Around them, the clatter of voices stopped as people waited to see what would happen.

'You can go to Hell for hypocrisy, too,' she declared. 'You were trading last Sunday yourself. I saw you. You sold Dalderby three ells of cloth at the butts.'

'That was an arrangement between friends,' said Dalderby. 'It was not trading.'

'You can go to Hell for lying, too,' retorted Ursula. Her brother suddenly became aware that she was the centre of attention, and hurried to her side.

'And *you* will burn for murder, madam,' retorted Kelby, pointing a finger that shook with rage. 'You had one death on your conscience with your careless use of cures, and now you have another. Poor Flaxfleete, murdered with poisoned wine.'

'Please, Kelby,' said Spayne quietly. 'This is no place for such a debate. Come to a tavern with us. I will buy ale, and we can discuss this like civilised—'

'So she can poison me, too?' demanded Kelby. 'No, thank you!'

'I have poisoned no one,' snarled Ursula. 'However, I heard Flaxfleete's death served a *very* useful purpose. It balanced out Aylmer and Nicholas Herl – both members of the Commonality.'

'What are you saying?' demanded Kelby furiously. 'That *I* murdered Flaxfleete, to disguise the fact that I also killed Herl and Aylmer? You have taken too many of your own potions, woman, because you are mad if you think I would harm a much-loved friend.'

'God will know,' said Ursula smugly. 'And He will punish accordingly.'

'Come, sister,' said Spayne. His face was taut with suppressed anger, although whether with Ursula or his rivals was impossible to say. He grabbed her arm and pulled; he was a strong man, and she could not resist him for long – at least, not without an undignified scuffle. She was livid as he hauled her away.

Meanwhile, Kelby spluttered with impotent fury. Bartholomew watched him thoughtfully, thinking he had guessed what Ursula's barbed comments had meant very quickly. Bartholomew himself had not understood her oblique insinuation immediately, and he wondered whether there was a good reason why Kelby had. He glanced at Dalderby, and saw him regarding his colleague with a troubled expression, as though the physician was not the only one asking the question.

Bartholomew left the *Pultria*, and went to the nearby Church of St Cuthbert, where he spent an hour standing at the back of the nave, mulling over what he had learned. He realised he had nothing solid to tell Michael, only more supposition and theories. He shivered in the damp chill, and emerged to find snow falling thickly. It coated the streets in a fluffy white carpet, which was soon churned to slushy black ruts by carts, hoofs and feet. Cynric had finished exploring the market, and was waiting for him, so they walked down the hill together. Spayne emerged from his house as they passed. His expression was grim, and Bartholomew supposed he had ordered his argumentative sibling to stay indoors. If so, it was good advice: the air of menace that had seethed when her accusations were levelled was tangible, and he sensed a violent encounter between Guild and Commonalty was looming fast.

Bartholomew smiled as Spayne greeted him. For good measure, he reached out and gripped the man's arm, to assess whether there was a bruise that might make him wince, but Spayne returned the gesture with what appeared to be genuine warmth. Bartholomew was not surprised: he had never shared Michael's conviction that Spayne would have attacked him.

'This snow,' said Spayne unhappily, glancing up to where the flakes were large grey puffs against the brightness of the sky. 'It is doing my roof no good at all. If I did not know better, I would say Kelby had asked the bishop to conjure up some foul weather.'

'But you do know better,' said Bartholomew. Spayne started to walk down the hill, and the physician fell into step with him, Cynric at his side. 'Gynewell remains aloof from this feud.'

'Actually, I meant that Gynewell would never petition the Devil for snow, because he hates the cold. If sweltering heat was afflicting us, I would have no doubt that he had been using his powers.'

'What powers?' asked Cynric immediately.

'I had an unpleasant experience last night,' said Bartholomew, afraid Spayne might be about to fuel the flames of Cynric's superstition. 'Felons attacked Michael and me in the Gilbertines' orchard.'

'The orchard?' asked Spayne, startled. 'What were you doing there?'

'Trying to reach the guest-hall,' supplied Cynric, his tone verging on the accusatory. 'The porter had been drugged, obviously to make sure they were obliged to go round the back, where someone was waiting to dispatch them.'

Bartholomew watched Spayne intently, but the man revealed nothing other than shock that such an incident should have occurred in the first place.

'It is not the first time decent folk have suffered the depredations of villains recently,' said Spayne worriedly. 'Miller's Market has encouraged some very rough men to visit our town. Last night, an alehouse quarrel ended in violence, and Chapman was badly injured.'

'Was he?' asked Bartholomew. 'Injured where?'

Spayne regarded him oddly. 'Outside the Angel.' He pointed to a sign depicting a debauched-looking cherub, which seemed to be the only thing in the city not coated with snow.

'I mean where on his body?'

Spayne gave a grin that smacked of relief. 'Of course, you have a professional interest in these matters. He was stabbed in the arm.'

'The arm,' mused Bartholomew thoughtfully.

'Surgeon Bunoun fears for his life,' Spayne went on.

'Then perhaps Miller might appreciate a second opinion,' said Bartholomew, aware of Cynric nodding eager agreement at his side. 'It sounds as though you were a witness to this attack.'

'I was elsewhere when it happened, but I saw folk milling around as I came home – the Angel is between where I was conducting my business and my house. Miller wants revenge, but I think I have convinced him to reflect on the matter before doing anything rash.'

'Revenge? Was it an attack on the Commonalty, then? You implied it was a tavern brawl.'

'It was, but Miller still wants someone to pay. Unfortunately, that is the way of things in this city.'

'It is a sorry state of affairs.'

Spayne grimaced. 'It is more than sorry – it is tragic. Lincoln is a lovely place, and I hate to see it torn apart by petty rivalries and jealousies. Look around you – indigent weavers who cannot feed their families; the Fossedike full of silt; beautiful buildings crumbling from neglect. If we were to put our energies into solving *those* problems, Lincoln would be great again.'

'It does look as though it has fallen on hard times,' admitted Bartholomew.

'I am sorry I cannot help you find Matilde,' said Spayne suddenly. 'I wish I could, but they are *her* secrets and it would be improper for me to betray her confidences. If she had wanted you to know, she would have told you herself. I know this is not what you want to hear.'

'Very well.'

'Do not be angry. I prayed to St Hugh last night, and asked for his guidance. No great insight came, but then I realised that *was* his answer: I should not intervene one way or the other.'

'Lady Christiana and Dame Eleanor are preparing me a list,' said Bartholomew, rather defiantly.

Spayne smiled. 'Good. I hope they tell you all I know and more. Then you will have what you want, and I shall have a clear conscience. It is the best of all solutions.'

They talked a while longer, and Bartholomew found Spayne hard to dislike. He wondered what it was about him that Michael had taken exception to, and was seriously considering his offer of a cup of wine when Cynric prodded him, to remind him of his duties to the monk and his investigation.

'Visit me soon, and I shall show you a scroll I bought recently,' said Spayne, disappointed by the refusal. 'It is by the Provençal Franciscan Francis de Meryonnes, and sheds a good deal of light on the mysteries of Blood Relics, which we discussed on Saturday. I would like your opinion.'

'I shall look forward to it,' said Bartholomew sincerely.

'Do not wait too long,' said Spayne. 'The only member of the Commonality with the wits to debate such a subject is Langar, but now his lover, Nicholas Herl, is dead, he has lost his zest for life. But, if you will not debate Blood Relics with me now, I should be about my business.'

'What business?' asked Cynric nosily.

'Mercantile affairs. It is dull stuff, and you would not be interested. Good morning, Doctor.'

'What I find interesting is for me to decide,' said Cynric, after Spayne had gone. 'Not him. And I certainly *would* be intrigued to know why he was passing the Angel last night. You have to go by there if you are walking between the Gilbertine orchard and his house.'

'And if you are walking between his house and a good many other places,' Bartholomew pointed out. 'Both are on the main street. Besides, it sounds as though Chapman has suffered a wound that may have been caused by a sword. We should speak to him before accusing Spayne of foul play.'

Cynric turned around and strode up the hill again, obviously disgusted that the strenuous detour had provided no clear evidence of the mayor's guilt. 'You were attacked by *four* assailants, and Chapman is only one man. And Spayne is furtive –' not telling us where he was last night. I know folk say he is decent, but he has thrown in his lot with some very dubious characters.'

'You dislike him because you think he should help me, but it is unfair to hold a grudge against a man who is acting as his conscience dictates.'

'I do not think so,' declared Cynric. 'Look! Here come Suttone, de Wetherset and Simon, fresh from being measured for new vestments. It is a good opportunity to ask Simon about his lovers and brothers.'

'Hardly,' said Bartholomew, 'because then he will know we have read his private prayer.'

'He should not have left it in a public place, then.'

'He did not leave it in a public place, Cynric.'

Cynric waved an airy hand, and the physician knew he would ask his questions if the occasion arose. 'Chapman's wound is an excellent excuse to visit *Adam Molendinarius, frater,*' he said with a predatory smile. 'And Simon, de Wetherset and Suttone will be our protection.'

Dean Bresley was with the three canons-elect. All four were in earnest conversation, and Bartholomew heard the dean clank as he walked, as if metal objects had been shoved down the lining of his cloak. The others seemed too intent on their discussion to notice.

'Think of an excuse to take the dean, too,' murmured Cynric in Bartholomew's ear. 'I heard he favours the Commonalty. You will be safer when you visit Miller if Bresley is with you.'

'No,' said Bartholomew, losing his nerve. 'I cannot do it. We do not know who attacked us last night, and de Wetherset is a complex man, well skilled in intrigue. *He* might have tried to rid himself of us, for reasons we do not yet understand.'

'De Wetherset?' asked Cynric doubtfully. 'Why would he do that?'

'He lies,' said Bartholomew. 'We caught him out over Simon's alibi, and I do not like his old association with Miller and his cronies. It is odd that he was a juror when they were acquitted, and all just happen to be in Lincoln now. And speaking of that trial, it is stupid to go to Miller's house. I am sure Langar did not believe me when I said I did not remember it.'

'They will not harm you in broad daylight,' argued Cynric. 'And I will be close. So will de Wetherset, Suttone, and Dean Bresley, if you tell them to accompany you.'

'I have decided to follow Simon's example, and present the cathedral with a gift at my installation,' announced Suttone to Bartholomew, as their paths converged. 'But what should it be? Simon and the dean suggest an altar frontal.'

'A relic is better,' declared de Wetherset in his dogmatic manner. 'An altar frontal will require a chest for storage *and* women to repair it when moths attack. These cost money. On the other hand, a relic will bring funds to the cathedral, because they attract pilgrims. Perhaps Simon will introduce you to the relic-seller who sold him the Hugh Chalice.'

'Yes,' said Suttone eagerly. 'An item as significant as the Hugh Chalice would be a perfect gift.'

'I cannot,' said Simon shortly. 'He has left Lincoln, and will never return.'

'You seem very certain of his plans,' said Bartholomew, astonished by the brazen lie.

'I am,' said Simon curtly. 'He has gone to . . . to Jerusalem, where he will retire. But the local relic-seller is Walter Chapman. He may have items to offer, although I have been informed that his wares are not always genuine, so you will have to be careful.'

'*I* can tell the difference between something sacred and something fraudulent,' boasted de Wetherset. 'Take us to him, Simon, and I shall give Suttone the benefit of my unique skills.'

'That may be difficult,' said Dean Bresley. 'The poor man was stabbed in a brawl outside the Swan tavern last night, and he is very ill.'

'The *Swan*?' asked Bartholomew. 'I thought it happened outside the Angel.'

'The Swan,' repeated Bresley firmly. 'I was a witness to some of the violence myself.'

'Spayne said it was the Angel,' breathed Cynric in Bartholomew's ear. 'He lied to you.'

'It may have been a slip of the tongue,' Bartholomew whispered back. 'It happens sometimes.'

'Taverns are turbulent places,' the dean was saying, while Cynric looked manifestly unconvinced by the physician's explanation. 'Surgeon Bunoun thinks Chapman might die.'

'If that is so, then discussing sacred objects will be good for his soul,' declared de Wetherset. 'And he may even *donate* something to the cathedral. Then Suttone will not have to part with his silver, but can still bask in the credit of arranging a gift.'

'That would defeat the purpose,' said Suttone. He reconsidered as avarice got the better of him. 'Although I imagine the cathedral will not mind who pays, as long as it receives something valuable.'

'True,' said the dean. 'Perhaps I should accompany you,

and point out that gifting a relic to St Hugh may effect a miraculous cure.'

'Come with us, Bartholomew,' ordered de Wetherset. 'You can tell him he is in danger of death, which will make him listen to us more readily.' He held up his hand when the physician demurred. 'It is *not* dishonest. It is for the good of the cathedral, so the end justifies the means.'

'If *you* go, Father Simon, you will be able to pay your respects to your brother,' said Cynric with a guileless grin that made him look slightly deranged. Bartholomew closed his eyes.

Simon stared at the book-bearer. 'What?'

'Your brother,' repeated Cynric. 'Adam Miller. I see the family resemblance now.'

There was an uneasiness in Simon's eyes that was apparent to even the least astute of observers. 'Rubbish! I barely know *anyone* from the Commonalty, and they are certainly not kin.'

'You know Chapman well enough to have bought the Hugh Chalice from him,' said Bartholomew. He disliked being told brazen lies – it suggested Simon thought him gullible and stupid.

Simon was outraged. 'I have already told you who sold it to me – someone who is no longer here.'

'My colleague does not believe you, Simon,' said Suttone, glancing at the physician. 'But that is easily remedied. Swear on the Hugh Chalice that Chapman did not sell it to you. He will believe you then.'

'You can swear that you and Miller are not kin at the same time,' added Cynric opportunistically.

'I shall do no such thing,' declared Simon. 'I do not have to prove myself to anyone.'

'You can do it without harm, Simon,' said Bresley, although his tone was more unhappy than malicious. 'It is not the real one, so you can safely prevaricate and not be struck down.'

'It *is* real!' shouted Simon angrily. 'Chapman told me . . . ' He faltered. 'Damn!'

'Damn, indeed,' said Bartholomew softly. 'Why did you lie?'

'Because of Chapman's reputation,' said Simon wearily. 'I *knew* the Hugh Chalice was real as soon as I saw it, but I also knew that no one else would think so, if word spread that it had come from him. So I invented a different relic-seller, to avoid such an outcome. I did what I thought was best.'

'We shall discuss the ethics of this tonight, by the fire,' said de Wetherset loftily, beginning to walk northward. 'First, however, we should see Miller. Do not dally, Bartholomew; we need your services.'

He strode away before the physician could tell him that frightening patients with gloomy prognoses went against all the oaths he had sworn at his graduations, but Cynric pointed out that they had needed an excuse to visit Chapman anyway, and pulled him after the portly ex-Chancellor. Bartholomew was surprised when Simon came too. The priest shrugged when he saw the physician's bemusement.

'Now you know the truth, it does not matter whether Chapman tells you he sold me the Hugh Chalice or not. And I am a cleric – if he is dying, he may require my services. He and Miller live in the parish of Newport, you see, and its vicar is Flaxfleete's cousin. He may decline to give Chapman absolution, although I have never had anything against the Commonalty.'

'And we know why,' said Cynric pointedly. 'What about Lady Christiana the elder?'

Simon looked at him askance. 'I have no idea what she thought of the Commonalty. What a bizarre thing to ask.'

'You knew her, then,' pressed Cynric. Bartholomew cringed at the bluntness of the interrogation.

'Of course. Why do you want to know?'

'Is the Swan tavern noted for brawls?' blurted Bartholomew. Cynric glared at him.

'It is a respectable place,' said Simon, still regarding Cynric with a puzzled frown. 'Miller and his friends went there last night, probably because they did not feel like sliding down the icy hill to the Angel, where they usually drink. Quarrel usually manages to keep everything in order, though.'

'He failed last night,' said Bartholomew.

Simon nodded. 'So it would seem.'

CHAPTER 9

The suburb of Newport comprised a ribbon of houses that stretched along the main road north, two churches and a convent of Austin friars. Like much of Lincoln, Newport was poor, and Bartholomew supposed its inhabitants were mostly farmers and their servants – and unemployed weavers. There was only one building of note, a handsome edifice surrounded by a sturdy wooden palisade. De Wetherset opened a gate, marched through the grounds, and tapped on the door.

'Several of the Commonalty, including Chapman, live here with Miller,' he explained. 'And Lora Boyner's brewery is near the stream over there. She claims the secret of her ale is that she uses water that has not yet flowed through the city.'

Bartholomew saw a neat, squat shed at the end of the garden. A horse was hitched to a cart, which was being loaded with barrels, and Lora was issuing orders to a pair of sweating apprentices. One keg was abandoned near the gate, and Lora and her people studiously looked the other way when a gaggle of women approached and began to roll it towards the nearest hovel. The weavers were proud, and Bartholomew was surprised the belligerent Lora should be sympathetic to their sensitivities.

'Lord!' said Suttone, gazing at Miller's home in awe. 'This is a mansion! Its owner must do very well at his trade – whatever it is. Is he a miller? There is a wheat-sheaf carved on his lintel.'

'I do not think so,' said the dean. He frowned. 'Actually, I am not sure what he does.'

De Wetherset was better informed. 'He is in the export–import business, although that cannot be easy with the Fossedike silting up. It means he sells things to people. In fact, if you express a desire to purchase anything, Miller is the man to get it for you. He has some very good contacts.'

'Father Simon?' asked Cynric innocently. 'Can you be more specific about Adam *Molendinarius*'s work?'

Simon scowled. 'I know nothing about his dealings. Why would I?'

The door was answered before Cynric could reply. A manservant conducted them to a solar, but insisted on remaining with them while a maid went to fetch Miller. It was an odd way to treat guests, but when Bartholomew looked behind him and realised Cynric had disappeared, he supposed Miller was right to be wary of men he did not know. He sincerely hoped the book-bearer would be careful, and refused to dwell on what might happen – to them both – if Cynric were caught snooping.

Within a few moments, Miller and Langar arrived. Both looked tired and pale, and Miller was oddly subdued. His voice was husky when he spoke, as though he had been shouting. Bartholomew looked at the daggers they carried in their belts and tried to ascertain whether they were the ones drawn against him and Michael the night before. There were no obvious signs that they had been used in a fracas, but he suspected that even if there were, Miller and Langar would claim they had resulted from the skirmish in the Swan tavern.

'Surgeon Bunoun says Chapman will die,' said Miller, when Suttone had explained why they had come. 'So he cannot show you his relics.'

'Does he need a priest?' asked Simon.

Miller smiled at him, revealing his four teeth. 'Not yet, although it is good of you to come.'

'Then perhaps I can help,' said Bartholomew, when de Wetherset shoved him forward with such force that he staggered. He had been watching the dean inspect a tray on which stood four gold goblets and a matching jug. 'I have some experience with wounds.'

'Recent experience,' added Suttone helpfully. 'He was at Poitiers, and his book-bearer says he treated many men with terrible injuries. He even managed to save a couple.'

'Did you?' asked Langar warily. 'You did not offer to help when Dalderby was shot.'

'Your surgeon was already there,' replied Bartholomew. 'It would have been impolite to interfere.'

'You are interfering now,' Langar pointed out, not unreasonably.

'He is here to provide a second opinion,' said de Wetherset smoothly. 'That is not interference.'

Miller regarded Bartholomew appraisingly, then blew his nose on his sleeve. 'Come upstairs, then. I will take you, and Langar can stay here with the others. We never leave visitors alone, because—'

'It would be rude,' finished Langar loudly.

'Right,' said Miller with a tired sigh. 'That is the reason. Not because we have anything to hide in our cellars. They are all empty, and we do not keep any goods of dubious origin in them.'

'You should rest, Miller,' said Langar sharply. 'You were up all night with Chapman, and the lack of sleep has blunted your wits.'

'Can we look at Chapman's relics while we wait for Bartholomew?' asked de Wetherset, while Miller stoically waved his lawyer's concerns away. 'Since we are here anyway?'

'Lora will bring them,' said Miller. 'Come with me, physician.'

Bartholomew knew he would be a fool to let Miller separate him from the others, but could think of no way to avoid it without arousing suspicion. He followed him up a narrow staircase to the upper floor, feeling increasingly nervous with each step.

'Father Simon tells me you and he arrived in Lincoln at the same time,' he said, to break a silence that was both oppressive and unnerving. 'About twenty years ago.'

It was a blunder of enormous proportion, and Bartholomew was heartily ashamed of himself for mentioning a date that held a far more meaningful significance for Miller than anything connected to Simon. Miller stopped abruptly and turned slowly to face him. Bartholomew felt the hairs on his neck stand on end as the man regarded him with considerable malevolence.

'What do you know about what happened twenty years ago?' he asked, removing a dagger from his belt and using it to pick one of his teeth.

'Nothing,' said Bartholomew, hoping he sounded calmer than he felt. 'I am just repeating what Simon said. It is called the art of conversation, Master Miller – two men exchanging meaningless pleasantries as a way to pass their time together.'

'Manners,' said Miller with a disparaging snort. 'Langar is always telling me I need to acquire some, but all they do is make a man something he is not. If I want to spit over my own table at dinner, why should I not do it? If I want to blow my nose and the tablecloth is available, why not use it? And what is wrong with drinking my pottage noisily? Dogs do it, and there is nothing wrong with dogs.'

'I suppose not,' said Bartholomew weakly.

'Father Simon and I *did* arrive here within a few weeks

of each other,' said Miller, replacing his dagger in its sheath as some of the anger left him. 'But we did not come together. I left Cambridge because I am a sensitive man, and I did not like what was being said about me after my acquittal. He came because he had been offered the post of parish priest at Holy Cross Church, Wigford.'

'Someone told me you were brothers,' said Bartholomew, attempting a smile.

'Well, we are not,' said Miller firmly. 'Do you want to see Chapman, or would you rather stand on the stairs and hone your "art of conversation" on me?'

Half expecting Miller to whip around and stab him, Bartholomew followed him up the rest of the stairs, along a corridor and into a pleasant chamber with real glass in the windows. A fire blazed in the hearth, and someone had set bowls of herbs on shelves, so the room was sweetly scented. Chapman lay on a fur-strewn bed, his arm heavily bandaged. He grimaced when he recognised the physician.

'Go away. I told you all I know about the Hugh Chalice. It is genuine, and I bought it in Huntingdon. And if you accuse me of foul dealings again, you will have Miller to answer to.'

'You questioned him about the cup?' asked Miller suspiciously. 'Why?'

'Curiosity,' said Bartholomew, wishing he had not let Cynric talk him into undertaking something so manifestly stupid. 'I wanted to hear for myself how Chapman came by such an important relic.'

'It was more than curiosity,' countered Chapman pettishly. 'You grabbed me by the throat and your fat friend lobbed rocks at me. It was not a pleasant encounter.'

'You were holding a dagger at the time,' retorted Bartholomew. He saw Miller's face assume its dangerous

341

expression again, and started to clutch at straws. 'And we are friends of Master Thomas Suttone, kin to the great Suttone clan. He would have been vexed had we allowed you to stab us.'

'Of course! You know the Suttones,' said Miller in understanding. 'It slipped my mind. Obviously, we would not want to offend *them* by knifing their acquaintances. At least, not unless it is absolutely necessary. Lie still, Chapman. Let him inspect you.'

Bartholomew sat next to the relic-seller and carefully removed the bandage, which was tight enough to have turned his fingers purple. It concealed a wound that was jagged, raw and already reddening from infection. When he looked closer, he saw specks of rust, and was able to conclude that it had not been the clean blade of his own sword that had caused the injury. *Ergo*, it had not been Chapman who had fought him in the orchard. The relic-seller chattered frantically as he worked, evidently to quell his nervousness at the treatment he was about to receive, and Bartholomew learned that the tavern brawl had occurred shortly before he and Michael had been attacked in the Gilbertine Priory.

'I was busy at the time,' said Miller cagily, just when Bartholomew had decided the Commonalty was innocent. 'And I came back to find him like this. Surgeon Bunoun has done his best, but he says there is no hope. It does not look very serious to me, and we have had worse in the past, but Bunoun knows his business. If he says a wound will fester, it nearly always does.'

'Is that so?' said Bartholomew, suspecting Bunoun had seen more than his share of sepsis, if he was given to stitching up dirty wounds. 'Is Bunoun the only medic to tend him?'

'Yes,' replied Miller, 'although a crone came and presented

us with a healing balm. Chapman is well liked, you see, and she wanted to help. Bunoun said it would make no difference one way or the other, but we slapped some on anyway. She was trying to be kind.'

'You could not be more wrong,' said Bartholomew, fetching water from the pot over the fire and beginning to bathe the wound. 'I can smell henbane in this salve, and that is poisonous.'

'Poisonous?' echoed Miller in shock, while Chapman lay back and groaned.

Bartholomew nodded. 'Will you send for more hot water and a clean cloth? This cut needs to be irrigated thoroughly and its edges resewn.'

'You will stitch me *again*?' asked Chapman, appalled. 'But it was agony the first time.'

Bartholomew was not surprised: Bunoun's handiwork was crude to say the least. 'What did the "crone" look like?' he asked, when Miller had finished issuing orders to a maid.

'Old,' replied Miller, after a moment of serious thought. 'She was crouch-backed and her face was covered by her cloak. She was just a crone.'

Bartholomew regarded him uncertainly, sure a man in the devious-sounding 'export–import business' would know about disguises. 'Tell me what happened in the Swan,' he said to Chapman, when Miller did not seem able to provide a better description. 'Who attacked you?'

'A man,' replied Chapman indignantly. 'I went outside to relieve myself, and he was waiting for me. He wore a hooded cloak, but there was something about him that made me think it was Dalderby.'

'How can that be possible?' asked Bartholomew. 'He was injured by an arrow, and is in no state to fight anyone.'

'He has recovered,' said Miller, in a voice that made it

343

clear he wished he had not. 'Langar should not have encouraged Bunoun to save him.'

'Langar is losing his touch,' agreed Chapman. 'He is full of bad advice these days. We were right to keep from him the business of . . . but we should not discuss this in front of strangers.'

'I was attacked last night, too,' said Bartholomew, speaking to fill an uncomfortable silence.

'Then you are lucky you did not end up like poor Chapman,' said Miller. His expression was impossible to read. 'Lincoln can be a dangerous city.'

Bartholomew turned his full attention to his patient, and asked Miller to see what had happened to the hot water. When Miller opened the door to bellow down to the kitchen, Bartholomew glimpsed a shadow in the corridor, and knew it was Cynric. His uneasiness intensified: they were playing a reckless game. He could hear de Wetherset and Langar arguing furiously, and hoped the row would not erupt into violence. Uncomfortable and unhappy, he pushed up Chapman's sleeve to inspect the wound more closely and gaped when he saw a blue mark on the man's shoulder. It was a chalice.

'What is that?' he blurted, before it occurred to him that he should have pretended not to notice.

'Something personal,' replied Chapman suspiciously. 'Why?'

'No reason,' hedged Bartholomew, trying to smile and failing miserably.

Miller stepped forward, and Bartholomew tensed, expecting to feel powerful hands lock around his throat or hear the sound of a dagger being drawn. His hand dropped to his own knife.

'Oh, that,' said Miller, when he saw what they were talking about. 'I have often wondered how you came by that.

344

Aylmer and Nicholas Herl had similar marks. I always thought they looked like cups.'

'Yes, symbols of good living,' said Chapman with a weak grin. 'Claret, you know.'

'Flaxfleete had one, too,' said Bartholomew, taking the bull by the horns. 'Is it a sign of alliance?'

Miller made a guttural hissing sound that Bartholomew assumed was a laugh. 'Flaxfleete hated the Commonalty – Chapman, Aylmer and Herl included. He would never have made an alliance with them, nor they with him. Eh, Chapman?'

'Of course not,' said Chapman shiftily. 'As I said, it is just something to express my fondness for wine. But I do not want to think about wine now, not when I feel so ill. Please stay with me, Miller.'

'If you insist,' said Miller reluctantly. He plumped himself down on the bed, and took the relic-seller's fluttering hand. 'Although I do not like surgeons and the grisly things they do to living flesh.'

'I am not a surgeon,' said Bartholomew. 'I am a physician.'

'University trained,' explained Chapman, when Miller seemed unaware of the difference. 'Surgeons just cut things off. Bunoun wanted to remove my arm last night, remember? You objected.'

'I was afraid he would make a mess on the rugs – the new ones, from Greece. But get on with whatever you plan to do, physician, or my resolve will fail.' Miller hawked and spat, making Bartholomew itch to point out that phlegm on his prize carpets was just as unappealing as gore.

Bartholomew unpicked the crude stitches, cleaned the wound, and sewed it shut in a way that left the lower part open for natural suppuration, following the accepted procedure adopted by all good medics. Each stage was accompanied by agonised shrieks from his patient, but it was Miller who grew steadily more pale, so much so that Bartholomew was afraid he might faint.

'Thank you,' said Chapman when all was finished, remarkably pert after the racket he had made. 'You did not hurt me nearly as much Bunoun did. We should reward him handsomely for that, Miller.'

'It sounded as though he was killing you,' said Miller, putting a hand over his mouth as though he might be sick. Bartholomew passed him a bowl. 'What do you want me to give him?'

'A relic,' replied Chapman. 'A bone, perhaps.'

'That is not necessary,' said Bartholomew quickly. Given Chapman's reputation, the gift would almost certainly be a fake, but Bartholomew did not want the responsibility regardless.

'A man not desperate for a fee,' mused Miller suspiciously. 'You are an odd sort.'

'Give him one . . . no *two* of those white pearls,' said Chapman, determined Bartholomew should not leave empty-handed. 'The ones that belonged to the Virgin Mary.'

'The Virgin wore pearls?' asked Bartholomew dubiously.

'Just on Sundays,' said Chapman. He settled down in his bed. 'If I live, I will give you two more.'

'And if he dies, I will bury them with you,' growled Miller, eyeing Bartholomew malevolently.

In Miller's solar downstairs, a vicious argument was in full swing. Suttone thought a reliquary containing Joseph's teeth was a suitable gift, while de Wetherset believed the cathedral would prefer a paten. Langar had taken Suttone's side, and de Wetherset archly demanded what a lawyer could know about the needs of a holy minster. When Bartholomew looked at the dean, to see where he stood

346

on the debate, he could not help but notice that there were no longer four gold goblets on the tray with the jug: there were three.

'That consultation sounded painful,' said de Wetherset, interrupting Suttone to address the physician. Having his own say then changing the subject before anyone could take issue was an annoying habit that Bartholomew remembered from Cambridge. 'Have you killed the poor fellow?'

'I hope not,' said Bartholomew uneasily. 'Master Miller will be vexed if so.'

'I will be more than vexed,' grunted Miller. 'I will ki—'

'He will pray to Little Hugh,' interrupted Langar. 'And if Chapman dies, and the physician follows him to his grave, do not come here looking for explanations. It will be what the saint has ordained.'

'If Chapman does die, it will not be Bartholomew's fault,' declared de Wetherset. 'He is a talented physician, but there is only so much he can do once a patient's humours are in disarray.'

Bartholomew was pleasantly surprised by the vote of confidence, especially since de Wetherset had never been one of his patients. He turned to Miller and Langar. 'Do not give Chapman *anything* brought by well-wishers. I will return tomorrow and change the dressing. Keep him warm and quiet, and let him drink as much as he wants – ale, though, not wine. Wine would not be good for him.'

Langar nodded. 'We can do that. What are his chances of life?'

'Fairly good, if you follow my instructions,' replied Bartholomew cautiously. He saw a flicker of movement in the passage outside the hall, and supposed it was Cynric again. He wished the book-bearer would hurry up and leave, and found his stomach churning in nervous apprehension.

'Here are your white pearls,' said Miller, going to a box on the table and picking out the two smallest. Bartholomew recalled that Sheriff Lungspee had received white pearls from Miller, too, as a bribe to see some member of the Commonalty acquitted of a crime he had almost certainly committed.

'Has Brother Michael found Aylmer's killer yet?' asked Langar.

Bartholomew dropped one of the pearls on the floor, to give Cynric more time to escape while he recovered it. 'I am afraid you will have to ask him. How about you? Have you discovered what happened to Herl?'

Langar smiled, although it was not a pleasant expression, and reminded Bartholomew of the lizards he had seen in southern France. 'You helped, when you inspected his body for that woman—'

'Sabina,' supplied Miller helpfully, bending to retrieve the gem from a gap in the floorboards and hand it back. 'His wife.'

Langar glowered at the hated name. '—and ascertained that he had been poisoned. It is odd that Flaxfleete died of the same thing. That woman said it is all to do with Summer Madness.'

'Perhaps it is set to return,' said Suttone, rubbing his hands rather gleefully. 'Like the plague.'

'Flaxfleete did *not* have Summer Madness when he set Spayne's property alight,' said Miller. 'So, Ursula was right to poison him in revenge. Do you think she killed Dalderby, too?'

'Ursula has not killed anyone,' said Langar warningly.

'So you say,' retorted Miller. 'Remember, though, that Dalderby was going around telling folk it was Thoresby who shot him, when he promised on his deathbed at the butts to forget their quarrel. She did not like that.'

'Dalderby is not dead,' said Bartholomew. 'The arrow wound in his arm was not fatal.'

'He died this morning,' explained Langar. 'Although I heard it was not his wound that killed him.'

'Perhaps Ursula knows it was Dalderby who stabbed Chapman last night,' said Miller flatly. 'And and the outrage was too much for her. It is certainly too much for me.'

Bartholomew could see Cynric lounging safely against the house across the street, and was desperate to be away from Miller. His thoughts churned in confusion. Who and what had killed Dalderby? Should he inspect the body, and try to find out? It might be pertinent if he had died from ingesting the same poison that had killed Flaxfleete and Herl, and that had been offered to Michael.

'I am needed back at the cathedral,' said Simon importantly. 'And we should let Master Miller be about his business. What will it be, Suttone? Teeth or paten?'

'Teeth,' said Suttone, ignoring de Wetherset's sigh that his opinion had been disregarded.

They took their leave of Miller. The dean disappeared on an errand of his own, and Suttone, de Wetherset and Simon followed the physician back towards the city.

'Thank you for speaking up for me,' said Bartholomew to de Wetherset as they went.

De Wetherset clapped him on the shoulder. 'You are welcome. I am sure you will remember my loyalty when I resume my duties as Chancellor at Cambridge.'

'When might that be?' asked Suttone in alarm. 'I intend to hold that post myself.'

'I have not decided,' said de Wetherset comfortably. 'So, the field is yours until I do. I may even vote for you – on the understanding that you vote for me when I make my bid for power, of course.'

They began to discuss strategies, all of which acknow-ledged the possibility that Michael might stand himself. Bartholomew suspected neither would succeed if the clever monk was a contender.

'Lord!' he muttered, when Cynric came to walk next to him. 'That was unpleasant. I was afraid for you, worried what these garrulous scholars might be saying to Langar, and nervous of harming Chapman. You should have heard him scream.'

'I did,' said Cynric dryly. 'And so did every other soul in Lincoln, I imagine.'

'Did you discover anything useful?' asked Bartholomew. Now the ordeal was over, his legs felt rubbery, and he hoped it had not all been in vain.

Cynric grimaced. 'There was a cellar, but it had a lock I could not pick. It is an odd room to secure, because most folk keep their valuables under the floorboards in their bedchambers. Burglaries tend to occur at night, see, and folk like to have their goods with them when they are asleep.'

Bartholomew recalled Miller's unconvincing claim that his basement was empty, and supposed he really did keep 'goods of dubious origin' in them. 'It is probably just as well you did not search it. You would almost certainly have found it stuffed to the gills with illegal imports, and perhaps even stolen property. We do not want to carry that sort of knowledge around with us.'

Cynric shrugged. 'Perhaps. It was galling to meet a door and not be able to get past it, though.'

'Right,' said Bartholomew, not entirely comfortable with this particular skill of Cynric's. 'Was there anything else?'

Cynric shrugged. 'Just this.'

He pulled something from under his cloak, and held it so only Bartholomew could see. It was a silver chalice, battered and dented, and identical to the one in the Gilbertines' chapel.

When Bartholomew, Cynric and the others reached the *Pultria,* the city felt unusually subdued for a weekday. The snow had stopped, but the sky was a dirty yellow-grey, suggesting there was more to come. Dusk would settle early, and Bartholomew was determined to be back inside the Gilbertine Priory before more would-be assassins could use the cover of darkness to strike at him.

'Miller denied being kin to Simon when I asked,' he said to his book-bearer. 'I am inclined to believe him, because there is no reason for either of them to lie.'

'There is,' argued Cynric. 'If *you* were a priest, would *you* admit that your brother is the biggest scoundrel in the city? And Simon has been a humble vicar for two decades, yet he can afford to buy relics and give them away. The reason he can do this is because his brother gives him money.'

Bartholomew was not sure what to think. 'Possibly, but—'

'There is a funeral procession,' interrupted Cynric. 'That explains why the *Pultria* is so quiet.'

'Flaxfleete's,' said Bartholomew, seeing Kelby carry the candle at the head of the cortege. Behind him, two guildsmen tolled hand-bells, and there were several cathedral dignitaries among the mourners. On top of the coffin was a large jewel-studded box.

'Do you see Kelby's candle?' whispered Cynric, pinching Bartholomew's arm. 'It is not lit!'

'It has blown out,' replied Bartholomew. 'It is windy this afternoon.'

'No, it is because *he* had a hand in his friend's murder and *God* extinguished it,' averred Cynric. 'God does not like hypocrisy at funerals. I heard Langar tell Miller what happened to Flaxfleete yesterday: Kelby is so scared that Miller might kill *him* to even the score for Herl and Aylmer that he killed Flaxfleete himself, to make amends. A sacrifice.'

'Langar must have been listening to Ursula,' said Bartholomew. 'That is what she thinks.'

'See that nice box on the coffin?' asked Cynric. 'That is the new reliquary for the Hugh Chalice. Flaxfleete was going to present it at the installation on Sunday. Quarrel at the Swan told me. It is being displayed now, so folk will know who donated it when Simon makes his presentation of the cup. It is the Guild's way of making sure they get credit, see.'

A number of people had gathered to watch the sombre ceremony. Among them were Dame Eleanor and Lady Christiana, who were in the unlikely company of Sheriff Lungspee. Bartholomew went to stand with them, Cynric at his heels, looking around for Michael as he did so. The monk was nowhere to be seen and, uncharitably, Bartholomew wondered whether he was sleeping off his exertions.

'A sorry business,' said Dame Eleanor quietly. 'Flaxfleete was too young to be taken to God.'

'We worked on your list today,' said Christiana, more interested in talking to the physician than watching the dismal spectacle of a casket borne through the wintry streets. 'Michael asked us to.'

Dame Eleanor smiled fondly, while Bartholomew pondered the familiar use of the monk's name. 'When you find her, you can tell her she will always be welcome to live in Lincoln.'

'And us helping you will show Spayne that not everyone is mean,' said Christiana. She tossed her head in a way that showed her long neck to its best advantage. Lungspee leered his admiration, and so did several men in the funeral procession. Christiana noticed, and a smile of satisfaction flitted across her lovely face.

'Look at this silver bracelet,' said Lungspee, tearing his eyes away from her as he proffered the bauble for everyone to see. 'Dalderby gave it to me last night, because he said he might need my help over accusations pertaining to the stabbing of Chapman. It probably means he did it. It is a good thing he passed it to me when he did, because he died this morning.'

Eleanor was shocked. 'Are you saying you accepted a *bribe?* Or did I misunderstand?'

'You misunderstood,' said Lungspee glibly. 'I never accept bribes. That would be illegal. This is not an inducement: it is a token of brotherly esteem.'

'What happened to Dalderby?' asked Bartholomew, before she could quiz him further. Squeamishly, he did not want to see what would happen when the saintly old lady learned of the sheriff's fondness for having the wheels of justice oiled.

'He suffered a hard blow to the head,' replied Lungspee, raking dirty fingers through his long hair. 'It occurred outside Spayne's house. He managed to stagger to Kelby, but said nothing before he died. It is a pity, since his death *and* Flaxfleete's mean a shift in the balance of power.'

'This horrible feud!' said Dame Eleanor with considerable feeling. 'I am heartily sick of it!'

'I shall do my best to avert a crisis,' said Lungspee, although he did not sound very keen. 'However, my sergeants have not been paid for two months, and they are becoming slow to follow orders.'

'I assume you intend to investigate Dalderby's murder, Sheriff,' said Dame Eleanor coolly. 'Or do you intend to pretend it did not happen?'

Lungspee grimaced. 'He almost certainly stabbed Chapman, so the culprit will be a member of the Commonalty or their supporters. I will ask a few questions, but I doubt I will ever learn the truth.'

'Were there any other wounds on him?' asked Bartholomew. If the fellow had been sufficiently recovered from his shooting to bribe sheriffs and ambush relic-sellers, then he was fit enough to stand in a dark garden and loose arrows at monks and physicians.

'I did not look,' said Lungspee. 'There was no need, not having seen the crack in his skull. Why?'

'He is a physician,' explained Eleanor. 'They are trained to ask odd questions. But it is nearing dusk, and I should return to my shrines for vespers. Will you escort me, Christiana?'

Before she left, Christiana showed Bartholomew and Cynric a small wooden carving of a soldier. 'I bought this for young Hugh today, and I cannot wait to give it to him. He will adore it, and it always gives me pleasure to see gifts so happily accepted.'

'Father Simon wrote some loving words to your mother today, lady,' said Cynric before Bartholomew could stop him. 'In a prayer.'

Christiana was surprised and touched. 'How kind. He always was fond of her.'

'I am sure of it,' said Cynric blandly. '*Very* fond, I should think.'

It was dark by the time Bartholomew left the *Pultria*. He could have forced his way through the crowds that had gathered to watch Flaxfleete's cortege, but the news of Dalderby's murder had unsettled him, and he did not want to draw attention to himself. He decided it was safer to maintain a low profile.

'Quite right,' said de Wetherset, when he voiced his concern. 'The city is often uneasy, but I detect something especially nasty in the air today. The deaths of Flaxfleete, Aylmer, Herl and now Dalderby have caused ripples that force men to take sides, even those who would prefer to remain neutral.'

Suttone agreed. 'And it would not do for us to make a bid for escape in the middle of a funeral, anyway. It will look as though we do not care about the soul of the deceased.'

'The crowds will be gone in an hour, and we can walk back to the convent together,' said de Wetherset. 'I doubt anyone will attack five of us, especially if one is a Suttone.'

'You are making the situation sound worse than it is,' objected Simon. 'It is uneasy, not perilous.'

'Matthew and Cynric would not agree,' said Suttone. 'Look what happened to them.'

So, it was well past four o'clock before de Wetherset declared the throng thin enough to allow them to leave. A spiteful wind brought heavy clouds from the north; they blocked out the moon and any light there might have been from the stars. There was a metallic scent in the air, and Bartholomew knew it would snow again that night. It was bitterly cold, and his thick winter cloak was doing little to keep him warm. He felt sorry for the beggars, who were gathering in doorways and the shelter of walls, certain some would freeze to death before dawn.

'There is Michael,' said Suttone, pointing down the hill. The monk had hired a boy to light his way with a lantern, although the lad was moving rather too quickly, and had to be called back every few moments. Bartholomew saw it was Hugh, making money after dark with what appeared to be one of the minster's ceremonial lamps.

'Gynewell came to see me this afternoon,' said Michael breathlessly, when their paths converged. 'I have been ordered to look into Tetford's death now, as well as Aylmer's.

He could have saved himself the journey: I feel honour-bound to look into it, anyway, as Tetford was my deputy. Furthermore, Bishop de Lisle is sure to want to know who killed his nephew, especially since Tetford came to me last night and claimed he was about to turn over a new leaf.'

Simon laughed derisively. 'And you believed him? Really, Brother!'

'I did believe him,' said Michael. 'I questioned his colleagues today, and he *did* close his tavern and sell his wine. His good intentions may not have lasted, but he was in earnest yesterday.'

'Did you ever visit his alehouse?' asked Simon. 'If so, you will know it was a lucrative business. He would have had to be *very* serious about reforming to give that up. I doubt he had it in him.'

'I shall not argue,' said Michael haughtily. 'However, I will make sure Bishop de Lisle knows that his nephew's last moments were full of noble sentiments.'

'However, these noble sentiments *were* expressed while he was giving you a poison-filled wineskin,' said Bartholomew, so only the monk could hear.

'And it is equally possible that the contents were intended for *him*,' Michael muttered back. 'Whatever the truth, I intend to find it, no matter where it leads.'

'Archdeacon Ravenser has the tavern now,' said Cynric. 'He invited us to visit it tonight, Brother. Perhaps we should go, so you can see it for yourself. We should be safe enough. After all, what harm can befall us in the Cathedral Close?'

'I shall accompany you,' said de Wetherset, while Bartholomew regarded the book-bearer askance: some of their best suspects for the previous night's attack were officers in the minster. 'I have never been in the Tavern in the Close, and I do not want my future colleagues to consider me aloof.'

'You have lived in Lincoln for years,' said Michael, surprised. 'Surely you have been to this alehouse before? It is very . . . well known.'

'I have not,' declared de Wetherset. 'Such places nearly always smell of wet dog, an odour I find inordinately distasteful. However, I shall put up with the unpleasantness this evening, just so I can say I have been, should anyone ever ask.'

'Then I will come, too,' announced Suttone. 'What is good enough for an ex-Chancellor is good enough for one of his successors.'

'They have no idea what they are letting themselves in for,' said Simon, watching Suttone and de Wetherset began to retrace their steps. 'Shall we tell them?'

'Wild, is it?' asked Cynric keenly. 'I like a tavern where a man can tell whatever tales he pleases.'

'You could say it was wild,' said Simon, regarding him wryly. 'I do not want to be caught there by Gynewell, though. He does not approve of it. I am going home.'

'You will walk to the Gilbertine convent alone?' asked Bartholomew uneasily. 'In the dark?'

'Yes, and the sooner the better. I can feel snow in the air already.'

'Be careful, then,' warned Michael. 'Do not forget what happened to us last night. We still have no idea who was responsible.'

'My chief suspect is Spayne,' murmured Cynric softly to Bartholomew.

Simon had sharper ears than the book-bearer had expected, and he heard the comment. 'I sincerely doubt it. He has never done that sort of thing before, and he has had plenty of provocation.'

'From whom?' asked Michael.

'Langar is not always a reasonable or pleasant ally, and

their rival Kelby can be nasty. I would be astonished if Spayne would attack you two after a few days, but has put up with them for years.'

'I do not think Spayne is responsible, either,' said Bartholomew. 'I grabbed his arm today, and there is no evidence of a bruise.'

'However, he admitted he was abroad last night, and refused to say where,' said Cynric, giving Michael a meaningful look. He and the monk were united as far as Spayne was concerned.

'He *did* say: he was at business,' said Bartholomew. 'And he was returning home when he saw the chaos surrounding Chapman's stabbing.'

'Outside the *Angel*, he said,' elaborated Cynric, still looking at Michael. 'However, Chapman was wounded outside the Swan. Spayne lied.'

Simon was dismissive. 'There will be a rational explanation. Spayne *said* the Angel, but *meant* the Swan. The Angel is where the Commonalty usually drink, so it is an understandable slip.'

'Perhaps Spayne was not the swordsman you wounded, Matt,' said Michael, not sure what to believe, 'but he might have been one of the three others.'

'He would have been a far more formidable opponent than any of them.'

'I doubt it,' said Simon, 'although that is not to say I think he is guilty. Spayne is not like you – the sons of wealthy landowners. He was an oblate at an abbey from the age of five. While you two were playing with wooden swords and learning how to ride, he was singing psalms. He later declined to take holy orders, and opted for a career in wool instead.'

'That explains his interest in Blood Relics,' said Bartholomew.

'The point I am making is that Spayne is unfamiliar with any kind of weapon,' said Simon. 'Lord, it is cold out here! The sooner I am home by the fire, the better. Do not stay out too late, not with a blizzard coming.'

Bartholomew watched him walk away. 'So, Spayne is in the clear. It was not he who attacked us, as I have been saying all along. He does not know how.'

'You are wrong,' said Michael. 'Simon's testimony suggests to me that Spayne might well have staged a feeble attack, then fled in terror when he realised he was out of his depth. But we will not agree, so we shall waste no more time debating. Let us go to this tavern, and see what the minster priests can tell us about Aylmer and Tetford.'

John was waiting to let the scholars in through the Close gate, stamping his feet to stay warm. Ravenser's tavern was larger than Bartholomew had expected, even bigger than the Swan. Lights burned within, visible under badly fitting window shutters, and there was loud, thumping music that included a flute and drum. Shouts and cheers accompanied the instruments, and it was a lot more rowdy than anything he had seen in the city. John excused himself before they entered.

'You will not join us for a drink, cousin?' asked Suttone. 'It will give us a chance to talk.'

John's tone was cool. 'A canon-elect can have nothing to say to a Poor Clerk with no prospects.'

'Talk to me instead, then,' suggested Michael. 'You can tell me about Aylmer and Tetford.'

John's expression was prim. 'Willingly, Brother, but not in there. I take no strong drink, and I am scrupulously celibate. Good night – and if you want me, I shall be praying at the High Altar.'

'Sanctimonious prig,' muttered Suttone, watching him

strut towards the cathedral. 'He always was that way, which has never endeared him to me. I prefer his younger brother, Hugh.'

'What do you think of Father Simon?' Bartholomew asked of de Wetherset, as they scraped mud, ice and ordure from their feet outside the alehouse door.

De Wetherset shrugged. 'He never misses an office, so will make a good canon. Can we discuss this inside? It is freezing out here. Ah, here is a charming young maid to take our cloaks. How kind. A warm welcome makes such a difference. And I cannot smell wet dog, either. Thank you, child.'

'That is all right, Father,' said the woman with a sultry smile. 'Welcome to Ravenser's House of Pleasure, which is the new name for the Tavern in the Close. I am Belle. What can I do for you?'

'I would like some ale, Belle,' said de Wetherset, rubbing his hands as he looked around him. 'Spiced, if you please, although not to the extent that you might flavour it for Bishop Gynewell.'

'The bishop will never come here,' said Belle ruefully. 'However, Ravenser said we must do *anything* he asks, if he ever does put in an appearance, even if it involves his pitch-fork. Gynewell wants this alehouse closed, you see, and us ladies thrown on the streets with nowhere to go.'

'Do not worry,' said de Wetherset kindly. 'There is always a demand for the labour of virtuous maidens.'

She shot him a bemused glance, then led them to a table near one of the room's two fires. The wood was well worn, and full of the kind of dents that said a good deal of jug-bashing had taken place on it. They sat and Belle fetched ale. She tripped as she approached, slopping some on Cynric's sleeve, and when she placed the other goblets on the table, she did so clumsily enough to spill more.

'Perhaps she *would* be unemployed if Gynewell

360

suppresses this place,' whispered de Wetherset. 'I do not like to be rude, but she is not very good at serving drinks.'

'I suspect her talents lie in other areas,' said Michael. He ordered food, and when the rabbit pie arrived, she slapped it down in a way that splattered Suttone's habit with gravy. He tutted in annoyance, but did not make the kind of fuss he would have done had an ugly boy been the culprit. When she wiped his lap with a cloth, taking rather longer than necessary, he forgave her completely.

'She is very obliging,' said de Wetherset to Bartholomew. 'Perhaps that is why she is so popular. Lots of Vicars Choral are calling to her, trying to attract her attention.'

'Good evening, sirs,' said another woman. The front of her dress was indecently low, and it became more so as she leaned across the table to refill their cups. Bartholomew saw de Wetherset's jaw drop. She ran her eyes across the gathering like a butcher looking for prime cuts, and her insolent gaze fell on Michael. 'Oh, my! You *are* a large man. Tetford was right.'

'Rosanna?' asked Bartholomew. 'The seamstress who adjusted Michael's ceremonial alb?'

'The very same,' she crooned, her eyes fixed on the monk. 'Now I see why Tetford insisted it should be so massive. Yours is an impressive figure, Brother.'

Michael preened himself. 'Some of my colleagues say I am fat.'

'Then they do not know what they are talking about. However, I imagine you have some *very* big bones.'

Bartholomew laughed, although Michael did not see anything amusing in the comment. 'Tetford fought Ravenser over a misunderstanding involving you,' said the monk.

She grinned mischievously. 'A mistake was made in booking arrangements. Tetford was nasty about it, and I

361

am pleased we now work for Ravenser. He will be a far nicer master.'

'You did not like Tetford, then?' asked Bartholomew.

'He was miserly and spiteful. Ravenser may seem wild, but he has a good heart. I think the tavern will do very well under him. For a few ghastly hours, we thought it might go to John Suttone.'

'John?' asked Suttone in surprise. 'He is not the kind of man who would run a . . . ' He waved his hand, not sure what to call it.

'He is good at administration, and the canons asked if he would consider taking on the responsibility. He would have bowed to the bishop's demands for moderation, though, and that would have been tedious. Now, whose company would you like? There is Belle from Wigford, and Jane and Agnes from Newport. And, since there are four of you, I shall make sure I am to hand, too.'

'To hand for what?' asked de Wetherset, bewildered. 'We have come for a drink.'

'Of course you have, Father. Now, you sit quietly and I will send Belle over. I think you have already taken a liking to her, and she certainly has to you. Look! She is waving.'

'I do not want the company of women,' objected de Wetherset, puzzled. 'I encountered a new argument pertaining to Blood Relics today, and I intend to practise it on my colleagues here. A lady would be bored with such an erudite discourse, and her restless shuffling might distract them.'

'Belle will sit still, if that is what you would like,' said Rosanna patiently, her eyes as old as the hills. 'Have no fear, Father. She will be very gentle with you.'

'Later, perhaps,' said Michael, smothering a smile. 'We would like to enjoy our ale first.'

362

'Very well,' said Rosanna. 'Call us when you are ready.'

'Ready for what?' asked de Wetherset when she had gone. 'This is a curious institution. I do not think I will be coming here very often, once I am a canon.'

'I might,' said Suttone perkily. 'It is a charming place.'

The evening wore on, and de Wetherset remained bemused by Ravenser's House of Pleasure. Most patrons were priests, although there was a smattering of secular clerks and servants. The atmosphere was raucous and dissipated, and even Cynric declared it too noisy. It was hot, too, which de Wetherset said explained why so many serving wenches were half naked. Cynric watched in shock, until one tried to sit on his lap, at which point he excused himself and scuttled outside, muttering something about his wife. Meanwhile, some of the men divested themselves of cloaks, tunics and even shifts.

'I would never have agreed to Tetford's nomination had I known he managed a place like this,' said Michael to Bartholomew, over the din of a drinking game taking place between Claypole and one of the Poor Clerks. 'There are limits, and this is well past them. Part of my reason for coming here tonight was so I could see if anyone caught my eye as a potential replacement for Tetford, but I do not think I want to hire a Vicar Choral who enjoys this sort of entertainment.'

'Do you think Bishop de Lisle knows what Tetford was like?' asked Bartholomew.

'I sincerely doubt it. If the establishment was discreet, he might have turned a blind eye, but this is brazen, to say the least. I hate to say it, but Tetford's death has spared me a good deal of trouble.'

'Here comes Ravenser,' said Bartholomew. 'He is no longer wearing his sword.'

'Good evening,' said Ravenser jovially. 'I am pleased you could come. I was afraid you might not, and tonight promises to be an excellent evening. Just wait until the amusements really begin.'

'Lord!' muttered Michael. 'This is more than enough for me already.'

'Is it like this every night?' asked de Wetherset, wonderingly.

'I hope so,' whispered Suttone, red-faced from ale and enjoying himself thoroughly.

Ravenser smiled. 'The Guild sent us a donation of wine when they learned I was to take over. Kelby wanted us to drink to Flaxfleete's memory.'

'I had forgotten the Guild provides the minster with money for its vices,' said Michael.

'The Guild is good to us,' said Ravenser, ignoring the censure in his tone. 'I hope the deaths of Flaxfleete and Dalderby do not upset the balance, and make it weaker than the Commonalty. I wonder if that was why someone tried to kill Chapman – to maintain the equilibrium.'

'Someone *was* determined he should die,' said Bartholomew. 'He was attacked with a sword, then provided with a poisonous salve. He is lucky to be alive.'

Ravenser excused himself when a roar of approval indicated that Claypole had won the round, and the scholars were left alone again. A woman called Jane of Newport insinuated herself next to de Wetherset, and her sister Agnes squeezed between Bartholomew and Michael. Suttone was dismayed, until Belle sat on his knee, claiming there was no room on the bench.

'Ladies, please,' objected de Wetherset plaintively. 'We are trying to discuss theology.'

'Is that so, Father?' said Jane, her voice low and husky. 'Then do not mind us.'

'Claypole is in good spirits,' said Bartholomew to Michael, watching the priest challenge another Poor Clerk to out-drink him. 'I wondered earlier whether he might be pleased by Tetford's death.'

'I saw him escort Christiana to the Swan for a cup of wine,' said Michael stiffly. 'She was not overly enthusiastic, but he was delighted. I imagine his success in spending an hour alone with her is the cause of his ebullience tonight. It is a pity she cannot see him now – depraved and reeling.'

'Is that Hugh?' asked Bartholomew, pointing to where someone was struggling to broach a barrel of ale. 'He seems to be everywhere – acting as a lantern-bearer, running errands for Gynewell.'

'It is because he is always in trouble,' said Agnes. 'He cannot resist playing pranks on his elders, and is always being ordered to pay fines. He needs every penny he can earn.'

It was not long before Hugh came to seek them out. His eyes were heavy and his hair tousled, as if he had been dozing somewhere when he should have been serving the tavern's thirsty patrons. He grinned cheekily at Michael. 'Can I conduct you to any merchants' houses, Brother?'

'You should be asleep,' admonished Michael. 'You have to rise early to sing tomorrow.'

'Ravenser said he will let me off prime the mornings after I work here,' said Hugh. 'I suppose he will make a decent inn-master, but I really wanted John to get the post.'

'I doubt John would have enjoyed playing the role of taverner,' said Suttone.

Hugh wrinkled his nose. 'Probably not, but *I* would have liked him to do it, because then he would have given me the best jobs. He says it is a duty to look after one's family.'

Suttone raised his eyebrows in annoyance, but Hugh did not seem to realise that the remark had been a barb directed at his cousin. 'Then when *he* is a canon, he can be as nepotistic as he pleases.'

The scholars' conversation had become desultory once the women had draped themselves around their table. Suttone tried to begin a debate about the causes of the plague, but Jane said the disease had left her with vile memories, and asked him to desist. Then de Wetherset said he would like to propound the notion of *creatio ex nihilo*, which he claimed was always a good topic to break the ice, and he and Michael managed a spirited argument until Agnes said she was bored and left. When Belle and Jane attempted to do the same, it was Suttone who persuaded them to stay.

'Here is Bresley,' said Michael, as the door opened and the dean walked in. Several men's hands dropped to their purses, and Ravenser went to a pot, where coins had been left for the women, and locked it in a cupboard. 'He will have something to say about all this racket.'

Instead of bringing the carousing to an end, Bresley strolled to a bench and sat, snapping his fingers at Hugh to bring him some wine. Agnes went to stand behind him, but he made no effort to move away when she flopped an arm across his shoulder. He rummaged under his robes and his hand emerged with something gold. His actions were odd enough to encourage Bartholomew to watch him.

Michael tried to peer around Jane, who was intent on crawling into his lap; the monk seemed powerless to resist her relentless advance. 'Can you see what he is doing?'

'He has just put something under Agnes's skirts,' replied Bartholomew. He laughed when Michael blushed modestly. 'Something metal.'

'We should leave,' said Michael uncomfortably. 'Simon was right: we should not be here. And I am surprised the dean dares show his face, given that he wants the place closed down. He is—'

'Madam!' shrieked de Wetherset suddenly, leaping to his feet. His face had flushed scarlet, and he was shaking. 'Madam!'

'What?' demanded Belle irritably.

'Your hand! It wandered a *second* time! The first I understand was an error, but to do it twice . . .!'

Belle frowned, puzzled. 'Rosanna told me to make sure you were happy.'

'I was happy,' yelled de Wetherset, 'until you . . . I shall not stay here to be molested. I am leaving!'

'What about my payment?' demanded Belle. Other women began to mutter ominously.

'Payment for what?' asked de Wetherset, amazed. 'Ravenser said the food and ale was from him.'

'We should all be going home,' said Michael hastily, pressing a coin into Belle's hand.

Bartholomew led the still-spluttering de Wetherset outside to where Cynric was waiting, his face a cool mask of disapproval.

'You lingered a long time,' he said, accusingly. 'I expected you to follow my example sooner.'

'She . . . she *touched* me,' stammered de Wetherset, outraged. 'And I am absolutely certain it was deliberate. She must have been trying to *seduce* me!'

'Do you see yourself as irresistible to lovely women, then?' asked Suttone sullenly. He had not been touched and seduced enough.

'Of course I am!' snapped de Wetherset. 'Powerful men are irresistible to people of either sex, but that is no excuse for her to make herself familiar with my person. We are in the sacred confines of a Cathedral Close! I certainly shall not visit *that* den of iniquity again.'

Agnes had followed them outside. 'Ravenser said you forgot this,' she said, passing the cloak de Wetherset had abandoned in his agitation. 'It is cold, and you will not want to walk home without it.'

Ungraciously, de Wetherset snatched it from her hand and strode away, Suttone hurrying after him when he saw him head in entirely the wrong direction in his agitation. While the monk watched Suttone herd the ex-Chancellor towards the right gate, Bartholomew made a grab for the folds of Agnes's unfashionably voluminous skirts. She started to screech, but stopped abruptly when he located a linen bag hidden among the pleats. It was suspended by a ribbon, and clanked in a way that suggested several items were contained within.

'That is mine,' snapped Agnes, trying to wriggle away from him. 'The men here sometimes do not have coins, so they pay with other items instead.'

Bartholomew tugged the bag, breaking the ribbon. Agnes hastened to snatch it back, but he fended her off with one hand and emptied its contents on to the ground with the other.

'This,' he said, grabbing a gold cup to wave at her, 'belongs to Adam Miller. It is one of a set of four, although the dean has ensured that Miller is now the perplexed owner of a set of three.'

'I will give it to the bishop tomorrow,' she said sulkily. 'There is a special box for anything from the dean, and Gynewell always makes sure it gets to its rightful owner. It is part of the arrangement of working here: anything from Bresley goes to the bishop, and the rest we can keep.'

'How odd,' said Michael, bemused.

'Bresley is ill,' explained Agnes. 'He does not know what he is doing. The bishop says he is a good dean, and does not want to find a replacement, although it means he is obliged to spend an hour of each morning returning borrowed property. That cup will be back with Miller by noon tomorrow.'

'And what is this?' asked Cynric, picking up another item. 'Did the dean give you this, too?'

Michael gazed at it in shock. 'That is the Hugh Chalice!'

'So is this,' said Cynric, producing the one he had taken from Miller's house.

'Lord!' exclaimed Michael, placing them side by side and inspecting them in the dim light of the lamp that burned above the tavern's door. 'They are identical. Which is the real one?'

'The one in the Gilbertine Priory presumably,' said Bartholomew. 'Unless all three are fakes.'

'Where did you get this?' demanded Michael of Agnes. 'Who gave it to you?'

'Tetford,' said Agnes reluctantly. 'After he had decided to close his tavern. He gave one to each of his favourite girls, and said we could sell them to keep us from poverty. He said they were the cups St Hugh used for his wild – but generally respectable – parties.'

'And how did Tetford come by them?' asked Michael, his face creased in confusion.

'He did not say. Why? Was he wrong about their value? The others will not be pleased, because they have already made arrangements with some of the city's convents. Lincoln's religious foundations are always eager to buy St Hugh's relics.'

'How many of these cups are there?' asked Bartholomew uneasily.

'He gave one each to me, Belle, Jane and Rosanna,' said Agnes. Her expression was hard and angry. 'He said there are no others like them anywhere in the world, but now I see he was lying as usual. God rot his filthy soul!'

* * *

369

It was past eight o'clock by the time Bartholomew, Michael, Suttone, de Wetherset and Cynric started to walk back to the Gilbertine Priory. Michael carried Agnes's bag, and in it were the four chalices Tetford had given to his ladies, along with the one Cynric had found in Miller's home.

'I do not understand,' said Bartholomew, speaking in a low voice because it was late and people in the houses they passed were asleep. Hard little pellets of snow swirled in all directions. They bounced across the frozen ground, where the wind blew them into dry, shifting heaps. 'These cups look similar – if not identical – to the one Shirlok was accused of stealing in Cambridge. What is happening?'

Michael was thoughtful. 'Someone has obviously been making copies of the real one in an attempt to make his fortune.'

'If there is a real one,' said de Wetherset. 'But regard-less, local convents will jump at an opportunity to buy a relic of St Hugh, especially if it is made of silver.'

'I doubt these are silver,' said Bartholomew. 'There is a spotting on them that suggests they are forged from some base metal.'

'Well, they *look* silver to me,' said de Wetherset, 'so they will *look* silver to potential buyers. I was right to be sceptical of Simon's chalice – the poor man was as deceived as those impertinent women. I always knew he did not possess my abilities.'

'What abilities?' asked Suttone sulkily. He had been enjoying himself in Ravenser's House of Pleasure, and held de Wetherset responsible for bringing a pleasant evening to a premature end.

'My talent for distinguishing genuine relics from false ones. It is a gift from God.'

Bartholomew was relieved when they reached the Gilbertine Priory, and even more relieved when there was someone waiting to let them in. Prior Roger had not liked the notion that his guests – especially Suttone – might abandon him, and was ready to do all in his power to keep them. He was so determined they should not be obliged to go through his garden a second night, that he had waited in the porter's lodge himself, to make sure the guard did not fall victim to another flask of drugged wine.

'There you are,' he said, leaping to his feet to usher them inside. 'I was beginning to be worried.'

'Yes,' said Michael. 'It is a dangerous—'

'Well, you are here now, thank the Lord!' Roger beamed. 'I hope you had a good evening. Is it snowing yet? I think we shall have a heavy fall before the night is out.'

'It is just starting again,' said Bartholomew. 'Is Father Simon in the guest-hall?'

Roger shook his head. 'Hamo saw him with you at Flaxfleete's funeral. Did you separate afterwards? That was unwise, given the number of villains arriving for Miller's Market.'

'*Hamo* saw us?' asked Bartholomew uneasily. He had not spotted the wet-lipped Gilbertine, and he disliked the notion that someone had been watching him without his knowledge.

'Simon has not returned?' asked Michael, equally unsettled. 'He left us hours ago, and said he was going to walk straight home. I hope he has not come to any harm.'

Eager to impress them with his level of concern for absent guests, Roger organised a hunt, sending his brethren out to make a thorough search of first the convent's buildings, and then its grounds. There was no sign of the priest, so Bartholomew offered to walk back to the city, following the route Simon would have taken. Cynric, Michael and three burly lay-brothers accompanied him, but they met with no success.

371

'His belongings are here,' said de Wetherset, when they returned, cold and tired. 'I have been through them, but there is nothing to suggest he intended to spend the night away. And Suttone and I have spoken to everyone here, and no one has any idea where else he might be.'

'He is local,' said Bartholomew. 'Perhaps he has gone to stay with friends.'

'He does not have any friends,' said de Wetherset. 'Besides, he likes the Gilbertines' daily offices, and he is a devout man. He will not miss a mass by sojourning with secular acquaintances.'

'He should have remained with us,' said Suttone, annoyed by the trouble the priest was causing.

'Perhaps he has less cause to be worried about being ambushed than the rest of us,' said Michael thoughtfully. He turned to de Wetherset. 'I want to know about his alibi for Aylmer's stabbing. Why did you lie about it? No, do not look shocked: this is important. You must tell me the truth.'

De Wetherset's expression was furious. 'I *did* tell you the truth. How dare you!'

'One on occasion you told me – rather smugly – that you had not attended the Gilbertines' prime since your first morning here. However, when we asked after Simon's whereabouts when Aylmer was murdered, you said you heard him singing in the chapel. You cannot have it both ways.'

De Wetherset sighed angrily. 'You always were a pedant, picking at details. As it happens, I *was* in the chapel that morning – I was speaking figuratively when I said I avoided *every* office after my first day. However, since you love irrelevancies, you should bear in mind my *exact* words when I answered that question: I said Simon had a loud voice. I did not say I had heard it, and the truth is that I cannot remember. Perhaps I heard him that day, perhaps I did not. I am afraid dawn offices tend to run together in my mind. However, he offered me a roof over my head at a very reasonable price when I first arrived in the city, and I decided to give him the benefit of the doubt. He is no killer.'

'I think he might be an arsonist, though,' said Bartholomew. 'He set his own home alight to hurry along the offer of a prebendal stall. It was not his house – it belonged to Holy Cross. Now the parish will have to pay for a new one.'

'I suspected at the time that he had had a hand in the conflagration,' admitted de Wetherset. 'We could have doused it when he woke me, but he told me to save my belongings first. By the time we had done that, the blaze had taken too firm a hold. Having said that, he intends to pay for a new building himself, out of his prebend, and it will be bigger and better than he one he burned. His only real crime was impatience – he wanted the promised stall sooner rather than later.'

'What shall we do?' asked Prior Roger unhappily, when he came a few moments later to see if Simon had been found. 'We cannot sit by the fire when the poor man is missing.'

'We have no choice,' said Michael. 'There is nothing we can do until daylight, and we—'

'We shall pray for his safety,' announced Roger. 'Ring the bells, Hamo. Rouse the brethren from their beds. We shall make sure *all* the saints hear our petitions.'

'Amen to that!' cried Hamo.

Not liking to sleep when everyone else was obliged to attend the impromptu service, Bartholomew trailed after Michael. Then, while Roger assembled his flock and the organ started to wheeze, he walked to the altar and looked for the Hugh Chalice. It was not there.

'Where is it?' he asked of Roger, breaking into the prior's first alleluia.

Roger gazed at the empty spot in horror. 'It was here this afternoon. I saw it myself.'

'Do you think Simon found out he had been cheated?' asked Michael. 'And tackled the culprit?'

'You mean Chapman?' asked Bartholomew. 'He is too ill for visitors, and I doubt Miller would have let Simon see him.'

'He might,' whispered Cynric. 'Why should he refuse the request of his own brother?'

'We can ask tomorrow, when I change the dressing on Chapman's arm,' said Bartholomew.

'Will they answer you honestly?' asked Roger worriedly. 'Why would they, if they murdered Father Simon themselves?'

CHAPTER 10

Simon did not appear for prime the following morning, and the Gilbertines declared they missed his booming voice. Candles were lit in St Katherine's Chapel, more prayers were howled and, at first light, Bartholomew went out again to see if he could find him. The promised snow had not materialised in any significant way, although there was a nip in the air that suggested the threat was far from over. He walked all the way to the Bail, asking everyone he met whether they had seen the priest, and returned via the frozen-edged Braytheford Pool and Simon's old church, Holy Cross.

The priest's successor, a fresh-faced youth proud of the fact that he had spent a term at the University in Oxford, said Simon had been kind to him, and had spent a lot of time making sure he understood his duties. The lad was staying with a kinsman until the burned house could be rebuilt, but claimed he had seen nothing of Simon for days.

'I am worried,' said de Wetherset, when Bartholomew reported his lack of success to the prior in his solar. Roger, Michael and Suttone sat in a row near the window; Dame Eleanor and Christiana were in chairs near the fire; and Hamo, de Wetherset and Bartholomew stood, because there were no more seats. Hamo kept rubbing his arm, as though it pained him. 'An attack on Simon is an attack on the cathedral.'

'How have you reached that conclusion?' asked Suttone, startled.

De Wetherset stifled a sigh of impatience. 'Because Flaxfleete is dead and Simon is missing. That means only Michael, you and I are left out of *five* canons-elect.'

'And two of your Vicars Choral are dead as well,' said Hamo, doing nothing to soothe the atmosphere of tense agitation. 'Aylmer and Tetford were—'

'As far as I can tell, the last time Simon was seen was when he parted company with you last night,' said Roger to Michael. 'You went to say prayers in the cathedral, and Simon walked home.'

'Perhaps he is still in the city, then,' said Bartholomew, noting Michael's sly glance at Christiana: the monk did not want her to know where he had really been. 'And we are searching the wrong—'

'You said he wanted to return here as soon as possible, because he thought it was going to snow,' interrupted Roger. 'Why would he have lingered elsewhere?'

'I hope nothing bad has happened to him,' said Eleanor unhappily. Christiana took her hand. The younger woman had forgotten to arrange her hair properly that morning, a sign of her concern.

Michael's expression was grim. 'And we should not forget that he is not the only thing missing: so is the Hugh Chalice.'

'It was there yesterday afternoon,' said Dame Eleanor. 'I saw it myself.'

'So did I,' said Roger. 'Therefore, it must have gone missing between then and midnight, when we all went to pray for Simon. That is a gap of about nine hours.'

'I have searched every building in the convent,' said Hamo. 'The chalice is not here.'

Michael rummaged in the bag he carried, and held a cup in the air. 'Is this it?'

'*You* have it!' exclaimed Roger, while Eleanor and

Christiana gasped in surprise, and Hamo looked peeved that he had wasted so much time searching for it.

'Examine it carefully,' ordered Michael. De Wetherset started to speak, but the monk silenced him with a glare. 'Is this the Hugh Chalice you have been minding since Aylmer was stabbed?'

Roger did as he was told. He tried to hand it to Dame Eleanor, but she hesitated to touch it, so he passed it to Hamo, and no one spoke until the Brother Hospitaller looked up.

'It is the one,' said Roger, while Hamo and Eleanor nodded agreement. 'Look at the engraving of the Baby Jesus. The artist gave him only three fingers on his left hand, which makes it distinctive and unique. Why do you want to know if we recognise it, when it is obvious we would?'

'Then what about this?' asked Michael, producing a second cup.

Hamo snatched it from him. 'They are the same! This babe has three fingers, too!'

Michael inclined his head. 'So which is the real one?'

'This,' said Hamo, pointing to the first. 'It is shinier than the second, and Simon kept it well polished. The other must be a copy.'

'And these?' asked Michael producing a third, a fourth and a fifth.

Dame Eleanor shook her head in appalled disbelief, while the two Gilbertines were more vocal, shouting their dismay and horror. Hamo stood all five cups in a line, and his face was white when he informed the gathering that Jesus only had a total of fifteen left-hand fingers: the 'unique' carving had been precisely duplicated. Then Roger covered his eyes while Christiana swapped them around, and the prior was forced to admit that he could not tell one from the other, and that he had no idea which of the five had been in his chapel for the past few days.

'If any,' said Christiana. 'Perhaps the original is with Simon – or with a thief who killed him and made off with it. *His* may be the real one, and these five are just poor imitations.'

'They are not *poor* imitations, My Lady,' countered Hamo. 'They are very good ones. However, Simon's must be the genuine relic one. Why else would it be stolen?'

'Perhaps none is the original,' suggested de Wetherset. 'Perhaps there *is* no original.'

'How many of these things are there, Brother?' asked Eleanor, after the monk had explained that Cynric had 'found' one and the others had been confiscated from cathedral 'seamstresses'. Bartholomew did not think he had ever heard so many euphemisms in a single sentence. 'Or do you have them all?'

'I doubt it,' said Michael. 'It was only chance that we happened to stumble on these. I would like to know how Tetford came to have four silver—'

'Metal,' corrected Roger. 'I know silver when I see it. These are probably tin.'

'—four *metal* goblets to give his sewing ladies,' finished Michael. 'And we are not in a position to make enquiries about the one Cynric "recovered", either. It is difficult to know how to proceed.'

'I am sure one of these cups was part of the property Shirlok stole in Cambridge,' said Bartholomew, speaking more to himself than to the gathering. Michael shot him a warning glance, but it was too late: Roger pounced on the slip, pointing out that the physician was morally obliged to share information that might reflect on the chalice's authenticity. Reluctantly, Bartholomew and de Wetherset gave an account of the trial. Bartholomew omitted what had happened to Shirlok at the end of it, and de Wetherset declined to mention that he had been a juror.

Hamo was gleeful. 'So, Miller *did* commit crimes of dishonesty and was brought to task for them!' he said, rubbing his arm again. 'The Guild was right all those years ago when—'

'The Hugh Chalice is worth far more than the twenty shillings paid by that Geddynge priest,' said Roger. 'It will make any priory or cathedral wealthy, from the pilgrims who flock to petition it.'

'Perhaps the *Hugh* Chalice is,' said Michael. 'However, we cannot be sure if any of the cups we have – or even the one from Geddynge – is the original, and—'

'One will be real,' said Roger firmly, 'although I cannot imagine how we shall identify which.'

'*I* shall do that,' announced de Wetherset. 'I told you: I have a gift for that sort of thing.'

Roger gestured to the five cups. 'Go on, then.'

'This is not helping poor Simon,' said Eleanor, after several moments when de Wetherset picked up each chalice in turn, but was obviously not going to be honoured with immediate divine insight. She stood. 'I am going to the chapel, to petition to St Hugh on his behalf.'

Bartholomew and Michael left Prior Roger's solar, and escorted Dame Eleanor to the chapel. They watched her walk to the altar and stand with her hands clasped in front of her. A psalm echoed around the building as she prayed.

'Her Latin is excellent,' said Michael. 'Better than some of our colleagues in Cambridge.'

'She likes to read,' said Bartholomew, recalling their discussion about Hildegard of Bingen. 'There is something I forgot to tell you yesterday, Brother. When I tended

Chapman, he insisted on paying me with pearls worn by the Virgin Mary.'

'The Blessed Virgin did not wear pearls,' said Michael scornfully. 'He tricked you, my friend.'

'White pearls were also among the goods Shirlok was accused of stealing with the chalice.'

'You think they are the same? Show me.'

Bartholomew handed them over. 'Do you think it is possible that Shirlok's hoard has been hidden somewhere, and is suddenly circulating?'

Michael stared at him. 'It might be! Cynric overheard Langar and Sabina say they think Shirlok is still alive – although Miller, Chapman and Lora disagreed. Do *you* think Shirlok is in Lincoln, selling the goods he once stole in Cambridgeshire?'

'It is possible, although I cannot imagine how he laid hands on them again. He ran out of the castle very quickly, and I doubt he came back.'

'But then the goods mysteriously went missing before they could be returned to their owners. Perhaps he *did* get them somehow.'

Bartholomew was thoughtful. 'Or Langar did. He was a castle official – in a position to make items disappear – and it seems he left Cambridge very soon after Shirlok's trial.'

Michael scratched the stubble on his cheeks. 'No connection was ever made, that I heard, between Langar's departure and the loss of this property.'

Bartholomew shrugged. 'Why would it? Langar was a law-clerk, a respectable man.'

'He has thrown in his lot with some very dubious characters since, though. It is entirely possible that his deviousness went unnoticed in Cambridge. You have said from the start that there was something odd about the way Miller and the others were acquitted. Now I am beginning to see why.'

Bartholomew nodded. 'Langar somehow arranged a favourable verdict, seized the goods Shirlok stole, and the entire group – minus Shirlok, presumably – came to Lincoln, where they accrued power through the Commonalty and merrily continued their illegal activities.'

'So, the cup was stolen *three* times: once from the friar-couriers, once from Geddynge and once after the trial. Chapman and the others made copies, intending to sell them as relics of St Hugh. They were not even subtle with the ones they hawked to Tetford, giving him four and claiming they were a set used by the saint at parties. How could Tetford have been so gullible?'

'Tetford loved revelry, and probably thought it great fun to possess something St Hugh had used to celebrate. Whoever sold them to him knew exactly how to persuade him to buy.' Bartholomew hesitated, as something else occurred to him. 'Sabina said Nicholas was a silversmith.'

Michael nodded. 'She thought the mark on his shoulder was a work burn. I see where you are going with this, Matt: *Hal* could have made the copies, because he had the skill to do so. Sabina did tell us he had been unusually busy over the last month. Perhaps he was in league with Chapman.'

'I am supposed to visit Chapman again today. I will ask him.'

'I do not like the thought of you in that house alone, so I shall come with you. I will tell a few lies about my imminent solution to Aylmer's murder. And then I will have to go to the cathedral and do penance at the Head Shrine for bearing false witness.'

The obvious place to look for Simon was the minster, where he would soon be made a canon, so Michael and Bartholomew decided to search it on their way to see Chapman. De Wetherset escorted them to the Gilbertines' gate, although he declined to join the hunt himself. He was clearly afraid to leave the convent, and Bartholomew hoped Michael would not pay for his greater courage with his life.

'Perhaps I will return to the University when this is over,' said de Wetherset worriedly. 'Lincoln has grown dangerous, and it was uneasy politics that made me leave Cambridge. If I am to be caught up with intrigue and plots, I might as well be where there is a decent collection of books.'

Bartholomew regarded him thoughtfully. '*Are* you caught up with plots and intrigue? It is odd that you happened to select Lincoln as a haven of peace, when you are tied to it by your appointment as a juror in Miller's trial all those years ago.'

De Wetherset's expression was cold. 'That was co-incidence, and I resent your implication that it was anything else. I told you – it was a shock to be confronted by men I had acquitted.'

Bartholomew was unconvinced. 'Miller tried to intim-idate me when he thought I might remember the trial. *Ergo,* I seriously doubt you escaped with nothing said – unless he *knew* he could trust you to reveal nothing harmful. Now why would he think that?'

'Matt,' warned Michael uncomfortably. 'De Wetherset is above suspicion.'

Bartholomew pressed on. 'Several pieces of informa-tion have just clicked together in my mind, and I now know something you would rather keep concealed. So does Miller, which is why he does not mind you being here.'

De Wetherset glared at him. 'And what might that be?'

'It concerns the goods that went missing after Shirlok's execution. We have just discussed the possibility that Shirlok may have been instrumental in their disappear-ance, but that is not the case.'

382

De Wetherset continued to glower. 'What does lost property have to do with me?'

'Matt,' said Michael uneasily. 'You are a long way from the mark with this.'

Bartholomew ignored him. 'After Shirlok was hanged, I remember the valuables being loaded on a cart. There were a lot of people milling around in the bailey, because Nicholas Herl and several others had just been released from gaol, and Miller had hired wagons to move their possessions, too.'

'Then you will also remember the line the sheriff drew in the mud with his boot,' said de Wetherset. 'No felon was permitted to cross it, on pain of death. None of them did.'

'But "felons" did not pile the recovered goods on the cart,' said Bartholomew. '*You* did – the only juror without an excuse good enough to let him evade the sheriff's demand for help. You were in a hurry, determined to finish and be about your own business as soon as possible. You put at least some of the items on the wrong wagon.'

'That is outrageous!' De Wetherset turned to Michael. 'If you are his friend, you will make him stop. Do not forget that I intend to be Chancellor again one day.'

'I do not think you did it deliberately,' Bartholomew went on, 'but you realised what must have happened when the news started to circulate about the goods' disappearance. You said nothing, and Miller must have had a lovely surprise when he reached Lincoln and unpacked.'

De Wetherset regarded him furiously. 'How dare you accuse me of being party to a theft!'

Michael's expression was troubled. 'He is not. He is just saying that haste made you inattentive.'

De Wetherset regarded Bartholomew with dislike. 'You cannot prove any of this.'

Bartholomew shrugged. 'I do not want to. It is irrelevant

now, and all it does is help us understand another step in the curious travels of the Hugh Chalice.'

'Perhaps St Hugh guided your hand, *forcing* you to put his cup on a cart bound for Lincoln,' said Michael, trying to pacify the furious ex-Chancellor. They had enough enemies, without making another. 'Perhaps he did not want it to sit in quiet obscurity at Geddynge. Bishop Gynewell himself told me that holy objects make their own way to the places they want to be.'

De Wetherset regarded him doubtfully, some of his rage lifting. 'Do you think so?'

'Why not?' asked Michael. 'It makes you an instrument of God.'

De Wetherset's temper cooled a little more. 'You have a point.'

'I hope you will remember who brought this to light,' said Michael, somewhat sternly. 'You cannot bear a grudge against Matt for pointing out that St Hugh selected *you* to do his will.'

'I do not mind him saying that,' said de Wetherset. 'I mind his accusatory tone.'

'It is not accusatory,' said Michael. 'He is just awed by the divine favour you have been shown.'

De Wetherset did not look convinced, but at least he was not scowling when they left the priory.

'Do you really believe all that?' asked Bartholomew, when the gate had closed behind them.

'Of course not,' replied Michael scornfully, 'but it may prevent him from doing something nasty to you at some point in the future. And you do not want *him* after your blood, believe me.'

The city felt uneasy as Bartholomew and Michael walked through it. Men were beginning to gather in huddles, and the alehouses were fuller than usual. Merchants scurried here and there with their heads down, as if they were afraid that eye contact might result in a confrontation that would see them deprived of their purses – or worse. Many of the better houses on the main road had kept their windows shuttered, and even one or two of the churches had firmly closed doors.

When the scholars reached the cathedral, and reported Simon's disappearance to Gynewell, the bishop responded by ordering his officials to search the Close, roping in Ravenser, John, Claypole, Choirmaster Bautre and even the boy singers. Dancing up and down on the balls of his feet with restless energy, Gynewell directed them to specific areas, although Bartholomew doubted the clerics could be trusted to be thorough. Ravenser looked as though he had imbibed too much of his own ale the previous night; John complained that the hunt would interfere with his library duties; and Claypole and Bautre carped about the inclement weather. Young Hugh was the only one who seized on the adventure with any enthusiasm, and Bartholomew was impressed by the systematic way the boy and his fellow choristers combed the land near the Vicars' Court.

'I am sorry, My Lord,' said Hugh a while later. He was soaking wet, covered in mud and close to frustrated tears. 'I was hoping *we* would be the ones to find him. Give us another area. I do not think Claypole scoured the Close churches, like you asked. We could look there for you.'

The bishop dismissed him to the kitchens to dry out, and ordered Claypole to return to the two Close churches – St Mary Magdalene and St Margaret – and search them properly. The priest slouched away resentfully, and Bartholomew suspected he had no intention of doing as he was told. Then Michael pointed out that the vain, self-important Simon was more likely to be in the cathedral than in a humble chapel, and proposed they look for him there themselves.

Bartholomew took the northern half of the building, Michael took the south, and they explored every nook and cranny. Bartholomew was near the Great Transept when he met Hamo and Roger.

'You seem to be in pain,' said Bartholomew, noting the way Hamo held his arm. 'Can I help?'

'I told you: I fell and bruised it,' said Hamo, moving behind his prior, as if for protection. 'I do not need poultices and purges, thank you.'

Bartholomew was not sure whether to believe him. 'On the night Brother Michael and I were attacked, you said you were both in the chapel. Did you notice any of your brethren miss—'

'No,' interrupted Roger sharply. 'No one was absent. We are delighted to have Master Suttone . . . I mean *all* of you in our convent, and would do nothing to make you want to leave. I assure you the ambush had nothing to do with us.'

'You will not be so delighted if Michael discovers Aylmer was stabbed by a Gilbertine,' said Bartholomew, knowing he was taking a risk by making such bald statements, but persisting anyway.

Roger licked dry lips. 'No Gilbertine killed Aylmer. Come, Hamo. We should visit the Head Shrine and pray for Father Simon's safe return.'

He left, but Hamo lingered, his expression as icy as the weather outside. 'I do not like your tone, physician, and nor do I like the way Michael leers at Lady Christiana. I do not like it at all.'

He stamped away, leaving Bartholomew staring after him unhappily. Could jealousy have been the motive for the attack in the orchard? Hamo fawned over Christiana, and it was possible that he was as smitten by her charms as was Michael. Had he gathered like-minded colleagues for the bungled ambush, hoping to prevent the monk from luring her away from the convent that had been her home for so long? And was Roger compliant, because he did not want to lose the valuable source of income Christiana had become? Miller thought the culprit was in holy orders; perhaps he was right.

Eventually, Bartholomew and Michael met by the shrine of Little Hugh. The cold weather had depleted the number of pilgrims, and it was deserted, except for Bautre, who was fortifying himself with Eleanor's holy 'water'. He blushed when he realised he had been seen, and scuttled away before they could talk to him.

'Cynric told me he found Simon's prayer for his brother Adam *Molendinarius* here,' said Michael. 'Did you see it? I am not sure I trust Cynric's Latin.'

'He read some of it aloud, but I did not look myself, obviously. I certainly did not believe his translation of the part that "proves" Simon was the lover of Christiana's mother.'

'Is it here now?' asked Michael, taking a dead twig from a wreath and trying to rake the petitions towards him. 'Do not look disapproving. I am a monk. It is all right for me to do this sort of thing.'

Bartholomew glanced through the railings. 'You are out of luck, Brother. Simon used some very white parchment, and I cannot see it now. Perhaps he noticed it in the wrong place, and retrieved it.'

'Or someone else got it, and decided Miller's brother is fair game in the city's feud. Here comes Archdeacon Ravenser. We shall ask him whether he has noticed anything untoward happening here.'

'All the time,' replied Ravenser, sounding surprised Michael should need to enquire. 'Visitors are always using the stems of flowers in an attempt to snag jewels and coins. However, Tetford was scheduled to tend Little Hugh this week, and he *did* fulfil his obligations – unusually for him. I saw him collect the prayers and read them all. He forgot to burn them on the altar, though, as we are supposed to do.'

Michael exchanged a glance with Bartholomew. 'What else did you see?'

'Nothing,' said Ravenser. 'No, wait! There was something. I saw Tetford talking to Miller later, and whatever he was saying made the fellow very angry.'

'He could have been telling Miller he was going to close the tavern,' warned Bartholomew, seeing Michael start to draw conclusions. 'And so would no longer buy Lora Boyner's ale.'

'You *should* look to the Commonalty for Tetford's death, Brother,' said Ravenser. 'You certainly should not search the cathedral for clues, and especially not around me. I know Bartholomew thinks I killed Tetford to get his alehouse, but he is wrong.'

'I shall bear it in mind,' said Michael. 'Is there anything else you can tell me?'

'Not really. Tetford spent a lot of time with Little Hugh the day he died. Thinking, probably. He kept reading the letter Bishop de Lisle sent him, and he drank a lot of the wine Christiana sneaks into Dame Eleanor's flask. Still, at least he had the decency to provide a replacement pot.'

He pointed to a flask, cunningly concealed at the back of the tomb. It was identical to the one in which Eleanor kept her holy water, and Bartholomew had seen others just like them for sale at the market the previous day. The physician retrieved it with difficulty, and Ravenser sauntered away. The dust Bartholomew had disturbed in laying hold of the container made him sneeze. He raised his hand to his face to stifle the noise, then recoiled in horror when his fingers reeked of fish. Thoughts tumbling in confusion, he inspected the jug's contents. Sure enough, it held poison.

'So, Tetford *was* trying to kill me,' said Michael indignantly. 'And here is his secret supply to prove it. He wanted me dispatched, in the hope that he would proceed straight to my stall.'

'He did say he wanted to advance quickly in the Church,' agreed Bartholomew. 'Can we be *sure* this belonged to him? A lot of people have access to this shrine. Anyone could have put it there.'

'Ravenser said Tetford was on duty here this week, and you have to admit it is a clever hiding place. He hatched his plot to kill me, but tried to blackmail Miller over the identity of his brother first. Fortunately for me, someone shot him before he could share his celebratory wine.'

Bartholomew shook the flask. 'We need to dispose of this before someone else dies – dispose of it properly, I mean, by pouring it down a drain.'

'They are all frozen solid, so it will have to go in the river. No, do not put it in your medical bag, man! We are about to visit Miller, and if he finds out you are carrying enough poison to murder his entire household, we will end up with our throats cut for certain.'

'Well, we cannot leave it here. We shall have to go to the river first.'

'There is no time. Did you not sense the city's restlessness this morning? I have the feeling that unless we resolve some of these crimes fast, the place is going to explode into violence. Push the flask as far behind the tomb as you can, and we will retrieve it as soon as we have finished with Miller.'

'Leaving poison lying around is not a good idea—'

'And neither is carting it around a city that is on the verge of a riot. Besides, it was Tetford's poison, and he is dead. Who else is going to use it? Do as I say, Matt. You know I am right.'

Bartholomew did know, but he was not happy about the decision, even so.

'I know I said time was short, but we cannot see Miller yet,' said Michael, as they left the cathedral. 'I am too confused. I need to sit quietly for a few moments and think. With a man like Miller, asking the wrong questions might see us in very deep water, and I do not want to make unnecessary mistakes.'

'Can you do it while we walk to the river?' asked Bartholomew, turning to go back inside and collect the poison.

'That will take too long, and I cannot think clearly when my heart pounds from scaling that hill anyway. We shall visit the minster refectory, and you can analyse what we have learned so far while I listen.'

'I cannot – I do not understand it myself. I do not even know where to start.'

'In Cambridge, twenty years ago. I have a feeling that is where this business originates.'

Bartholomew was thoughtful. 'No, it begins in London, before the Cambridge trial. The two friars were given the Hugh Chalice to transport to Lincoln, but Shirlok relieved them of it when they broke their journey at Cambridge. Shirlok then sold it to the priest at Geddynge, and within a few days had taken it back to sell again, with the help of Lora Boyner.'

'Shirlok was caught and decided to name ten accomplices in an attempt to mitigate his sentence. Meanwhile, Chapman told us the two friars were killed on their way back to London – he said by robbers, but I suspect by Miller's gang. Come with me, Matt. It is too cold to think out here.'

Bartholomew followed him into the refectory that served

the cathedral's officials, where they found a table near a fire. The windows were shuttered against the bitter weather, and the room was lit and warmed by the braziers around the walls. A servant brought bread, cheese and ale, then left them alone. The physician was silent for a moment, then began again.

'The accomplices Shirlok named were Nicholas Herl and Sabina – not married at that point – Miller, Chapman, Aylmer, Lora Boyner and four others, including Miller's brother. Langar was the clerk who recorded the case.'

Michael took up the tale. 'The appellees were acquitted, despite the fact that some were known felons: Herl had been accused of robbery the year before, but was released for lack of evidence; Sabina's first husband was hanged for theft and she was implicated in his activities; and Chapman could not leave Cambridge with Miller, because he was in gaol on another charge.'

'Shirlok was hanged, but miraculously escaped. Then the recovered property went missing, thanks to de Wetherset. Perhaps it was then that Herl, Chapman and Aylmer marked themselves with cups. Miller did not, because he said he had always wondered what the symbol meant. Later, Flaxfleete joined their ranks, although by the time we met him, he was their enemy.'

'When they arrived in Lincoln, Miller and the others took over the Commonalty. A feud was already bubbling, and the intervention of ambitious upstarts from another county will have done nothing to calm troubled waters. How did they come to amass so much power?'

Bartholomew watched Michael eat. 'They have had two decades to do it, and I imagine it is easy when you have lots of money. When people died and the two sides became uneven, Spayne elected to support Miller, not from any sense that Miller is good or right, but to maintain the equilibrium. Then we come to the first death. Nicholas Herl was poisoned three days before we arrived.'

'You are moving far too fast, Matt. We were told it was the suspicious demise of the wicked Canon Hodelston that escalated the rivalry between the factions. *His* was the first death, and I suspect there have been others, too. However, the next incident pertinent to us occurred in the summer, when Flaxfleete burned Spayne's storerooms, causing such an inferno that Spayne's roof is set to collapse.'

'And around the same time, Thoresby threatened to behead Dalderby. Yesterday, Dalderby gave Sheriff Lungspee a bribe, and it is obvious that *he* stabbed Chapman – and that he expected his crime to be exposed. But Dalderby is now dead, killed by a blow to the head, but he was able to stagger to Kelby's house before breathing his last. Under the circumstances, we should not forget the rumour that Kelby killed his own friend Flaxfleete as a sacrificial lamb, to prevent Miller from avenging Herl and Aylmer. Perhaps Kelby killed Dalderby for the same reason.'

'You are still going too fast, Matt. Herl's death came before any of this.'

'Herl ingested poison after drinking ale in the Swan tavern, and either fell or was pushed into the Braytheford Pool. A few days later, Aylmer, having renounced his life of sin, was stabbed while holding Simon's goblet – which may or may not be the Hugh Chalice.'

'Now you have left something else out,' said Michael. 'The chalice was stolen by Aylmer once before, when it was in Kelby's possession. Remember?'

'I remember Gynewell saying an accusation had been levelled, but that Flaxfleete had agreed to drop the charges. Gynewell had found it in the cathedral's crypt.'

'And Aylmer – in holy orders – had access to the vault.'

'That thing certainly circulates,' said Bartholomew in

392

distaste. 'Then we have another odd connection: Aylmer, Flaxfleete, Herl and Chapman have drawings of cups on their shoulders, and all – except Herl – have been in possession of the chalice.'

'Herl *did* have it. We think he may have been the silversmith who made the fakes. Next, Tetford was shot. Like Aylmer, he had decided to turn over a new leaf, but was killed before he could do it. The consensus is that he *was* sincere, but that he probably would not have succeeded.'

'He died while giving you poisoned wine. That does not sound like a new leaf to me. It was the same kind of poison that killed Herl and Flaxfleete, and we have just found a large pot of it in a place where Tetford spent most of his last day. Perhaps he is our culprit, and your case is solved.'

'Or perhaps he was killed because someone objected to the fact that he shut the Tavern in the Close. His ladies were none too pleased, for a start. Perhaps the poison belongs to one of them. Or to Ravenser, because he wanted to run the alehouse.'

Bartholomew sighed. 'We have worked out a logical sequence of events, and we have unearthed new connections between victims and suspects, but none of it tells us the identity of the killer. Anyone could have poisoned Flaxfleete's wine keg while it was waiting to be delivered; Herl drank his ale in a tavern full of people; and the Gilbertine Priory is so lax in its security that anyone could have wandered in and stabbed Aylmer. Our suspects still include virtually everyone we know.'

Michael grimaced. 'You are right: we *are* no further forward, but at least my thoughts are clear now. So, let us see what we can learn from Master Miller.'

*　　*　　*

Miller was waiting for Bartholomew, staring out of the window at the palisade of pointed stakes that protected his house. Langar was with him, and together they escorted physician and monk to the sickbed. Chapman smiled warily when he saw them, and said he was feeling better. Bartholomew removed the bandage and was pleased to find no signs of mortification. As he worked, Miller, Langar and Michael formed a looming wall behind him, and Miller spat on the floor.

'I promise not to hurt him,' said Bartholomew, not liking the way they hemmed him in. He sat back, bumping into Langar as he did so. 'There is no need for you all to stay.'

Miller's eyes narrowed, and he removed his dagger to pick one of his four yellow teeth. 'Are you trying to get him alone? To ask him about matters that are none of your concern?'

'Of course not,' said Michael scornfully. 'Very well. We shall all watch, if that is what you want, although we should step back and give him room to work. We can talk about Aylmer while we wait.'

'Do you know who killed him?' asked Miller eagerly.

'Not yet,' replied Michael, 'although I know a good deal more now than when I was first asked to investigate. However, you can help me advance even further by clarifying a few points.'

'That depends,' said Miller. 'I am not talking about Cambridge, if that is what you have in mind.'

'He has met that woman – Sabina.' Langar spoke the name with utter contempt. 'She has been gossiping, telling him how you were once accused of heinous crimes. *She* should not have been released with the rest of you, *she* should have shared the fate of her first husband. She turned very odd after Aylmer retook his vows a month ago, and I do not trust her. So, we *will* answer the monk's questions, Miller, to make sure he has the truth.'

'Sabina did mention a misunderstanding in Cambridge,' said Michael cautiously. 'She also said you were not guilty. Shirlok was hanged, though.'

'I deplore hangings,' said Langar with a shudder. 'I could not bring myself to watch.'

'I could,' said Miller, 'but I missed that one, because it took place sooner than I expected.'

There was a tap on the door and Sabina entered, bringing food on a tray. She was surprised to see the scholars, and Bartholomew was startled to see her: he had been under the impression that she had broken away from the Commonalty. She saw what he was thinking and explained.

'I came when I heard Chapman was unwell. The others do not know how to care for a sick man, and I do not want the poor fellow to die for want of gentle hands.'

Langar sneered. 'She told you her decision to leave us and lead a blameless life, did she, physician? I doubt she will endure it long.'

She glowered at him. 'I am doing very well, thank you.'

Langar regarded her with contempt. 'You are not here for Chapman, but because you detect unease in the town and you want our protection. Your past association with us means you are still considered fair game by the Guild. You own allegiance to one person only: yourself.'

'She can stay until Lincoln is calm again,' said Miller, cutting across her response, and silencing Langar's objections with a glare. 'I would rather have her where I can see what she is doing, anyway.'

Sabina shot the lawyer a triumphant look, then addressed Michael. 'Have you come to tell us who killed my Nicholas?' She smiled spitefully when Langar winced at the use of the possessive.

'The monk has been looking into Aylmer's murder,' snapped Langar. 'Nicholas's was mine to explore.'

'And have *you* learned anything useful?' Sabina asked him mockingly.

He ignored her and addressed Michael. 'I visited all the apothecaries, and asked whether they have sold any fishy poison recently. None have. *Ergo,* the toxin came from another source.'

'Why would an apothecary own such a thing?' asked Miller, puzzled.

'It can be used as a medicine,' explained Bartholomew. 'I suspect the killer collected black rye grains in the summer, though. These can be crushed and added to wine or ale. With alcohol, they combine to deadly effect, which is why both Herl and Flaxfleete died so quickly.'

'Then anyone might have done it?' asked Miller. 'Anyone who knew which grains to use?' When Bartholomew nodded, he grimaced his disappointment. Then he blew his nose in a piece of linen, and shoved it up his sleeve to use again later. The physician looked away, revolted.

'Tetford had some in his possession when he died,' said Michael casually. 'But he is dead, so we have no way of knowing whether he was aware of the fact.'

'Tetford,' mused Miller softly. 'He was an unpredictable devil. He told me he planned to close his tavern and buy no more of Lora's ale, but would not say why. Then Ravenser renewed the Close's order for ale, so all is well again.'

Langar walked to the window, flung open the shutter and stared out, gazing thoughtfully into the yard below. Michael started to ask something else, but Miller raised an authoritative hand, and the monk faltered into silence. Sabina watched Bartholomew bathe Chapman's arm without a word, and it seemed the Commonalty was used to being quiet when Langar was deliberating. The tension was stifling, and just when Bartholomew felt he could stand it no longer, the lawyer spoke.

'You seem to think Tetford killed Flaxfleete and Nicholas, because you found poison among his belongings, but you are wrong. First, he was not brave enough. Secondly, he liked Flaxfleete, because Flaxfleete donated wine to his brothel. Thirdly, Nicholas once gave him a shilling when he was destitute, and he never forgot the kindness. Fourthly, he seldom read, so I doubt he knew what the physician has just told us about the poison. And fifthly, he was in holy orders, which moderated his behaviour to a degree: he would never have committed murder and damned his immortal soul.'

'The cathedral,' said Miller bitterly. 'That is the cause of this trouble. Aylmer was perfectly normal until he began frequenting the minster. Then he started to repent his sins, and other such nonsense.'

'You probably think we killed Flaxfleete to avenge Aylmer,' said Langar, 'but we did not. We have allowed *his* murder *and* Nicholas's to go unpunished, because we do not want a bloodbath.'

'We debated it for hours,' elaborated Miller, 'but Langar said that if we kill a guildsman, the situation would spin out of control, and he says we cannot be sure of winning an all-out war yet. I think we can, but he does not.'

'There is no point in risking all on a battle with an uncertain outcome,' said Langar irritably. 'Besides, I do not want random guildsmen dispatched. I want the real killer.'

'What about Dalderby?' asked Michael. 'Did someone in the Commonalty kill him?'

Langar pursed his lips. 'I have just explained why it is unwise to engage in unfocused violence, and you immediately ask that question. Of course we did not kill him, although Kelby thinks we did.'

Miller was becoming restless. He turned to Bartholomew. 'Chapman is on the road to recovery?'

Bartholomew nodded. 'As long as he is not plied with salves from anonymous donors again.'

'We do not know who did that, either,' said Miller. 'Langar says the "crone" I saw was wearing a disguise, so it could have been anyone. Even a man.'

The comment sparked a three-way debate between Langar, Miller and Sabina as to which guildsman or cathedral official might have delivered henbane to an ailing man, and Michael inflamed the discussion by suggesting several names. He moved away, drawing the others with him and shooting Bartholomew a glance that said he was to question Chapman while his friends were preoccupied. Bartholomew hastened to oblige, leaning close to the relic-seller so his voice would not carry.

'This chalice you sold Father Simon,' he said, trying to keep the urgency from his voice. 'We found another five last night, virtually identical to it.'

Chapman gaped at him. 'That is impossible! The cup I sold Simon is unique.'

'You lied when you said you bought it in Huntingdon, though. It was one of the items stolen by Shirlok. So how did it come to be in your possession?'

Chapman was not well enough to prevaricate. His expression was resigned. 'All right, I admit the Hugh Chalice *was* part of Shirlok's hoard – although *he* did not know it – but it surfaced later, as stolen goods always do. I sold it to Simon, because it is sacred, and I knew he could be trusted to donate it to the cathedral.'

'I thought you did not like the cathedral.'

Chapman's voice dropped further still, so Bartholomew had to strain to hear him. 'I do not like the men who *infest* the minster, but I revere St Hugh with all my heart. I wanted his chalice where it belongs – at his tomb. I did it for the benefit of future generations.'

Bartholomew was not sure whether to believe him. 'And the mark of the cup on your shoulder?'

'That is part of it,' said Chapman. 'I—'

'What are you whispering about?' demanded Miller, breaking away from Michael when he became aware of what was happening. 'It had better not be anything about my import–export business. I do not want to go on trial for theft again, just because I happen to give you the occasional—'

'The occasional drink in the Angel,' interrupted Langar sharply.

Michael drew his own conclusions from what was not quite said. 'Because you give him the occasional item to sell for you? Does this largess extend to objects from a hoard that disappeared twenty years ago? One that contained white pearls, like the two you gave Matt?'

'No,' said Miller coldly, while Bartholomew came to his feet fast. Michael's question had been too blunt, and trouble was inevitable. 'We do not mean those objects.'

Langar was gazing at Michael with eyes that were hard slits. 'Those pearls came from an old woman who needed ready money to repair her roof. They are most certainly not part of any hoard that went missing twenty years ago.'

'No,' agreed Miller, but unconvincingly. He began paring his nails with his dagger, but his hands were unsteady and Bartholomew saw blood. 'And neither did the Hugh Chalice. It is not the same cup that Shirlok agreed to steal from Geddynge.'

'*Agreed* to steal?' pounced Michael.

'He means *arranged* to steal,' said Langar, stepping in quickly to minimise the damage, while Bartholomew thought that manoeuvring Miller into a position of power in the Commonalty must have been a daunting task. He decided Langar was either a genius or blessed with the patience of a saint.

'It should be in Lincoln,' said Chapman softly. 'Not Geddynge. It belongs with St Hugh.'

'Does St Hugh really want it?' asked Michael. 'It has been handled by some very devious folk.'

Miller led the way down the stairs and opened the door to usher the scholars out, while Sabina remained with Chapman, who said he felt weak and needed a woman's soothing touch. Trailing at the end of the procession, Bartholomew was about to step into the yard, when he happened to glance along the hallway to his left and notice the cellar door ajar. He wondered whether it was the same one that Cynric had complained about not being able to open. Then his stomach clenched in alarm when he noticed a familiar – and far from pleasant – odour.

Michael and Langar were engaged in a sniping, dangerous debate about Shirlok's hoard. They were intent on worming information out of each other, and the confrontation looked set to continue for a few moments more, so Bartholomew told Miller that he had left the knife he used for cutting bandages with Chapman. Miller indicated, with an impatient flick of his head, that he should go and fetch it. Heart thudding, Bartholomew stamped up the stairs, then tiptoed down them again and approached the cellar door. The smell verged on the overpowering.

He listened hard, hearing Michael's voice raised imperiously and Langar clamouring to make a point. He glanced down the steps and saw a lamp burning in the room at the bottom. There were soft, scraping sounds, too. Someone was there. He began to descend, aware that he would have no excuse if he were caught. He moved as quickly and quietly as he could, then almost ruined his efforts by skidding on ice near the bottom. It was cold in the cellar, and a damp patch had frozen hard.

At the foot of the stairs, there was a second door, also ajar. He peered around it into a long room. Someone was at the far end, masked against the stench. It was Lora Boyner, her back towards him as she laboured over a still figure that lay on a table in front of her. Bartholomew took a step closer, determined to know what she was doing. A sliver of ice cracked under his boot.

'Who is there?' Lora called, looking up immediately. She squinted, because the light at the table was bright, but the stairs were in darkness, and while the physician could see her, she could not see him. As she started to walk towards him, he saw the face of the person on the table for the first time. She strode closer, so he turned and bolted up the steps as fast as he could. He was walking towards the front door, feeling sweat trickling down his back, when Miller spotted him. At the same time, Lora emerged from the dungeon steps, dragging a scarf away from her nose and mouth.

'I dropped it outside Chapman's room,' said Bartholomew, waving his knife and hoping the smile he gave did not reveal the depth of his shock at what he had witnessed.

Lora narrowed her eyes. 'Have you *just* come from upstairs?'

Bartholomew's heart was pounding. 'Where else would I have been?'

'There is ice on your boot.'

Bartholomew shrugged. 'It is cold today, so there is frost everywhere. Look.' He touched his toe to a place where water had frozen in a corner of the corridor. However, there was no earthly way it could have transferred itself to anyone's foot – at least, not someone walking normally.

Miller accepted his explanation, although Lora remained suspicious. 'So there is,' he said, spitting at the ice and scoring a direct hit. 'Thank you for seeing to Chapman, but he is

401

better, so do not come back. We will bring you the other two pearls when he is on his feet.'

'Very well,' said Bartholomew, hoping he did not sound as relieved as he felt. While he disliked the notion of abandoning a patient quite so early on his road to recovery, he was perfectly happy never to set foot in Miller's lair again. He escaped from the house without another word, and walked briskly around the nearest corner. When Michael found him, he was leaning heavily against a wall, shaking violently.

'Whatever is the matter?' asked Michael, regarding him in alarm. 'Chapman is not worse, is he? Langar just told me that Miller will kill you if he dies after enduring your ministrations.'

'Shirlok,' said Bartholomew, gulping fresh air. 'He is in Miller's cellar. Dead.'

Michael took Bartholomew's arm and strode towards the city. It was mid-afternoon, but the clouds were a sullen grey-brown, which meant some of the shops on the main street were already lit with lamps. Bartholomew tried to explain what he had seen, but Michael stopped him, claiming that it was not safe to speak on roads that teemed with weavers. One might overhear the discussion, and report to Miller that things had been seen that he might prefer to keep concealed.

They passed through the crowds that had gathered to watch a fire-eater in the *Pultria*, ducking into the porch of St Cuthbert's Church, when they saw Kelby and a sizeable contingency of guildsmen processing towards them. Behind was a coffin, and Bartholomew supposed Dalderby was about to be buried. The merchants' faces were bleak and watchful, expressions that did not go unnoticed by the weavers. Inside the chapel, a priest told Michael that

Dalderby's murder was considered an act of war on the Guild, and that he expected revenge to follow shortly. A weaver overheard, and slipped away quickly. Bartholomew saw him talking to several of his fellows outside, and knew it would not be long before the priest's prediction became hard fact. There was menace and fear in the air, and he sensed it would take very little to spark off the kind of riot he had experienced in Cambridge.

When they reached the Swan, Michael pushed the physician inside and took a table near the fire, calling to the potboy to bring them wine. The tavern was warm after the chill of the December afternoon, and the braziers on the walls emitted a cosy red glow. Bartholomew found he was shivering, and wondered if it was the cold or a reaction to what he had seen in Miller's cellar.

'You are as white as a corpse,' said Michael, when the boy had gone. He poured dark claret into two goblets as he grimaced an apology. 'Sorry – that was an unfortunate analogy. Drink some wine; it will make you feel better. Cadavers are never very nice to behold.'

'It was not the corpse,' said Bartholomew shakily. 'I have seen too many for them to shock me. It was the whole business of sneaking down the steps, and expecting to be trapped between Miller and Lora. I do not understand how Cynric has the nerve for that sort of thing. It was worse than a battle.'

'What was Lora doing?'

'Wrapping Shirlok's body in a winding sheet. I suppose they intend to bury him somewhere, because he is beginning to reek.'

'If he smells as strongly as you say, it means he has been dead for some time.'

Bartholomew nodded. 'Especially as cold weather tends to retard that sort of thing. No wonder Lora – along with

Chapman and Miller – was able to declare Shirlok dead when Cynric overheard her discussing him in the Angel tavern. She had his body in her basement!'

'But Langar thought Shirlok might still be alive,' said Michael, rubbing his flabby cheeks. 'Which means he may *not* know Shirlok is currently in need of a shroud. This suggests the other three killed him without their lawyer's knowledge.'

'Langar is clever, Brother. He may have killed Shirlok himself, and left the body for his friends to dispose of. If we were in Cambridge, I would suggest lying in wait with your beadles, and catching them red-handed when they go to bury Shirlok, but not here. We do not know who is a friend.'

'Gynewell,' suggested Michael. 'He stands aloof from the city's feud.'

'We *think* he is aloof, but we cannot be sure he will not go straight to Miller.'

'Prior Roger and Hamo, then. They are not too deeply embroiled in the dispute.'

'But Aylmer and Tetford were killed in *their* convent; Herl died in the Braytheford Pool – a stone's throw away; and their guest Simon is missing. Also, Hamo does not approve of your liking for Christiana, and he injured his arm on the night we were attacked. We cannot trust them, either.'

'Well, I do not think we should involve Sheriff Lungspee. It might be Miller's turn to bribe him.'

'You would overlook a murder?' asked Bartholomew.

'What is to say Shirlok was murdered? Perhaps he just died.'

'There was a noose around his neck, Brother. He had been hanged.'

Michael regarded him askance. 'Are you saying you were mistaken twenty years ago, when you saw him run away?

They exhumed him and brought his bones here for some odd reason?'

'I am saying he was hanged in the last few weeks. He is older and greyer – like all of us – but it is him without question. His face has been etched into my mind ever since he "died" the first time.'

'And you are sure he is dead? He will not leap up and run away again?'

'No, Brother. He is beginning to rot.'

Michael sipped his wine. 'So, let us assume he stayed low after escaping from Cambridge, living the life of a travelling thief. Eventually, he arrived in Lincoln, perhaps by chance, but perhaps because he heard Miller and his cronies are now influential citizens. Once here, he demanded money for his silence about their past. You seem sure they were guilty of the charges he levelled against them, so perhaps he felt they owed him something.'

'Yes, but in Cambridge, he tried to save himself by exposing their roles in his crimes. Even a stupid man will know that sort of behaviour will not see him welcomed with open arms.'

'How long did you say he has been dead? Exactly?'

'I did not say – I cannot, not after the merest of glimpses. The smell suggests weeks, though.'

'So, his death could coincide with the first appearance of the Hugh Chalice, about a month ago?'

'It could.' Bartholomew drank more wine, and his thoughts wandered to another matter. 'Those symbols on Chapman, Herl, Aylmer and Flaxfleete *are* significant: you do not make permanent marks on yourself for something inconsequential. The only one of the four still alive is Chapman, and he keeps telling us how important the Hugh Chalice is. Those signs *must* represent that cup, Brother.'

Michael agreed. 'However, Miller could not dispose of it

as long as Shirlok was alive and waiting to accuse him again, and its public appearance would certainly have attracted Shirlok's attention. I think it – along with the rest of Shirlok's goods – has been languishing somewhere, all but forgotten.'

'That assumes Miller knew Shirlok's execution was unsuccessful.'

'He did. Langar had a friend who was witness to his escape, if you recall.'

'But Cynric overheard him tell Langar that Shirlok was definitely executed.'

'And when did Cynric hear this? *Two days* ago – and you have just said Shirlok has been dead weeks. Of course Miller knows Shirlok is dead *now*, because the corpse is in his cellar.'

'All right,' acknowledged Bartholomew. 'So, Shirlok arrived in Lincoln unexpectedly, Miller hanged him properly, and he and Chapman were free to sell the goods at last. Chapman has a special interest in the chalice, because I think he really does believe it is sacred. He sold it to Flaxfleete – another man who carries the mark of the cup.'

'Then it was stolen, perhaps by Aylmer, although nothing was ever proved.' Michael snapped his fingers suddenly. 'I see what happened! The bishop found the chalice in the crypt. And who has access to the cathedral vaults and owns a penchant for the belongings of others? Besides Aylmer?'

Bartholomew sighed. 'The dean! I saw him steal a goblet from Miller myself, and everyone at the cathedral seems aware of his "illness". It is obvious now: the dean took the cup from Flaxfleete, and Gynewell returned it on the understanding that the matter would be quietly forgotten.'

'Aylmer had been unjustly accused, and perhaps being blamed when he was innocent shocked him into wanting to turn to a new page in his life. Then what? Did Flaxfleete sell it to Simon?'

'I think he probably gave it back to Chapman, although I doubt we will ever know why. And Chapman sold it to Simon, knowing he would donate it to the cathedral, where he thinks it should be.'

Michael rubbed his chin. 'We can make a few assumptions about Herl now, though. He became disenchanted with the "chalice fraternity" and scraped off his mark, suggesting he no longer believed in it. Then he crafted copies of the cup and sold them to Tetford – and probably to others, too.'

'I do not think Chapman had anything to do with that, because he was horrified when he learned there were replicas. He reveres the thing too much for skulduggery.'

'I agree. So, I suspect Herl was killed by another member of the fraternity – for his sacrilege.' Michael finished his wine and stood. 'We should return to the Gilbertines, and see if they have news of Simon. He may be able to answer some of our questions, and I would like to see his shoulders.'

'He denied having a mark when you asked him about it.'

'And I stopped him before he could remove his habit to prove it. Perhaps I should not have done.'

They left the tavern, Bartholomew light-headed from gulping too much wine too quickly. It was dark, and he wondered whether they should pay some of the itinerant weavers to escort them home, in the hope that their presence would avert another attack. Then it occurred to him that the weavers might owe allegiance to the ambushers, and would melt away at the first sign of danger. On reflection, he decided they would be safer alone. He rested his hand on the hilt of his sword, only to find it was not there: he had forgotten to bring it with him. He stumbled across a frozen heap of entrails outside a butcher's shop, drawing a worried glance from Michael.

'That wine did not taste of fish, did it? There was no poison?'

'I saw Quarrel giving other customers wine from the same jug, so it should be all right. Of course, if it were poisoned, you mentioning it now would do us no good. It would be too late.'

Michael blew out his cheeks in a sigh. 'This business is unnerving me. I am seriously considering locking myself inside the Gilbertine Priory until Sunday, then jumping on a horse as soon as I emerge from my installation and riding as fast as I can to Cambridge.'

Bartholomew glanced at the sky. 'It is snowing again, and a heavy fall will block the road. It would be unfortunate if you were to dash away in all your splendour, only to be turned back by drifts.'

'It would be embarrassing,' conceded Michael. He frowned unhappily. 'Do *you* think I am justified in abandoning my investigation? I know I am under an obligation to help Gynewell, but this is not my city, and I do not understand its intrigues and plots. Things are different in Cambridge, where I have beadles and a sheriff to protect me. But then I remember that Tetford is Bishop de Lisle's close kin, and—'

Bartholomew stopped suddenly. 'Tetford! We were supposed to collect his poison on our way back, and drop it in the river, but Shirlok knocked it from my mind. We shall have to go and get it.'

'Not tonight, Matt,' said Michael firmly. 'It would mean toiling back up that hill, and it is already too late to be out. Besides, you hid it very well. I will destroy it first thing tomorrow—'

'Brother, look!' hissed Bartholomew suddenly, gripping his friend's arm. 'There is Simon!'

Michael followed the direction of his finger and saw the

priest walking briskly along the road in front of them. Michael opened his mouth to yell, but Bartholomew warned him to silence.

'He is moving furtively – he does not want to be seen. We will follow him and see where he goes.'

'You must be drunk,' said Michael uneasily, 'or you would not suggest such a thing.'

'We will just see where he is going,' said Bartholomew. 'Come on.'

Michael was about to object further, but the priest was striding down the road he and Bartholomew needed to take anyway, so it was no inconvenience to stay behind him. There were a few footpaths off the main track, leading to the river in one direction and the parallel dike in the other, but Simon took no detours. Eventually, he reached the place where the road crossed an odorous ditch called the Gowt. He glanced behind him, but the night was dark, and Bartholomew and Michael had been careful to stay in the shadows.

'He is going inside Holy Cross,' whispered Bartholomew, hanging back.

'His old church,' murmured Michael. 'He keeps looking around him in a very sly manner.'

'Yes, he does,' agreed Bartholomew. 'So do not walk so fast, Brother, or he will see you.'

'I do not like this,' grumbled Michael. 'I am too heavy-boned for stealth, and Cynric told me I look like a hippopotamus when I tiptoe. Shall we follow him inside?'

'Is the building open? It is well past sunset, so it should be locked.'

Holy Cross was a dark mass against the night sky, and the charred remains of Simon's old house comprised a sinister blackened shell. The priest walked across the churchyard and fiddled with a chancel window. After a moment, there was a hollow, echoing clank as a bar fell away on the other side. He glanced around quickly, then climbed in. Moments later, Bartholomew heard him unlock the door.

'He knows that window is a weak point,' said Michael. 'He went straight to it.'

'He worked here for twenty years, so that is not surprising. However, he must be expecting company, or he would not have opened the door. What shall we do? Clamber through the window, and hope he does not see us? Or wait out here, to see who comes to meet him?'

'You said we were just going to see where he went,' said Michael accusingly. 'Well, we have done that, and it is too cold a night for lurking in icy churchyards. We should return to the Gilbertines.'

'We should find out what he is doing. His intentions are not innocent, or he would not be breaking in – he would have asked his successor for the key. Watch the door while I go through the window.'

Michael sighed testily. 'This is *not* a good idea. Hurry up, then – and be careful.'

Bartholomew scrambled through the window, wincing when his feet scraped noisily on the sill, then dropped lightly to the floor on the other side. It was warmer in the church than it was outside, although not much, and the air was still and damp. It was also pitch black, and he waited for his eyes to adjust.

The nave walls were stone, but its floor was of beaten earth, which served to muffle his footsteps. He moved slowly, afraid of making a sound that would alert Simon to his presence. He found him at the altar in the chancel, kneeling with his hands clasped in front of him and his eyes fixed on the wooden cross. Bartholomew eased into the shadows to watch, but Simon remained in an attitude of prayer for so long that the physician became uncomfortable with what he was doing. He had assumed Simon was up to no good, but now it appeared he had just been coming to his old church to pray, and no one had any right to spy on him. He began to edge away, intending to leave the way he had come. Then there was a sudden clamour of voices from outside.

'No!' yelled Michael, and there was a clash of arms.

Abandoning any pretence at stealth, Bartholomew bolted towards the door. He collided heavily with someone coming in, and was bowled from his feet. He scrambled upright, instinctively fumbling for his sword before realising again that he did not have it. Hands snatched at him, but he struggled away from them, tearing the clasp from his cloak and leaving the garment behind. He dashed outside, and saw Michael doing battle with a man who held a sword. The monk had grabbed a shoe-scraper, and was managing to fend off the blows, but only just.

Bartholomew hurtled towards them with a battle cry he had learned from Cynric. The swordsman turned towards him with a start, and raised the weapon to defend himself. Bartholomew swung wildly with his medical bag, and caught the fellow on the side of his head, sending him reeling. Then someone leapt on the physician from behind. He went down hard, and his mouth and nose were suddenly full of suffocating snow.

CHAPTER 11

Someone was grabbing the back of Bartholomew's tunic, pulling him away from the choking coldness of the snow. He tried to struggle to his knees, but the fall had winded him, and it was some time before his senses cleared and he was able to look around.

'Matt!' said Michael. 'Stand up, or you will ruin your new hose in all this filthy sleet.'

'Where are they?' Bartholomew asked, staggering to his feet and more concerned about the men who had attacked them than the welfare of his clothes.

'Gone. They ran off when you gave that battle screech you seem rather fond of these days. It was loud enough to wake the dead, and now half the parish is here, demanding to know what happened.'

Bartholomew saw a crowd of people standing in a tight knot, as if they thought such a formation might be safer. 'We should follow the swordsmen. See where they go.'

'They are long gone. It was a stupid idea to follow Simon. I should never have listened to you.'

'He was only praying,' said Bartholomew. 'Where is he? Did he run away with the others?'

'He is still in the chancel. The new priest is giving him last rites.'

Bartholomew gazed at him, mind reeling. 'He is dying? How? I do not understand.'

'He took an arrow in the innards. Even I can see the

wound is mortal, although he lingers yet. Will you see if you can help him?'

Bartholomew tottered unsteadily to the church door, Michael at his side. Simon was lying on his back near the altar, and Bartholomew could see the barb protruding from his stomach. It was an ugly place to be shot, painful and almost invariably fatal.

'After you drove that sword-wielding lunatic away, a second fellow appeared,' explained Michael, as they approached the stricken cleric. 'He attacked you from behind, and I lobbed the shoe-scraper at him when it looked as though he was going to smother you.'

'Were they two of the men who attacked us before?'

'It was dark, so I could not see, but I imagine so. There cannot be that many people who want us dead. When they had gone, I heard a lot of shouting from inside the church. I ran towards the door in time to see two men bowl out as though they were on fire; Simon was here, lying as you see him. I could not make out more than shadows, but one was larger than the other, and they were both armed.'

'So, there were four of them again,' mused Bartholomew. 'Just like last time.'

Michael nodded. 'And none appeared to be the worse for wear from our last encounter. Your bruising of the swordsman's arm was obviously not as serious as you thought.'

'I have finished,' said the young priest, white-faced with shock. His term at Oxford had not prepared him for the murder of his predecessor. 'I sent for the surgeon; he should be here soon.'

Bartholomew knelt, trying to assess Simon's wound without touching it and making it worse. He asked for the lamp to be brought closer, and wondered if he should try to extricate the missile. It would tear the organs it had

413

penetrated, but he could repair them. The more serious problem would be the infection that always set in later, something he had no idea how to prevent.

'Give me something,' whispered Simon. 'For the pain.'

Bartholomew produced a phial of poppy and mandrake juice from his bag, dribbling it between Simon's lips, but pulling away when the priest grabbed his wrist and tried to swallow the whole pot.

'Can you save my life?' breathed Simon.

'I do not think so,' replied Bartholomew honestly.

'Then I will wait for the surgeon. Bunoun cured Dalderby of a near-fatal wound recently, and might be able to do the same for me.'

'Dalderby's was not a serious—' Bartholomew began, before biting off the words. Simon would be more likely to recover if he thought he was in the hands of a genius, and perhaps the surgeon would work a miracle where Bartholomew could not.

The door opened, and Bunoun bustled in. Without a word, he opened his bag and laid his implements on the floor. They were rusty and stained black with old blood. He took the arrow with one hand and waggled it about, holding Simon still with the other. Bartholomew winced at the screams that echoed around the church, and Michael put his hands over his ears.

'Gently,' said Bartholomew, unable to stop himself. 'And do not pull obliquely. You need to trace the path the missile took when it entered, or you will cause more damage.'

Bunoun did not appreciate the advice, and gave an experimental tug on the quarrel that made Simon shriek. 'I know what I am doing.' A gout of blood spurted over his hands. 'Let me do my work, physician. You can write his horoscope when I have finished.'

'When you have finished, he will not need one,'

muttered Bartholomew, gritting his teeth when Bunoun pulled hard enough on the quarrel to make Simon's body rise off the floor. The missile was obviously barbed, and tugging it out was not a good idea.

'Enough,' gasped Simon, trying to fend off the surgeon with scarlet hands. 'No more.'

'I shall prepare a poultice,' announced Bunoun loftily. 'It will draw out the poisons, and tomorrow morning, the quarrel will be extracted without pain or loss of blood.'

He moved away, using a nearby bench as a table for his preparations. The only sound in the church was Simon's laboured breathing and the clink of pots and phials as Bunoun worked.

'Where have you been these last two days, Father?' asked Bartholomew gently, hoping to distract the priest from his agonies by talking. 'We have been worried about you.'

'Praying,' replied Simon, relaxing slightly when he saw Bunoun had gone. 'I had second thoughts about your invitation to the tavern, and realised I should not alienate new colleagues by being aloof. I slipped in at the back, where a lady called Agnes came to greet me. She said it was customary for new patrons to please her with gifts, and showed me the kind of thing she accepted.'

'A cup,' surmised Bartholomew. 'A Hugh Chalice?'

Simon nodded weakly. 'And she said her friends had similar ones. I grew alarmed for my own, so I hurried back to the priory and took it from the chapel. I did not want the Gilbertines to know I was in an agony of doubt over its authenticity, so I slipped in and out without being seen. Then I went to the minster, hoping St Hugh would send a sign to let me know I had the real one. I do not want to present the cathedral with a fake, not after all these years of waiting.'

'No one saw you,' said Michael doubtfully. 'And people have been looking everywhere.'

'The cathedral was too noisy, too distracting, so I went to St Margaret's in the Close instead.'

'Claypole searched for you there,' said Michael. 'He said it was empty.'

'No one came, not even St Hugh, who chose not to answer my prayers. So I wrote to Chapman, and asked him to meet me here. I was going to demand the truth about how he came by the cup.'

'All these years of waiting,' echoed Bartholomew suddenly, leaning forward to push Simon's habit from his shoulder. The mark was fainter than it had been on Aylmer, as though it had been etched tentatively, but was clear, nonetheless. 'You *are* a member of this fraternity. You said you were not.'

Simon grimaced. 'I knew if I offered to remove my clothes to "prove" I was free of symbols Michael would stop me. He knows the dangers of cold air on a singer's throat. We took a vow, you see, to keep our group a secret.'

Michael did not say he had demurred because he had not liked the look of the priest's scaly legs. 'Is it still a secret, or can you tell me now?'

Simon gave a mirthless smile. 'I know we sound an unlikely alliance – me, Aylmer, Chapman, Flaxfleete, Herl and many others – but we all swore a sacred oath to see the Hugh Chalice in the minster one day. There were two score of us – guildsmen, Commonalty, clerics, weavers, all with the mark. But then Canon Hodelston was poisoned, and some members began to think the feud was more important than their duty to the saint. Friends became enemies, and only a few of us remain faithful.'

'You should rest now, Father,' said Bartholomew gently. 'Save your strength for—'

416

'No!' Simon gripped his hand, to prevent him from leaving. 'I want to talk, and there are things you should know. I feel no pain anyway, just a great weariness of body and spirit.'

'Are you sure?' asked Michael. The priest nodded. 'Then I do not think Chapman *sold* you the chalice, as you claimed. I think he *gave* it to you, so you could present it to the cathedral in a ceremony that would venerate it. I imagine that is why Flaxfleete returned it to Chapman after the incident with the dean: Flaxfleete could *donate* it to the cathedral, but you could make it part of a major rite.'

Simon coughed weakly. 'It was why I agreed to be installed as a canon.'

Bartholomew had also been thinking. 'Aylmer was dishonest *and* he was in Cambridge two decades ago. I think *he* was one of the friars charged to bring the cup from London – I recall thinking at the trial that he looked like a fallen priest. He was weak and corrupt, and he sold the chalice for twenty shillings, a paltry sum for such a venerable object. The friars were not murdered by robbers or struck down by an angry St Hugh on their way home. They just began new lives in another place.'

'No,' breathed Simon. 'Shirlok *stole* it from Aylmer. Aylmer told me so himself.'

Michael frowned. 'Shirlok always denied taking the chalice, although he admitted to making off with the other items. I think Matt is right: Aylmer sold the chalice to Geddynge for fast money. And he lied to you about it – lied to *you*, Simon, because *you* were the other friar.'

'Of course!' exclaimed Bartholomew, seeing the priest's expression of resignation. 'It makes sense now. You came to Lincoln because you had nowhere else to go. You could not return to London, given that you had failed to deliver the relic. And you felt guilty about losing it, so you decided to live here, where you could dedicate your life to the saint whose chalice you had mislaid. Plus there is the fact that Miller is your brother. Cynric was right: Adam and Simon *Molendinarius* were named by Shirlok as his accomplices.'

'You doubtless stayed with your brother in Cambridge on your journey north,' Michael continued, when the priest said nothing to indicate they were wrong. 'You told him about the sacred task with which you were entrusted. The rest is obvious. Miller helped Aylmer sell the chalice to a gullible priest – Geddynge was chosen because it is a safe distance from Cambridge, making it more difficult for the crime to be linked to him – and Shirlok was charged to get it back again. But Shirlok was caught, and the whole miserable tribe was in trouble.'

'Adam and I are *half*-brothers,' whispered Simon. 'Neither of us had anything to do with removing the chalice from Geddynge, though. I was terrified when we were ordered to appear at Cambridge castle. It was a dreadful day.'

'I do not remember you,' said Bartholomew. 'And Miller said his brother died in prison.'

'I do not remember you, either, but that is no surprise after all this time.' Simon closed his eyes for a moment, rallying his strength, then began to speak again. 'When we arrived here, Adam and I decided to conceal our relationship until we had found our feet: he was to say his brother was dead and no one ever asks about a priest's family. Later, we maintained the pretence, because *I* do not want to be associated with criminal activities, and *he* finds it embarrassing to have kin in holy orders.'

Michael was puzzled. 'Why did you elect to live in the same place, if you then denied knowing each other? What could be gained from that?'

'I came here because St Hugh appeared to me in a

dream, and said I could make amends by serving as parish priest to Holy Cross. When the chalice finally reappeared and I was nominated as a canon, I knew he had forgiven me at last.'

'And your brother?'

'He liked the sound of the place when I described it to him, and he had nowhere else to go. So, I *was* the other courier, Brother, but Aylmer and I were *robbed.* We did not *sell* the Hugh Chalice. We have lived with the shame of losing it for twenty years. Aylmer's sorrow led him to a libertine life, but he retook his priestly vows when the cup arrived in Lincoln recently.'

'You credit him with too much decency,' said Michael. 'He was never anything but a felon.'

Simon did not seem to hear him. 'I founded the "fraternity", as you call it, to look for the chalice, and we have been searching ever since. Chapman and Adam found it four weeks ago.'

'Adam is not a member,' said Bartholomew, not mentioning that Miller had probably known for the best part of two decades that his brother's holy grail was not lost at all. 'Why not?'

'Because that would have put us too much in each other's company, and I did not want him to reveal our relationship in a moment of carelessness. You may have noticed that his wits are not the sharpest in the town. Poor Aylmer. He died trying to protect the chalice . . . '

'You said he was trying to steal it,' said Michael.

'No, I did not. Others did, but I said we should give him the benefit of the doubt. I never believed he was acting dishonestly. I have no idea who killed him, though. Did Chapman shoot me? He must have done, because no one else knew I would be here. I paid young Hugh a silver penny to deliver him a letter, asking him to come.'

'Can we be sure Hugh delivered it to the right house?' asked Michael, troubled.

By the time Bunoun declared himself ready to apply his salve, the priest was sinking towards death. Unwilling to see Simon subjected to painful treatment that would make no difference to the outcome, Bartholomew told the surgeon his chances of success were slim and suggested he abstain from spoiling his good record. Bunoun was experienced enough to know he spoke the truth, and packed up his equipment before going outside to declare that he had been summoned too late to effect one of his miraculous cures. Since there was no more to be done at Holy Cross, Bartholomew and Michael left Simon in the care of the parishioners he had served so long, and returned to the Gilbertine Priory.

'I think he was telling the truth about the Hugh Chalice – at least, the truth as he knows it,' said Bartholomew, as they walked. 'It is obvious to us that Aylmer sold it to Geddynge, and Shirlok was asked to get it back again, but Simon harboured no such suspicions. He founded his fraternity to hunt it down and bring it to where he thinks it belongs.'

Michael nodded. 'I am sure you are right.'

'Aylmer was too cautious to sell it as the Hugh Chalice, but was quite happy to collect twenty shillings for a silver cup. He may have had redeeming thoughts towards the end of his life, but he was a despicable man.'

Michael sighed. 'Simon confided a few other things while you were consulting with Bunoun. I asked why folk had joined his group, and it sounded as if he had applied a good deal of moral pressure. I suspect that is why they fell away so readily – their allegiance was not willingly given. Still, at least we know what the mark means. I assumed it was sinister, but it was not. He also denied impregnating

Christiana's mother, but admitted to setting his house alight – for the Hugh Chalice.'

'How did he think that would help?'

'As we suspected, Gynewell had intimated he might be in line for the Stall of Sanctae Crucis, so he burned down his home to draw attention to himself. It worked: he was offered the post in a matter of days. It meant full-time duties in the cathedral where the cup was to be displayed, and would have allowed him to guard it.'

'Where is the chalice now?' asked Bartholomew. 'Simon's, I mean, not the others.'

Michael removed something from under his cloak, and Bartholomew saw the familiar, dented vessel with its worn carving. 'He asked me to make sure it is presented to the cathedral on Sunday.'

'It looks just like the others,' said Bartholomew warily. 'And I thought he was uncertain about it.'

'He claims it *is* the real one, because St Hugh would not let him die without seeing it after his years of devotion. So, I shall put it in St Katherine's Chapel with the others, and de Wetherset can decide.'

Prior Roger was full of questions when Michael presented a sixth cup for his growing collection, and it was some time before he allowed the monk to go. Wearily, Michael returned to the guest-hall, where he found Bartholomew already asleep. The monk had often envied his friend's ability to doze through all manner of commotion, and in this case, the chamber in which he rested contained de Wetherset and Suttone, who had lit several candles and were making no effort to lower their voices. Cynric was honing his sword on a whetting stone, and Whatton and a few friends had just started to bellow psalms in the building next door.

'He refused to tell us anything,' said de Wetherset, indicating Bartholomew with an angry flick of his thumb. 'He said he was tired, and that we would have to wait until tomorrow. Then Whatton came to tell us Simon is dead, and invited us to sing songs for his soul. Is it true?'

Michael nodded. 'And I do not want to talk tonight, either. However, here comes Hamo. As he was outside his prior's door when I gave my account of what happened, you can ask *him* about it.'

Suttone regarded Hamo in surprise. 'I thought you would have abandoned eavesdropping, considering you had an accident the last time you did it. How is your arm, by the way?'

'You hurt yourself listening to private conversations?' asked Michael disapprovingly.

'It happened the other night, when you and Matthew were assaulted,' elaborated Suttone. He gave a rather malicious smile. 'Hamo was so determined to hear what Prior Roger was saying to Whatton in the Lady Chapel that he tried to climb the ivy on the wall outside – I could see him through the window. And all the time, you were in the orchard, fighting for your life.'

'Our Lady Chapel is a difficult challenge for eaves-droppers,' said Hamo, making it sound as though the fault lay in the building, rather than the activity. 'And the only way to monitor discussions is to go outside and scale the wall. I heard the clash of arms as you fought off your attackers, and I was so frightened that I fell and stunned myself. By the time I had recovered, Cynric was saying that you had escaped and Tetford was dead.'

'Why were you trying to listen to your prior?' asked Michael curiously.

'He wanted to know whether Whatton was going to be promoted to Brother Cellerer,' supplied Suttone helpfully. He assumed a pious expression. 'Nosy men will die when the plague comes again.'

Michael smiled, noting that the timing of the incident eliminated Hamo, Roger and Whatton as candidates for the ambush. He wished Suttone had mentioned it sooner. 'Would you mind extinguishing the lamps and going downstairs to talk? Matt will snore through the trumpets of Judgement Day, but I require silence and darkness for my slumber. Good night, gentlemen.'

He lay on his bed and hauled a blanket over his face. He did not think he would sleep, because his mind teemed with questions, but he did not want to spend the night chatting to de Wetherset and Suttone, either. He needed time alone, to consider what he had learned and try to instil some order into it. Therefore, he was surprised when he opened his eyes to find the room full of daylight.

'Roger ordered the bells silenced this morning,' explained de Wetherset, watching him look around in confusion. 'You seemed so exhausted last night, that I thought you might appreciate longer in bed.'

'It was our suggestion,' said Suttone shyly. 'Roger was set to produce some really loud music today, as he now has six Hugh Chalices lined up on his altar, but we persuaded him that your repose was important to solving the mysteries that have beset his city. Grudgingly, he agreed.'

Michael sat up and scrubbed his face. Bartholomew was shaving in some hot water Cynric had brought, and had changed his clothes. By comparison, Michael felt soiled and grubby. He swung his large legs over the side of the bed.

'I have a lot to do today,' he said ungraciously. 'You should not have let me waste time.'

'Your wits will be sharper with the additional rest,' said de Wetherset. 'I am trying to help you, Brother. If I am an instrument of the saints, then I should put my talents to good use.'

Michael glanced sharply at him, but could see no trace of humour in the ex-Chancellor's face. His ploy to prevent de Wetherset from harming Bartholomew at some point in the future had worked better than he had anticipated.

'Roger invited Gynewell to come and hear your account of Simon's death,' said Suttone. 'I heard him arrive a few moments ago.'

'He heard cloven hoofs rattle across the cobbles,' murmured Cynric. He was in a foul mood, furious that he had not been there when Michael and Bartholomew had been attacked a second time.

Michael stood, stretched and performed his morning ablutions. Then he donned a fresh habit and asked Cynric to air the one he had been wearing, so it would be clean for the Sunday celebrations – if he lived that long. In an attempt to alleviate the guilt he felt for not protecting his scholars, Cynric went to the kitchens and forced the cook to prepare the best breakfast the convent could provide, fingering his dagger meaningfully as he recited a wholly unreasonable list of demands. The meal took three men to carry, and won Michael's instant approval.

'It is healthy to consume a decent breakfast,' he declared, when Bartholomew warned that he might be sick if he ate more than a dozen eggs. 'I am sure Surgeon Bunoun would agree.'

'Bunoun is an excellent *medicus*,' agreed de Wetherset. 'Look what he did for Dalderby, although the reprieve was only temporary. I heard Miller killed him, by hitting him over the head with a stone.'

'It is a bad time for men to slaughter each other,' said Suttone worriedly. 'In four days, we shall have our installation, the General Pardon and Miller's Market, all at the same time. If there are tales that the Guild and the

424

Commonalty have been killing each other, blood will flow for certain.'

'The city felt very uneasy yesterday,' agreed de Wetherset. 'Men were gathering in groups, according to affiliation, and that is always a bad sign. I remember it from my Cambridge days.'

When Michael had reduced Cynric's fine spread to a few gnawed bones and a sizeable midden of eggshells, the four scholars walked across the snow-covered ground to Prior Roger's solar, where Bishop Gynewell was prodding the fire into a furious glow that was too hot to be comfortable for anyone else. Prior Roger stood near a window he had eased open, and Hamo was pouring cups of wine and readying platters of pastries. Bartholomew saw they were expected to consume yet more of the Gilbertines' hospitality, and hoped Michael would not make himself ill.

'There you are,' said Gynewell, bouncing across the floor to offer them his ring. 'It is a cold—'

'There was a lot of snow last night,' said Roger. 'Have you seen the thickness of it on the chapel roof? I do not think I have ever known such weather. Well, there was last year, I suppose. And Fat William died on an equally bitter night the year before that, God rest his soul.'

'Fat William died of a surfeit of oysters,' explained Hamo when Gynewell looked bemused. 'He was feeding quite happily, when he started to gag. Then he shuddered, gasped and drummed his feet until he died. Poor Fat William!'

He crossed himself, while Bartholomew wondered whether Fat William's oysters might have been tainted with the same poison that had led to Flaxfleete's demise. The symptoms sounded very similar.

Gynewell manoeuvred a chair directly in front of the hearth, sprang into it, then listened carefully while Michael outlined what had happened in the Church of the Holy Cross.

'That leaves just you three,' he said to Michael, de Wetherset and Suttone when the monk had finished. 'You must promise to be very careful over the next four days. I do not want to tell the hopeful crowds that the ceremony is cancelled because all the canons-elect are dead.'

'You are expecting crowds?' asked Suttone in surprise. 'I assumed everyone would prefer Miller's Market.'

'Dean Bresley suggested we hold the service earlier,' explained Gynewell. 'Now people can attend the ceremony first, and go to the fair afterwards.'

Michael was horrified. 'The previous timing meant the two factions would remain separate, but now everyone will go to both, and fights will be inevitable. What was Bresley thinking?'

'That he does not want anyone to know which side is the stronger,' explained Gynewell. 'He says the more powerful one will see it as a favourable omen for war. In this way, the two parties will never know the extent of each other's army, and he thinks it is the best way to keep the peace.'

Suttone swallowed nervously. 'Who knows with this city? It is worse than Cambridge!'

Michael turned his thoughts to his investigation. 'Before he died, Simon gave us several clues, and I mulled them over at breakfast this morning. I now know enough to begin the process of unveiling Aylmer's killer.'

Bartholomew regarded him in astonishment. 'Do you? Last night you were ready to give up.'

'Food, Matt,' said Michael. 'It does wonders for a man's mind. I mean to start with young Hugh.'

'My cousin, the choirboy?' asked Suttone in astonishment. 'I do not think *he* killed Simon!'

'No, but he will know who did,' replied Michael. 'The

426

message Simon asked him to deliver to Chapman was intercepted by someone – and that same someone then arrived with armed cronies at Holy Cross. I shall have this killer yet. He will not outwit Cambridge's Senior Proctor.'

Bishop Gynewell wanted to witness the impressive sight of six Hugh Chalices standing in a row in the Chapel of St Katherine, and his companions were more than willing to escape the stifling heat of Prior Roger's solar and walk in the cold church. When they arrived they found Dame Eleanor on her knees before the altar and Christiana sitting at the back, waiting for her to finish. She had been slouching, and hastened to adopt a suitably elegant pose when she saw admirers might be watching her.

'Dame Eleanor says it is not for a poor woman to say which is the real cup,' she whispered, as they came towards her. 'So she is praying to them all.'

Michael rested an unnecessary hand on her shoulder. 'I am sure she is right, and there are almost certainly more to be found. We happened on these by chance; logic dictates that there will be others.'

Gynewell was unhappy. 'I am afraid I cannot tell which is the original one now. I suppose we will have to send them all to Avignon, and let the Holy Father decide.'

'There is no need for that, My Lord,' announced de Wetherset. 'I told you, I have a talent for detecting an air of sanctity in such things. If there is a real chalice, I shall be able to identify it for you. I know I could not do it yesterday, but I have recited several very eloquent prayers since then, and I am sure St Hugh will help me now.'

He went to stand at the altar, where his shuffling presence disturbed Eleanor. With a sigh, she rose and joined the others in the nave, hobbling slightly after kneeling so long.

'I have been praying for Simon. And the others who have died – Aylmer, Dalderby and Tetford.'

'We all need to pray,' said Hamo. He raised his hands in the air, and closed his eyes. 'In fact, we should praise the Lord with—'

'Alleluia,' agreed Roger with enthusiasm. 'Let us lift our voices to the Heavenly King.'

'Dame Eleanor has been petitioning St Hugh on my behalf, too,' said Christiana to Michael, as the Gilbertines began to rail. 'She has asked him to send me a good husband. I am not sure I shall follow your advice of taking the veil and soothing my loneliness with lovers.'

'I did not put it quite like that,' said Michael, startled. 'I said there are ways to—'

'We have learned a good deal about the Hugh Chalice,' interrupted Bartholomew. He did not think Michael should have that sort of discussion with a bishop standing within earshot. 'We know Simon and Aylmer were the friars charged to bring it to Lincoln, but that Aylmer sold it because he could not resist the temptation of easy money.'

'Twenty shillings,' said Suttone, shaking his head. 'He could have had ten times that.'

'Perhaps he did,' Bartholomew pointed out. 'We do not know the Geddynge priest was his first and only victim. It is possible that he had already sold it several times before.'

'And it has languished in Lincoln for the last twenty years,' Michael went on, reluctantly dragging his attention from Christiana's kirtle and focussing on his investigation, 'because Miller knew Shirlok had escaped hanging, and did not want to attract his attention by hawking the goods that had been used to convict him. Meanwhile, the fraternity was Simon's idea. Aylmer joined so as not to reveal his role in the original theft; Chapman enrolled because he sincerely believes it belongs here; and I suppose Flaxfleete and Herl subscribed later.'

'Flaxfleete always was an ardent devotee of St Hugh,' said Gynewell. 'He was distraught when the chalice failed to arrive from London two decades ago, and wanted to serve the Head Shrine when he became a canon. This did not occur to me when we discussed the mark on his skin a few days ago, but on reflection it is obvious that he would have belonged to such a fraternity. He founded the Guild of Corpus Christi to emulate the saint's good deeds.'

'And Herl would have enrolled because aligning himself with powerful men might have brought him wealth,' said Roger. 'I am afraid he was a greedy, selfish man.'

'But Shirlok has since died,' continued Michael. 'And Chapman saw it was finally safe to bring the stolen goods – including the Hugh Chalice – out of his cellar. Flaxfleete offered to "donate" it to the cathedral, but the dean visited him . . . '

Gynewell grimaced. 'Poor Bresley. He has an uncontrollable urge to lay hold of items that do not belong to him, but he puts them in the crypt, so I can return them to their owners. He thinks he will be *unable* to steal the real chalice, which is why he is so certain Simon's is a fake.'

'He believes it will cure him?' asked Bartholomew, suddenly understanding some of the dean's curious remarks about the relic.

Gynewell nodded. 'He removed the cup from Flaxfleete when he went to inspect it on the cathedral's behalf, and I was obliged to take it back the following day. Aylmer was blamed, although he was innocent. The next I heard was that Flaxfleete had given it back to his relic-seller for reasons he declined to share, but that the relic-seller had approached Simon instead.'

'It was during this time that Herl confused matters,' said

Michael. 'He made copies of the cup and sold some to Tetford, who gave them to his . . . '

'Seamstresses,' interjected Bartholomew.

'Simon and Chapman knew nothing about these duplicates, though, and nor did Aylmer.'

'How are you able to conclude that?' asked Gynewell curiously.

'Because both Simon and Chapman were appalled by the prospect of replicas, and Simon *died* trying to learn the truth. Meanwhile, Aylmer was trying to protect the chalice when he was stabbed: you do not lay down your life for something of no value.'

'Who *is* this vile killer?' asked Gynewell tiredly. 'I would like an end to this before Sunday.'

Michael smiled. 'You will be the first to know, My Lord. We will talk to young Hugh, and—'

'Hugh?' asked Eleanor, appalled. 'He can know nothing about this! He is a child!'

'Do not worry,' said Michael reassuringly. 'He is not on our list of suspects. All we need from him is the identity of the person who might have read a letter he was supposed to deliver to Chapman. And when he tells us, we shall be a step closer to catching this fiend.'

Gynewell approached the altar. 'Well, de Wetherset? Which is the real Hugh Chalice? It is time it was in the cathedral, not lurking in dungeons and at the scenes of murders.'

'I have not received divine inspiration yet,' said de Wetherset with a pained expression. 'Give me time. I *shall* give you an answer.'

'I am sure he will,' said Bartholomew to Michael, 'but how will we know if it is the right one?'

While Bishop Gynewell questioned de Wetherset about his preliminary conclusions on the six chalices – the ex-Chancellor had managed to eliminate two – Bartholomew and Michael left the priory. They had taken no more than a few steps towards the city when Bartholomew saw Sabina Herl kneeling by the Eleanor Cross, opposite the Gilbertines' main gate. It was a cold place to pray, and he supposed it was some sort of penance. Michael went to find out.

'Your prayerfulness does you credit, madam,' he said softly, 'but beware of telling lies to God. He is no bumbling monk, to be deceived by claims of false repentance.'

She gazed at him. 'I do not know what you are talking about.'

'Then let me enlighten you. You said you had broken away from Miller, but you leapt at the opportunity to tend Chapman. You are no more a good Christian woman than I am.'

Her expression was rueful. 'What Langar said was right, although I would never admit it to him: I *have* been associated with the Commonalty too long, so I *am* considered a viable target by the Guild. Thus I *do* need Miller's protection, and I intend to have it until the current crisis is over. And *then* I shall continue with my fresh start.'

Michael frowned. 'And you have elected to atone for past sins because . . . ?'

'Because of Shirlok, Brother,' said Bartholomew. He watched the surprise on her face that he should know. 'I suspect she was uncomfortable with what happened in Cambridge twenty years ago, but she put it behind her, as did everyone else. Then, a month ago, Shirlok appeared in Lincoln – alive.'

She lowered her head. 'It was a terrible shock. Unlike Langar, Chapman and Miller, *I* did not hear the rumours about his miraculous resurrection. I thought he was a ghost, come to haunt me, but he was flesh and blood, and he was demanding reparation. We had let him take sole blame for the crimes we all committed, and he wanted us to make it right.'

'How did he know you were here?' asked Michael.

'He fled to Essex after his trial, where he eventually settled. Then his family died in the plague and he took to wandering; by chance, his travels brought him here. He wanted to be paid for not telling *his* side of the story to the city where his co-accused are now fine, upstanding citizens.'

'Did Miller kill him?' asked Bartholomew, not pointing out that no one would be overly shocked to learn the Commonalty had criminal pasts.

'I learned yesterday that it was Bunoun. He was one of the ten people Shirlok named, and he had more to lose from Shirlok's blabbering than the rest of us. Who will hire a surgeon with a dubious ethical history? Anyway, suffice to say that Shirlok died with a noose around his neck.'

'Bunoun?' asked Bartholomew in astonishment. 'But de Wetherset said that, of the ten accused, two had died in prison, and two were taken by fever . . . '

'That is what Miller tells everyone. I suppose de Wetherset believed him, although Father Simon did not die in prison, and Bunoun did not die of a falling pox.'

'And Shirlok is why you broke with the Commonalty?' asked Michael.

She gave him a pained smile. 'I was always uncomfortable with Miller's activities, but when I met Shirlok a month ago, and I heard what he intended to do, I decided to distance myself from them. Then Lora told me – just yesterday, when I was tending Chapman – that Shirlok was no longer a problem.'

'That is partly true,' said Bartholomew, 'but your good intentions coincide with the reappearance of the Hugh Chalice, which was irrelevant to you, but very important to someone else: Aylmer. The cup's return, along with Suttone's unexpected invitation to be his Vicar Choral, made him rethink his life. He decided to revert to the cleric he once was, and you saw he would never be with you.'

'I was married to Nicholas. I could not have been with him anyway.'

'Your marriage to Nicholas was a sham, because *his* real love was Langar,' said Bartholomew. 'Perhaps you married Nicholas to shock Aylmer into taking you more seriously, but found yourself trapped when it did not work. Then, when the chalice reappeared and Aylmer began to collaborate with his fraternity to see it in the cathedral, you saw it was finally time to give up on him.'

'All right,' she agreed cautiously. 'That is true. So what?'

'Were you really caught kissing him behind the stables?' Michael answered his own question. 'No. Your "penance" was an excuse to be inside the Gilbertine Priory, near Aylmer. You were eager to know what had happened to the man you loved – and I do not mean your husband.'

She gazed at the ground. 'Yes, I wanted answers. Aylmer's rebirth was genuine, and I never believed he was trying to steal the Hugh Chalice when some vile killer stabbed him in the back. And although Nicholas and I were not man and wife in the proper sense, we were friends; I do not want him buried in unconsecrated ground without good reason.'

'Again, that is partly true,' said Bartholomew. 'There is also the fact that anything *you* learn about Nicholas's death will annoy Langar.'

She shrugged. 'It is the only way I shall ever hurt him, and I really do loathe the man. When we first arrived in Lincoln, I wanted to live quietly, but he insisted on taking over the Commonalty and ruling the city. He ruined all our lives with his filthy ambition, and he has brought us to the brink of civil war. The feud between these two

433

factions would have faded years ago, if *he* had not come along.'

The bishop and Lady Christiana emerged from the priory as Bartholomew and Michael finished talking to Sabina, and joined them as they walked to the cathedral. Unwilling to leave his friends in the company of Satan, Cynric followed at a distance. Michael was delighted to escort Christiana – she was going to light candles at the Head Shrine for her mother, as she always did on a Tuesday – although the pace she set left him with scant puff for talking, and he soon fell silent, concentrating on not appearing too winded in front of her. He was relieved when Spayne hurried from his house, indicating that he wanted to speak, because it gave him an opportunity to catch his breath.

'Have you reconsidered your decision yet?' he gasped. He watched Gynewell go to assist Canon Stretle, who had lost his footing on ice and lay sprawled on his back. 'About Matilde?'

Spayne was startled. 'I never intended to rethink it, Brother. I made up my mind, and it was final.'

'It is not a very charitable stance,' said the monk accusingly.

'No,' agreed Christiana, shooting the merchant a glance that was far from friendly. 'These men want to trace Matilde because they are concerned about her. Michael is right: you should reconsider.'

'You can berate me all you like, My Lady,' said Spayne with the tone of the wounded martyr. 'I will not go against my conscience.'

'I suppose it does not really matter,' said Michael. He smiled at Christiana. 'Other people have offered to make us a list of the places she might be instead. We do not need you, Spayne.'

Christiana nodded, eyes flashing as she regarded the mayor defiantly. 'Dame Eleanor and I will tell Michael and Matthew what they need to know. And I hope, with all my heart, that they find her.'

'Fine,' said Spayne in an icy voice. His face was hard, and Bartholomew wondered whether Michael had been right after all: there *was* an element of spite in his refusal to help. He was not the only one who detected the chink in Spayne's moral armour. Christiana's expression became flinty, and she looked the hapless mayor up and down like a hawk with a rabbit.

'You lied to Matthew the other day,' she said. Bartholomew wondered what she was talking about. 'Cynric told me. When Chapman was stabbed, you uttered all manner of untruths.'

'That is right,' said Cynric, willing to join them as long as Gynewell was occupied with his floundering canon. 'You spun tales that were pure fabrication.'

'I assure you I did not,' said Spayne indignantly. 'I simply described what I saw.'

'And what was that, pray?' demanded Christiana. Michael regarded her in astonishment; he had not known she could be pugnacious.

'That Chapman was attacked with a knife outside the Angel tavern,' replied Spayne. 'I happened to pass by shortly after, and although I did not see him wounded, I saw the fuss of the aftermath. I was returning home from conducting some business.'

'What business?' asked Cynric immediately.

'Wool business,' replied Spayne shortly. 'Not that it is any of your affair.'

'Unfortunately for you, Chapman was *not* hurt at the Angel,' said Christiana. 'We all know it is the Commonalty's usual drinking place, and you would normally be right in assuming he was there. On this occasion, however, he went to the Swan, because the weather was too cold for the longer journey to the Angel. You made an assumption, and it showed you to be a liar.'

'She is right about the tavern,' said Bartholomew, when the merchant looked as though he did not believe her, 'but I have been telling them it was a slip of the tongue . . . '

'Yes,' said Spayne, relieved. 'It was—'

'No, it was not,' said Christiana sharply. 'You lied, because you did not want Matthew to know what you had really been doing – this "business" you are so keen to keep to yourself.'

'It really has nothing to do with you, madam,' said Spayne, shooting the scholars an uncomfortable glance. 'And I was trying to assist Brother Michael with his enquiries.'

'Spinning yarns does not help me,' said Michael, standing with Christiana. 'It confuses the issue, and makes it even more difficult to distil the truth.'

'It *was* the truth,' snapped Spayne. 'However, I admit that I was not the eyewitness: it was Ursula. She was coming home from visiting a friend, but declined to tell you what she had seen. I did it in her stead, so you would have the information – albeit scant – she had to offer. I was trying to be useful.'

'Why would Ursula want to hinder my investigation?' demanded Michael.

'Because Chapman was the victim,' replied Spayne impatiently. 'A man who has earned her contempt by selling fake relics. I thought that if I could pass off her intelligence as mine, the Spayne household would not be responsible for impeding your work. Obviously, I did not listen carefully enough to her account, and I told you the wrong tavern.'

'Good,' said Christiana sarcastically. 'The truth at last, My Lord Mayor. Now let us have a little more. Tell Brother Michael *why* you could not have witnessed what happened to Chapman. Your "business" was in the east of the city, not the south as you claimed, so you passed neither the Angel nor the Swan.'

'That is none of your—'

'You were visiting a woman called Belle,' Christiana went on relentlessly. 'But you do not want these scholars to know about that, do you? It throws a rather different light on your reputation as a grieving, celibate man who will not look at another woman now Matilde has gone.'

Spayne was white. 'It is hardly—'

'I see,' said Michael with a smug grin. 'You hired a whore! Well, you should be grateful to Lady Christiana. When we caught you in lies and a refusal to explain your where-abouts, I immediately assumed you were out a-murdering. Now I see you are not a deadly adversary, but a feeble man, who is obliged to pay for his pleasures.'

Spayne's shoulders slumped, and the commanding pres-ence that had so impressed Bartholomew on their first meeting began to deflate in front of his eyes. 'But I pay her very well.'

Michael was delighted with the confession Christiana had forced from Spayne, gratified that the paragon of virtue Bartholomew had championed had transpired to be something rather pitiful. Bartholomew was sorry for Spayne, although Michael murmured in his ear that if the merchant was ready to lie about that, then what else might he be hiding? Reluctantly, Bartholomew conceded that he might be right.

'We make a good team,' said Michael to Christiana. 'We must work together again.'

She smiled, and there was a coquettish bounce in her step as she turned to resume the climb to the cathedral. 'As often as you like, dear Brother.'

Spayne caught Bartholomew's arm as he started to follow. 'Actually, I came to ask if you would spare a moment. My sister is unwell. Surgeon Bunoun tended her earlier, but I do not like the look of the potion he prescribed. It is not urgent, but we would appreciate a visit. Today, if possible.'

He began to walk away, and Bartholomew trotted after Michael, thinking he would see Ursula after they had spoken to Hugh.

'Go,' said Christiana, pushing Bartholomew gently in Spayne's direction when he explained why the mayor had intercepted them in the first place. 'He may be sufficiently chagrined about my exposure of his frolics with Belle to let something slip about Matilde.'

'That is true, Matt,' said Michael, keen to have him out of the way and develop his new working relationship with Christiana. 'I do not need you with me when I speak to a child.'

'I will come,' said Cynric to Bartholomew. 'Spayne will not attack you with me there.'

'He will not attack me anyway. If he was being entertained by Belle when Chapman was stabbed, then it means he cannot have been at Holy Cross. So, if he was not one of the four men who killed Simon, then he cannot be one of the four who ambushed us in the orchard, either.'

'That is probably true,' conceded Michael, albeit reluctantly. He turned to Christiana. 'I am grateful to you for showing Spayne to be a liar, but you seemed angry with him. Is it because Ursula harmed your mother?'

She was startled by the question. 'Of course not! He cannot be held accountable for his sister's actions. Anyway, as I have already told you, I think my mother knew exactly what she was doing when she asked Ursula for that particular tonic.'

Michael regarded the hill without enthusiasm. 'Shall we be on our way to the top, then?'

Christiana hesitated. 'However, just because the Spaynes had nothing to do with the death of my mother does not mean I consider them harmless innocents. You do not become mayor by being nice, and Spayne is just as ruthless as Miller, Kelby and anyone else you care to name. I am sure he is jealous of your friendship with Matilde, and may decide he does not want you to find her.'

Michael nodded. 'That is true, Matt, so be careful. Do not let him send Cynric to the kitchens for refreshment with the servants, or some such nonsense.'

'I shall come with you, then,' said Bartholomew, pleased to be in a position to chaperon Michael. 'And we can visit Ursula together on the way back.'

Christiana shook her head. 'You should go now, when he is flustered. And you should accompany him, Michael – both to pit your clever mind against his defences and to make sure nothing happens to Matthew. With men like Spayne, there is always safety in numbers.'

'I would much rather escort you to the cathedral,' objected Michael, his face falling.

Gynewell had finished helping his bruised canon, and heard the monk's remark. 'I can do that, Brother. Her virtue will be safe with me. I have no interest in women. Except for their souls.'

Cynric gaped at him, then jabbed Bartholomew with his elbow, to ensure such a sinister remark did not go unnoticed.

'It is for the best,' said Christiana, seeing Michael's disappointment and seeming to share it.

'You had better appreciate this, Matt,' grumbled Michael, as they made their way to the mayor's house. 'I am fond of you, but you are a poor second to Lady Christiana.'

'Go with her, then. You can retrieve that poison from the shrine at the same time. Besides, Spayne may employ prostitutes, but he is no killer. And Cynric is here.'

Michael regarded him thoughtfully. 'No, I will stay. If you still cannot see the real Spayne under his amiable façade, then you are not in a position to defend yourself. I cannot leave you.'

Spayne had seen them coming back, and was standing by his door, ready to usher them in. He had gone from pale to flushed, and Bartholomew saw he was acutely embarrassed.

'It is only occasionally,' he murmured, as they stepped across the threshold and stamped their feet to get rid of the snow that adhered to them. 'Belle, I mean.'

'Your vices are not our concern,' said Michael coolly.

'I do not want you to think badly of me,' Spayne continued uncomfortably. 'Since Matilde left, things have been difficult and . . . but you are right, my problems are not your concern. Please see what you can do to help my sister. Your book-bearer can take some refreshment in the kitchen with the servants while you are occupied.'

'No, thank you,' said Cynric, immediately suspicious. 'I do not want anything.'

Spayne gave a tight smile. 'Then you can wait outside. I do not allow men from the lower classes into my hall.'

He slammed the door in the startled Welshman's face, and led Bartholomew and Michael to the main chamber, where Ursula reclined on a cushioned bench. A bucket stood on the floor nearby, but Bartholomew saw it was placed to catch drips from the ceiling, not for the patient. A cold, heavy droplet landed on Michael's tonsure with a sharp click, and he glowered at the mayor, as though he had made it happen deliberately. Ursula was white-faced and frightened, and it was obvious she was more unwell than her brother had led them to believe. Bartholomew knelt next to her and began to ask questions. She had eaten nothing different, and had barely left the house, because of the cold.

'I had a little milk yesterday,' she said, clutching her stomach. 'I suppose that was unusual.'

'You do not normally drink milk?'

'I love milk, but Surgeon Bunoun says it is responsible for blockages, so I only have it as a treat. I had some yesterday, though, to celebrate Dalderby's funeral.'

'Ursula!' exclaimed her brother. 'That is a terrible thing to say.'

'Well, it is true,' she said, unrepentant. 'I am pleased he is dead. It will weaken Kelby, and that is a good thing for us. Miller knows I like milk, and he left it for me.'

'Left it?' echoed Bartholomew. 'Left it where?'

'On the doorstep. It was good milk, too. Full of cream.'

'Do you still have the jug?' asked Bartholomew.

She gazed at him. 'It is in the parlour. Why? You do not think . . . ?'

Frowning, Spayne left the hall, and returned a few moments later holding a pitcher. There was not much of an odour, but fishy poison was in it nonetheless. Bartholomew mixed Ursula a tonic containing charcoal, thinking that the fact that she had not noticed what was a very distinctive odour suggested she was not as competent an apothecary as she liked people to believe.

'You have not ingested much,' he said. 'And if you drank it yesterday, you are already over the worst. Do you not know it is unwise to consume gifts left on doorsteps, no matter who you think they are from?'

'Especially in a city that boils with hatred,' added Michael.

'I have learned my lesson,' said Ursula bitterly, lying back against the pillows. 'The burning is passing now, and I feel better. Thank you for your kindness.'

'Would you be prepared to reciprocate?' asked Michael. 'With a little information about Matilde?'

'I cannot,' said Spayne before she could reply. 'And I have explained why.'

'Oh, tell them, Will,' snapped Ursula. 'Share whatever it is you are hiding. Matilde may welcome enquiries after her well-being from these scholars, and you owe her nothing, not after all these years.'

Spayne appeared to be in an agony of indecision. 'All right. Let me think it over. I shall ask St Hugh's advice. If he does not make his displeasure felt, I shall tell you what I know.'

'That is good news, Matt,' said Michael, when Spayne had closed the door behind them and they were out in the street again. 'If he was going to ask for a *positive* sign, I would say you can forget about having his help, but he said he would share his knowledge if St Hugh *does not* object. Signs at Hugh's shrine are rare, and you may be in luck at last. The man's resolve is weakening.'

'He will send you somewhere dangerous,' said Cynric, who had not appreciated being shut out. 'He cannot be trusted. Did he try to harm you while you were in there?'

Bartholomew shook his head. 'He kept his distance, and—'

He glanced up at an odd scraping sound above his head. Cynric suddenly leapt forward to shove Michael to one side. Then there was an almighty crash.

'Lord!' breathed Michael, looking at the shattered rooftile that lay on the ground. 'That might have killed me! It is heavy, and it came plummeting down like a . . . Dalderby!'

Bartholomew sighed when he understood what had happened. 'Dalderby was "attacked" right here, killed by a blow to the skull from a stone. Sheriff Lungspee said he managed to reel to Kelby's house, but died without speaking, and there were no witnesses. Kelby lives next door.'

'Is that too far for an injured man to stagger?' asked Cynric.

Bartholomew shook his head. 'We saw Sir Josquin de Mons lurch twice that distance at Poitiers, and there was an axe embedded in *his* pate. So, we can explain Dalderby's death, at least. The weight of snow on a roof already damaged by fire has caused the tiles to slip. No one killed Dalderby. It was an accident.'

'You could say Flaxfleete was responsible,' said Michael, still looking at the broken stone. 'It was *his* inferno, after all.'

As they left Spayne's abode, Bartholomew became aware that the situation had changed since they had gone in. There were a number of men loitering outside Kelby's home and, judging from the buzz of voices, there were a lot more inside. Further down the street, people stood in small, uneasy groups next to shops and houses. Most were well dressed, and Bartholomew was puzzled.

'Is there a Guild meeting today?' he asked. 'There are a lot of trader-types in this part of the city, but there is not an unemployed weaver in sight.'

'It looks as if the Guild has claimed the area around the *Pultria*,' said Cynric. 'The Commonalty must be gathering near Miller's house. In Cambridge, men assemble in clans like this when there is a riot in the offing.'

'Lord, you are right!' muttered Michael. 'Will you warn the sheriff while we speak to Hugh?'

The book-bearer nodded. 'You may not have another opportunity to wander where you like, if the city turns violent, Brother, so make the most of your time. I have a feeling we might be spending the next few days in the Gilbertine Priory, hoping the fight does not spill across the city walls.'

When Bartholomew and Michael reached the cathedral, Gynewell was waiting to tell them that Hugh was at choir practice. The boys' voices soared along the vaulted ceiling, although Michael pointed out that the lower parts were under-represented – a number of Vicars Choral and Poor Clerks were missing. Bartholomew saw why when they passed the Head Shrine: Christiana was there, and several men who should have been singing hovered around her. Ravenser was polishing a brass cross, Claypole and John were pretending to read psalters, and Bautre was inspecting the offerings left by pilgrims. When Christiana raised her head and said something, all four scurried to a nearby cupboard, and there was a good deal of elbowing as each tried to grab the candles she had requested. Her smile suggested she expected no less.

'Hugh is a rascal,' said Gynewell. 'When I heard a kinsman of *his* had been appointed to the Stall of Decem Librarum, I was afraid your Suttone might be an adult version of him. He seems a decent man, though – more like John.'

'He is all right,' said Michael begrudgingly. 'Although rather preoccupied with the plague.'

'Who is not?' asked Gynewell. 'I lost two-thirds of my clergy, and all but two of my canons. I was afraid the balance of power would tip so far that Lincoln would be ruled by Miller, but the Commonalty also lost men, and the equilibrium was maintained.'

'It is a pity these factions exist,' said Bartholomew. 'A pity for Lincoln.'

'Yes and no,' said Gynewell. 'When the balance is in

effect, it is a good system, because one side holds the other in check. I have heard your University has amassed a lot of power in Cambridge, to the detriment of the merchants. That is not good, either.'

'The merchants do not think so,' said Michael comfortably. 'I am more than content.'

'Moderate yourself, Brother. You will find it pays in the long term.' Gynewell cocked his head. 'I hear this *Gloria* coming to an end, so you should nab Hugh before he escapes to do something else.'

He was right, and Michael was hard-pressed to waylay the boy before he could disappear with his friends. Hugh looked particularly angelic in his white alb, although mischief winked in his eyes.

'Father Simon gave you a letter to deliver last night,' said Michael without preamble. 'What did you do with it?'

'It was for Master Chapman,' piped Hugh.

'Yes,' said Michael patiently, 'but to whom did you take it? Chapman is unwell, so I doubt you would have been allowed to give it to him personally.'

Hugh shuffled his feet. 'He said he would give me two pennies. And Father Simon had already given me one, which made three! That is enough to buy seven arrows for the butts.'

'Who offered you twopence?' asked Gynewell. 'Speak up, Hugh. This is important.'

'Master Langar,' said Hugh reluctantly. 'But it was not my fault! He refused to let me see Chapman, so I had no choice. He promised to pass the message to Chapman, and said I had fulfilled my duty in bringing the note to the house. Then he gave me a marchpane, too.'

'Did you eat it?' asked Bartholomew uneasily.

Hugh grinned. 'Yes, and it was a good one – from the best baker in the city.'

He scampered away, and Bartholomew watched him dart to Christiana's side. She smiled at him, but did not stop her prayers.

'I will go and drag him away from the poor lady,' said Gynewell with a sigh. 'She will have no peace if he is hovering like a fly. What will you do now? Go to see Langar?'

'We have no choice,' said Michael unhappily. 'It is the only way forward.'

'Well, there is your Welshman with his sword,' said Gynewell, nodding to where Cynric was waiting. 'I strongly advise you to take him with you.'

'We should give Gynewell that poison we found,' said Bartholomew, as he and Michael walked along the South Choir Aisle. 'He can dispose of it, because we cannot leave it here another day.'

Michael agreed, and watched as Bartholomew knelt by the Shrine of Little Hugh and pushed his arm through the gap at the back. He frowned when the physician drew his dagger and used it to fish about, lying full length on the floor to extend his reach. 'Hurry up, Matt. We do not have all day, and I want to get this interview with Langar over with as soon as possible.'

'I knew we should have taken the time to deal with the flask yesterday,' said Bartholomew, standing empty-handed, covered in dust and thoroughly alarmed. 'Because now it is no longer here. Someone has taken it.'

CHAPTER 12

Bartholomew and Michael left the Close and walked to Miller's fine house in Newport. Remembering what he had seen the last time he had been there, Bartholomew was grateful Cynric was with them. As they moved farther north, an increasing number of weavers and their families thronged the streets. They spoke in low voices, and there was a distinct aura of fear and uncertainty. Miller's house and enclosure was like a castle under siege. Armed guards lurked outside, and there were even archers on the roof, training their weapons on passers-by. The grinning Thoresby patrolled the grounds with a black dog that snarled at anyone who came too close.

'I do not like this,' whispered Michael. 'Miller has helped the weavers over the years, and it looks as though they are going to show their appreciation by massing against the Guild.'

'And the Guild is ready to resist,' said Cynric. 'The two sides are fairly evenly matched.'

'You are wrong,' said Michael, surprised. 'The Commonalty's supporters outnumber the Guild by at least five to one – there are far more poor in Lincoln than merchants.'

'The guildsmen have better weapons, though,' argued Cynric. 'And they have horses and hired mercenaries. I would not risk a single penny by betting on the winner: the outcome is too uncertain.'

He led the way across Miller's yard, ignoring the way

the dog slathered at him, although Bartholomew made sure Michael was between him and the creature; it did not look as if Thoresby had it fully under control. No one spoke as they approached the door, although dozens of eyes watched. Cynric rapped with his dagger, and when it was whipped open, Miller's face was as black as thunder.

'I told you not to come back, physician,' he snarled, 'or have you come to gloat over sending Chapman a few steps nearer the grave?'

'He is worse?' asked Bartholomew, concerned. A fever was often the outcome with dirty wounds – and then there was the poultice of henbane. Perhaps he had not cleaned it all out.

'Bunoun said Chapman would have recovered by now, had you not meddled,' said Miller furiously. 'We sent for you at dawn, when he became sicker, but the Gilbertines said you were not to be disturbed, so we summoned Bunoun instead. Thank God we did.'

'Is there a suppuration?' asked Bartholomew. 'That is always a danger with—'

'Do not blame it on the wound,' snapped Miller, hand dropping to the dagger in his belt. 'Bunoun said you poisoned him. You are lucky I do not run you through!'

Cynric drew his hunting knife, daring him to try, while Bartholomew's hand slipped into his medical bag and the various implements it contained. He had forgotten his sword again.

'Young Hugh brought a message last night,' said Michael, before Bartholomew could embark on a complex explanation of wounds and their consequences that Miller would not understand. And Cynric had been right: the looming riot would bring an abrupt end to his investigation, and time was short. 'It was for Chapman, and asked him to meet Simon in the Church of the Holy Cross.'

Miller regarded him frostily. 'Do not be stupid. You know

Chapman could not go to Holy Cross or anywhere else. He is too ill.'

'So you have said,' said Michael. 'But I want to know about the note. When was it delivered?'

'There was no note from Simon,' said Miller firmly. 'I would have remembered, since he so seldom bothers to acknowledge me these days. After all I have done for him, too.'

Langar had heard the shouting, and came to see what it was about. Ink stained his fingers, and he carried a quill in one hand and a sword in the other. Behind him were the hefty Lora Boyner and Sabina. Lora carried a bowl of water, and her blunt features were tear-stained.

'Master Langar,' said Michael. 'Did *you* see a note from Simon last night – for Chapman?'

Langar frowned. 'There was no letter from Simon – for Chapman or anyone else. The man is a coward, afraid to put pen to parchment, lest the Guild wins the confrontation they are itching to provoke. He is too cunning to leave documentary evidence of his real allegiance.'

'The Guild will not win,' snarled Miller. 'God is on *our* side. Chapman said so.'

Lora looked the scholars up and down. 'You are brave. Miller promised to kill you if Chapman dies, and here you are on his doorstep, *asking* to be executed.' Her eyes watered, and Bartholomew saw the relic-seller's sufferings had pierced her tough façade. 'It was the wine you sent yesterday afternoon that did the damage. You said he should not have claret, but then you had a flask delivered and ordered him to finish the whole thing.'

'I did not send anything,' said Bartholomew, puzzled. He jumped back when Lora emptied the bowl, narrowly missing him. 'And I specifically told you not to give him wine – only ale.'

449

'The prescription accompanying the jug was signed with your name,' snapped Miller, not believing him. 'One of the priests from the cathedral brought it. You left it with him, because you could not be bothered to walk the extra distance to hand it to us yourself.'

'And you gave this potion to Chapman?' asked Bartholomew, appalled. 'After I expressly warned you against feeding him anything from outside?'

'Do not blame it on us,' said Sabina, indignantly. 'You—'

But Bartholomew was livid, both by the slur on his skills and on behalf of his patient. He went on the offensive, startling them with the ferocity of his attack. 'You ignorant fools! Chapman narrowly escaped the first time someone tried to poison him, and now you have let the killer strike again. I thought he would be safe here, among friends concerned for his welfare, but I was wrong. I should have taken him to the Gilbertines' hospital, and tended him myself. You are—'

'Easy, Matt,' said Michael, afraid he might push them too far. 'It is clear a mistake has been made, and yelling will not help us understand what has happened. Do you still have this flask, Master Miller? If so, then perhaps we can see it.'

'You had better come in,' said Langar reluctantly. 'This is not a conversation we should have in the open, not with the city on the brink of civil unrest. We want to avert a riot, not encourage one.'

'Do we now,' sneered Miller, suggesting that Langar would have his work cut out for him if he intended to act as peacemaker. 'Fetch that wineskin, Lora. I want to know what is going on here.'

While Lora went to find the offending container, Bartholomew looked around Miller's hall. Changes had been made since their last visit. Window shutters had been

450

reinforced with planks of wood, and water-filled buckets stood in a row near the hearth, in case of fire. A pile of crossbows lay on the table in the centre of the room and several men were sharpening bolts. Uneasily, Bartholomew wondered whether they had defence or attack in mind.

'Old models,' muttered Cynric in Bartholomew's ear. 'Unreliable. These will not change the odds in their favour. They are still about even with the Guild.'

Michael surveyed the scene with monkish disapproval. 'Perhaps you would tell me something while we wait, Master Miller. Yesterday, Ursula de Spayne was sent milk that was tainted with poison. She drank it, because she assumed it was a gift from you.'

'Ursula likes milk, bless her,' replied Miller. 'It is bad for her innards, though, and I stopped sending it when Surgeon Bunoun told me it blocks her bowels. So you can accuse someone else—'

'Ursula is not the only one who has been fed fishy poison,' Michael went on. 'First, there was Herl, then Flaxfleete, then it was in Telford's wineskin.'

'And now Chapman,' said Bartholomew, taking the pitcher Lora handed him and sniffing it carefully. The poison did not smell as rank as it had in Flaxfleete's barrel, but, like Ursula's milk, it was still strong enough to be noticeable. He supposed it had come from the pot they had left at the cathedral – the one they should have destroyed.

Miller was confused. 'This note is from you,' he said, snatching a piece of parchment from Lora and waving it in Bartholomew's face. 'See your name signed at the bottom, nice and big?'

'I never write it like that,' said Bartholomew, regarding it in disdain. 'And nor would my prescriptions encourage a sick man to "swallow the lot", as is so prosaically written there. I did not send Chapman the wine, just as you did not send Ursula the milk.'

'This is Kelby's doing,' said Lora, turning angrily to Miller. 'It must be. He killed Herl, then Aylmer, and now he is after Chapman. Where will it end? When he has dispatched the lot of us?'

Suddenly, there was a sword in Miller's hand. 'I will not wait meekly to be struck down by poison. Round up the men, Langar.'

'Not yet,' said Langar. 'We should wait until Sunday, when we have a better idea of numbers—'

Spittle flew from Miller's mouth as he spoke. 'We could all be dead by Sunday.'

Langar scowled, angry in his turn. 'Very well, we shall have a war, if that is what you want. However, I need an hour or two to take a few steps of my own – to increase the odds in our favour.'

'What do you mean?' asked Michael nervously.

'I have trained men to spread rumours that will shake our enemies' confidence,' explained Langar. 'And one or two highly placed guildsmen have been in my pay for years. I shall summon them and learn Kelby's secret plans.'

'If he has any,' said Sabina reasonably. 'He may be like us, waiting to see what will happen.'

'You *would* say that,' said Langar, turning on her. 'You abandoned us, and only returned when you became frightened for your life. You are not here for friendship or loyalty.'

'That is not true,' lied Sabina. 'I came because Chapman is ill.'

'Nicholas should never have married you,' said Langar, working himself into a temper. 'We were happy until *you* came along with your sordid offer of "marriage". And you did *not* do it to save him from Kelby's accusations of lewd behaviour with me. You did it because you wanted to share his house and the money he had from his trade.'

Sabina shot him a look full of loathing. 'His house was a hovel and he earned a pittance.'

'He was not a dedicated silversmith,' admitted Langar. 'However, he was content until you started criticising his work, demanding to know why he did not make more money. You corrupted his mind, and it led him down a dark path.'

'A dark path whereby he made copies of sacred relics?' asked Michael guilelessly.

'What?' asked Langar, put off his stride by the question. He opened his mouth to resume his attack on Sabina, but she spoke before he could do so.

'That is *exactly* what he did. And it was not right. The saints do not approve of that sort of thing.'

'Are you saying Nicholas made copies of the Hugh Chalice?' asked Langar. 'Is that what he was doing, night after night in his workshop for the last month of his life, when he would not see me?'

'He made bad replicas,' said Sabina spitefully. 'Only a fool would have been deceived by them – they are made of tin, for a start. And there are mistakes in the carving.'

'He gave Jesus three fingers,' said Michael.

'Oh, he took that from the original,' said Sabina scornfully. 'He was not *that* inept.'

'Where are they?' asked Langar, looking around as though he expected them to appear. 'I sincerely hope Chapman has not sold any. We do not want our Commonalty stained with that sort of thing. People have scruples where relics are concerned.'

'Chapman did not sell them,' said Lora disdainfully. 'He believes the Hugh Chalice is sacred, and refuses to have anything to do with Nicholas's work. Nicholas was so angry that he tried to scrape the mark off his arm.'

Langar frowned. 'He told me Sabina caused that injury, by throwing a hot pan at him.'

'How many did he make?' asked Michael, while Sabina shot Langar a derogatory look.

'A number,' replied Lora evasively.

'He died with four in a bag around his shoulder,' said Sabina. Her expression was spiteful; she was enjoying Langar's hurt shock as he learned things his lover had kept from him. 'Tetford was kind, though: he helped me toss them in the Braytheford Pool, where they belong. As a reward, I gave him a cope, given to me by that horrible Canon Hodelston, as payment for—'

She stopped speaking abruptly. 'As payment for providing him with information about the Commonalty?' asked Langar softly. 'We always did wonder how he and the Guild always seemed to know our plans. It almost saw us destroyed during the plague.'

'That is the garment in which you will be installed, Brother,' whispered Cynric, lest the monk had not made the connection. 'Tetford's tale about the chest in his tavern's attic was a lie. And now we know how he came by the four chalices for his women, too.'

'We do not have time for this,' said Miller, pacing restlessly. 'Kelby wants to slaughter us all, and the longer we stand here chatting, the more time he will have to organise it.'

'Please,' said Sabina, going to place her hand on his arm. 'Do not walk the road to violence. Lives will be lost on both sides, and our town deserves better. Spend your money on helping the weavers.'

'Sabina seems rather ready to persuade us to stand down,' said Langar icily, 'just as she was six years ago, when Canon Hodelston brought us to the brink of ruin. You should ask yourself why.'

'Do not listen to him,' said Sabina, while Miller and Lora

454

regarded her with sudden suspicion. 'He wants to get rid of you, so he can take your place as head of the Commonalty. He is telling lies, to confuse you and make you look inept.'

'I have no reason to doubt him,' said Miller coldly. 'And perhaps he is right about you.'

'I am here to help Chapman,' sighed Sabina impatiently, as if she was becoming tired of repeating herself.

'Kill her,' said Miller to a man with a crossbow. The response was so immediate that Bartholomew wondered whether summary executions had been ordered before. One moment, Sabina was opening her mouth to protest her innocence, and the next she was lying on the floor with a bolt in her throat. The room was silent except for an unpleasant choking sound, which stopped before Bartholomew could do more than kneel beside her.

'Damn,' breathed Langar, rubbing a hand across his mouth. He glanced uneasily at the scholars. 'That was inopportune, Miller.'

'Rubbish,' snapped Miller. 'I have never trusted her, and should have listened to your concerns years ago. What is wrong with you? I thought you would be pleased.'

Langar shot the visitors another uncomfortable look, then headed for the door. 'I cannot say I will miss her, but this was not how I envisaged the problem being solved. But we can discuss it later; now we must be about our business, if we are to survive this confrontation.'

Miller sneered disdainfully as the lawyer swept from the room. 'We will do more than survive – we are going to *win*. Thoresby, rally the men. Lora, go to Spayne, and tell him we have need of his help.'

'Wait,' said Michael finding his voice at last. 'This is not the way to resolve a dispute. We—'

'Out of my way,' said Miller, shoving him to one side. 'We have work to do.'

'Please,' begged Michael. 'Let *us* talk to Kelby and—'

'I am inclined to dispatch you, too,' said Miller, regarding Michael and then Bartholomew with his small eyes. He spat on the floor. 'Especially as you have just witnessed what you probably regard as a murder. You are lucky that I do not want to annoy the Suttones by shooting their friends, so I shall let you go. However, the physician can consider it a temporary reprieve.'

'What do you mean?' asked Michael in a low voice.

'I mean that if Chapman dies, then so will he.'

Cynric bundled Bartholomew and Michael out of the house and down the nearest alley as fast as he could, afraid that if they tried to reason with Miller he might change his mind about letting them go. Even Bartholomew's recent battle experiences had not steeled him for a murder ordered in front of his eyes, and he was deeply shocked. Michael was more concerned with the lives that would be lost if Lincoln went to war, and was ready to do anything to stop it.

'You did your best to make him see sense,' said Cynric, holding the monk's sleeve when he attempted to return to Miller and argue the case for peace. 'So did Langar, but *he* has the wits to see he was wasting his breath. And look what happened to Sabina when she argued for moderation.'

'Cynric is right,' said Bartholomew shakily. 'We are completely helpless. If we warn Kelby, he will summon his own troops, and there will be a skirmish for certain.'

'Sheriff Lungspee will not help, either,' said Cynric. 'When I told him his city was about to erupt into civil war, he asked whether I thought his gate would withstand invaders. He intends to lock himself in, and only emerge when the battle is done and he knows which side to favour.'

Michael peered around the corner, watching the scurrying preparations around Miller's domain. Bartholomew stood next to him, seeing ancient weapons pulled from storage, and men assembling so quickly that he could only assume they had been waiting for the call. He was alarmed: he had not anticipated that Miller's friends would be so numerous. He saw several traders among them, looking terrified, and suspected they had been forced to show their colours against their will.

'Not everyone wants this fight,' he said. 'The more militant of the workless weavers have little to lose, and rich guildsmen will be desperate to protect their houses from looters. But most people are frightened, because they do not know where this dispute will take them – no matter who wins.'

'What can we do?' asked Michael, appalled. 'This is our fault, for going to Miller without thinking the situation through. We must stop him, or the blood will be on our hands.'

'No, it will be on that killer's, Brother,' said Cynric practically. 'It was him who unleashed all this mayhem with his poisoned wine. You are innocent.'

'Well, I do not feel innocent,' stated Michael. 'I repeat: what can we do?'

'Find the real killer,' said Bartholomew. 'And then hope Kelby and Miller will listen to reason.'

'How?' cried Michael, frustrated. 'I thought we had our answer when Hugh said he delivered Simon's letter to Langar, but all we have is another attempt on Chapman's life.'

'I think I know who it is,' said Bartholomew quietly.

Michael whipped around to face him. 'You do? I suppose we may have enough clues to allow a logical deduction now. Who is it? It *must* be someone from the cathedral, since we have eliminated the Gilbertines, and I do not think Miller and his people would try to kill Chapman,

457

because he is one of their own. Well, Sabina might have done, I suppose. Is it her?'

'I do not know how to say it,' said Bartholomew unhappily. 'You will not be pleased.'

'Gynewell!' said Cynric in satisfaction. 'I always said there was something odd about him.'

'Not Gynewell,' said Bartholomew.

'The dean, then,' said Michael. 'Yes, that makes sense. The night we were attacked, it was *Bresley* who said we did not need an escort, and that we would be safe walking to the Gilbertine Priory alone. He had henchmen waiting, and he intended us to be murdered.'

'The dean has no reason to want us dead,' said Bartholomew. 'On the contrary, he wants you to stay in Lincoln and help him keep order among his unruly clerics. I imagine he was more worried about the bishop's safety when he told Gynewell not to accompany us – there will not be another prelate so understanding about his stealing. I am afraid the culprit is someone clever enough to stay one step ahead of us today. It is someone who deliberately sent us to Miller's house in pursuit of the letter Simon sent Chapman – the missive Langar never received.'

Michael regarded him with round eyes. 'You think young Hugh is the killer?' He started to laugh. 'Really, Matt! He might have lied about giving it to Langar – God knows, he has fibbed before – but his motive would have been mischief, not malice. Besides, he is a child.'

'Of course I do not think it is Hugh,' snapped Bartholomew impatiently. 'But our culprit learned that we wanted to speak to Hugh this morning, and managed to reach him first. I think Hugh was *ordered* to lead us astray by saying Langar accepted the letter.'

'It may have been Langar doing the lying,' Cynric pointed out. 'He *is* a law-clerk.'

'I believe he was telling the truth. The note was intercepted by someone who then killed Simon and tried to do the same to us. Ineptly.'

'Spayne,' said Michael with great delight. 'He enticed us away from Hugh with tales of an ailing sister, and sent a crony to tell the boy what to say.'

'Not Spayne,' said Bartholomew. 'We did not tell him our plans, so he could not have known them. However, there was one person who knew exactly what we intended to do, and who encouraged us *both* to visit Spayne before interviewing Hugh. She did it so she could speak to him first.'

Michael narrowed his eyes. 'I sincerely hope you are not referring to Lady Christiana.'

Bartholomew saw it was not going to be easy to convince him. 'She insisted we visit Ursula. Then she asked Hugh to lie about delivering the note to Langar, because the truth is that Hugh gave the note to *her* – the woman who buys him wooden soldiers.'

'This is rambling from a deranged mind,' said Michael, beginning to walk away. 'I will not listen.'

'It is true,' said Cynric gently to Bartholomew. 'You cannot be right.'

'I *am* right,' said Bartholomew, gripping the monk's sleeve to prevent him from leaving. 'You saw what Hugh did when he had finished speaking to us: he darted straight to Christiana. And she *asked* to accompany us to the cathedral when she heard what we were going to do.'

'She went to pray,' said Michael coldly, freeing himself. 'As she does every Tuesday.'

'And she has others who do her bidding, too,' continued Bartholomew, 'such as the "priest" who delivered the poisoned wine to Chapman. Only an hour ago, we saw Ravenser, Claypole, Bautre and John follow her about like lovesick calves. They do anything she asks.'

459

'Christiana has no reason to kill Chapman,' said Michael. 'You are deluded.'

'The poison is unusual,' said Bartholomew, thinking aloud. 'Yet it features in the deaths of Herl, Flaxfleete and Tetford – and now the attempts on Ursula and Chapman. *And* there was the man who died during the plague . . . '

'Canon Hodelston,' supplied Cynric. 'Rapist, thief and extortionist.'

'And I think Fat William had some sort of toxin-induced seizure, too. Perhaps this poisoning has been going on for years – ever since she arrived in Lincoln – and we shall never know how many have really died.'

'Then what about the possibility that Ursula may have given herself a non-fatal dose because *she* knows we are coming close to the truth?' demanded Michael archly. 'She certainly has a knowledge of poisons, because she dispatched Christiana's mother with some.'

'*There* is Christiana's motive for trying to kill Ursula,' pounced Bartholomew.

'Christiana thinks her mother killed herself,' said Cynric doubtfully. 'She does not hold Ursula responsible.'

'She is lying,' said Bartholomew, 'so she will not be a suspect when Ursula dies.'

'That is ludicrous!' exclaimed Michael. 'I suppose she took her bow with her when she killed Simon and Tetford, did she? Or do you think Dame Eleanor is the archer? I would not put it past her: the elderly are known to be very deadly.'

'She does not need Dame Eleanor. She has willing priests from the cathedral to help her. Claypole is tall, so perhaps he is the swordsman. And John and Ravenser were the others.'

Michael was so disgusted, he could find no words to express himself. Cynric spoke for him. 'The cold must have addled your head,' he said, concerned. 'We should return to the Gilbertines, and—'

Bartholomew ignored him. 'Christiana spends a lot of time at the tomb of Little Hugh, where we discovered that poison. *Now* I see why it was in Tetford's flask. It was not to harm you, but was intended to kill him.'

'Why should she want to do that?' demanded Michael, finding his voice again. 'You just said she recruits men like him to go around ambushing people for her.'

Bartholomew could think of no good reason. 'Perhaps he refused,' he suggested lamely.

Michael pulled a face to indicate he did not consider the theory worthy of further discussion. 'Hundreds of people visit that shrine, and the poison could belong to any one of them. Everything you say about Christiana is arrant nonsense.'

'Miller is innocent in all this,' said Bartholomew. 'Well, as innocent as such a man can ever be. He did not poison Flaxfleete, he did not kill Aylmer or Herl, and he did not send tainted milk to Ursula.'

'He and his cronies just hanged Shirlok, shot Sabina and are planning to plunge a city into civil war,' said Michael tartly. 'Aside from that, Miller is as pure as the driven snow. And now you must excuse me, Matt, because *I* have a killer to catch.'

Bartholomew ordered Cynric to stay with Michael, over-riding the book-bearer's objections that he preferred to be with the man who had lost his wits. He believed the monk had allowed passion to interfere with his reason, and was convinced he needed protection from a very ruthless criminal. Michael flounced down the hill, indignation in his every step, with Cynric trailing reluctantly behind him. Bartholomew watched them go and wondered what to do. Should he confront Christiana, since it was clear Michael would not do so? Or should he try to gather more evidence first? What he had was flimsy, and he did not see her giving herself up when presented with it.

He started to follow Michael, glancing up when something brushed his face; snow was falling again. He shivered. It was bitterly cold, and he would have preferred to return to the convent, to sit in front of the fire and discuss Blood Relics with Suttone. He had had very few intellectual debates over the past year, and was surprised how much he had missed them. A cold winter's day, with a blizzard in the offing, meant the best place for any scholar was by a hearth with like-minded company. But he was unsettled and troubled, and felt compelled to discover more about the killer.

It was a dull morning, so lamps were burning in some houses, and the air was thick with wood-smoke as people lit fires to ward off the chill. The snow began to fall in earnest, which meant it was difficult to see Michael and Cynric, even though they were not far ahead. Through a whirl of white, he watched the monk skid and Cynric jump forward to catch him. Roughly, the monk shoved him away, and Bartholomew saw his theory about the identity of the killer had genuinely enraged him.

The streets were curiously empty of people, and Bartholomew's immediate assumption was that the blizzard had driven them indoors, and that snow might accomplish what peacemakers could not. Then gradually he became aware of furtive movements in the shadows of the darker alleys, and the few people who were out were heavily armed. He was about to hurry forward and suggest he, Cynric and Michael return to the Gilbertines while they could – to sit out the storm caused by Miller and the weather at the same time – when a figure loomed out of the swirling whiteness. It was John.

'Have *you* seen my brother?' he demanded. 'Bautre

462

wants him to learn the solos for the installation ceremony on Sunday, but he has slunk off on business of his own. I cannot find him anywhere.'

'I last saw him with Christiana at the Head Shrine.'

John's harsh expression softened at the lady's name. 'She is good with him, and he is much better behaved when she is around. You owe me your thanks, by the way. I delivered that flask to Chapman, to aid his recovery, just as you asked. However, there is a rumour that it did not work, and that Chapman is dying. I am sorry.'

'That claret was not from me. And it was tainted. Who told you I wanted it delivered to Chapman?'

John's jaw dropped, and he started to back away. 'No! There must be some mistake . . . '

Bartholomew grabbed the front of his habit. 'Who?' he repeated angrily.

'I cannot . . . I did not . . . I see the answer! Someone must have deceived Christiana, and she in turn deceived me, although she did it unknowingly. We are *both* innocent of wrongdoing.'

Bartholomew released him. 'You had better find Hugh. A child should not be out in this weather.'

'He will be all right,' said John, backing away before he was grabbed again. 'He has an uncanny instinct for his best interests, and he is almost fourteen years old, anyway, a child no longer.'

'Speaking of his best interests, he thinks you will make a better brothel-keeper than Ravenser.'

John's expression was spiteful. 'The same could be said about anyone in the city, regardless of talent, because Ravenser is dead. Someone shot him.'

Bartholomew gazed at him. 'Another death?'

'The first of many today, I imagine. Miller and Kelby are mustering forces, so there will be a fight. I intend to be

463

in the cathedral before it starts, and I recommend you do the same.'

'Do you think Miller's men killed Ravenser?'

'Probably, since Ravenser announced today that his so-called House of Pleasure will not be buying any more ale from Lora Boyner. Kelby threatened to withhold donations to the cathedral if Ravenser continued to purchase ale from a Commonalty brewer, so he really had no choice. And now, if you have finished manhandling me, I shall be on my way.'

Bartholomew watched him stagger up the hill, skidding on the slick surface. The snow was coming down harder, and it was not many moments before he was out of sight.

'There he is!' came a sudden yell. 'There is Chapman's murderer!'

Bartholomew glanced behind him to see Lora, with Langar at her side. She wore a leather jerkin, military style, and held her sword as if she knew exactly how to handle it. She surged forward, and Bartholomew was fortunate snow had rendered the ground slick underfoot, or she would have been on him before he had had time to turn and face her. He scrabbled in his bag for a surgical knife, although he doubted it would do him much good against a sword.

'Chapman is dead,' she shouted, feinting at him and forcing him to take several steps back. 'He died in the throes of a fit. Miller said we were to kill you.'

'Hurry up,' ordered Langar. 'This is a major thoroughfare, and although it seems deserted, you never know who might come along. The longer you take, the greater our chances of being seen.'

'So, you want no witnesses to your crime,' said Bartholomew, backing away and holding his bag in front of him like a shield. 'That should tell you your reasons for murdering me are flawed. If it was a justifiable killing, you would not care who saw it.'

'A scholar's logic,' sneered Langar. 'Hurry up, Lora. At this rate, we will be pursuing him all the way to Cambridge.'

'I am doing my best,' muttered Lora, struggling to keep her balance. 'I am unused to men who jump away from me. Most stand and fight, because they assume they cannot lose against a woman. Few survive to warn others never to underestimate the fairer sex.'

Bartholomew had no intention of underestimating the fairer sex, and he knew better than to engage an experienced sword-wielder with a dagger. His only option was to stay out of blade range for as long as possible, in the hope that someone would see his plight and come to his rescue – or distract Lora for the split second that would allow him to turn and run for his life.

'Which of you killed Shirlok?' he demanded, hoping the certainty in his voice would throw her off her stride. 'He arrived in Lincoln recently, and you were afraid he might destroy all you have built. You hanged him, making sure it was done properly this time.'

Langar gazed at him in surprise. 'Shirlok? I thought I saw him in the Angel, but everyone told me I was mistaken. I knew he had survived his execution, but he would be a fool to come here and—'

'Bunoun did the honours,' said Lora. She shrugged when Langar gaped at her. 'He said no one would hire a surgeon with a criminal past, and Miller did not like being blackmailed, either. There was no need for you to know, Langar, although I am surprised you have not smelled him. He reeks, and Miller said it was only a question of time before you investigated the basement.'

Langar continued to stare, and Bartholomew took the opportunity to spread dissent. 'There are other things they

465

have kept from you, Langar – such as the Hugh Chalice being in Lincoln for the last twenty years. Where was it, Lora? In the cellar?'

Lora grinned. 'Yes – and you have no idea how surprised we were when we arrived here, and found a chest containing the lion's share of Shirlok's treasure among our crates. We did not *steal* it, though, so we have done nothing wrong.'

Bartholomew had continued to slither away, but he had reached the hill and moving down it backwards on the slippery snow was not easy. 'Then I imagine you were delighted when Bunoun eliminated Shirlok. It meant you could sell the Hugh Chalice at last.'

'*Is* it the Hugh Chalice?' asked Lora. 'Chapman believed in its sanctity, but the rest of us are sceptical. And now we are done talking, because if I slide all the way down this hill, I shall have to walk up it again, and I need my strength for slaughtering guildsmen.'

'Will you let her murder me?' asked Bartholomew of Langar. He could hear the desperation in his own voice. 'She who has kept secrets from you, and has hidden the bodies of murdered men in your home? She and Miller obviously do not trust you, or they would have shared this information.'

'They often keep me in the dark,' said Langar with a shrug. 'It makes it easier for me to defend them in court – I do a better job if I do not *know* they are guilty. But hurry up and make an end of him, Lora. There is a lot to do, if we are to stand any chance of winning against Kelby.'

Lora launched herself forward with single-minded determination, and Bartholomew scrambled away from a swing that was intended to decapitate him. He turned, intending to make a run for it while she was off balance, but his foot slipped, and he stumbled to one knee. He tensed, anticipating her blade would be driven into his back, but Lora was overly eager, and when she dived forward, ice sent her sprawling flat on her face. Bartholomew struggled upright, but Langar grabbed his cloak, yanking it hard enough to drag him off his feet again. Lora took her sword in both hands, while Langar held the physician down, to make the killing easier for her.

Bartholomew kicked out as hard as he could – not at Lora, whom he could not reach, but at Langar, causing the lawyer to crumple across him. Langar shrieked in pain and shock as Lora's sword bit into his shoulder. He released Bartholomew's cloak, and the physician rolled away, cursing when the snow stopped him from gaining his feet as fast as he would have liked. Lora ignored her groaning colleague, and came after Bartholomew with a series of hacking blows, swearing when her blade hit the wall of a house and sent pain shooting up her arm. She dropped the weapon and clutched her wrist. Bartholomew clambered to his feet and ran as fast as he could, trusting he would soon be invisible in the swirling snow. He heard Langar and Lora yelling at each other as he disappeared.

He was near Spayne's home, so he located the narrow alley that separated it from Kelby's house, and ducked inside, praying no one would follow the footprints he had left. Moments later, Lora lumbered past, eyes fixed on the road ahead. Langar was a considerable distance behind, hand to his injured shoulder, and the lapsed time was enough for wind and snow to have masked the tracks to some extent. Cynric would not have been deceived, but Langar was not the book-bearer, and he staggered past without noticing. Then they were gone, and Bartholomew heaved a shaky sigh of relief.

He moved farther down the alley when he heard

shouting, afraid Langar had met with reinforcements, and found himself in the yard at the back of Spayne's house. The remains of the blackened storerooms were smothered in snow, and he supposed Spayne would be alarmed for his roof. More yelling told him that he would be wise to stay out of sight for a while, so he huddled against the back of the house, near one of the window shutters. He wondered how long it would be before the trouble eased, and considered taking refuge with Spayne. But their last encounter had been uneasy, and he was not sure his welcome would be a warm one. Indeed, Spayne might even betray him, so he would not be asked to reveal what he knew about Matilde. He decided to stay in the yard, wrapping his cloak more closely around him, and pulling his hat down to cover his ears.

But the hollering was becoming more agitated, not less, and he saw he was going to be in for a long wait. Eventually, he heard the bells chime for a cathedral ceremony he knew was due to take place at two o'clock, and ventured out to assess the road. It was fortunate he had moved stealthily, because Miller himself was standing near the end of the alley, in conversation with Spayne. The two men nodded agreement and separated, Spayne to go back inside his home and Miller to address a group of weavers. Bartholomew retraced his steps and hunkered down in his chilly refuge again.

It began to grow dark, dusk coming early because of the low clouds. He felt the cold seep into him, and hoped the weather would drive both sides back into their houses for the night. Then there was a hissing sound from above, and he leapt up in alarm when he recalled how the tile had almost killed Michael earlier. But it was only snow, sloughing off to land in a slippery pile near Spayne's rear door. Heart thumping, he decided to abandon the yard. The falling flakes and encroaching night might be enough to hide him, but if not, then Lora's sword was a better end than being buried alive. He was just rubbing life into his frozen legs in anticipation of escape, when he heard a familiar voice. Spayne had guests.

' . . . is the pity of it,' came Christiana's clipped tones. 'I do not know what else to say.'

'It was an accident, I swear,' replied Ursula, her voice unsteady. 'I did not mean to harm her.'

Bartholomew frowned, wondering why Christiana should be visiting the sister of a man she so obviously despised. He put his eye to the gap under the shutter, to see inside the house.

'You *did* harm her, though,' Christiana was saying flatly. 'Matilde was right.'

'She was not,' shouted Ursula. 'She was misguided and spread vicious rumours about me.'

'You have been telling everyone that your mother asked Ursula for cuckoo-pint deliberately,' came Spayne's voice. He sounded confused. 'You believe she *wanted* to die.'

Christiana's voice was colder than Bartholomew had ever heard anyone speak. 'My mother had everything to live for. She would *never* have entertained suicide. I spread that tale so no one will look to me when Ursula dies.'

A dark chill gripped Bartholomew as he knelt in the snow. He had hoped for proof that Christiana was the killer, but he had not expected it to come in the form of another death. He comforted himself with the knowledge that Spayne would not allow his sister to be dispatched – or would he? He recalled what Simon had told him: that Spayne had been an abbey oblate, and knew nothing about arms and fighting. Perhaps he would be powerless to prevent it.

'Your mother and I were friends,' said Ursula wheedlingly. 'Why would I harm her?'

'Because she was going to marry Kelby,' said Christiana in the same icy voice. 'And her dowry would have made him stronger and richer than your brother. You could not stand the thought of that, so you intervened in a spectacular way. You killed her.'

Bartholomew poked the window shutter with his knife, grateful to find it rotten. Quickly, he bored a hole, so he could better see what was happening within. He winced when the hinge protested at the pressure, but the room's occupants were more interested in each other than in strange sounds from outside. When he put his eye to the hole, he was astonished to see not three people, but four. Spayne and Ursula sat side by side on a bench on the far side of the hall, while Christiana stood near the hearth. Hugh was with her, and Bartholomew saw he held a small bow – the kind children used when they learned archery. His face was alight with curiosity, and Bartholomew supposed he should not be surprised the boy would be out when mischief was in the air.

'The sadness is that it was unnecessary,' said Christiana quietly. 'My mother did not love Kelby and would never have wedded him. She was going to ask Prior Roger to marry her secretly to the man who had captured her heart – the man whose babe she carried.'

'Did she tell you?' asked Spayne, and the expression on his face was both stricken and guilty.

'I am her daughter,' said Christiana. 'Of course she told me.'

Bartholomew's thoughts reeled as he tried to understand what they were saying. Then he looked at Spayne, and had his answer in the way the mayor's eyes flicked around the room: a man who enjoyed prostitutes, but who

470

had declared himself celibate. Bartholomew found his hands were shaking, and wondered whether Matilde had known that Spayne had lain with her closest friend.

'My mother was pregnant with your child,' said Christiana softly. 'But Matilde held your heart. You were in a quandary. Should you do the dutiful thing and allow Prior Roger to marry you to my mother? Or should you put your own happiness first, and wed Matilde?'

'It was not like that,' said Spayne miserably. 'Not so . . . sordid. And I did not want to hurt either—'

Christiana's voice was loaded with disgust. 'My mother's death left you free to take Matilde, as well as preventing Kelby from getting her dowry. You were even vulgar enough to propose on the day of the funeral. I am not surprised Matilde refused you. She fled the city, and I lost a valued friend.'

Suddenly, there was a rap on the door. In his agitated state, Bartholomew jumped violently enough to rattle the window shutter, but the occupants of the room did not notice.

'If you call out, I will kill you,' said Christiana sharply and, for the first time, Bartholomew noticed that Spayne and his sister were bound hand and foot.

'I must answer,' said Spayne desperately. 'It is probably Miller, and talking to him will give me another opportunity to urge him to stand down. And *then* you and I will discuss ancient history.'

'It is not ancient,' snapped Christiana. 'It was six years ago. But I have finally obtained the evidence I need to convict you, Ursula. We all know you fed my mother cuckoo-pint – that was never in question – but we have never been able to prove you did it knowing it would kill her.'

'That is because I am innocent of malicious intent,' insisted Ursula. She licked dry lips.

'Why have you waited so long to voice these vile accusations?' asked Spayne. His strangely furtive expression suggested to Bartholomew that he had known exactly what his sister had done.

'Because I had no proof before. I have it now, though. Matthew was the key, although he does not know it.' The physician was startled, but then recalled the discussion he had had with Dame Eleanor. They had talked about wake-robin, and how it was used to expel afterbirth. Wake-robin was another name for cuckoo-pint. 'He told Eleanor that all good midwives know to give cuckoo-pint in small amounts over a number of hours. However, you gave my mother her potion in one large dose. You knew exactly what you were doing.'

'Prove it,' challenged Ursula, but Bartholomew could see she was worried.

There was another knock, harder this time. Someone was becoming impatient.

Christiana ignored it. 'Once I knew what to ask, I was able to go to midwives and apothecaries, and discuss with them the correct way to administer it. They all said the same: bit by bit. My mother was the only one who received hers all at once. Matilde was right after all.'

'So what if she was?' demanded Ursula, suddenly defensive. 'No one cares about this now. And no jury will ever convict me.'

'I was not thinking of going to a jury,' said Christiana in a soft voice that made Bartholomew's blood run cold. 'I was thinking of dispensing my own justice. I tried with the milk, but that did not work, because I could not use a strong enough dose – you would have noticed.'

The hammering came a third time. 'Spayne?' came Michael's voice. 'I know you are in there, because I can see your lamps. We are looking for Matt. He is missing and I am worried.'

'Lady Christiana might know where he is,' shouted Ursula, before Christiana or Hugh could stop her. 'Come in and ask her yourself—'

She fell silent when Hugh leapt towards her and placed a dagger under her chin. 'That was stupid, lady,' he whispered fiercely. 'We asked you to keep quiet.'

'It was not stupid at all,' said Ursula defiantly. 'It was extremely clever. Now the monk knows she is here, and if I come to any harm, *she* will be his prime suspect.'

'Christiana is with you?' With relief, Bartholomew recognised Dame Eleanor's voice – the one person who could talk sense into her misguided friend.

'Let them in,' said Christiana to Hugh. 'Ursula is right. We cannot let Michael go, having heard that. He is tenacious, and I do not want him investigating my affairs.'

'We could kill him later,' suggested Hugh. 'After we have finished here.'

'We will do it now,' said Christiana. 'We have already made two unsuccessful attempts to dispatch the fellow, and learned to our cost that he is not an easy target. Claypole's arm is still bruised, and I was almost brained twice – once with the branch of a tree and once with a shoe-scraper.'

'What about Dame Eleanor?' asked Hugh nervously. 'She might not like it.'

'She will be no trouble,' replied Christiana.

When Christiana moved towards the door, Bartholomew pushed away from his window and tried to run to the front of the building, to warn the monk. The snow had drifted, so it was knee deep and like wading through mud. He tried shouting, but there was too much racket on the main road, and he knew Michael would not hear him. He took only a few steps before realising it was futile, and struggled back to his vantage point, defeated.

It gave him no pleasure to know Michael would soon see he had made a dreadful mistake with the woman he had admired, and he was disgusted with himself for dismissing Hugh's role with the letter so readily. He was a child, it was true, but one with an eye for mischief, and also one who was a talented archer, as Bartholomew himself had witnessed at the butts. And, like many other males at the cathedral, Hugh was captivated by Christiana.

By the time he reached the hole in the window again, Michael and Eleanor were inside the hall. The monk beamed at Christiana, and Bartholomew saw Hugh had hidden his weapon. He considered bursting through the shutter, but a bar had been placed across the inside that would seriously hamper any attempt to enter quickly. He had also lost his bag with its arsenal of surgical blades, and there was a limit to what an unarmed man could do against a bow.

'I am glad you are here, Michael,' said Christiana, indicating he should sit on the bench opposite Spayne and Ursula. 'We have been discussing murder.'

'Have you?' asked Michael. Something in the tone of her voice had alerted him to the fact that all was not well. He was an astute man, and immediately became wary. 'Well, in that case I shall leave you, and resume my hunt for Matt—'

Hugh moved quickly to block the door. 'You must stay here.'

'Why?' asked Michael. He had noticed that the Spaynes were trussed up like chickens.

'Because Hugh will shoot you if you try to leave,' said Christiana, as the boy snatched up his bow. 'And he is very good, as Simon and Tetford can attest. Now, sit down.'

'Christiana?' asked Eleanor, startled. 'What are you doing?'

'Ursula confessed,' blurted Christiana, suddenly tearful. 'She is proud of herself for eluding justice, and her brother feels no guilt at all for his role in my mother's murder.'

'That is not true,' cried Spayne. 'I am wracked with self-reproach. Why do you think I have never married? It is nothing to do with Matilde, but because I have a nagging sense that I will be damned in the sight of God if I find wedded bliss with another woman.'

'I do not know what is happening, but I am sure it can be resolved peacefully,' said Michael, edging towards the door. 'And I cannot stay here. I need to find Matt before—'

Hugh aimed his bow, and Michael flopped hastily on the bench when he saw the determined gleam in the child's eye. Christiana moved forward, and Bartholomew was impressed by the speed with which she secured the monk's hands. She left his feet free, though, and Bartholomew was under the impression she did not intend to wait long before making her move. He looked at Dame Eleanor, willing the old lady to bring the confrontation to an end, trusting her quiet saintliness would make Christiana see reason.

'What is happening here?' asked Michael with quiet calm. 'If it involves violence, I beg you to reconsider. Too many men have lost their lives already.'

'We are working to the glory of God,' replied Christiana, moving away from him. 'And it is time to avenge my mother's murder at last.'

'Hugh,' said Dame Eleanor, turning to the boy. 'You know what to do.'

Bartholomew watched aghast, as the boy raised his bow and shot Ursula in the chest. She made no sound as she slumped to one side. Christiana and Eleanor glanced at each other, and smiled.

* * *

'I doubt St Hugh will be very impressed by that,' said Michael in the shocked silence that followed. 'Your actions will have him weeping in Heaven.'

'On the contrary,' said Dame Eleanor. Bartholomew's heart sank when he saw the old lady's eyes fill with the light of religious fervour. 'I have served him for sixty years, and I know what he wants.'

'He wants this?' asked Michael, nodding towards Ursula.

'He wants justice,' said Eleanor coldly. 'And he sent Christiana and Hugh to help me in my quest. *That* is how I know I am doing what he desires.'

'You have corrupted them,' said Michael. 'A child and a vulnerable, grieving woman. You have murmured your deranged ethics into their ears, and turned them evil.'

Eleanor grimaced. 'Rot! They know I am right, and they are only too happy to help me.'

'She is a saint,' said Hugh simply, while Christiana nodded agreement. 'One day she will have a shrine in the cathedral, and we will be recorded by the chroniclers as her helpmeets. People will revere us for taking a stand against sin.'

Bartholomew moved away from the window, and put his hands over his face. He had been wrong: Christiana was just a foot soldier, and the real power behind the murders that had so mystified them was the saintly Eleanor, with her wise eyes and kindly smile. He was in an agony of indecision. Should he burst into the hall and attempt to disarm Hugh? Should he run to the Gilbertine Priory or the cathedral for help, or would that take too long? He staggered back along the lane into the main street, trying to decide which option would give Michael the best chance, then stopped abruptly when a figure loomed out of the swirling snow, just visible in the faint light from the lamp above Spayne's door. It was Lora, who greeted him by hurling her dagger. He threw himself to one side, and it landed quivering in one of Spayne's windowsills.

'Fetch Miller!' he called urgently, staggering to his feet with his hands full of snow. 'Spayne is being held captive in his house by the people who killed Aylmer and Herl.'

'I do not believe you.' She moved towards him with her sword.

Bartholomew had not imagined she would. He lobbed snow at her as hard as he could, first with one hand, then the other. Both landed square in her face, making her gasp in shock. While she was reeling, he landed two quick punches that knocked her flat on her back.

'Summon help,' he ordered, when she gazed at him in stunned surprise. 'At once.'

He did not wait to see what she would do. He grabbed her dagger from the sill, knowing that Michael's rescue – he did not care what happened to Spayne – was down to him alone. He tried peering under the shutters at the front of the house, but they fitted better than the ones at the back, and all he could see was Hugh and his bow. There was no time for rationalisation. He waded to Spayne's front door and kicked it hard. It flew against the wall with a resounding crack, and he marched inside.

'Sheriff Lungspee is on his way,' he declared. 'He will be here any moment, so put up your weapons and bring an end to this before anyone else is hurt.'

'Do not treat me like a fool,' said Eleanor coldly, neither surprised to see him nor unsettled by his announcement. 'Lungspee is hiding in his castle, waiting for the city to grow peaceful again.'

Bartholomew raised the dagger, intending to hurl it at Hugh and force him to drop the bow, but Eleanor moved fast, and he saw something flash through the air. There was a resounding thump under his arm, and he jerked

477

backwards, staggering against the brace near the hearth. It groaned alarmingly, and there was a short silence. Then Hugh laughed and Michael groaned in despair.

'Did you mean to do that?' asked Christiana of Eleanor, going to close the door. When Bartholomew recovered his wits sufficiently to understand what had happened, he found himself pinned to the pillar with a knife. It had passed under his elbow and caught the material of his tunic.

Eleanor grimaced. 'I was aiming for his heart, but he moved. Still, he is rendered harmless, because my knife has nailed his arm to the wood, so the outcome is the same.'

Bartholomew flexed his hand to make sure she was wrong. It would not be difficult to rip himself free, but then she would hurl a second blade at him, and this time she might damage more than his clothes. He sagged slightly, trying to give the impression that he was injured, while his mind worked feverishly for a way out of the predicament. He could see none.

Michael's face was white, and his voice was barely audible over Spayne's heartbroken sobs. 'Matt worked out what you had done, but I did not believe you capable of such wickedness.'

Eleanor glanced at Bartholomew. 'What did you work out, exactly? You may as well tell us. We will not kill you as long as you are talking, and you are vain enough to think the delay may provide you with an opportunity to escape. What do you have to lose?'

'Do not humour them, Matt,' said Michael harshly. 'Let them continue to wonder what you know and who else we have told about it.'

Hugh aimed his bow at the monk. 'I will kill *him* if you do not answer, physician. Dame Eleanor says shooting evil men is good for my soul, so I am not afraid to do it.'

'I know,' said Bartholomew, deciding to accept the challenge. Lora might do what he had asked, and the longer he talked, the greater the chance of her arriving in time. 'You shot Tetford, because he closed his tavern – you earned pennies as a pot-boy and did not want to lose the income. Since then, you have learned there is always a need for pot-boys, and that murder was unnecessary.'

'He is a child,' said Michael, joining in reluctantly. 'And it did not occur to his unformed mind that the tavern would be taken over by another landlord. Then, of course, he realised he might do better under his brother than with Ravenser: John is always talking about looking after the family, and Hugh has high expectations. Did he tell you he shot Ravenser today?'

'Did you?' asked Eleanor, regarding the boy admonishingly. 'You cannot go around killing for personal gain – only for greater purposes.'

Hugh was sullen. 'Ravenser paid me less than his whores.'

'You ordered Hugh to shoot Michael – after you had rendered the guard insensible so our knocks at the gate would go unheard,' Bartholomew went on, 'but Tetford happened to be with us, and the temptation was too much. You have created a monster.'

'A soldier,' corrected Hugh. 'Not a monster. And I did not mean to shoot Tetford: he just got in the way. It was dark, and I could not see very well.'

'And then you ran away,' said Michael contemptuously. 'You are happy to kill with bows, but too cowardly to fight with blades. No wonder no one has given you a sword. You do not deserve one.'

Hugh was outraged and his weapon started to come up. Eleanor pushed it down again. 'Not yet. I want them to tell us what they know about Tetford.'

'You were going to kill him anyway,' said Bartholomew.

479

'You had put poison in his wineskin – we found the secret supply Christiana keeps at Little Hugh's tomb. You could have saved yourself the bother of the orchard ambush. Tetford offered that wine to Michael, and he would have swallowed it, if Hugh and Claypole had not loosed their arrows.'

Christiana frowned. 'That was what Dame Eleanor originally intended: the two of them poisoned while toasting Tetford's latest insincere attempt to be a good man.'

'I was annoyed when Claypole and Hugh acted too soon,' said Eleanor. 'Tetford was a wicked young man, and I intended to prevent him from becoming a Vicar Choral in my cathedral. And I did not want you interfering with the saint's will by exposing me, Brother, so you had to die, too.'

'If you attacked us in the orchard, then you were also responsible for the episode at Holy Cross,' said Michael. 'The pattern was the same: two bowmen, someone with a sword and someone with a dagger. You three and Claypole. No wonder you did not best us. So, we know why you killed Tetford and attempted to dispatch me, but what about Father Simon? What had he done to incur your wrath?'

'He engaged in skulduggery,' said Eleanor angrily. 'And I am tired of it. Hugh showed me the note he wrote, inviting Chapman to discuss the Hugh Chalice, so I decided to make an end of them both.'

'I see why you deplore Chapman,' said Michael. 'I dislike relic-sellers myself. But Simon—'

'Chapman is not a relic-seller,' said Eleanor. 'He is a felon who sells stolen goods for Miller. Worse yet, he dared lay his sinful hands on the Hugh Chalice! When my henbane salve did not work, Christiana arranged for John to take him some wine instead. There has been nothing but theft and wickedness ever since the cup made its appearance, and it is demeaning. St Hugh does not approve.'

Bartholomew flexed his elbow. The material was pinned very firmly to the wood, and he was not sure he could free it without anyone noticing. The brace creaked and Eleanor glanced sharply at him. He tried to look helpless, hoping she would not come and inspect her handiwork. 'And you think he approves of murder?' he asked, to distract her.

'It is not murder,' she said firmly. 'It is justice.'

'And I suppose "justice" led you to poison Herl and Flaxfleete, too,' said Bartholomew. 'The toxin is an unusual one. Did you read about it when you were trying to understand how Ursula had killed Christiana's mother?' Eleanor inclined her head. 'And I suppose you murdered Herl because you learned he had duplicated the Hugh Chalice?'

She nodded a second time. 'He tried to sell me a copy. And Aylmer was on the verge of stealing the real one—'

'So, you stabbed him in the back,' said Bartholomew. 'We thought it was someone who either took him by surprise or who he did not expect to hurt him. Both are true in your case. Sabina said he was killed with his own dagger. You grabbed it and knifed him before he knew what was happening.'

'The pity of it is that Aylmer belonged to a fraternity dedicated to placing the chalice in the cathedral,' said Michael. 'As did Simon. Aylmer contrived to be at the Gilbertine Priory to *help* Simon, not to steal from him.'

'He was holding it when I caught him,' objected Eleanor. 'He had taken it from Simon's bag and it was cradled in his hands. Everyone else was in the chapel, so it looked suspicious, to say the least. And I acknowledge that this fraternity was dedicated to the chalice, but it was not selfless. Simon wanted it presented at a ceremony that would glorify him, and Flaxfleete intended to present an ostentatious reliquary at the same time. It was wrong.'

'I know how you killed Flaxfleete,' said Michael. 'The

481

keg was not poisoned when it sat by the door of the Swan, as we assumed, but when it was still in the cellar. The inn is owned by Christiana, so she can come and go as she pleases.'

Bartholomew's legs were beginning to shake from standing at an awkward angle, and he shifted his weight. The roof creaked, and he had a sudden memory of Michael leaning against the sapling in the Gilbertines' garden when he was interrogating Chapman. He wondered whether he could bring down the roof. But then he and Michael would die, too. So would Spayne, who had said nothing since his sister's murder, and who sat with his eyes glazed in helpless shock.

'You might have killed the entire Guild,' Michael went on. 'Although when you poisoned Herl's ale – also in the Swan – you were more careful.'

'All for St Hugh,' said Eleanor. 'I am weary of evil men, but no matter how many I dispatch, there are always more to take their places. I started with the sinister Canon Hodelston, during the plague—'

'Lungspee said Hodelston's death took the feud to a new level of violence,' interrupted Michael accusingly. 'And I suppose next on your list was Fat William, who died eating oysters.'

'Fat William was a glutton who ate food designated for the poor, but he was not the second or even the third. However, I have learned all I need from you now. It is time to end this.'

'We are going to set a fire,' chirped Hugh. 'And you will all die in it.'

'St Hugh would be appalled by what you have done in his name,' said Michael. 'It is time to stop.'

'I cannot,' said Eleanor. 'Not as long as my saint's city is infested with sinners. Shoot them, Hugh. Michael first.'

Hugh raised his bow and Bartholomew saw he could not fail to miss. He leaned as hard as he could on the post. There was a low groan.

'The roof!' cried Spayne, in a voice that cracked with tension and distress. 'Do not lean on the brace – the ceiling will cave in!'

Bartholomew pushed harder and beams began to sag.

'Stop!' screamed Eleanor. 'Hugh! Shoot him!'

Hugh was more interested in ducking away from the clumps of plaster that were dropping around him. He dropped his bow and scampered this way and that, like a rat in a cage. With a bellow of fury, Christiana dived for the weapon and snatched it up herself. Summoning every last ounce of his strength, Bartholomew shoved the pillar until it popped out of its holdings and crashed to the floor. It dragged him with it, so Christiana's shot went wide.

'Run!' he yelled to Michael, trying to free himself.

The monk leapt to his feet as timbers fell.

'You are a fool!' said Eleanor to Bartholomew, standing immobile among the chaos. 'Tonight, Christiana and I were going to tell you where we think you will find Matilde. We know you love her – your determination to find her is too strong for mere friendship.'

Bartholomew ignored her as he struggled to free himself. She staggered as a piece of plaster struck her, and the physician raised his arm to protect his head as chunks of stone began to rain down. She dropped to her knees, blood streaming from her scalp, while Christiana hurled the bow at the monk and aimed for the door. Michael reached for the old lady with his bound hands, intending to drag her outside, but she snatched up a long splinter of wood and threatened to stab him with it.

'I will not be exiled to some remote convent when all I have done is obey the saint's will.'

'Get up!' yelled Michael, backing away and turning to Bartholomew. He hauled ineffectually on the dagger that pinned the physician's tunic to the fallen support. 'Hurry!'

'You killed my sister,' said Spayne to Christiana, blocking her path. His hands and feet were still tied, but when she tried to duck past him, he launched himself forward and knocked her over with his body. She cried out in pain when she fell on her own dagger, and gazed in horror at the blood that stained her hand. Bartholomew could not see whether it was a superficial wound or a mortal one.

Eleanor turned to him in anguish. 'I have chosen to die here, but you must save her. You see, we did not *write* our list – it is in her head. You must take her with you if you want to find happiness.'

Bartholomew finally ripped his tunic free and headed for Christiana, but before he could reach her, she disappeared under a billowing cloud of debris that drove him backwards. The air was full of thick, choking dust.

'Matt!' screamed Michael, who had gained the door. 'The whole thing is going to fall!'

'They do not know where Matilde went,' said Spayne hoarsely. Bartholomew spun around and saw the mayor's legs were trapped under a massive beam. It was too heavy to move, and he was going to die in the collapsing building. 'No one does, except me. I am the only person she ever told about a friend in a certain city. I am sure she will be there now.'

'Come away, Matt!' howled Michael.

Spayne had used Christiana's dagger to free his hands. 'I will tell you my secret if you help me escape. If you refuse, I will throw this blade, and you will not reach the door alive.'

Bartholomew hauled on the beam with all his might, but knew it would not have budged had he been ten men.

He glanced up and saw the sky through holes in the ceiling. A tile crashed into his shoulder, knocking him to the ground. Dizzily, he put his hands around the wood again, barely aware of what he was doing.

'It is hopeless,' said Spayne, his voice cracking with despair. 'All right, come closer. I will tell you what you want to know, but only if you promise to tell Matilde I still love her.'

Bartholomew nodded, willing to agree to anything.

'She is . . . ' began Spayne. 'No! For the love of God, no!'

His head jerked back as an arrow slapped into his throat. Bartholomew gazed at Spayne in shocked disbelief, then turned to see Cynric at the door, a bow in his hand. The book-bearer clambered across the wreckage and grabbed Bartholomew's arm. There was another groan, and more timbers dropped

Bartholomew jerked away, appalled that Cynric should be the instrument that had destroyed his last hope. 'He was going to tell me where to find Matilde!'

'He had a dagger,' said Cynric, fighting his way across the wreckage and dragging the physician with him. 'He was going to stab you as soon as you leaned close enough to hear what he was saying.'

Bartholomew shook his head, feeling numb. 'He was—'

There was another groan from above. Cynric shot through the door, pulling Bartholomew after him. With a tremendous crash, the last of the roof gave way and collapsed in a billow of snow and tiles.

EPILOGUE

The day of the installation was bright and clear. Michael, Suttone and de Wetherset made their oaths of canonical obedience to Gynewell in the Bishop's Palace, then went outside to join the magnificent procession that was to walk to the cathedral for the formal ceremony. There was some jostling and confusion among the participating dignitaries and officials – the number of people involved was considerable, and protocol and rank needed to be scrupulously observed – but eventually, everyone was in his designated place, and the bells began to ring in a jubilant, discordant jangle.

'What shall we do about the Hugh Chalice?' asked Gynewell, while they waited for the choir to line up. 'In all the excitement following the deaths of Dame Eleanor, Lady Christiana and the Spaynes, I clean forgot about it. Simon was going to donate it to the cathedral today, but obviously he is in no position to do that now.'

'I have some bad news,' said de Wetherset. 'I spent a good deal of time with all twenty-two of the cups you retrieved, but none is the genuine item. They are *all* fakes.'

'How do you know?' demanded Suttone. 'What tests did you perform?'

'I can tell by their feel,' replied de Wetherset loftily. 'I cannot explain it any better than that. I just sense, with all my heart, that none of these goblets is the Hugh Chalice.'

'Then you are wrong,' said the dean. He held up a tarnished vessel, although Bartholomew had no idea whether it was one he had seen before. 'I also subjected the cups to rigorous examination, and I sense – with all *my* heart – that this is the real one.'

'How?' asked de Wetherset, startled.

'Because it is the only one I do not desire to own myself,' explained the dean. 'I am content to see it stand on the High Altar, whereas while I feel obliged to take the others to the crypt.'

De Wetherset weighed it in one hand, then the other. 'I suppose it may have a certain something,' he conceded eventually. 'Although, as an instrument of St Hugh myself, I expected the sensation to be a good deal stronger.'

'Perhaps the saint has abandoned you,' said Suttone unkindly. 'He does not want you to stand as University Chancellor against a Suttone, and this is a sign of his displeasure.'

'It is tin,' said Bartholomew, watching Michael take the cup from the spluttering de Wetherset. 'I thought the real one was supposed to be silver.'

'Details, Matt, details,' said Michael. 'If the dean says it is holy, then that is good enough for me.' He passed it to Suttone.

'It *is* holy,' declared Suttone, although he was no more qualified to make such a proclamation than Michael. 'This is the real one, without the shadow of a doubt!'

'Oh, yes,' agreed Choirmaster Bautre, eager to please the Michaelhouse scholars because they had exposed Claypole's role in the murders, thus ridding Bautre himself of the man who was plotting to overthrow him. 'I can *see* the holiness radiating from it.'

'So can I,' said John sombrely. 'Our dean speaks the truth.'

'Good,' said Gynewell, pleased. 'But none of you has answered my question: what shall we *do* with it? I have no idea who owns legal title. Does it belong to the Old Temple in London? The Geddynge priest who bought it from Shirlok? Are we actually entitled to display it in the cathedral?'

'I think so,' said the dean. 'And if anyone else lays claim to it, then I swear, by all I hold holy, that I will bring it back again by any means possible. It belongs here. I *feel* it.'

'It can be a part of the procession, then,' said Bautre. 'One of my lads can carry it, holding it aloft all the way through the ceremony. It will be an arduous task, so I shall allot it to Hugh – the first of many such duties he will have to endure as penance for listening to bad advice from Dame Eleanor.'

'Putting a holy thing in the hands of such a person might see him struck down,' said Suttone uneasily. 'I would not like my day marred by an effusion of blood.'

'I would not mind,' said Michael venomously. 'It would be divine justice, and I do not see why he should escape unscathed while his co-conspirators lie dead. It was clever of Dame Eleanor to leave that document claiming full responsibility, and maintaining Hugh was not present at any murder, but it was unwise. She wanted to leave Lincoln a better place, but she has unleashed a devil in it.'

'Let John carry the Hugh Chalice,' suggested Suttone, after a moment during which everyone looked sombre. 'He is an upright fellow, and I intend to make him my Vicar Choral.'

'You are too late,' said Michael smugly, while John looked suitably modest. 'I have invited him to be my deputy, and he has accepted. You must find another.'

'You cannot have Bautre, either,' gloated de Wetherset. 'He is mine.'

The dean smiled suddenly. 'This business may have been unpleasant, but it has rid me of some very turbulent priests.

Tetford, Aylmer and Ravenser are dead, Claypole is in prison. We shall have a staff worthy of this fine cathedral yet.'

Suttone pouted sulkily. 'You two were securing yourselves Vicars Choral when you should have been praying, like me. Dame Eleanor was right: this *is* a corrupt place.'

'Not as corrupt at Cambridge,' said the dean indignantly. 'And it was there that this business began. De Wetherset was telling me about it yesterday.'

De Wetherset shrugged when everyone looked at him. 'You all know that Miller, Lora and Langar died in that riot the other night, and that Master Quarrel of the Swan has been elected head of a new Commonalty, which includes guildsmen. Well, now their black shadows have gone, I am free to reveal what I recall of the incident twenty years ago.'

'You mean about the carts in the bailey?' asked Bartholomew. 'And the box that you—'

'No,' said de Wetherset sharply. 'I refer to the trial. Shirlok told the truth when he named those ten people as his accomplices, and everyone knew it. Why do you think they left Cambridge immediately after? Not because they were shamed by the accusations, but because an arrangement was made.'

'What sort of arrangement?' asked Michael icily, angry that there was still information that had been kept from him.

'One whereby they would leave Cambridgeshire if they were acquitted.'

'How?' asked Bartholomew. 'The trial was in front of a jury, and—'

'And juries are made up of men,' interrupted de Wetherset. 'Men can be bribed. The first jury comprised Miller's friends and relations, but Shirlok recognised them and exercised his right to object. So, Langar was obliged to find replacements. They had to be folk who could be bribed, which is more difficult than you might imagine – people are afraid of being caught.'

'And you think Lincoln has problems!' breathed Bresley.

'Not all the jurors were tainted,' de Wetherset went on. He addressed Bartholomew. 'Your brother-in-law's ethics are somewhat fluid, but they do not stretch to corruption on that scale. However, eight of the twelve – including Morice and Deschalers the grocer – agreed to return a verdict of not guilty.'

'I thought so,' said Bartholomew. 'Miller paid them, just as he has been offering "tokens of his affection" to Sheriff Lungspee here.'

'It was not Miller,' said de Wetherset. 'It was his brother, Simon.'

'Are you sure?' asked Bartholomew, startled.

De Wetherset nodded. 'Yes I am. I even know why. You have already ascertained that Aylmer sold the Hugh Chalice to Geddynge for twenty shillings. However, it was not *Shirlok* who stole it from Geddynge and gave it to Lora to sell again: it was Simon. Miller had commissioned Shirlok to do it, but Simon did not trust him, so he did it himself.'

'No,' said Michael, shaking his head. 'Simon wanted the Hugh Chalice to be in Lincoln so much that he carved one on his body. He would never have passed it to Lora to sell a second time. Besides, he would have told us as he lay on his deathbed.'

'Not necessarily,' said Bartholomew thoughtfully. 'He admitted his involvement in various plots, but not once did he acknowledge doing anything felonious. His "confession" only went so far.'

'He *did* want the cup in Lincoln,' agreed de Wetherset.

'However, do not forget that he hailed from a criminal family, and was more than happy to make a profit along the way. He confessed it all one night, when we were drunk together in his Holy Cross house. I doubt he remembered our tête-à-tête the next morning. In fact, I doubt he remembered his crime when he was sober at all – I think he probably pushed it into the deepest recesses of his mind.'

'I suppose his suppression of these memories might explain why he was such a convincing liar,' said Michael doubtfully. 'Why did *you* not mention this sooner?'

'And have Miller come after me?' asked de Wetherset scornfully. 'Do not be an ass! But to return to our drunken heart-to-heart, Simon described how he gave the chalice to Lora to sell, and then he bragged about how he had expected to steal it back again.'

Bartholomew understood what had happened. 'Unfortunately for him, Shirlok was arrested on a different set of charges and named Lora as a regular handler of his stolen goods. Even more unfortunately, Lora happened to have the Hugh Chalice in her possession at the time. Simon's simple plan to make a few shillings had gone disastrously wrong. So, of course he needed to hire a corrupt jury to acquit him.'

'Why did he arrange for all ten appellees to be released?' asked Suttone. 'Why not just himself?'

'Now that *would* have looked suspicious,' said de Wetherset. 'And he could not leave his brother to hang, anyway. Langar obliged him by appointing malleable jurors, but added a proviso: they would have to leave the county afterwards. That was self-interest on Langar's part – he was afraid that if any of the felons bragged about evading justice, then he would hang, too. And besides, he had plans of his own – to leave his clerking post and rise to power on the backs of loutish men.'

Michael sighed irritably. 'You should have told me this before, regardless of the risk to yourself. I might have solved the case in half the time – and perhaps even saved some of the lives lost.'

'Well, it is over now,' said Gynewell, before de Wetherset could object to the reproof. 'And virtually all these wicked men are dead. I expect the Devil is devouring their souls as we speak.'

He did a curious jigging dance, banging his crosier on the ground. Cynric watched expectantly, and Bartholomew recalled that the book-bearer had predicted the bishop would explode in a puff of red smoke that morning. He edged away, not wanting to be caught in the crossfire.

'I am sorry about what happened to Christiana, Michael,' he said in an undertone, as the others moved away. Since her death, the monk had spent all his time either at the cathedral preparing for the installation, or sitting quietly in St Katherine's Chapel. There had been no opportunity to talk. 'I know you were growing fond of her.'

'I am a monk, Matt, sworn to a life of chastity. How could I be "fond" of a woman?' Michael smiled, but the expression did not touch his eyes. 'And I am sorry I did not believe you when you saw the truth. None of this was her fault, you know. She was seduced by that evil old lady's deranged lies.'

Bartholomew nodded, but made no other reply. He did not want to spoil the day with an argument.

'Is my cope straight?' whispered Michael, plucking nervously at his robes. Rosanna had done a fine job, and he looked magnificent in his vestments. 'Damn this breeze! It is ruffling my hair.'

Bartholomew gave the heavy garment a tug that jerked it from perfectly even to a decided list to the left. Suttone sniggered.

'You should go,' advised de Wetherset, before the physician could do any more damage. 'Or you will not find a good place to stand. Obviously, you will not want to miss anything.'

Bartholomew walked up the winding path to the cathedral and found the building full of people. It was so packed that he considered seeing the procession inside and then slipping away. He did not feel equal to the occasion, and wanted time alone, to absorb the fact that his quest to find for Matilde was at an end. Unfortunately, he was spotted by Prior Roger, who invited him to the South Transept, an area that had been reserved for special guests.

'What a fine day God has created!' bawled the prior, making several merchants jump in alarm. 'I am looking forward to raising my voice in praise today! The choir will appreciate a little help, I am sure, given that so many of their number are either dead or in prison.'

Bartholomew tried to think of an excuse to leave before the music started, but then Hamo approached and pulled him to one side.

'I cleared out the rooms of Dame Eleanor and Lady Christiana this morning,' he said. He no longer rubbed his arm, because Roger had ordered him to submit to a medical examination, and Bartholomew had removed the splinter he had acquired while eavesdropping. He was astonished that he could be so painlessly 'cured', and had been gratefully obsequious to the physician ever since. 'I found this.'

He passed Bartholomew a piece of parchment. It contained a long list of names Matilde had mentioned to the two women, and the settlements where they might be found. Bartholomew's hopes soared when he realised Eleanor's declaration that there had been no written

493

record had been a desperate ploy to force him to save Christiana. Then they plummeted again.

'I have already visited all these people.'

'I am sorry,' said Hamo sincerely. 'I was optimistic when I discovered it. Dame Eleanor was not a bad woman, and spent more than half a century serving the cathedral. Do not judge her too harshly.'

'She murdered Herl, Aylmer, Chapman, Flaxfleete, Simon and Ursula, and she admitted to dispatching many more – including your Fat William. She looked the other way while Hugh rid himself of Tetford and Ravenser, and she tried to hurt Michael. And it was her killing of Canon Hodelston that inflamed the feud that has ravaged the city ever since. It is hard to see her as a saint.'

'Her motives were pure,' argued Hamo. 'She really thought that ridding the city of wicked men would benefit everyone. And she had a point – no one she killed will be bound for Heaven.'

'I have heard murderers use these justifications before, but who was she to judge?'

Hamo acquiesced. 'You seem sad and preoccupied. Why?'

'I cannot stop thinking about Spayne, and how he was about to tell me Matilde's secret when Cynric shot him. It makes me wonder whether I should abandon my duties in Cambridge and continue my search. There is still more to be learned about her.'

'Spayne had no answers,' said Hamo. He shrugged when the physician showed surprise at the confidence of his words. 'He knew nothing that would help you, and your book-bearer was right to shoot him before he could harm you with his dagger.'

'How do you know?'

'Because I am good at hearing conversations not intended

494

for my ears, as you know.' Hamo patted his arm ruefully. 'And I happened to chance upon a discussion between him and Langar once. He was telling the lawyer all the places he had looked for Matilde, but said there was one he would never search, because it was where he had been an oblate and it held too many unhappy memories. I imagine *that* is where he was going to send you – if indeed he was ready to confide. I am inclined to believe Cynric: he was trying to make sure you died with him.'

'Where was he an oblate?' asked Bartholomew eagerly.

'I asked around, but no one seemed to know, so I spent all day yesterday trawling through the cathedral's records. I found the answer late last night. It was Stamford, but that is on Christiana's list, and you just said you have visited everyone on that. *Ergo*, I do not think you would have learned anything useful from Spayne.'

Bartholomew sighed. He was disappointed, but at the same time relieved. 'Thank you. At least now I will not spend the rest of my life wondering.'

That morning, he had been surprised to wake up and find himself looking forward to returning to Cambridge and his teaching. There was a desperate shortage of University-trained physicians, and Suttone had been talking about the imminent return of the plague only at breakfast. Reinforcements might be needed soon, and in Cambridge he could do some good. He would see his patients, teach his students and write his treatise on fevers, and in time the wound Matilde had left would heal.

He was about to ask Hamo whether *he* had heard any rumours regarding the pestilence, when there was a sudden, ear-shattering blare on a trumpet that had all the Gilbertines grinning in delight. The procession began to pass through the great west door. At the front was Hugh, struggling under a massive cross, and following him was the choir. Then came the Vicars Choral, dissolute and slovenly, and the canons. Michael winked at Bartholomew, de Wetherset nodded, and Suttone gave him a self-satisfied smile. Then came the relic-bearers, which included John toting the Hugh Chalice, men carrying St Hugh's head, a fat canon with Joseph's teeth, and the dean with the gospels. Gynewell, hopping impatiently from foot to foot, brought up the rear, his mitre sitting incongruously atop his curly head and his heavy cope dragging the ground behind him.

The ceremony was as grand and impressive as any Bartholomew had witnessed. Gynewell had a good voice, and his careful Latin was a pleasure to hear. The physician began to lose himself in the beauty of the place and the occasion, closing his eyes to listen to the music soaring through the nave. When he opened them, he noticed some of the choristers were becoming restless. Two seemed to be playing a game with pebbles, studiously ignoring Bautre's warning glares, while Hugh had abandoned his place altogether. Bartholomew hoped his absence would not herald the beginning of some piece of mischief that would spoil Michael's day.

In the South Choir Aisle, unseen by prying eyes, Hugh shrugged out of his choir robes and hid them behind the tomb of Little Hugh, recovering his cloak at the same time. Then he inserted his new sword – the one Christiana had been going to give him for his birthday – between two stones at the base of the shrine and levered, making sure to do it when the dean was reaching a crescendo to mask the noise. The stone popped out, and Hugh dropped to his knees, to rummage in the recess it revealed.

First out was the Hugh Chalice – the real one, which Eleanor had acquired from Herl after he had made his copies. She had immediately brought it to the cathedral, where Hugh had adapted the plinth so she could keep it safe from wicked men. They were the only two who knew about the hiding place, and it had proved useful for concealing one or two other items, too – such as the white pearls Hugh had stolen from Bartholomew's medical bag during the confusion following the collapse of the Spayne house. These went quickly into the purse at his belt.

Finally, he extracted two flasks. One contained the wine-and-water mixture Dame Eleanor had swallowed to fill herself with holy strength, and the other held the poison she had used to kill Herl, Flaxfleete and countless others; she had asked Hugh to secrete it inside the plinth when a smattering of dust had told her someone had discovered its usual hiding place. The two cheap pots looked identical, and Hugh wondered how she had known them apart. He sniffed them gingerly, but they both smelled foul, as far as he was concerned.

He unwrapped the Hugh Chalice and stared at it for some time, trying to decide what to do. Eventually, he put it back inside the tomb. It would be safe there until he had secured a wealthy buyer. Perhaps he would try the Old Temple in London, where St Hugh had died. Then he placed the two flasks in his hat and slipped out of the nearest door. He skipped down the hill to the Bishop's Palace, and let himself into the kitchens, where food and a large keg of wine stood, waiting to be served to the newly installed canons and their guests. He sniffed the flasks a second time, taking his time to decide which was which, although it was not easy.

Looking around quickly, to make sure no one was watching, he emptied the contents of one pot into the bishop's wine. Then he took a long draught from the second, to fortify himself for the long journey he was about to make. He grimaced at the flavour, but he was not afraid. Dame Eleanor would watch over him, as she had promised. And she was a saint, after all.

HISTORICAL NOTE

John Gynewell, Bishop of Lincoln from 1346 to 1362, had a terrible time with his cathedral officers. As early as 1347, he records trouble with the Vicars Choral and Poor Clerks: they neglected to attend their offices, they talked and wandered off during the ones they did keep, and they skulked about at night bearing arms. Worse was to come. In January 1359, the episcopal register indicates that Gynewell had twice issued orders asking for women – who ran taverns and encouraged licentious behaviour – to be ejected from the Cathedral Close; three months later, it was discovered that prostitutes had even been admitted to the dean's house. The dean at this time was Simon de Bresley, who died around 1360.

The records are full of clerics charged with insolence, irregular behaviour, 'evil lives', negligence, debt and immorality, and in 1350, a clergyman called John Tetford was found guilty of brawling and keeping a tavern. No doubt part of the problem lay in the papal and archiepiscopal power of provision, which meant popes and archbishops were free to appoint canons and other officials as favours, and as a consequence many were foreigners and cardinals who never had any intention of visiting the minster. Vicars Choral were appointed to manage the religious side of things, but the dean needed canons in residence to help with discipline, and too many were absent.

Michael de Causton and Thomas Suttone, both of whom were associated with Michaelhouse in the 1350s,

499

were made canons of Lincoln, and were almost certainly non-residentiary. Michael was elected to the Stall of South Scarle, valued at £11 in a tax survey of 1292, while Suttone's Stall of Decem Librarum was worth £6 18s 7d. Both were busy men with careers to further, and would have hired deputies to fulfil their religious duties, paying them a pittance and pocketing the rest. There is no record of Richard de Wetherset holding office as a canon, although he was Chancellor of the University at Cambridge during the Black Death, and probably again in 1359.

The Suttone, or Sutton, family was one of the great dynasties in fourteenth- and fifteenth-century Lincoln. One John Sutton (died 1391) represented Lincoln at Parliament in 1369, and he and his father were generous to the parish church of Holy Trinity, Wigford (demolished due to neglect in 1551, but holding a good many Sutton tombs) and St Katherine-without-Lincoln, the Gilbertines' chapel. Oliver Sutton was Bishop of Lincoln (1280–1299).

Other fourteenth-century cathedral officers were Archdeacon Richard de Ravenser and Nicholas Bautre, who was Master of Choristers after 1354. John Claypole held the office before Bautre. The Shrine of St Hugh in the chancel, the Head Shrine in the Angel Choir, and the tomb of Little Hugh would have been important sites for pilgrims, although contemporary Vicars Choral were unimpressed: they complained that draughts blew the Host about the altar top. They were also in the habit of stealing sacramental candles from each other.

The Gilbertines owned a site about a mile and a half south of the cathedral, which incorporated the Hospital of St Sepulchre, and was known as the Priory of St Katherine-without-Lincoln. They enjoyed royal favour, and the first of the Eleanor Crosses – the monuments raised by Edward I to honour his dead wife – was built outside their gates. The Gilbertine Priory was wealthy in its early years, but a combination of the Black Death and some bad business investments had reduced them to poverty by the end of the fourteenth century. The prior in 1351 was Roger de Bankesfeld; John (de) Whatton occurs in the clerical poll taxes in the 1370s, and Hamo of Sutton was prior by 1388.

A woman called Christiana de Hauville came to stay with the Gilbertines in 1319, on the orders of the King, while she recovered her senses and finances after losing her husband and three sons in the wars against the Scots. Five years before, one Eleanor Darcy had been appointed a canoness for life.

In Lincoln itself, there was a dispute as to who should be mayor in 1354. Walter de Kelby, a merchant-bailiff wealthy enough to lend money to the Exchequer in 1359, was elected, but he was displaced by William de Spayne. Spayne held office until Robert Dalderby overthrew him in 1359, then returned for two years until he was succeeded by Kelby. Other powerful men were Robert de Hodelston, who died in the plague, Thomas de Flaxfleete and Robert Quarrel. In the 1350s, John de Thoresby was accused of trying to extort money from Dalderby – by threatening to burn down his home and chop off his head. Thoresby was pardoned in 1353.

Lincoln had been a powerful and prosperous city until the end of the thirteenth century, when it began to decline. The causes were various, but the silting up of the Fossedike (Fossdyke) and the collapse of the weaving industry were certainly significant. By 1356, the city would have been suffering from the general decay and poverty that afflicted it until its fortunes began to rise during the agricultural revolution in Georgian times.

The medieval chronicler Henry Knighton records that

in the summer of 1355 people ran mad all across the country. He describes a sickness that made people deranged, some shunning other human contact to live in remote woodlands, and others harming themselves with knives or teeth. Many were taken to churches for relief. It is possible the outbreak of 'summer madness' was hysterical in origin, although the symptoms described are similar to ergotism. Ergot is a fungus parasite that infests grasses such as rye, and was known as Holy Fire (*Ignis sacer*) or St Anthony's Fire.

Meanwhile, back in Cambridge in the 1330s, a series of cases was heard by Justice Sir John de Cantebrig. All were faithfully recorded by his clerk William Langar, and are now in the archives of the Public Record Office. Several trials revolved around one John Shirlok, who was accused of theft. Shirlok turned approver, and named eight men and two women, probably in an attempt to avoid hanging. He appeared in front of one jury, but seems to have objected to some of its members, and was returned to prison until another could be summoned.

Shirlok would not have been pleased with the outcome of his second court appearance. Although the evidence suggests a well-organised criminal gang was operating, he was the only one found guilty. The others were acquitted, with the exception of two (including Simon Miller) who had died in prison. The remaining eight – Nicholas Herl, John Aylmer, Adam Miller (*Molendinarius*), Lora Boyner, Walter Chapman, Walter Bunoun, John le Taillour and Sabina Godeknave – were allowed to go free with no questions asked. Sabina Godeknave's first husband was hanged for a theft in which she was implicated, and Chapman was detained on another charge after the others had been released.

The items listed stolen by Shirlok at his trial included a chalice from Geddynge (Gidding), valued at twenty shillings and white pearls valued at one hundred shillings. It is a curious case, and no reasons are recorded as to why these people were set free. Shirlok's attempts to save himself lay in tatters, and he was hanged a few days later.